THIN
GIRLS

THIN
GIRLS

A NOVEL

DIANA CLARKE

HARPER ⬤ PERENNIAL

NEW YORK • LONDON • TORONTO • SYDNEY • NEW DELHI • AUCKLAND

HARPER ⬤ PERENNIAL

A hardcover edition of this book was published in 2020 by HarperCollins Publishers.

HarperCollins books may be purchased for educational, business, or sales promotional use. For information, please email the Special Markets Department at SPsales@harpercollins.com.

FIRST HARPER PERENNIAL EDITION PUBLISHED 2021.

Designed by Elina Cohen

Library of Congress Cataloging-in-Publication Data has been applied for.

ISBN 978-0-06-298669-6

21 22 23 24 25   LSC   10 9 8 7 6 5 4 3 2 1

For my ma and for my pa

God gave a Loaf to every Bird —
But just a Crumb — to Me —
I dare not eat it — tho' I starve —
My poignant luxury —
                                —Emily Dickinson

Either the well was very deep, or she fell very slowly, for she had plenty of time as she went down to look about her and to wonder what was going to happen next.
                                —Lewis Carroll, *Alice's Adventures in Wonderland*

It is dark: I cannot see myself anymore. And what do the others see? Maybe something hideous.
                                —Simone de Beauvoir, *The Woman Destroyed*

THIN
GIRLS

I always thought anorexia was a dinosaur. Some relative, maybe a second cousin, of the Tyrannosaurus rex. There she is, pale beige and beautiful. Long neck, slim build. She looks like a horse if only a horse were taller and transparent and not a horse. It's okay if you can't see her, she might've already gone.

She's an herbivore, of course. How she cranes her neck to nudge the leaves of a ginkgo with her snout, knocks fruit free, sends it tumbling down the trunk for fellow creatures to feast. How she blinks, slow as her lope. How she tiptoes despite the size of her feet.

She wants to make no mark on this world, anorexia, not even a footprint in long grass. If you want to be graceful, it's best not to exist. She has always been more idea than animal.

The group leader gives me this journal and tells me, "Write it all down."

The weight of a book—I flex my hands. I tell her, "I wish I had no hands."

She says, "You do, so use them." She used to find me charming. My quirky condemnation of corporeality. I never meant to be cute. I meant that I, too, wish to be more idea than animal.

The group leader says that anorexia is a memory. Find what planted the seed of the disease in your mind and only then can you start to recover.

"Write it down" is what she says. "From the beginning."

1994 (5 years old—Lily: 55 lbs, Rose: 55 lbs)

I told Lily that, if she didn't eat the broccoli off my plate, I'd hold my breath until I died. She laughed until my cheeks bruised blue. Then she ate.

PART ONE

The group leader is showing us how to pre-eat.

"Preheat?" I say.

"Pre-eat," she says.

"Pre-*eat*?" I say.

"Yes. Pre-eat."

"Oh. *Pre-eat*. Okay."

She lifts her hands into parentheses, as if she were showing us the size of a fish. Not a very big fish. A minnow, maybe.

The other girls in the group follow suit, lifting hands, curving fingers, all trying to be one another. I follow along, too, making brackets with my palms. I'm just trying to be like everyone else. Isn't everyone? Isn't it the impetus behind laughing when happy, crying when sad, shaking hands and bless you, how are you, good thanks, fine thanks, behind driving single file, walking down the sidewalk single file, the impetus behind wearing capris and then ripped jeans, sideburns then bangs, behind liking Abba, no, Ariana Grande, and toe rings and adult coloring books and Facebook? The humanest of instincts is to follow. And the group of us, all of us, we're just trying to be human again. So we do it. We follow.

I relax my fingers into wilted versions of themselves. I, too, can hold space. The air between my palms feels important. I stare at it, claim it. My air. My nothing.

"Now," says the group leader, her voice meant to be calming, tender and slow as a tidal change. "Imagine what might be between my hands."

"A chain of paper dolls," says a thin girl, whose name I don't know.

I stopped bothering with names after a week or two. They die or they leave. These are the options for thin girls in the facility. Not me—I've been here an entire year!

It's inappropriate to think of your endurance here as an achievement, the group leader likes to tell me.

I like to tell her, *Would you tell the pyramids of Egypt that their endurance is an inappropriate achievement?*

Then the group leader says something like, *Perhaps we should unpack this strange comparison you have made between yourself and one of the great wonders of the world.*

I hate to unpack! I haven't unpacked since I got here. I like the ephemeral feeling that comes with a full suitcase. The in-betweenness of it. I'm not thin enough for my body to shut down, too thin to live in the real world. I'm not dying, not living, I'm surviving. Welcome to my purgatory. I'm Rose.

"No, it can't be a chain of paper dolls," says the group leader, and just like that, the paper dolls of our collective imagination vanish. Poof! "It has to be food," says the group leader. "Pre-eating."

"You didn't say that when you said the rules," says Sarah, my only friend. Her eyes bag like a basset hound's, and she's younger than most of us. Only eighteen, skin still acned all over, bubble wrap. I like her, Sarah. The way she pops her knuckles every hour, on the hour, clockwork. The way she peels tiny licks of skin from her lips. Plucks her eyelashes, one by one. She can't leave herself alone. As if she needs the constant reminders: *This is your body. Do with it what you will.*

"Let's just imagine it's a sandwich," says the group leader and we all agree that there could plausibly be a sandwich between her parenthe-sized hands.

"Can you see it?" says the group leader. "Can you see the sandwich?"

I can't, of course, because there isn't one, but I do want to impress her, and I do want to recover, and so I nod. I nod and say, along with the crowd, "Yes, I see it, I see the sandwich, yum!"

The group leader smiles, and I feel glad to have made that smile.

"Now," says the group leader. "Now I want you to try not to think about calories," she says. "Don't think about the calories in this sandwich."

Which is easy because the sandwich is air.

"Think about something else, girls," she says.

1999 (10 years old—Lily: 88 lbs, Rose: 88 lbs)

We'd just finished a stint at summer camp, Lily and I, and we had furious sunburns, our noses shedding old skin, our shoulders alive with that hot itch. We had new freckles sprinkled across our cheeks, and even the sun knew to kiss us with symmetry.

Our parents liked to send us to camp whenever possible. They told us, when we whined, not wanting to go, that it would teach us independence. "And new skills!" they said. "Like tying knots!"

On parents' day, when each kid was meant to lead their mother by the hand, show their father how they could build a raft from only branches and twine, they didn't come, our parents. On mail day, which happened once a week, the other kids opened letters sealed with the lipstick kiss of their mothers, signed roughly by their fathers' gruff hands, the camp counselors sometimes offered Lily and me a letter printed on Camp Coromandel stationery, from the camp staff, who felt sorry for us.

After four weeks in the New Zealand woods, our young faces were striped with nature's grime. A lick of mud across the brow, twigs braided into matted curls. We were identical, even in our disguises.

Our parents picked us up and we were on our way back to the city, Dad in the driver's seat, Mum sitting shotgun, and Lily and I tangled in the back, holding hands, my head on her lap, our legs coiled around one another like climbing ivy. We smiled, luxuriating in the alone time we had been waiting for.

When we stopped at a gas station, Mum turned to us, entwined in the back seat, and said, "Want a drink, girls? Bottle of water? Diet soda?"

"Sausage smoothie!" said Lily.

"Anchovy juice!" I countered, and we fell into our laughter.

"You two are impossible." Mum sighed. But we barely heard her.

Back then, my favorite color was pink because Lily's was. I liked cucumber sandwiches because she did. I went on playdates because Lily was invited to them, and I had friends because she hung out with other kids, and I hung out with her. We were inseparable, and we lived for moments like these, in which we existed on our own frequency, a station between channels that sounded like nothing more than raw static to others.

Dad filled the car. Mum ran inside for gum and cigarettes, because even back then she was dieting. Lily and I opened our doors to let the summer air circulate, let our bitten skin breathe. It was the kind of summer day that wraps itself around you, bandages you with its wet heat. The kind that feels like forever. Like we would never go back to school, like the season would forget to change.

To keep ourselves occupied, we played one of our favorite games: Sister Says.

"Sister says, put my hands on your head!"

She did.

"Sister says, put your elbow on my knee!"

I did.

"Sister says, put your arms in the air!"

She did, and then Dad slammed Lily's door, jamming her fingers in the metal seam. She screamed. The heat on my tongue was immediate, like chewing on a handful of jalapeños. I gasped.

Her fingers, stuck in the door, looked bisected—they disappeared at the knuckle, every digit beheaded at once. Her arm went limp and she turned to me, eyes damp and begging. Things happened in slow motion—the significance of a memory tends to weigh it down, slow its pace. Before asking Lily whether she was okay, instead of reaching over her to open the door and free her, I raised my own hand—*Sister says, put your arms in the air*—I slammed my door shut, making sure my fingers would fall victim to the attack.

"Jesus Christ, Rose!" Mum shouted.

As soon as my tears started, Lily's stopped. She reached for my injury, so careful. My hand throbbed, heartbeat in my fingernails. Dad shook the gas nozzle and returned it to its bed. "What'd I miss?" he said, settling into the driver's seat, fastening his seat belt.

"The girls," said Mum, as if it were an answer. She turned over her shoulder to look at me. "If Lily jumped off a bridge, would you do that, too?"

"Yes."

Lily sat for the rest of the journey home, nursing my slow-swelling hand in hers, our identical constellations of freckles aligned. We watched our matching bruises fade from red to purple, this gorgeous skin sunset.

Even hurting, I was happiest when we were in sync. We bled together, my sister and I.

Back then, the only difference between Lily's body and mine was a mole. Hers. She kept it on the left side of her lower back. I hated to see that mole, perfectly round, slightly raised, the size of a chocolate chip plucked from a cookie. Every birthday, blowing out the candles, I'd wish that blemish away.

There's a knock on the door to the group session room, and we all turn, invisible sandwiches suspended, mouths wide and about to bite.

She's standing in the doorway, tall and thin. She looks like a streetlight. She's wearing a top hat and a bow tie, to hide her balding, her bones, respectively. She can't fool us thin girls with that gaudy getup; we've tried every trick in the book to keep our starvation to ourselves.

Her eyes are rimmed with black pencil, and it makes them look cartoonish, like those animated eyes that can boing out of a skull in surprise. She's so elegantly ugly, this new thin girl. And familiar! I look around at the other sandwich holders, and they, too, are squinting with recognition.

She lifts a hand and her sleeve falls and her wrist is crisscrossed with raised white scars. Her wave is a flicker of fingers. "Kat," she says. Then she licks her palm and uses it to bat at a feline ear that isn't there. "Like cat," she says.

It's that, the kitsch gesture, the voice so low it crawls, that makes our eyes widen. We know this thin girl. Kat Mitchells. Child star. Her song, the only one she ever released, maybe, appears like an unwanted guest. The chorus, something about falling in love with a girl.

There was outcry about the sexualization of the singer, Kat Mitchells, who was thirteen and wearing golden hot pants onstage. There was more outcry about the sexual orientation of the singer, Kat Mitchells, who called herself a lesbian on live television.

"She's a kid!" the people said. "How can she possibly know she's gay!"

"How can your kids possibly know they're straight?" said Kat Mitchells, in a talk-show interview that took over the world for a moment. Then she stuck out her tongue. It was pretty, pink, studded silver, and it drew to a point at the tip.

Kat Mitchells was so cool. You know Madonna? Mariah? Miley? Kat Mitchells was cooler. She was the first face of hair mascara and stick-on earrings and temporary tattoos. She had her own line of tube tops that said things like COOL CHICK and BITE ME. She was the celebrity face of Kit Kats and released her own customized raspberry bar called the Kit Kat Mitchells. The Kat Mitchells Barbie wore fishnets and a leather miniskirt and came with a headset microphone and if you tugged her ponytail, she'd belt out a few robotic notes. Kat Mitchells wore men's jackets wide open with nothing underneath. She dyed her hair neon and shone like a nightclub. She looked like a fucking Friday night. She chewed gum like it was part of her biology and blew big pink bubbles that never splattered over her face when they popped. Parents hated her. We were in love.

Lily and I watched the show from our bundle on the threadbare couch, eyes and mouths wide.

I once read about the Ain Sakhri, sculpted in the year 9000 BC. It is the first known artistic depiction of sexual intercourse, and the sex of each figure is indeterminate. It is often believed to be the first portrayal of queer lovemaking, but the statue, body tucked into body, could also be a pair of twins in the womb, fetal and joined.

• • •

And now here she is. Kat Mitchells. *The* Kat Mitchells! At the facility, *my* facility, standing in the doorway, older, thinner, uglier.

"Welcome, Kat," says the group leader, gesturing to a spare chair. "Welcome to Intellectual Eating. Please, take a seat."

"I'd rather not, darling. Actually, I'd rather perform fellatio on an aroused gorilla." All the moisture has been wrung out of her voice. I want to lotion her throat.

The group leader raises her eyebrows. "Sit." She doesn't care that Kat Mitchells is a celebrity. This facility has a way of equalizing everyone, not communism but cloning. We all become one another in here— sick is all that we are.

Kat sighs into the seat next to me. I shuffle my chair away.

"What's wrong, baby?" Kat leans over and whispers in my ear as she folds her long body into the too-small chair. "Do I scare you? You think I'm gonna bite?" She snaps her teeth closed, and, if she'd been holding a sandwich like the rest of us, she'd have just taken a large mouthful.

"No," I whisper. My cheeks hot, palms spiked with sweat. Kat smells of peppermint and vomit. Fresh and stale. I inhale. "I'm Rose," I say. "I'd shake your hand, but . . ." I nod at the way we are all still holding our imaginary sandwiches.

Kat smiles, her teeth sepia as an old photograph. A purger. I check her knuckles, and sure enough, they are the color of concrete, calloused and dry.

"Are you thinking about calories, Rose?" the group leader asks, inspecting my expression with a suspicious brow.

I want to tell her that I'm only thinking about calories, when she says the word *calories*, but I also want to please this whisper-haired woman. It's her hair, so sparse it looks accidental, that makes me think she's recovered from the battle we're all fighting.

Anorectics experience extreme weight loss. But you lose more than that. Hair, fingernails, teeth. You lose your friends, family, yourself.

You lose your sense of the world. Of what is important beyond the not-eating. And, eventually, you lose it all. Your life. She's greedy, anorexia is.

Now, the recovered group leader wears scrubs around us, as if she believes our thinness to be contagious. Her new body shape is that of someone unafraid of carbohydrates—a little swollen, like a human allergic reaction, but not in a bad way.

"No," I tell her. "I'm not thinking of calories even a bit."

Kat laughs, the sound, the rattle of the last mint in the tin. Even though she's barely famous anymore, barely recognizable, she still has the jaw of a famous person. The way celebrity chins are all sharp angles compared to the rest of us, soft. I reach for my neck, and the flesh there feels like fat.

The group session room looks like a classroom. We sit in a circle, on little chairs, behind little tables. The walls are elaborately dressed in motivational posters featuring photographs of landscapes, mountains, forests, lakes, the sorts of scenery people might describe as *tranquil*. Superimposed over the images are a series of words in bold fonts. INSPIRE: AWAKEN YOURSELF, GRATITUDE: THANK THE WORLD, PEACE: NOT HARM. We are being monitored by abstract nouns.

"Good," says the group leader, a parabolic smile. "Now," she says. "Now, open your mouths wide, girls."

Everyone does. Too many teeth are rotten, given our ages, which are mostly twentysomething. Our smiles are expired corncobs. Every fourth tooth, blackened.

I turned twenty-four a week ago. On my birthday, there was cake. I blew out the candles, laughed when they sang to me, then took a slice of chocolate gâteau. Someone had made it with such care, as if the only thing keeping me from recovering was a decadent sweet. The right recipe, the proper ratio of sugar to cocoa, flour to butter, and see how I would wolf it down! Cured!

While the others played party games, I snuck morsels of cake into the neck of my sock. Trafficked the whole slice out of my own party, unnoticed. Happy birthday to me!

"Great!" says the group leader. She thinks she can exclaim us into eating. "Take a big bite of that sandwich, girls!" she says, taking a big bite of hers. She thinks this is so easy! I hate her. Her face. I hate how her cheeks are always dusted red, boasting her healthy blood flow. I hate how when she talks, she chews on her words, as if her consonants are especially sticky, syllables gluing to her teeth, toffee.

This accumulation of negativity is unproductive is what the group leader would tell me if she weren't so insistent on pre-eating. I close my eyes and breathe. *Negativity is unproductive*, I say to my own self. *Negativity is unproductive*. I open my eyes, all negative thoughts banished.

"Follow me," says the group leader, and I want to! I want to follow her! Following is the easiest thing to do!

But, sitting in that skinny circle, holding my air sandwich, I'm afraid of the space between my bracketed hands. I worry that calories have grown there, that I've conjured them up like some spell between my palms. Of course, I know better. Air is air is air. I look at the others for support, but they, too, are looking around, nervous.

Kat is the only one not holding a sandwich. Instead of semicircling her hands, she's examining her wrists, running long fingers along each scar, tracing their paths like a maze in an activity book. Under the table, she shifts her leg, rests her thigh against mine. Her skin is cold and soft. Have you ever felt the icy suede of a snake sliding over your skin? She's reptilian, this new girl.

"Did you hear?" Sarah, on the other side of me, hisses, breath hot, rough lips against my ear. Grateful for the distraction, I turn to her. Her eyes flash with conspiracy and she whispers, "There's a lesbian in our midst."

In high school, we were taught about the USA's Founding Fathers. About how, in 1779, Thomas Jefferson's suggested punishment for lesbianism included cutting a hole in the perpetrator's nose cartilage, at least a half inch in diameter.

The next day, every popular girl's nose piercing had been removed. *No lesbians here*, said their unstudded nostrils.

"What do you mean?" I say to Sarah, a whisper. "What do you mean a lesbian?"

"Did you say lesbians?" Kat leans across me, ignoring my clutched sandwich. "Are you talking about me, darling?"

"What? No?" says Sarah. "There have been moans coming from the supply closet. Everyone's talking about it."

"Well, this place just got a little more interesting," says Kat, taking a tube of lipstick from her breast pocket and crayoning her mouth a shouting red. "Thank god, I'm already bored. Who's the dyke, then?"

I swallow and look around at the group. Try to see them as individuals, try to remember their names, but it is so hard to tell human skeletons apart. I give up and return to my not-meal.

Scientists can easily tell an anorectic's skeleton. Saw any bone in two and see how it is porous as honeycomb. Cannibalistic mandible, the jaw has eaten only itself.

"You're so close, pumpkin," the group leader says to Sarah, who is about to not-eat. She is! And thank god, I feel like I've been here, here holding this not-sandwich, for hours! My arms ache!

Sarah's lips are nearly touching the space between her hands by now, and I hold my breath. Others do the same. It's a habit among us. Breath holding. We love to feel in control.

"That's it," says the group leader. "Nearly there, honey. Nearly there, sugar." They like to call us food nouns, as if they think that hearing the words might make us want to eat them. That we might absorb the calories aurally.

Sarah's mouth rests, closed, on the crust of the nonbread. We stare. See how things move in slow motion in here?

Kat snorts. She takes an imaginary sandwich from the table in front of her, a giant sub. Look at it! Eight inches long! She inspects its fillings, licks her lips, opens her mouth, wide as the night, and bites down on the air between her palms. She chews, chews, swallows, and then shows us her clean pink tongue, its silver stud rusted orange.

Sarah, who was so close, puts her sandwich down.

Kat's done it. She's not-eaten. We applaud, forgetting our held sandwiches, which must fall to the ground as we clap and clap for this new thin girl.

"Well done, honey!" says the group leader.

Kat stands, takes an elaborate bow. The neckline of her T-shirt hangs open, and I see all the way through, a tunnel of cotton. She's not wearing a bra and her nipples are raisined with cold. I look away.

"Oops, pick up your sandwiches, girls," says the group leader.

We do, dusting them off—five-second rule. "Now everyone try it! Everyone take a big bite. Ready?"

I am. We are. We bite the air, chew the oxygen, swallow the nothing, and we are victorious. We raise our fists into the air, sandwiches forgotten, and we celebrate. We will recover, we know it. If we can eat not-sandwiches, then we can eat not-anything.

"Now," says the group leader. "It's time for lunch, ladies. Who's hungry?"

"Oh," says our favorite brave idiot, Kat, her eyes alight and pretty. "I couldn't possibly, darling. I'm so full from all of this pre-eating."

I nod. We nod. We agree. We, too, are full from pre-eating.

This facility—us thin girls lovingly call it *The Facility*—feels like white space. White walls white floors white. I feel like a single dark letter in the center of a blank page. I am so lonely!

In the daytime, we're meant to socialize with one another, all crowded together in our hollow common room. It's called a common room not because it's a room we have in common but because we all have hollow in common: us girls and the space.

Numerous studies have been done on the collective behaviors of animals. A tiger cub added to a litter of puppies will teach itself to bark. An orphaned lamb among piglets will learn to nose the ground, snoutless. It's nature versus nurture. We behave like those around us. As anorectics among anorectics, we starve.

We sit in a tangle, stringy limbs knotted together. This is our brand of support. We gather; we flock. People often come to see us thin girls. New patients. Loved ones. Not mine. They stand in the hall and peer through the glass like watching an attraction at the zoo, hands cupped over eyes, squinting into our darkness, they say, "Is she that one?" and, "Look, that other one just moved."

They're parents, they're families, and they don't recognize us anymore. We watch the watchers, our eyes wide in loose sockets, hair erect, teeth bared, but the snarls come from our stomachs.

The other girls look like freeze-dried humans. Like sacks of flesh once bloated with liquids and solids and gases, now punctured, deflated, their skin falls limp and flaccid, empty but for slow-eroding skeletons. I know I must look like that, too, but we're not allowed access to mirrors in the facility, so I can't know for sure. We're the same, all of us thin girls. Birds of a feather forced together. Community is not always a choice.

Birds flock when they fly for two main reasons. The first is that it's easier for everyone except the bird flying at the front of the V formation. The leader flaps its wings and creates uplift for those behind it, the followers are buoyant in their front-runner's wake. The second reason is that flocking makes it more difficult for predators to concentrate on a single victim. It's the logic of girls moving in groups: there's safety in numbers, even in the sky.

For anorectics, though, flocking is futile. We stare as others starve. We cheer as others purge. We are a supportive suicide squad, and we don't care about anything but for our own thinness.

A man, surrounded by nurses, passes by our common room. We stop to stare from inside our enclosure, watch his plank-walk down our glass-lined hall. He walks with his head down, as if expecting there to be cracks in the carpet. We can only see his profile; he's almost two-dimensional. He's beautiful. Less a person than a sketch of one.

"Newbie," says one girl.

"Not many men in here," says another.

He stops as if he heard us—surely not, still, he turns toward the glass. I stand to face him, and there we are, nose to nose, like looking in a mirror. He pushes his hair back, rubs his eyes with balled fists. I push my hair back, rub my eyes with balled fists, smile. He cocks his head, smiles. A nurse puts her arm around his shoulders, ushers him off, down the hall, away.

"Have I just not seen a man in a while or was he, like, really hot?" says Sarah.

"Men, shmen," says Kat. "So what do you ladies *do* all the time? Measure each other's waists with strings of pearls? Drink champagne and barf it all back up again? Suck one another's clits and call it eating out?" She's lying on her back on the floor of the common room, watching the blades of the ceiling fan chase one another, her hip bones reaching skyward. She's an exaggerated version of us. Maybe that's what celebrities are. Human hyperboles.

"We just hang out," says Sarah, taking her knuckles and pulling each one, pop, pop, pop. I want to take her hands and hold them in mine. Keep her safe from herself.

"Why are you here?" I say to Kat, who frowns.

"Same reason as you, I'd imagine, baby." She sounds like an expensive engine. "We're all just learning how to be human, aren't we?"

"This is such a shitty facility. Why aren't you at some fancy place?"

"Ah. So you *do* recognize me. Bravo."

I say nothing.

Kat waves her hand. "Oh, please. Everyone knows about this place. Everyone knows that this is the recovery center to go to if you don't want to recover. It's infamous, darling. It's the worst-run clinic this side of the equator. No one comes out of here healthy."

She's right. It is a badly run facility, this one. Poorly funded by the government, who want to *say* they support mental illness institutions more than they *want* to support mental illness institutions. The other main problem with the facility's function is that the nurses don't understand us. Most of them have never needed thinness the way we do. They don't know the lengths to which we will go. Sometimes they pick up on our tricks, sure, but they don't understand our minds. They don't understand how we will do anything to vanish.

"I do want to recover," I say.

"Sure you do, baby."

I say nothing. I don't believe me, either.

"Plus, I mean, it was one song. It's not like the cash could last forever, darling. Not with my lifestyle. Designer pills. Designer shoes. Designer designer. It all adds up." Kat straightens her bow tie. Clears her throat. "I make most of my money off cheap endorsement deals now."

I want to grab her. I want to say, *Be normal!*

"It's good to have you here," says Sarah. She's smiling at Kat, and I don't like the smile. The way it makes her eyes shine hopeful.

"So, how often do you have to do that pretend-eating shit?" Kat asks.

"Pre-eating," I say. "We do group sessions once a day."

"Sounds fucking tedious." Kat strokes her hip bones. Pets them like pets.

"It's not that bad," I say. "You get used to it."

Kat sighs. "My god, this is boring. I'm bored! Let's go check out the supply closet. Maybe a little voyeurism will lighten the mood." She rolls onto her stomach, clambers to her knees, her bones clacking together like a wind-up toy. "Didn't you say that's where the excitement's happening, Sarah, baby? The supply closet?" When she wiggles her eyebrows, they disappear beneath the brim of her hat.

A bell sounds, and I stand, relieved. "It's the bedtime bell," I say, when the ringing gradients out.

Disappointed, Kat's body concaves.

"Oh well." I smile, then reach to help Sarah off the floor, pull her upward and groan from the effort. I give her a half hug, like embracing a flagpole. "Good night." I kiss her temple. Her skin, dry. "Protect your own peace," I say. This is the facility's mantra. Protect your own peace. It means almost nothing, but it's nice to say. Rolls about on the tongue, soothes the throat, like a lozenge.

"Protect your own peace," she replies.

Kat reaches for me, and I take her hands, help her off the floor, too. This is what us thin girls do for one another. This is our supportive environment.

"So," Kat says, her hands still in mine. "Were you a fan? A Kat Mitchells groupie? One of those tragic little girls who'd fall to their knees at my feet and beg to lick my pussy on the spot?"

I swallow, silent, as the thin girls dwindle out of the room, calling, "Protect your own peace!" and "See you at breakfast!"

Kat lingers, and, eventually, we are the only two left in the common room. She's standing too close. I've forgotten how to move. She traces her fingers up my arm. "You know," she says, "I could see you before breakfast, if you want?"

I reclaim my arm and am surprised to find that her fingertips haven't stained my skin. I swallow and step away from her touch. "I don't think so." I smile. "I'm not, you know. Well. Anyway. Protect your own peace, Kat!"

"You're not fooling anyone, Slim," she calls after me. I say nothing, I don't even turn around.

Each morning, I mark days on the wall of my room, despite the cliché of it. A prisoner might have counted in coal or bark. An especially obvious inmate might have used their own blood. I use ketchup from the dining hall. I like the way it tattoos my plaster wall pink.

I'm not counting down the days; I'm counting up. I've given up all hope of recovery by now, and a life in the facility wouldn't be so bad. It's like its own little world in here. Smaller. Less frightening. Our worlds are only as big as the spaces we create for ourselves.

It's okay. My life won't be a long one. I have a list of things to do and then I'll be on my way. I've never wanted to outstay my welcome.

GROCERIES:
1. Feel what it is to be in love. Head-in-lap love, kiss-on-the-forehead love, the kind of love they write books about.
2. Make sure Lily is safe and happy and well.
3. Make sure Sarah is on the path to recovery.
4. Finish reading *Animal Behaviors*. I'm not one to leave things open-ended.

There's no rush. My life oozes like a wet wound. Everything is fine! I don't mind living so much. See, it's sunny today! Warm! This world is a beautiful one, I know it. Still, the possibility of death has always felt like a pending exhale.

Before breakfast, as I add the 367th notch to my tally, I notice a light on across the courtyard. I notice it because it's bright out. To add to the sun, suggest its inadequacy, seems greedy. I frown out the window, furious.

We must, the group leader always tells us, *be actively grateful for life.*

This light consumer is not(!) being actively grateful for life.

The lit room is identical to mine—bed, desk, closet, and an identical human sitting on the foot of the bed. That room has been empty for as long as I've been here, but now it is occupied and it is occupied by him. By *him*! Handsome, tall, lean, his dark hair hanging long and heavy like expensive curtains. I stare and he stares. My insides shift and I feel like a chicken ruffling her feathers. Proud? Ridiculous.

I stand from my bed; the man stands, too. I press my hand against the glass; he does the same. I smile and he smiles. I wave and he waves. This is what we call a meet-cute.

We wave for a long time, until our wrists ache and the gesture becomes foreign, artificial, like smiling too long for a photograph. Neither of us wants to be first to break the interaction. It's a test. Whoever stops waving first will be responsible for the end of this relationship.

Eventually, the man retreats into his room, opens his closet, takes a square of lilac fabric and dangles it at me. I laugh, effervescent with excitement, then take a Kleenex because I don't own a handkerchief. I hold it up for him to see.

We stand at our windows, waving our handkerchiefs at each other like eighteenth-century women at a parade. This, I think, elbow aching from the exercise, must be the love of my life.

"What took you so long?" I say to the window, the man, the first item on my to-do list. "I've been waiting for you!"

I go to the cafeteria, giddy with daydreams of new love.

A crush must have been named for how all-consuming the feeling is. The way new passion covers the skin like a sweat, wear it and glow. The way people say, *It's just a crush*, but have you ever seen an object crushed? It's never *just*.

Normal people are frightened for us thin girls, frightened *of* us, and fear is no foundation for a relationship. To be with another thin person is probably my most feasible chance at love, and I want to be loved. What else is there to be?

The man across the courtyard, the way his eyebrows, thick and dark, frame his eyes like awnings, he and I could eat celery sticks and drink lemon water on date night, curl up on the couch, all bones and sinew, tough body wound around tough body, like an old rope tied into a knot. I imagine our thin wedding. Like someone had drawn the occasion using stick figures.

We would drink herbal tea for the rest of our lives, the thin man and I. We would sit on our porch in rocking chairs, him reading the newspaper, me knitting, our hair falling out in clumps, our stomachs twisted into tight, constipated fists. A love for the ages!

Everyone would point at us as we strolled down the street, hand in hand, counting expended calories beneath our shallow breaths.

Look! they'd say. *Look, she finally found a man to spend her life with.*

Kat is already sitting at breakfast with Sarah, my Sarah. They're sitting in the seats Sarah and I always sit in. Our seats! They look as if they've been friends forever. The table is full of thin girls who want to be near Kat. Our brand-new celebrity.

My hands, fists.

What our group leader would say: *The only thing you can control is your own joy.* She thinks I have a problem with control. She thinks we all have problems with control. They think that's why we do it, starve, so that we can be in control of something in this world. They might be right. Or at least, that might be how it starts, but us thin girls, we lost control long ago. She's at the wheel now, anorexia is, and us? We're held hostage in the back of our brains, arms and legs bound, tape over our mouths, we've stopped our thrashing. It's dark back here, and quiet, and no one can hear us over the boom of her presence.

The group leader always says, *Let go.* She says, *It's okay to let things happen.*

Once, as kids, five years old or maybe six, Lily and I switched places, a cliché of our twinness. She brushed my hair out, Lily-like, and left hers in a matted knot. She rolled matching frilled socks up my ankles and dressed her own feet in my ratty sneakers.

At school, I watched as she shared crayons with a girl I hated, as she handed a drawing of our family, so unrealistic—they didn't even have feet—to the teacher, my name scrawled in the bottom corner. It was like watching myself from a distance, like watching myself do all these things I didn't want to be doing, unable to control her, me, unable to speak.

Not even our parents realized we'd switched, even when, at dinner, Lily ate every vegetable off her plate. Our mother: "Good girl, Rose! You're learning to like vegetables!"

I left my green beans untouched. Our mother: "Eat up, Lily. Be more like your sister."

She was always saying it. *Be more like your sister.*

I climbed into my own bed, thinking the swap was over, but Lily joined me.

"That was fun," she said to the nape of my neck, her stomach pressed against my back. Sometime, late that night, in the depths of a dream, I pushed her matching body out, onto the floor.

I breathe. Smile. "Hi," I say, pulling up a chair on the other side of the table. It's okay.

"Hi," Sarah and Kat say in near-perfect synchronization.

Sitting across from them, I feel strange. An audience. Watching this relationship begin from the outside. I miss the warmth of Sarah at my side, and she's hardly even warm!

Kat is wearing a different top hat today. It's sequined pink. She has a long pearl necklace on, and, for a glimpse of a moment, I imagine pulling on it until she clutched at the beads, cried my name.

Breakfast is peanut butter on toast—an easy one—I make sure the supervising nurses are preoccupied and peel off a section of bread, lift my T-shirt, let the condiment act as glue, and stick each piece to my stomach, mosaic my torso with toast.

I want to recover, I just hate to eat.

French philosopher Simone Weil died from anorexia at age thirty-four. For her, bodily hunger signified a void in the self in which god could reside, but I don't want god inside me, either. The weight of omnipotence—imagine!

I look up to see whether Sarah is copying my mosaicking, the way she always does, but she isn't. Instead, she and Kat are whispering.

"I'll teach you how, baby," Kat says.

"I've never been able to," says Sarah. "It grosses me out."

"I'll teach you. It's so easy. And it means you get to eat something."

"What's so easy?" I say. "What're you teaching her?"

"Never you mind, Slim!" Kat says, lifting a slice of toast, inspecting it, inhaling, then taking a large bite.

I frown at her. Doesn't she know that our ecosystem is fixed? Sarah is mine; she is under my wing. She is not in the market for another mentor. Kat catches my gaze and raises an eyebrow. A *something wrong?* eyebrow. I add another segment of toast to the artwork on my stomach.

"Oh my god," says Sarah, and, when I look up, she's chewing. I've never seen her chew before, and it's all wrong. "Oh my god, it's so good," Sarah says.

I swallow nothing but my own saliva and frown at Kat, who has finished every crumb of bread and is now busy licking peanut butter off her plate.

Finished with my process, I push back my chair and stand, leave the cafeteria alone, but not before I hear Sarah ask, "So is it true that you're, like, a celebrity?" She's too young to understand that Kat Mitchells is irrelevant.

"Mouth," says a nurse as I exit the dining hall.

I open wide. Lift my tongue. Show her the insides of my cheeks.

"Hands."

I lift my fists, unfurl. My fingernails have left tiny red smiles on my palms. The nurse, satisfied with my empty-handedness, waves me through.

I walk back to my room gently, so as not to disrupt the toast, tiptoe past the supply closet. Its door is ajar.

5

Lily visits, wearing yellow. She wears so much yellow that her body shouts its existence. People often tell her she's brave for wearing such bright hues, or that they wish they could be as confident as she, and she takes it as a compliment, but what they mean is that fat bodies shouldn't wear bright colors. I've learned to absorb the verbal slap for both of us.

Today her yellow is a floor-length dress. She bought it from a store that specializes in dressing very big bodies. It's sleeveless. Her arms wave like flags.

We were once identical, Lily and I, both with loose brown curls and too-big noses. We were identical until I stopped eating and she started. After that, I seemed to lose whatever weight she gained, an exact trade, as if, perhaps, what she was eating were me.

"My baby sister!" Lily calls, before perching on my bed, taking me into her arms. Her hug is like being swaddled and I am safe in her bright embrace. "Did I see that singer in the hallway? The girl who sung that old 'Girls on Girls' song? Remember that? You had that poster of her in our room. Is it her?"

"No," I say. "I don't know. No. Why?"

"A lookalike, then." Lily smiles. "Anyway, how are you?"

"Balmy," I say.

Her eyes peruse my body as she checks off a mental list: cheeks, chest, biceps, hands. These are the only parts of me showing. I am drenched in gray. A gray T-shirt, gray yoga pants, gray socks that hide my protruding anklebones. I would have worn sleeves, but we're not allowed. Sleeves can hide smuggled food, untaken pills, attempts to raze the body from the outside in.

"Weight?"

"I weigh exactly the same as I did yesterday," I tell her. It's true. I'm surviving.

"Good. Hey, do you know what I feel like?" She sits, her body corrugates, and she adjusts her dress so none of the fabric is tucked into her skin's folds. "A cake frosted in gravy!"

I laugh. This game has always been our sanctuary. "Do you know what I feel like?" I scrunch my nose, sifting through menus. "Pickle pie!"

2003 (14 years old—Lily: 99 lbs, Rose: 99 lbs)

The popular girls would sit, before classes started each morning, in a coven in the corner of the classroom. They made lists. The ten hottest actors. The ten hottest pop stars. The ten hottest boys in our class. The ten grossest. Lily was sometimes allowed to join the circle, and they tolerated me sitting just behind Lily. If I sucked in my breath, deflated myself, I might be able to wedge my body between my twin and the next girl, able to fit into the closed shape.

Jemima Gates was the leader of the popular pack. She was rich. Her grandmother was the founder of Absolute Abs, a fad workout from the '90s, and Jemima got a healthy cut of the royalty checks.

Jemima was the sort of girl who swished her blond hair over her shoulder like an expensive satin scarf. The sort of girl whose mascara-dressed eyelashes seemed to grow, floral, toward the sun. Who varnished her long legs in an oil that smelled of Pacific islands and then slipped like a fish, brushed up against any bare-skinned boy like an eel, just to show that she could. She looked like Scarlett fucking Johansson, and she slathered on lip gloss, thick as frosting, and called herself sweet. It shone red and smelled of fake cherry, the gloss, and she liked to kiss the soft inner wrists of her chosen few friends, stamp them with her own sticky red seal.

She was the alpha, and, those mornings before class, she was the one with the pen and paper. The rest of us could only watch as she wrote down the social law.

"Obviously Justin," said Jemima.

"He was the hottest guy last week," said Jemima's favorite minion, Lauren, who was a draft of Jemima gone wrong. She was blond, too, but her hair was more yellow than gold. She wore lip gloss, too, but she always colored outside the line of her mouth, leaving her face sticky, as if she'd just mauled a mango.

"Yeah, well, he didn't get uglier," said Jemima, applying a new layer of Cherry Chap, pouting, kissing the air.

"This game is boring if we keep the same order every time," said Lauren.

"Be supportive or leave, Lauren," said Jemima. "Maybe Lily can take your spot at our table."

Offended by the threat of social demotion, Lauren scowled at Lily, but Lily didn't notice. She was busy staring up at Jemima, her eyes hopeful and glassy with affection for our leader.

"And anyway," Jemima was saying, "Justin and I are a thing now, which gives him extra hot points." We watched as she etched Justin's name at the top of the list. She drew a heart over the *i*. That was the kind of girl she was.

"Who's next?" she said when she finished writing. "Who's second hottest? Lil?"

"Nick Lawrence?" Lily tried.

"Yes," I said. "Totally. Nick Lawrence. He's so cute."

Jemima wrote the name in the second slot. "Okay then, Twin Two," she said. "If you have so many ideas. Who's third?"

I swallowed. Looked at Lily. Her eyes were wide on mine. I didn't know how to tally a boy's features like these other girls did. Their game always seemed more raffle than reason to me, but I understood that, if I ever wanted to be liked, it was important to play the game.

My problem was that I made people uncomfortable. Strangers could only meet my eye for moments at a time, and even then their gazes skated over mine, too afraid to look too deep. Scared of what they might find in there. I was intense. I considered small talk to be a barrier to productive discussion. Niceties a distraction from what really mattered. Manners a Band-Aid over our very humanity. *Everyone*, I told Lily when she suggested I bring up the weather with strangers instead of polling for opinions on abortion rights, *already knows that it's sunny outside. Why would we talk about it?*

I just mean that you could lighten up. Lily was always telling me, *Lighten up a little.*

Another reason I made people uncomfortable was because I was not quite Lily. So like her in so many ways, but not quite her. I was her stunt double, her stand-in, her understudy. People looked at me and saw almost Lily, her in every way but for her air, her demeanor, our main differentiating feature, something intangible. Like an artist had painted a perfect portrait of my sister, but in the wrong color scheme, too dark to capture her properly. I was her wax replica in one of those museums. I made people question themselves, and people don't like to be questioned, especially by themselves.

"Um," I said. "Hm, let me think." I tapped a finger against my chin as I scanned the classroom, searching for any hint of attraction. Two girls, Fiona and Freya, sat at the front of the room. They were best friends, and they wore matching clothes most days. Jemima called them freaks, but I admired their attempt at twinship.

"George," Lily's voice in my ear, a life raft, barely a breath. I turned to her. She widened her eyes. I turned back to the group.

"I think George is third," I said.

Jemima only shrugged. "Not bad," she said.

"Yeah," I said, high on the affirmation. "George Bailey is so hot."

Lily groaned. Jemima snorted. I swallowed.

"Wait," said Jemima, clutching at her throat. "George *Bailey*? Oh my god. You think *George Bailey* is hot? I thought you meant George *Setter*! George Bailey is a total troll."

I closed my eyes.

"Lil," said Jemima. "Do *you* think George Bailey's hot? Is this some kind of weird twin crush?"

I looked at Lily, hopeful, asking for her hand, for her to join me on my social descent, but she refused to meet my eye. "No," she whispered. "I don't think George Bailey is hot. I think George Setter is, though." Treason.

"I know, right!" Jemima added George Setter's name to the list. "George Bailey." She tutted, shook her head. "Gross. At least one of the twins has some taste in men."

Lily wouldn't even let her eyes blink in my direction. Embarrassment burned my cheeks. Lily, too, was flushed, but I couldn't tell whether the humiliation was her own or just the overflow of mine.

"Come here, Lil," said Jemima, beckoning Lily toward her. I watched, my stomach a well. "Here," Jemima said, taking Lily's arm and flipping it, vein up.

Have you ever heard a kiss happen to someone else? The sound is lonelier than silence.

The deal was done. Jemima winked. Lily shone. I tugged the sleeve of my cardigan up to my elbow, held my arm out for a matching kiss, but Jemima only smirked and took her pen. "Freddie Weiss is next," she said. My forearm throbbed with lack.

Our teacher started roll call, and Jemima rolled her eyes at the interruption. She went to take her seat, ponytail swaying.

"Here," said Lily, taking my arm and pressing hers, lip gloss side down, onto my skin. The stamp of cherry felt a shadow of the way I thought it would, like nearly being chosen, nearly being liked.

Lily smiled when she saw that the kiss had transferred onto my skin. "There," she said. "Now we're the same again."

"Lil," shouted Jemima, from her seat at the back of the class. "Come sit with me!"

There was one seat available. The other free desk was at the very front of the room.

Lily shrugged. "Sorry," she whispered, but I was already licking the pad of my thumb, rubbing the kiss from my flesh.

Before Lily left to take her seat at the back, I hissed in her ear, "Traitor."

At lunch that day, I went and sat in the library.

Lily and I usually sat at our own table, close to the popular girls, just the table over, but not with them. Theirs was always full, and we were the most dispensable members of the group.

We were not popular, Lily and I, but we were popular adjacent. As in, if it weren't for my existence, Lily would have been popular, but, as it was, I was there, clinging to her, a blemish that kept her from being invited into the club of pale, ponytailed, thin things who already kissed boys and threw secret parties on Friday nights.

I was too quiet to be popular, too shy, too something. If we were all walking down the sidewalk and the path narrowed, I would be the one to drop back, to walk behind the bunch. If we had to get into groups of five in class, I was the sixth. I didn't mind. I preferred to live in Lily's shade. Lily was the one who knew how to smile, when to laugh. Lily was the one unafraid to speak her thoughts and joke with others.

Lily was always one notch better. I was smart, but Lily was smarter. I was pretty, but she was prettier. She was sportier. Cooler. Friendlier. When people asked how she was, she said, *Living the dream.* Lily learned how to form opinions from a young age. Whenever someone brought up a topic, Lily would have ideas about it. I had trouble forming opinions. I took in information like a spill, absorbing every new liquid it comes across, but I could never take a stance on anything. When people asked how I was, I said, *Fine.* Anyway, Lily's ideas always sounded good to me, and I didn't mind being the follower, her double, her shadow. I was good at agreeing. *Be more like your sister.*

Lily spoke in plurals so that I didn't have to. She said, "We love the Spice Girls" and "We're not good at math" and "We'd love to come for a sleepover." I watched her, in awe. She was so human.

I didn't hate Lily for being the better one, and I wasn't jealous. I didn't exactly love her, either, or I did, but in the way you love one of your own limbs or the air you breathe. Ours was such a self-sustaining love that it never had to be said. Or maybe it wasn't a love as much as it was a need; there was no one of us without the other.

But that day, I sat on my own, curled into a corner of the library, reading a romance in the hopes of feeling something like desire. I tried to concentrate on the boy meeting the girl, but a small smile of vengeance hijacked my lips every time I pictured Lily sitting there, eating all alone.

"So, I met this guy," says Lily from her seat at the end of my bed.

I can taste her joy, butter bubbling in my mouth. I have nearly gathered my response, which is to say *Me too* and tell her about my handkerchief waver, but Lily continues, "And, Rosie, I think I might really like him."

Lily hasn't dated anyone in a long time. She used to date men the same way I starved, consistently and determinedly. She is a sommelier of love. She can recite every rom-com monologue, voices and everything. She reads Mills & Boon and cries until the ink of each page swims. She examines every man she meets with the critical gaze of a job interviewer, and she doesn't think there's any point in singing if it's not a love song. All she wants is to be loved. What else is there to be?

All throughout high school, throughout college, she dated, dated, dated, she moved from man to man. The energy of a new love was her drug of choice and, without one, withdrawal, miserable and trembling until she found someone new.

But not since I was admitted to the facility. She's been single for a year and I've always thought it was because of me. That her celibacy was some sort of solidarity. But here she is, silly with new love.

What I want to feel: happy for her.

What I feel: left behind.

"Who is he?" I say.

"He's so dreamy. A little older. Fiftysomething. But who can put an age on love, right?"

I nod and nod. *It is important to support the ones we love* is what the group leader tells us. "True," I say. "Who can?"

"He's a businessman. Tall. Handsome. Last night, he took me out to this fancy restaurant and ordered for both of us. There was champagne! It was so romantic, Rosie."

She's shining. Her eyes glinting and dancing, sunlight on water.

"I don't want to jinx it or anything, but I really think he could be the one."

"Maybe!" I say, wanting to encourage, to hearten, but this is how she always is, my sister. She thinks they're all the one. If a man holds out a hand, she'll take it without question. For her, the most important character trait is desire. If he desires her, she's infatuated. She's all or nothing. Me? Nothing. "He might be, Lil!"

"He's so funny, Rose. And he's so smart. And successful. A businessman!" She sighs. "You know when you meet someone, and it just feels right? You sort of click into place, you know?"

"Yes," I say, nodding, sighing, gossiping. "I do. I know that feeling."

"Do you?" says Lily. A frown.

The story of my new love, my across-the-courtyard suitor, is itchy on my tongue, but Lily's incredulous brow, her patronizing smile, the way her arms are crossed over her breasts, closed . . . She thinks her new love is better than mine, more real, more likely. I keep my mouth shut. Shrug.

"I meant I know *of* the feeling." I wear my best swooning smile. "I hope this guy's the one, Lil."

Lily nods. "God, I know. Me too, baby sister. And do you know what? He really might be. I can really see a future with this one."

I bite the insides of my cheeks to keep from questioning. From calling her crazy. Her skin is lit, luminous. It is so important to support the ones we love.

A nurse arrives with my CalSip, a calorie-laden drink that tastes of old milk and cardboard and comes in a juice box meant for children. I'm meant to drink two CalSips a day, and my consumption of them is monitored.

Once upon a time, I would have locked my jaw closed. I would have thrown the drink at the wall, stomped on the box, and watched as the calories exploded from their cage, seeped into the carpet. I would have screamed and cried. I would have refused. A year ago, when Lily graduated from college and I was condemned to be an inpatient, I decided to eat. I decided to eat the way most people decide to diet. Over and over and over again. Each time I failed to let anything pass my lips, the world's most vigilant bouncers. They let nothing in.

But now I'm recovering, and I want to recover. The group leader tells us, *It is so important to want to recover*, and I do! I want to recover just as long as I don't grow, and so today, I take the plastic-wrapped straw, open it with only a wince, pierce the box, and drink. I'm used to the flavor by now; it tastes like safety. It tastes like the knowledge that drinking just two of them per day, so long as I'm escaping most of my meals, will not add to my size.

"He's a student's father," Lily is saying. "His daughter is gorgeous. Just such a cutie. You know how I've always wanted kids."

Kids? Has she? Sometimes I don't know her at all. I look up. I can only control my own joy. A march of termites makes their daily commute across my ceiling.

Termites eat their whole lives. They never stop consuming. They don't care what they eat, which is lucky, because they are blind. Their hunger does not discriminate. If it exists, it is edible. If it exists, they will eat it.

Tired of the quiet that's settled in between us, comfortable as a pet, but boring to Lily, she takes a cell phone from the depths of her purse. I wait for her to make a call, but instead she just holds the phone in the palm of her hand like she's showing me a frog she found.

I finish the CalSip, shake the box to show its emptiness; she smiles.

"I got you this," she says.

"Lil, I'm not allowed a cell phone in here," I say. "I need to protect my own peace."

"I know."

"You know?"

"But I got you one anyway."

"Thank you," I say, taking the phone from her outstretched palm. It's an old flip phone. I flip it open and then closed. I do it again. "I can't use it. I'll get in trouble."

"You're an adult, Rose. You can have a phone."

"A phone might disrupt my peace." I need to protect my own peace.

"Seriously, you can do what you want," she says. "You're a big girl now."

I swallow Lily's disapproval, which tastes of soap, and say, "Okay."

"Don't tell anyone," Lily says, and I nod, stashing the phone beneath my pillow. "It can be our secret. Call me whenever you want, okay?"

"But, Lil," I say, "you're here all the time. Why would I need to call?"

Lily shrugs. "I don't know. I'm just, you know, I'm seeing this guy now and, if I can't visit for some reason, I want you to be able to contact me."

"You're going to stop visiting?"

"No!" Lily's cheeks are bright. "Of course not! It's just in case, okay? It's a just-in-case phone."

I nod. I can only control my own joy. Lily stands to hug me goodbye. I hold on to the embrace for too long, as usual, hoping to absorb her via osmosis.

Over her shoulder, I see my handkerchief-waving lover in the window, standing in his room, watching my sister and me. I wave behind Lily's back. He waves, points at Lily, then flips his palms to the ceiling and shrugs an exaggerated shrug. *Who's that?* he's asking in our own special silent tongue. He wants to meet my family! Love moves so fast! But I don't want to introduce him to Lily. Not yet. She'll steal men from anyone, even me, I'm sure of it. It's not her fault. She's an addict, she gets high on testosterone, high on feeling wanted. I maneuver her to the door, push her out into the hall, bid her good night.

Alone, I look at the phone, my phone. I know only two numbers by heart. Lily's and another. The other, I know everything about her by heart. She lives there, in my chest.

I call and hang up before the first ring.

"Protect your own peace," I whisper to me.

I call again and hang up again and call and hang up and hang up and hang up and I don't even lift the phone to my ear once. I feel like a desperate rom-com teenager. Us girls—we're so silly!

The phone blinks an angry red. I've already exhausted its battery.
I whisper an apology to the screen and flip it closed. Tuck it beneath
my pillow to rest, keep it alive, even if just barely.

My room's ceiling sags in the center, a smile, as if made of fabric,
threatening to smother me in the night.

I dip my finger in the pot of ketchup, stolen from the dining hall,
and add another stripe to my tally. 368. But when I draw the line, the
wall gives, my finger breaks through the wallpaper, and then my hand
is inside the house.

The termites have eaten the house's organs, skeleton, and all that
remains is a flimsy skin. It must feel so light, this house. Empty as
the sky.

6

I'm changing for dinner when a knock from the other side of my room startles me. My handkerchief-waving lover is standing in the court-yard, palms pressed to my window, breathing fog onto the glass. I rush to him. My love! He's handsome, even from such a close distance, a proximity at which most people become ugly, even yourself. Have you ever kissed a mirror?

But my new lover is gorgeous. See how his cheekbones run straight as ramps. His smile is adoring; he loves me. I am wanted.

I hold my hands against his, just the width of the glass between us, and think that this is a good analogy for how I live. A window width away from everyone else. Like being with beloved friends who are somehow speaking French. Like the whole family eating around the dining table, but the table is rectangular and the rest of the family is clustered at one end and I am a long stretch away, too far to make out what anyone is really saying. Like sitting inside on a gloomy day with sunglasses on, seeing only the shadow of everything. I experience life from a distance, just the width of an eating disorder away from everyone else.

A nurse taps my lover on the shoulder. His expression is pained as she ushers him from my window, a husband being torn from his wife. This is how war must feel. I miss him immediately. I do!

I have Kat's stupid song in my head. The nursery rhyme jingle of it. Something about the girls at school, *soft lips, softer hearts.* Stupid! I shake my head to erase the tune, the world's worst Etch A Sketch.

"Thought Diversion" is what our group leader would advise. This is how we deal with our problems in the facility. We think about not-problems instead. Like my new love, for example!

I begin a letter to the thin man.

~~Hello—~~

~~My name is Rose. What's your name? A few things about me: I enjoy~~

When we were kids, our teacher wanted us to be pen pals with the students of our sister school in Fiji. We were meant to write a list of things about ourselves that we wanted our new friend to know. My pen pal, Talia, wrote about her parents, who worked as cleaners at a fancy tourist resort. Her cat, unnamed, who slept in the crook of her neck each night. She wrote about her walk to school, the way she would steal a banana from a roadside stall for breakfast. She wrote about not having siblings. Not even one. I never finished my response to Talia. I didn't need another friend. I had Lily, and she already knew everything.

Different people seek different species of love. This is something we learned in a group session. *While you might prioritize one type of love, it's important to acknowledge all of them* is what the group leader told us. The types of love are these:

1. Monogamous love—People who desire monogamous love want to love and be loved by one person.

2. Small circle love—These people want to be loved deeply by a small number of people, maybe a partner and a couple of friends, parents, siblings.

3. Large circle love—These people want to be loved by many. They might be considered social butterflies. They would prefer to be loved widely rather than deeply.

4. Celebrities—People who want to be adored by the world. They do not require depth to their love but would prefer that a large population admires them from a distance.

5. Self-love—People who prioritize self-love tend to seek relationships that will contribute to their self, help them better love themselves.

• • •

I'm pleased to see that Kat isn't at dinner yet. Sarah is sitting alone.

Us thin girls carry our plates to the cafeteria line, and a nurse with a face like a bulldog heaps two ladles of mashed potatoes, side by side, mocking our breastlessness, onto the plastic.

They gave up on porcelain plates a long time ago. New girls would drop their meals before they learned that the nurses would just replace their plates with other, bigger, fuller plates. So we eat from plastic like infants, and we use plastic cutlery, because we can't be trusted with metal. After all, we starve ourselves; who knows what else we're capable of?

"You're going to eat all of that today, aren't you, Rose?" says the supervising nurse. She is pointing at the piles on my plate.

"Oh, yes." I nod, lick my lips, smile. "Yes, I am, yum!" I do so like to please these women. I am their most amenable anorectic.

I take my plastic tray, balanced across both hands like a scale, to a long dining table and sit beside Sarah, eager to tell her about my romance. My handkerchief-waving lover. About how when I get out of here, finally graduate from the facility, I will be released into the arms of a man. Imagine how happy I will be. My cheeks will hurt from smiling! They'll use my photograph as the stock image in picture frames for sale! People will get suspicious of me: *What does she have to be so happy about?* Love!

"Guess what," I say, but Sarah is busy shaking her leg beneath the table's surface. It's not a syndrome, she knows she's doing it, and she's smiling about the secret exercise no one has yet noticed. On top of the table, she's flattening her mash with her fork, watching it squash between the tines like Play-Doh. But I get started on the process straightaway. The nurses are still serving, and their attention is divided between slopping meals onto plates and supervising our activity. I plunge my hands into my mashed potatoes and store as much as possible under my fingernails.

"Sarah," says a nurse. "Sarah, stop that."

Sarah halts her knee, but she's smiling. She doesn't care. She's already lost at least five calories, two and a half Tic Tacs. She takes to tugging on her eyelashes instead.

While Sarah is being talked to, I take two handfuls of potatoes and slap them under my armpits, then press my elbows to my sides as if using a knife and fork like a Proper Lady. I pretend to lift bites to my lips. I pre-eat my meal.

"Hey." A nurse frowns, pointing at me. "Don't forget your pills."

There's a cocktail of capsules, white, yellow, pink, green, piled next to my water glass. I don't trust them. There's no nutritional information on most vitamin containers. They could be calorie-laden, and no one would ever know.

At the turn of the twentieth century, tapeworms were sold in pill form. The advertisements, I can imagine: pretty women in their stiff collars and broad hats, smiling, cake-laden forks raised to curled lips. *Eat more and lose weight!*

The tapeworm diet was banned when doctors found the worms to be growing into eight-meter-long snakes, slithering through skinny bodies, feeding on flesh.

The fad diets have changed, the advertisements have not. Everywhere you go: *Want to lose weight? How to get your summer beach body fast! Lose those extra pounds in three simple steps!*

The media: promotional parasites.

Lily always loved the mole on her back. The one physical difference between us. Her love for it became a tic. When she stood, absent-minded, hand on hip, she'd trace the circumference of it with her fingertip. Circled, circled, circled, framed it over and over again, just to make sure it was still there, to make sure she was still not me.

One day, Jemima Gates asked Lily to go shopping after school, and Lily went. She didn't invite me, didn't even ask if it was okay for her to go, just told me to walk home without her.

"No," I said. "I'll come with you."

"Not this time, Rosie."

"I'll scream."

"So scream."

I stared at her, and she stared back.

"Why are you doing this to me?" I said.

"I'm not doing anything to you. This isn't about you at all."

That night, Lily came home with a bag from an expensive store.

"How did you afford that?" asked our mother.

"Jemima got it for me," said Lily. "As a gift." She turned to me. "How was your afternoon, Rosie?" There was a waver to her voice, and the waver was fear. I said nothing. If she wanted to spend time without me, then I'd show her time without me. I wouldn't speak to her until she begged.

Before bed, I caught Lily trying on her purchase in our shared bathroom. It was a crop top, spaghetti-strapped and slutty. The hem barely came to her belly button. From behind, I could see her mole, decorating the stripe of flesh between the top of her jeans and the bottom of the new tank.

"That's hideous," I said.

"Good night, Rosie," she said.

I couldn't stop thinking about the top all night. About how she might wear it to school, parade her mole around the halls. Everyone who usually confused us, stuttered between names, they'd know. They'd be able to tell us apart.

It was three a.m. before I decided on a course of action. I unplugged our night-light from the wall to use as a lamp and took the scissors from our shared homework desk. Lily was fast asleep on her stomach, and she barely shifted when I lifted her pajama shirt.

I opened the scissors, only a sliver, and carefully lowered the blades around the mole. Then, in one quick motion, I pinched the scissors closed. Lily screamed awake. The mole was still there, now surrounded by two bloody gashes. I dropped the scissors to the floor.

"I'm so sorry, Lil," I said, already in tears. "Oh my god, I'm so sorry. I don't know what I was thinking. Oh, Lil."

"What the hell were you doing?"

"I'm so sorry, Lil." The sobs shook my whole body. I was sorry. I never meant to hurt her. "I just felt so left out. I don't know why I did that. I'm sorry. I'm sorry."

Over time, the cuts faded into red slits, then white traces, then nothing at all. The mole, though, it stayed, so proud of itself.

"So," says Sarah, when the nurse finishes scolding her. "Who do you think they are?"

"Who do I think who is?"

"The lesbians?"

"What?"

"The supply closet lesbians?"

This facility runs on gossip. It's what keeps these girls alive. What is the caloric value of a rumor? High in protein and fiber, low in fat—hear one a day to boost your metabolism!

"How do you even know it's lesbians?"

"I heard the moaning myself. So did Kat."

I ignore the mention of Kat Mitchells. Who cares. Not me! "Maybe someone was just masturbating in there."

"Gross," says Sarah. "And anyway. If it was just, you know, *that*, wouldn't she have done it in her own room?"

She has a point. I look around the cafeteria, as if I could *Where's Waldo?* the lesbian. As if I expect her to be wearing a white-and-red striped suit or a sandwich board that says, IT'S ME! I'M GAY! No. Only thin girls staring at their plates, hoping they might ogle the food away.

Before I was admitted, I had to answer a questionnaire:

Do you monitor what you eat?

Do you count your caloric intake?

Do you think you need to lose weight?

Do you skip meals on purpose?

Do you feel fat?

Ask any woman these questions. Admit us all to the facility! This is what you have done to us. This is your monster, and it's starving.

"My darlings!" Kat calls as she carries her tray to our table. She's wearing a lipstick so scarlet it looks painful. Her mouth is pretty and pouted, the shape of a rose. "My loves!"

Thin girls, those scattered around other tables, watch as their new idol weaves her way through the cafeteria and toward us. The type of love that Kat Mitchells seeks is Celebrity.

"I'd think Kat was the lesbian in the supply closet if she didn't just get here," I whisper from the peripherals of my lips.

Sarah laughs, and the laugh sounds like a victory. Mine.

"Hey," I smile, polite.

"What'd you say, baby?" Kat frowns. "You just said my name."

I swallow. Sarah is looking at me, waiting. I could lie, but dishonesty is frowned upon. What the group leader tells us: *Deceit begets harm. Truth begets health.* It is important to be honest. "I said that, if you didn't just get here, I'd think you were the lesbian who's been fooling around in the supply closet."

Kat laughs a bark and pleats her long body into the chair beside me. "Oh, honey," she says, lifting her cutlery. "I've been out of the closet since before you were born." Then she leans over her meal, inhales the damp scent of powdered mash. "I fucking love potatoes," she says, scooping a forkful between her lips. "Especially when they're vodka."

I look at Sarah, eyes wide, and she looks at me, eyes wider.

"Eat something, Sarah, baby," Kat says, mouth padded with potatoes. "Mash is an easy one to get rid of. Comes right up. Like barfing clouds, darling. It's gorgeous."

Sarah eyes her meal as I eye Sarah. The only thing I can control is my own joy.

Kat eats and talks, all at once. "So, guess what, I'm working on a secret project," she says. "It's so exciting, darling, it's going to liven this dud of a place right up. I can't say much yet, kitties, I'm keeping mum about it for now. Just for now! But I'll let you ladies in on it as soon as I have the logistics sorted out."

"What is it?" says Sarah. "You can tell us. We won't say anything." She looks especially young today. "We promise. Right, Rose?"

"I said," Kat reaches out and tweaks Sarah's nose, "I'll let you in on it once it's all planned out, baby." Her plate is clean. She stands. "Anyway, gotta go," she says. "Kisses!"

We watch her dart between tables, show her empty plate to a nurse, who waves her out of the cafeteria. The nurse mustn't notice Kat's fingers, preemptively raised to her lips, poor girl. I turn back to say something to Sarah, something about bingers and purgers, but her mouth is full of food.

"Can you believe Kat Mitchells is in *our* facility?" a thin girl leans over to hiss. "*The* Kat Mitchells. I always wanted to be her."

"Well, congratulations," I say, standing from the table. "You did it."

2003 (14 years old—Lily: 101 lbs, Rose: 101 lbs)

Lily and I were invited to Jemima Gates's sleepover. Or, Lily was invited, and I packed my bag, too. She didn't go places without me. Especially overnight.

"Rosie," said Lily, as we tucked toothbrushes into side pockets. "Can you do something for me?"

"Anything."

"Can you just try to be normal, tonight?" Lily sucked her lip. "Just, I just mean, I don't mean that you shouldn't be yourself. I just mean, can you be a more normal self?"

"My normal self?"

"Well, no."

I zipped my bag closed. "Never fear, Lil," I said. "I'll be nothing more than your shadow. You say jump, I'll jump."

"Just try not to say anything, okay?"

Jemima's house was big. This sprawling white brick mansion that, compared to our two-bedroom home, seemed palatial. Dad dropped us off and told us to ring the bell. He'd driven away before Jemima opened the door.

"Lil!" Jemima hugged Lily and kissed her on the cheek. She did things like this. She'd probably been to Paris and learned how to cheek-kiss from a French man twice her age. "Oh! You brought your sister," she said, her smile tightening.

I raised a hand in a nearly-wave. I did not receive a cheek kiss.

"Okay," said Jemima. "That's fine. The more the merrier, I guess, right? Come in. The girls are in the basement."

The foyer, a room that seemed to have no function except to hold removed shoes, was so huge and empty it felt as if the house was abandoned.

"Are your parents home?" I asked as I added my shoes to the pile. Jemima ignored me.

"Are your parents home?" Lily repeated.

"Oh no." Jemima laughed, shaking her head. "Hardly ever. It's so cool. I get to do anything I want."

I looked at Lily.

"The housekeeper's upstairs, though," said Jemima, nodding at a long, curved staircase that looked straight out of the movies. "She won't bother us. I told her to keep to herself."

I made a sound. It was a laugh of disbelief I'd attempted to stifle, but the resulting noise was a snort. Lily elbowed me.

"Is your sister okay?" Jemima asked Lily, as if asking me directly could put her at risk of contracting loser.

"She's fine," said Lily. "She's cool. You're cool, right, Rosie? She's cool. Let's go downstairs."

The girls welcomed Lily and politely ignored me. They sat around, all wearing fluffy robes in feminine shades. Lily and I didn't own robes, and when I suggested we change into our matching Elmo pajamas, she shushed me.

The basement was dark but for the twinkle of white festive lights. There was a table adorned with pink candy and pink-frosted cupcakes and a large chocolate cake that had Jemima's name written in a loopy pink cursive, a font reserved for pretty girls.

At school, on tests, in birthday cards to relatives, I always wrote my name in capital letters. *ROSE*, I shouted to everyone. *ROSE, ROSE, ROSE.*

Music was playing, a song I recognized. Kat Mitchells crooning about kissing girls. It was everywhere right now. Our parents called it *that gay girl song* whenever her sandpaper voice bellowed out the opening notes. We weren't allowed to sing along, but Lily and I knew every word, lip-synced the lyrics to each other—she was the only audience I ever needed.

Lily poured a cup of lemonade, my favorite, and dug a pack of cards out of her bag, ones she must have packed especially. She handed both to me.

"You play solitaire over here," she whispered. "And drink this. I'll be just over there, okay?" She was pointing at the herd of girls, who sat in a circle, chatting and sipping on sodas spiked with vodka. I nodded and started to shuffle.

Time passed in won games. Twelve. Mostly, I managed to tune out the warble of girl gossip and giggling.

"Rose," said a voice that wasn't Lily's. I stopped dealing cards and turned. It was Jemima, and she was looking at me. Talking to me. On purpose! "Come here," she beckoned.

I stood, moved forward a single step, untrusting.

"We need you to be the lookout."

"The lookout?"

"That's right." Jemima spoke to me slowly. As if talking to a child. "The lookout. Go stand at the top of the stairs," she said. "And shout if the housekeeper is coming."

"Why?" I said.

"Just do it, Rosie," said Lily, with a smile. "You're part of the game."

"The most important part of the game," said Jemima.

"Really?" I said, skeptical.

"Really." Jemima winked.

"Okay, I'll do it. I'll play." I hurried up the stairs and stood on the landing. "Ready!" I called. "What now?"

"Now wait up there!" yelled Jemima.

I sat, my back against the wall, and waited. Time ached. I braided my hair, unraveled it, and braided it again.

There was a lot of laughing, yelping, squealing, all coming from the basement. I peered down the stairs, but it was dark. They'd turned the lights off, and I couldn't see anything. There was a gasp. A scream. I stood, slipped down the stairs silently, squinted into the black.

"I dare you to kiss me." The voice was Jemima's.

"Kiss you?" said my voice, which meant Lily was talking. "Like on the mouth?"

"Duh," said Jemima.

"Uh."

"You'd only be afraid if you were a lesbian," said Jemima. "Are you?"

"No," said Lily. "I'll do it."

I could make out the shadows. My sister's silhouette, so like mine, and Jemima's, curvier, more adult. Then the space between them disappeared. Their shadows combined, and there was a wet smacking sound that made me wince.

"Lil?" I said, and the shapes leapt apart.

Someone hit the lights and I squinted into the new brightness.

"Why are you watching us, lesbo?" said Jemima, wiping her lips with the back of her hand. Her eyes, a terrible cliché, sparkled. They really did!

"We should go," said Lily. "We'll go home. Come on, Rosie." She took my hand, chose me, and led me back up the stairs. We only needed each other. The type of love we needed was Monogamy.

Us thin girls are always full of food when we leave the dining room. We wear it like fashion. Sauces striped down our arms, sticky sleeves. Cheese pressed to our chests until it clings, a gluey bra, to breasts that have long been flattened, concave as DIET buttons on soda lids. We smile as we strut, single file, from the room. The strut, of course, an internal one, for one cannot stride well with a slab of hamburger meat clutched between her thighs.

Sometimes we're caught in the act—steak-handed—but we're clever. We morph, mutate, like a strain of the flu. Tricks get trickier. We traffic our meals, chipmunk-like, in our cheeks. We tie our hair in buns, tuck stray vegetables into brunette caves. We plug our nostrils with peas. Fold deli meat small enough to insert into our ears. Store lumps of meat in our throats and cough them into our pillowcases once we are safely in our rooms. We'll do anything to keep from eating. We will rest our heads on sacks of rot each night.

As I walk past a potted plant, I drop dollops of potato into the soil and smile.

As I walk past the supply closet, I press my ear to the door, listen for a moan.

When I was admitted to the facility, the group leader gave me a list of my issues and a list of mantras to deal with them:

1. Control—You can only control your own joy.

2. Dependence—You are your own self.

3. Abandonment—You are your own forever.

4. Emotional manipulation—You are responsible for only your own life.

5. Self-destruction—Protect your own peace.

Your own your own your own your own. What does that mean? My own? I've never been my own.

As kids, Lily planned our wedding. We would, she assured me, meet twin brothers. They'd be handsome. A whole foot taller than us, with eyes so green they looked enchanted. We'd get married on the same day! Our vows would be said in unison! She made a wedding book. We chose dresses, hers a dessert-looking gown and mine a simple white A-line.

"Now pick a husband," she told me, opening a magazine to the best suits worn at the Oscars that year. "Any of them. You can pick first."

The men looked the same, all in their monochrome costumes. It was as if they wanted to be interchangeable. I shrugged. "Him?" I pointed at the first suited man. He was so tall and slender he looked as if he'd been stretched.

"Oh, oops," said Lily. "That's actually a woman. Tilda Swinton."

"A woman?" I said, lifting the page, bringing Tilda Swinton's face up to mine, so close I could see her pixels. She was beautiful. I didn't want to change my answer.

"Who do you want to choose instead?" said Lily.

"You pick for me," I said. "I don't mind."

Lily chose Hugh Jackman to be my husband, even though he looked more like my father. She glued a photo of my face onto a bride's body and cut and pasted Hugh Jackman beside me. For some reason, the image of her and Orlando Bloom looked like a wedding. The one of me with Hugh Jackman, my young face, my virginal frock, looked more like a sacrifice.

It's Relaxation Hour, and usually Sarah and I would be sitting in the common room with books, her head in my lap, or mine in hers, reading aloud whenever we came across something noteworthy. But today I am alone. My book on animal behavior, called *Animal Behaviors*, is in my hand. I sit on the floor and look for somewhere to rest my head.

Halfway through the hour, Sarah arrives, hand in hand with Kat. They're giggling, shoulders trembling with happy. Sarah wipes the corner of her mouth and Kat picks something off her T-shirt, flicks it to the floor. A fleck of dried vomit, I'm sure of it.

I pretend not to see them. The only thing I can control is my own joy. I smile and return to my book.

Adélie penguins use rocks to elevate their nests higher above the ground. This way, when the snow melts, the egg will not be drowned. Lazy Adélie penguins, when building their nests, do not go to the shoreline to collect stray rocks, but instead steal the stones from neighboring nests.

7

Lily visits. Leans against the door frame, takes a cigarette from behind her ear, the world's worst magic trick, and a lighter from her breast pocket. She lifts the cigarette to her lips.

"What are you doing?" I say. She lights up and inhales, coughs, scrunches her nose, and snuffs the cigarette on my empty CalSip box. "I didn't know you smoked," I say.

"I don't," she says. "I'm trying to pick it up."

"You're trying to pick up smoking?" I look at my sister, at the door, wonder whether Lily has been replaced with some terrible doppelgänger, and wonder whether I would even realize if she had been.

Lily's changes are always so abrupt, disruptive as that of a caterpillar. When she was at university, she became a vegetarian overnight. Switched her degree from law to primary school teaching because of a handsome professor. One day she'd be a fierce feminist and the next she'd be dating the world's most malicious misogynist. When we were kids, she was so herself that I could be her, too. I wonder whether the reason she's always changing is to keep me from copying her. *Be more like your sister*, people would always tell me. Maybe I'm so herself that she feels like she can't be.

I never change. I'm the base. The constant. The placebo. I can measure how much Lily changes by how far she strays from me, how many standard deviations she's wandered. She always comes back.

"You're trying to pick up smoking?" I say. "In 2013?"

"The guy I'm seeing smokes," she says. "It's just something I'm trying out. Don't overreact. Don't freak out."

I say nothing.

"He's not, like, pushing me to smoke or anything. That's not what this is. Don't put this on him."

"I wasn't. But why?"

She shrugs.

"You know you don't have to be exactly like him in order to love him, right?"

Lily barks a laugh, as if the idea is ridiculous, but I've felt it, the desire to become the person I want to be with. Being a twin is being so similar to another, so close to another, that being as close to someone else, even a lover, is almost unimaginable. The kind of love she seeks is Monogamy.

Lily thinks she will better love this man if she becomes more like him. Smoking and all.

In the 1920s, doctors prescribed cigarettes as a weight-loss tool. *They curb the appetite*, those doctors would say. *Too much food can kill you.*

"They're an appetite suppressant, you know?" Lily says. "Cigarettes are."

Of course I know. I know every trick in the book. It's my bible, that book. I keep it on my nightstand. "Are you trying to lose weight?"

"I don't know." She shrugs, attempting casual, failing. "Maybe? I'm trying this new holistic health guide. It's called YourWeigh. It's not a diet, it's more like a lifestyle."

My stomach aches. My sister, the advertisement. "And cigarettes are part of your new lifestyle diet?"

"Well," Lily says. "Not cigarettes explicitly. But anything that stunts the appetite is encouraged. You know, black coffee, herbal tea, all that. I figure smoking can only help, too. Right? I figure it'd be good to lose a few pounds. You know, for my health."

The words coming out of her mouth belong to me. Lily has never dieted. I know she's trying to please because I can taste the citrus tang of her desperation deep in my throat, its light vibration clings to my tonsils. I want to tell her that she doesn't need to lose anything. Instead, I say nothing. I can only control my own joy.

"Anyway, so, my new guy? Phil? He wants to meet you," says Lily, her cheeks flushed with romance.

"What?"

"Phil. That's his name. Phil Bright," she says. Proud.

"Phil Bright? Isn't that, like, some kind of scholarship?"

"Can you not?"

"Why does he want to meet me?"

"I don't know." Lily shrugs. "Things are getting serious, I guess. I know it's moving quickly, but we just had this immediate connection. You should hear how we met. He came to parents' night with a bottle of wine and a card that said, *For all the stress my kid has caused you.* I thought it was so funny. His kid isn't even one of the bad ones."

"He has a kid."

"So then I asked if he wanted to share the bottle and one thing led to another."

I hadn't asked for the story. It tastes of old meat. A steak left in the sun. Something is off. "That's nice, Lil," I say. "What are you keeping from me?"

"Keeping from you?"

I pull a hangnail too far down. String cheese. The blood is immediate, and my instinct is to suck on my finger, lick myself clean, but the calories. What is the nutritional content of your own blood?

"You're not telling me the whole story."

She sighs. "You'll judge me."

"He's married," I tell her.

"He's married."

"He's married," I say.

"He is," she says. "Married."

"But?"

"He's not happy. They're not happy. They're basically only still together for the kid."

"He's married."

"Rose."

• • •

The cuckoo is a bad mother. She tricks other mother birds into rais-ing her babies by laying her eggs in a nest that isn't her own and flying away, freeing herself of any and all responsibility.

"Is this why you're dieting, too? This Phil Bright person?"

"No. I'm doing it for me." The lie is sour as a lemon. She tucks her hair behind her ears. "But Phil did say I'm looking good lately. He thinks I've already lost at least five pounds. I think he's the motiva-tion I need, you know? I've wanted to lose a few for a while now, and my doctor's been telling me I should try to eat healthier." She runs a hand over her stomach, pinches the flesh that resides there. "I just, you know, I want to look good for him."

"For Phil," I say. It is important to support the ones we love.

"Exactly. For Phil. He's so dreamy, Rose. And he's crazy about me. The way he looks at me. He's just—"

"He's married."

"Over fifty percent of marriages end in divorce, baby sister." She stands, taps my nose, kisses my forehead. I am a child to her! "Now, I have to go. Phil and I are going out for Italian. Ciao bella."

Someone said the difference between hunger and greed is the line at which the human body feels full. I don't eat when I'm hungry. Lily eats even when she isn't. She desires everything in excess. Men, food, love. She dates the way she eats. With a ravenous passion.

Our mother monitored our caloric intake from a young age. If we were dining at a restaurant with a choice of sides, our mother chose for us, the green salad, every time. At the ice cream store, we were given frozen yogurt. Soda was forgone in favor of its diet counterpart. Low-fat, zero-sugar, no-carb—most of the food we ate boasted the absence of something.

She was creating us in her image, attempting to make dieting something hereditary. The way she ate was like this: if we had lasa-gna for dinner, she ate only the sauce. If we had a roast, she'd eat a scoop of peas or cut a wedge of squash into tiny scraps and eat them one by one. If we were having burgers, she ate the vegetables from inside and left the burger and patty, still an entire hamburger in itself, assembled and everything. She ate quickly, our mother did, darting fork to plate and back again, mechanical, robot, the calculated up and down of her jaw, precise on its hinge. By the time her throat swelled in swallow, her fork had already punctured the next bite.

Whenever Mum went away for work, our father changed into a different version of him. A lighter version, one who smiled, who laughed. The three of us would wave goodbye to her as we all stood on the porch, watched as she drove off to whichever conference the pharmaceutical reps were going to this time, then he'd turn to us and raise his eyebrows. "Junk night?"

Junk night went like this: Dad got on the phone and ordered the most calorie-laden takeout from our favorite restaurants. Nachos from the Mexican place down the road. Fried rice from the Chinese shop on the corner. Pizza. Burgers. Fries. Milkshakes. While he reeled off orders enough for fifty, Lily and I skipped across the street to the convenience store, where we stocked up on pints of ice cream, bags of candy, chips, cookies, chocolate bars. We carried the plastic sacks home slung over our shoulders like twin Santas and when Dad opened the door we rubbed our bellies and ho-ho-hoed.

We were allowed to choose the movie, which meant *I* was allowed to choose the movie, which meant that we watched *The Shining.* I liked the twins, how they leaned into their sameness. We ate until our stomachs hurt. We groaned around on the floor, feeling ten times our size, laughing and happy.

"Do you girls want another slice?" Dad would ask.

"No!" we'd shout together, holding our bellies.

"Are you sure?" he'd say, lifting a slice and swimming it toward us. "No!"

He'd chase us around and around the coffee table, slice of pizza held like a weapon. We played until we fell asleep stretched out on the couch, legs tessellated together.

In the morning, when we woke, all the food would be magically gone, hidden or tossed, out of shame, out of fear. Dad would be at work. We got ourselves ready for school, skipping breakfast, the memory of the previous night's binge still curdling in our stomachs.

If Lily's new romance really is love, and it sure tastes like it, then she will have a family, a new family, one complete without me. Mother, father, daughter, what a perfect fairy tale of a life. They'll get married in a church, they'll smile in family portraits, send quirky Christmas cards each year, *Look how happy our life is in these matching Santa hats!*

I'm jumping to conclusions, again, I know. I mourn any object prostrate on the street as roadkill long before I get close enough to learn that I've been grieving a trash bag or a stray shoe. I jump from conclusion to conclusion like a flea. A great athlete. I'd win medals! One jump extinguishes about a tenth of a calorie. It adds up, after a while—

8

The next morning, there's an envelope on the floor of my room. Lying on the carpet, slipped beneath my door. It's unopened, and beneath the address, my address, a red kiss. I lift it, slip my finger beneath its seal. The adhesive strip is still wet and the way it whispers open, labial.

R—

Did you call me? I got all these calls from an unknown number and I just thought that maybe . . . I don't know. It seemed like such a Rose thing to do. I answered every time. I hope you're doing okay. Your sister wouldn't tell me which facility you're at, so I sent this letter to every facility in the area. There are eleven!

I'm not sure if you're allowed to write me back, maybe you could just call again? Call and hang up? It'll be our secret code. I'll know what it means.

—M

The one person I'm not allowed to speak to, to think about. The reason I divert every thought. I swallow and press the paper to my cheek. It's soft. I touch the letter to my tongue, but it tastes only of dust. Maybe it's the taste of love. If something is dusty, it's been sitting around for a while. I want a love that sits around for a while.

Lily would tell me to shred the letter and then forget it ever came.

Our group leader would tell me to keep the letter only if it brought me no triggering feelings.

Kat, I imagine, would wiggle her plucked-thin eyebrows, knowing.

I pick up the cell phone and stare at its screen. I run my thumb over the buttons, the formula that would call. Our secret code. *I'll know what it means.* But would I know what it meant?

I tuck the note into its envelope and then both the envelope and the phone under my pillow. I lie down. The letter feels big and obvious, the princess and the pea, I can feel its outline, rectangular, hard against my skull.

There's a line from one of Kat's songs orbiting inside me. *I'll hold my tongue if you let me hold yours.* I remember hearing it for the first time, the way my breath caught in my throat, as if hitched on something, mid-inhale.

Thought Diversion is what the group leader would say.

A fling is what the girls in the movies would say. Gossiping girls huddled around their heartbroken friend. They'd eat whole pints of ice cream and cry over romantic comedies and stroke tears from each other's cheeks. This is how you be a girl, we are taught.

You have to get back out there, they'd say, and oh, how they'd nod.

The only way to get over someone is to get under someone, they'd say, and oh, how they'd laugh.

2003 (14 years old—Lily: 101 lbs, Rose: 101 lbs)

Jemima Gates lived in our neighborhood. Sometimes, in the summer, when Lily and I walked the block to the community pool to swim, Jemima would already be there, stretched out over her towel like a sacrifice. She wore a teal bikini, because even then she was edgy, while Lily and I wore our matching pink one-pieces.

Lily had begged for bikinis. *We can even get matching ones*, she'd pleaded with me, appealing to my preference that we matched our clothes each day. *But please can we get bikinis? Everyone has bikinis now, Rosie. Look how cute!* She held a bikini set in each hand, yellow with little red strawberries all over. I shook my head. A bikini would reveal her mole, our difference.

One-pieces or nothing, I said. *I'll scream.*

Rosie.

I'll scream, and Mum will make us leave the store with nothing.

We tried on the pink one-pieces. *We look so cute,* I said, untwisting the strap of Lily's. *So cute. Just the same.*

I loved to wear our matching suits, like tiny synchronized swimmers, but Lily always slumped her way into hers.

We were at the dawn of puberty, and Jemima would sunbathe, body bare and bared, sipping on lemonade, shades on, watching the boys play soccer beside the pool. I tried not to stare, but it was impossible. Watching Jemima was like watching a celebrity. She sometimes caught me looking, winked, and said something like, "You like what you see, Rose?"

My skin tightened. I closed my eyes.

Cognitive behavior therapy is used to help people deal with unwanted cravings, desires, and urges, in three ways: redirect, distract, visualize.

Redirect: Think about something else until the urge passes.

Distract: Do something else until the urge passes.

Visualize: Imagine yourself in a different scenario until the urge passes.

Each of these methods assume an urge to be in motion. Each of these methods assume that, at some point, the urge will pass. Whether quick as a car zipping past on the highway or slow as a cloud lumbering by overhead. Cognitive behavior therapy does not account for those urges that stay stuck still, mountains, immense, unmoving.

Lily and I, when we were alone in the pool, liked to play Sister Missed-Her, a Marco Polo spin-off that included Lily hiding somewhere around the pool's circumference, and me closing my eyes, spinning in circles, then asking, "Sister?"

Lily would reply, "Sister!"

I listened, stopped spinning, and pointed to where Lily's voice had come from, called, "Sister!"

If I guessed the right spot, opened my eyes to see Lily at the end of my outstretched finger, then I won. If I missed, then Lily would shout, "Missed her!" and I lost.

When Jemima was there, boy-watching and snide, she would yawn at the game and tell us to grow up. Then she'd lie on the pool's edge and tilt her sunglasses to get a better view of the boys playing soccer on the other side of the fence.

The summer after Jemima's sleepover, the grass yellowing in the heat, teeth going bad, Lily and I were playing Sister Missed-Her when Jemima came sauntering through the pool's gate. I stared. Her body was already swiveling and stretching in adult places.

"Hey," she said, flipping her sunglasses up onto her head and pushing her hair back like a celebrity. I wondered how she knew to do these things. Things that made her audience immediately aware of her superior femininity. "Can I play?" she said, dipping a toe into the pool.

"We're playing Sister Missed-Her," I said, wary.

"Yeah," said Jemima, her eyes blinking to the soccer boys, who were roaring at a goal. "I know. Can I play?"

"If you want," I said.

"Rosie," said Lily. "I don't know if that's such a good idea. Why don't we just play Hot or Not again? Jemima loves Hot or Not." She was using the voice she used when I was meant to listen to her. More nasal than usual. Like some ghost hand was pinching the bridge of her nose. I hated that voice.

"No," I said. "That's a boring game. Sister Missed-Her is fun. And anyway, we were halfway through a game." I turned to Jemima. "I'll teach you the rules."

"Rosie," said Lily, using the voice she used when I was meant to seriously listen to her right now, low and controlled as a train on its tracks. "Don't," she said.

But I was already giddy at the thought of Jemima learning the game, learning to love it, learning to love me. Lily rarely ditched me for the popular girls, even though I knew she could if she wanted to, but now, if I could just show Jemima that I wasn't weird, that I was normal, fun, even, just like Lily, then I had a chance to be friends with the popular girls, too. Lily and I could both be cool, together. Twins.

A stray soccer ball rolled through the pool's gate. Jemima picked it up. A boy stood, hands wide and waiting.

"You want this?" Jemima said, a smile.

The boy only nodded.

"Come and get it, then."

The boy, our age, neared slowly, untrusting. Jemima flipped the ball from hand to hand. Her eyes on the boy the whole time. He paused.

"I said come and get it," said Jemima.

He stood, hands dangling. The air, it throbbed.

Eventually, Jemima tired of the game and tossed him the ball. The whole world sighed.

"So are we playing, or what?" said Jemima, when the boy turned and ran back to his game.

"Come on, Lil," I said, trying to communicate beneath my words, some kind of spontaneous Morse code. *I am doing this to help you*, I wanted her to hear. "Don't be a bummer," I said.

Jemima nodded. "Yeah, Lil," she said, a sneer. "Don't be a bummer."

Lily's eyes were a warning, but then she shrugged, a surrender. I happily reeled off the rules to Jemima, who nodded and nodded, an eager learner. But once I was done with the basics of the game, she held a hand, fingers spread, a stop.

"Did I miss something?" I said.

"No," said Jemima. "I have an addition to the game."

Lily sighed, and I swallowed.

Jemima went on. "This new game is called Sister, Missed-Her, Mister Kisser."

"Mister Kisser?"

"Yeah," said Jemima, her smirk evolved into a smile. "If you're accidentally pointing at the soccer boys, you have to go kiss one of them."

"Kiss one of them?" I said. "A boy?"

Jemima smirked. "As opposed to what?"

Lily's cheeks flushed.

"Wait," I swallowed. "If we're accidentally pointing at the boys on the road, we have to go kiss one of them?"

Jemima looked at Lily. "Is she stupid?"

Jemima, unlike the rest of the world, had always treated Lily and me as separates. She refused to let me be part of Lily's extroversion, her likeability, her personhood. She saw me for who I was on my own, which was an undesirable. Jemima started a rumor that I had a crush on Lily, and for a good six months, the popular kids at school called me Incest.

What Jemima Gates didn't understand: I didn't want Lily; I wanted to be her.

Lily crossed her arms. "Rosie," she said. "Maybe we should just go home. It'll be dinnertime soon." She was chewing her lip, the way she did, waiting to see what I would do, whether she would be required for damage control, or whether she could continue on with her day. I didn't want Lily to be concerned for me. I didn't want to embarrass her. Not ever. Not now. I wanted to do this *for* her, to be popular *for* her.

"No," I said. "We're playing." I looked at Jemima. "Stupid rule. But I'll do it. The kissing part."

"You will?" said Lily.

"You will?" said Jemima.

"Yeah," I said, shrugging in a way that I hoped seemed nonchalant despite my rioting stomach, the way my lips tingled and stung with anticipation. I had never kissed anybody besides Lily before. Not even my parents, who were self-described nontouchers.

"Okay," said Jemima. "I'll go first."

She spun. "Sister?"

Both Lily and I, hiding in the same spot, in the opposite direction from the boys on the road, replied, "Sister."

Jemima smiled as she pointed directly at the makeshift soccer goal, 180 degrees from our hiding spot. "Sister?"

"Missed her," murmured Lily.

"Mister kisser." I laughed.

Lily, of course, must have realized that Jemima had chosen the boys on purpose, but I couldn't imagine ever wanting to kiss one of them, my body didn't work that way. I chuckled at how bad Jemima was—perfect little Jemima, so bad at our game!

She levered herself out of the pool with grace, stood, jutted her chest. Magicked a tube of Cherry Chap from somewhere, slathered it thick, then walked, headfirst, toward the soccer game.

"Hey!" she called as she neared the boys. "Stop!" And they did. All standing, mouths agape at Jemima's near-naked body. She walked right up to the kid nearest the curb, took his face in her hands, and kissed him on the lips. She let her mouth linger there, like a movie woman, and then stepped away, pinched his cheek in a way that was so adult and condescending. She strutted back to us, dove into the pool, and surfaced, raking fingers through her hair.

"Who's next?" she said, as the boys whooped and cheered.

"I'll go," I said, just a moment before Lily said, "Not Rose."

"Why not Rose?" said Jemima, turning on Lily.

"Yeah," I said, raising a brow at my sister. "Why not me, Lil?"

Lily chewed her lip so hard I expected to see blood begin to drool down her chin. I reached for her cheek and tugged it the way Jemima had done to the soccer boy. It had the desired effect. Lily's lip was saved. "Please be normal, Rose," she whispered.

"I'm fine," I said, before closing my eyes and spinning.

Even in the dark, it was clear that Jemima was the only one playing. I could feel Lily's presence behind me, and I could tell she was unhappy by the way my mouth tasted metallic, blood-filled.

We had been tasting each other's emotions all our lives. It was irritating, oftentimes nauseating, but when Lily was happy, filled with joy, I savored the flavor and salivated. Each Christmas, Lily's favorite holiday, I sucked on my tongue, marinated in melted butter all day long.

"Sister?"

"Sister," said Jemima, and her reply came from the same direction as the boys.

I swallowed, pointed. "Sister?"

There was a snicker, a series of splashes, and then, "Missed her," said Jemima. "Mister kisser."

I opened my eyes to find Jemima standing in a spot that was not where her voice had come from. I was pointing at the soccer game.

"You cheated," I said to Jemima. "You moved."

"No, I didn't," said Jemima. "I didn't, did I, Lily?"

"Did she, Lil?" We both turned on my sister, who was sucking her lower lip again.

"I don't know," said Lily. "I don't really know."

"How could you not know?" I said. "You were watching, weren't you? Did she move or didn't she?"

Lily's cheeks reddened and I felt a twinge of pain in my mouth. My tongue. Lily had bitten through her own flesh. Her eyes filled with rain. I held my breath, the way Lily had taught me, and counted to five. My anger subsided, a sun shower. I exhaled.

"Okay," I said. "That's okay. Doesn't matter."

I smiled at Lily, willing her to relax, willing the lip from between clenched teeth, and it worked. Lily's poor, battered lip popped out of her pout, an embarrassed red, purpled with bruise. "I'll do it," I said. "I'll kiss one."

"Rosie, you don't have to," said Lily. She knew I had never been kissed. We had never been kissed.

"Yes, you do," said Jemima. "That's the game."

I stood from the pool, pulling pink goggles from my head and releasing my hair from its braid. I combed the strands loose with my fingers and tried to appear calm. Cool.

The girls were silent as I marched over the grass verge, made my way to the game.

"Stop!" I shouted, the way Jemima had, but the soccer continued. I turned back to the girls and grimaced. Lily was hugging herself; Jemima was folded in laughter. "Hey!" I shouted again. "Stop!" Still, nothing. The boys kept running, darting around one another, zipping away from me like mosquitos. I shrugged and decided on the goalie, the only boy standing still.

"You," I said as I neared him. Then I took his child-chubby face in my hands, leaned in, and slapped my lips against his. It felt like kissing a fish; he was slimy with sweat, and his mouth was salted. When I pulled back, the boy wiped at his face with the back of his hand.

As I walked away, I heard the boys' laughter start like a storm. Clapping and snorting. Then the goalie: "Why'd Mike get the hot one and I had to kiss the fat one?"

I thought I would cry until Jemima wrapped herself around me. Whispered, "Proud of you, babe," into my ear. I could smell the fruit on her lips.

I stand, open my door, and peer into the hallway, which is empty. I walk softly. These halls are carpeted to keep a creak from sending some thin girl over the edge at the reminder of her body. The supply closet door is closed, and I stand, not knowing what to do, and I am still standing, standing still, when I hear the choking gasp.

Then I am flattened, on my stomach, a soldier in combat, my eye pressed tight to the gap between door and floor. It's dark in there, too dark to see, but, listen, the breathing strangled with pleasure, the sighs inflated with want.

I sit up, lean my back against the door, ear to the sound, and reach into the waistband of my leggings. My heart rate picks up when the sounds do. I try not to think of Kat, her lips, butterflied, beautiful. When I masturbate, I conjure up scenarios in my mind, elaborate scenes, more intricate than any porn plot I know, more nuanced, less obvious. I can't stand those clunky narratives, a pizza delivery guy who rings the doorbell to find a topless girl, who, shocked despite having opened the door herself, is so overwhelmed with desire for the delivery man that she drops to her knees on her very own doorstep. My scenarios have realism and character development. A woman notices a man out to lunch with another woman. The first woman is sitting at her own table, nursing a cup of green tea. The tea has long since gone cold, but the woman, our protagonist, the porn star, is besotted by the beautiful couple. She watches as the other woman spoons her minestrone and blows on it with such tenderness before lifting it to the man's lips. When he tastes the soup, he smiles and says something, an exclamation or a positively connoted adjective. It's important not to get too specific, given the distance between our star's table and the couple's, and given that the restaurant is busy and there are servers moving between the watcher and the watched all the time. Verisimilitude is key to a well-directed pornographic film, not many people know.

The man leans over to whisper something in the woman's ear. She laughs. They are so happy, this couple. So happy and beautiful they could be the couple that are in the frame before you replace the stock image with your own, less perfect photograph. The couple continue to share their meal, they joke with their server, and it's clear that they are his favorite table to wait on.

Their dessert arrives, a brownie as big as your head, and they finish the whole thing between them, feeding each other carefully curated mouthfuls of chocolate and vanilla ice cream from their forks. Usually, that dessert scene will finish me off.

I don't often see myself in my pornographic fantasies, but when I am there, it's very clear that I'm Lily. I can tell by the mole above her left butt cheek. The one physical difference between us.

For example, now, as I imagine my across-the-courtyard lover knocking on the door to my room, and I imagine myself standing from my bed, where I had been reading about animal behaviors, and he embraces me and I notice his erection, grown from nothing but the intensity of his desire for my body, I zoom out, a long shot, and the woman there, standing there, embraced by such a thin man, is smiling and rosy-cheeked. Her hair is still full-bodied and her skin isn't grayed as old snow. Suddenly the couple starring in my fantasy are naked, and there it is, the mole, the landmark of her back, announcing her name. Lily. My body trembles in time to the closeted couple's grunts. And when they come to a stop, I do, too.

I wonder how many calories an orgasm expends.

Don't think about calories, our group leader says. But it's Psychology 101: the human mind doesn't register the negative well.

• • •

Test subjects are presented with the sentence: *There are no birds in the sky!* The same test subjects are presented with two images, one showing a bird in his nest, the other showing the bird in the sky, and, every time, the subjects associate the sentence with the picture of the bird, flying, skyward.

Instead of *Don't think about calories*, try *Think about elephants*.

Instead of *Don't think about her*, try, *Think about rabbits*, or *food*, or *a man*.

9

The days on which we're allowed to move are rare, but cleaning day is one of them. Today, we're cleaning our common room, which, like the rest of this place, has a termite infestation. The bugs are so methodical. They march, their trail so consistent in its single file that it looks as if the ceiling is perforated, as if the left side can be torn from the right.

The nurses dress our hands in latex gloves that feel like wearing another skin. A blue, smooth, rubbery skin, plump and full. Sometimes girls shriek and let the gloves fall from their hands afraid that the latex might adhere to them and hide those sharp bones protruding from their wrists forever. I keep mine on, suctioned tight to my body, the elastic grip reminding me that I exist.

2003 (14 years old—Lily: 103 lbs, Rose: 103 lbs)

On the first day back at school each year, disposable-gloved cafeteria workers served mince on toast for lunch. *As a special treat!* they told us.

After the Mister Kisser incident, Jemima bumped two other girls from her table to let Lily and me sit with her. She stopped spreading rumors about me being in love with Lily, and she stopped faux-gagging every time I started to speak. I was so grateful for the pause in cruelty that it almost felt like kindness.

"Rose," Jemima called when we arrived in the cafeteria on the first day of term. "Lily."

I tried not to feel smug at the order of our names, Rose, then Lily, it meant something. With Jemima, everything meant something. She thought out every detail of her day like a chess match. Who she'd sit next to at lunch, who she'd ask to accompany her to the bathroom, who she'd borrow lip gloss from. Like stray dogs, she gave us all just enough attention to keep us whining for more. The type of love that Jemima Gates sought was Large Group love. The order in which she spoke our names was a calculated move. I had won.

"Come sit with us," she said. "There's space here." She pointed to the sparc seats at her table.

The table talked around me, I almost felt as if I weren't there, about blow jobs.

"You start like this," said Jemima, lifting her banana and running her tongue around the stalk. "You can't just go right into it." We lifted our bananas, ran wet tongues around the stalks. "Then lick all the way up the underside," said Jemima. "Like you're trying to stop a popsicle from dripping."

We did. We licked.

"Then you take as much of it as you can into your mouth."

We opened wide, we inched the bananas back, like pointing a revolver up, toward the brain. The fruit felt too big for my mouth, but I didn't mind. This was how to be popular! Practice oral sex at lunch! The hardened tip nudged the back of my throat, and I gagged.

"That's my girl," said Jemima, laughing and removing her own banana from her mouth. "That's the kind of dedication that'll get a man to fall in love. Doesn't it feel good?"

My throat felt wounded. The banana's head was red with blood—mine. "Yes," I said. "It feels so good."

"Hear hear, sister," she said, toasting me with her bottle of orange juice.

See how easy it is to be normal? Agree and agree and agree! This was something I could do, keep doing. This was a sustainable personality. The new me! Blow-job-loving, oral-sex-wanting, Jemima's-best-friend me.

"Now you have a decision to make," said Jemima, her eyes starry. "Spit or swallow." Us popular girls, we looked around at one another. This was an ultimatum, no one had to say.

Lauren, the minion, gulped. Lily quickly copied, swallowed. I glanced at Jemima Gates, whose smile faltered, just a little, but enough for me to know. I took my single-ply napkin and held it to my mouth, spat once, twice for good measure, into the paper, and balled it in my fist. Jemima winked, spat into her napkin, and folded her arms across her chest. "You two just drank jizz," she said, with a performative gag.

The other girls stared, their eyes seething, I could almost hear the feline hiss. Lily knew I knew nothing about blow jobs. Her stare was a chill on my cheek, but I was busy basking in the light of Jemima's approval, and I could barely taste my twin's disappointment as Jemima took my hand in hers, flipped my arm, soft side up, and pressed her mouth to my wrist. My first kiss.

"So, I read about this new diet," she said, turning back to the table, our interaction over. I mourned the moment immediately. The way an extra must feel when the star of a show interacts with them briefly, just to order coffee or push past them on the bus. A fleeting fame.

Jemima told the table of a diet she'd read about in one of her mother's magazines: the Apple-a-Day Diet. The diet's title was also its rule book. Simple. Foolproof. Eat one apple per day for ten days.

"What do you think, girls? It's the diet Kat Mitchells is on, and have you seen her? She's so skinny."

"So pretty," the table agreed.

Jemima tucked her hair behind her ears. "Okay, then." She smiled, her lip gloss glinting in the sun. "Are you in?"

When Lily turned to me, eyebrows raised in proposition, I nodded, eager to do the things these better girls did.

"Lil?" said Jemima, already pushing her lunch tray away from herself, demonstrating the start of her diet.

"I'm in," Lily said, looking at me, then Jemima, then back at me.

"We're in," I said.

"Diet starts today, ladies," said Jemima, taking only the apple from her tray and smiling at the group as, one by one, each popular girl picked up her apple. "We're gonna be Kat Mitchells skinny!" She bit into the apple, and the sound was a sharp crack.

The rest of the table lifted their apples, our apples, to our lips. We bit, chewed, and it was almost as if we were one mouth, a communal swallow. Lily and I looked at each other and smiled. We were in.

We're armed with spray bottles and scrubbing brushes, and the nurses tell us, "Go, clean!" And we do. Say what you want about us thin girls, but we can clean. We scrub at the floors, at the walls, at the tables and chairs. We scrub and scrub at the imperfect and then at the perfect just the same, our skewer arms threatening to bisect all the while. It's how we earn our keep in this place we don't want to be kept.

I love cleaning day. I count lost calories in Tic Tacs. One Tic Tac = two calories. It takes ten minutes of scrubbing to lose one Tic Tac. I scrub the mints out of me and watch them tumble to the floor, scatter, and then I scrub those away, too.

After school on the day the apple diet started, our parents ordered a pizza and left it on the table for us to find before going out on a date night.

We were accustomed to being home alone. Our parents had always treated us like each other's babysitter. When they decided to have a kid, they thought it would bring them together. A filling for the sandwich that was their marriage. But then they had twins, and Lily and I were a ready-made family. We didn't need them the way an only child might. We only needed each another.

Lily opened the box and inhaled. "Pepperoni," she said.

"We're not eating, remember?" I took a glass from the cupboard and filled it with water, calorie-free and diet-approved.

"Don't be stupid." Lily lifted a slice, used her palm as a plate. "Jemima was joking around."

"I don't think so," I said. "I'm not risking it."

"You're so weird about Jemima Gates," said Lily. "That whole banana-blow-job thing today. It's like you have a crush on her or something."

She watched for my response so carefully.

"Me?" I said. "You're the one who starts giggling whenever she kisses your wrist."

"Whatever." Lily finished her slice and took another. "You're seriously not going to eat any of this?"

I shook my head and sat at the table, sipping water, watching Lily. She ate and ate, slice after slice, she ate her way through the entire thing. I could almost feel the ache in my own belly, but she pretended to be barely full.

"Yum." She wiped her lips with a napkin and closed the empty box. "All done."

Lily went to watch TV, and I printed a poster of Kat Mitchells in a miniskirt and tank top. Her hip bones splayed out of her body like wings. Her clavicle, sharp cliffs over her chest. I hung it above my bed and smiled up at her, the pop star, so thin. I could look like that.

As we brushed our teeth before bed that night, I noticed Lily's stomach in the mirror, swollen, a tiny bulge under her T-shirt. I stroked my own torso, flat.

When we look in the mirror, we see inverted versions of ourselves. In a photograph, flattened versions of ourselves. The closest anyone can come to seeing themselves is still only a manipulation of the self. The closest I can come to seeing myself is Lily.

Something that happens when you start dieting: You notice bodies. You notice everybody. You notice every body. Everyone has a body and they bring it with them everywhere they go. You notice fat bodies and remember who you were, and you notice thin bodies and remember who you want to be. You notice gaps between thighs, cellulite on stomachs, arms that tremble, knees that bulge. You notice your mother's bony fingers and your father's drooping chin. You notice the body that swells over too-tight jeans and the one whose ribs can be counted all the way up to her neck. Everybody has a body, but you will always feel like an intruder in yours.

Sarah wipes down windowsills as I polish the glass.

"A married guy?" she says, when I finish my recount of Lily's visit. "So what?"

"He's married."

"Sure, but I thought she always dated terrible guys? I thought terrible was like, her type."

"Yeah, but this seems different," I say. "She's got these shiny eyes. She's—"

"Happy?" says Sarah.

I spray solvent onto already-clean glass and wipe the splatter away. "Maybe."

"If she's happy, then why do you care? I thought you wanted her to be happy."

"Because he's married!" I climb down from the stool I'd been using as a ladder. "And he's a *smoker.* She's smoking, like, cigarettes."

"I miss cigarettes."

She looks so eighteen I could cry. Instead, I forge on. There is a point to be made! "It's like she can't see that this relationship has an expiry date. She's going to get her heart broken."

Sarah circles an arm around my waist and pulls me close. Her breath smells of sick, and I wonder how she managed to purge when every bathroom visit is supervised by a nurse. Kat must have a secret spot, but I'm not worried. She'll be found out. They always are, the purgers. Vomiting into their own shoes or the suitcase they brought here. You can only hide the tang of sour sick for so long.

"Listen," Sarah says. "Focus on you for now. Your sister will be okay. You need to figure out your own stuff before you think about hers."

She rests her head in the crook of my neck. She's right, and I thought that Lily and I had come to that very agreement, although never explicitly: that we would focus on my health until I was better and then our lives could be taken off hold. But now she's dating. Moving on. Without me.

"She's so lucky to have you," says Sarah. "I wish I had someone like you."

Her hair is soft against my cheek, and, as I rest my chin on the crown of her head, the vomit becomes something softer, still bitter and fermented, but in a way not unlike a glass of wine. Maybe a chardonnay.

"You do," I say. "You have me."

The window is so clean now that if I squint, I can see the blur of our outline, me and Sarah. We look similar.

"Hey," comes a shout from the door. "You two want to get a room? I can't offer a penthouse at the Four Seasons, but my room could do with a good old-fashioned christening."

I turn, we turn, Kat, standing smug, leaning against the door frame, latex up to her elbows, elegant as opera gloves on her skinny arms. She smiles. Her teeth hemmed brown from her own barf.

Kat. So determined to disrupt our ecosystem, this carefully curated boredom we inhabit. Do you see how slowly time passes in here? Minutes drool. We like it. Everything is predictable, and we can watch life pass, like sitting at the window and seeing how the day turns dark.

"It's not like that," Sarah whispers, too quietly.

"Shut up, Kat," I say, too loudly.

I once read about a science professor at a prestigious university who suffered from a depersonalization disorder. One morning, he woke up and he didn't recognize himself in the mirror. He thought his reflection was an intruder and punched the glass. Then, once his hand stopped bleeding, he decided that his estranged reflection must have been a version of himself in a different dimension. He wrote a long academic paper and had it published in esteemed journals. He won a big award. It took months for anyone to realize that his groundbreaking research was based on a personality disorder rather than multidimensional physics.

Our group leader is teaching us how to pre-drink.

You lose your identity in the facility. Your *I* and *me*, your *my* and *mine*. You become a *we* and an *us*.

It is important to be part of something bigger than you is what the group leader tells us.

We sit in our room, surrounded by pictures of mountains and forests and lakes, words that say DREAM and HOPE and LOVE, these things that are meant to inspire us, meant to make us feel something other than hungry. We focus on the drinking glasses in front of us.

The group leader takes a carafe of water and drops two slices of lemon into it. She fills our glasses halfway then sits at the head of the circle. Circles, if drawn properly, should not have a clear summit, but they all do. In every circle, there is a leader. Ours is lifting a glass to her purple-painted lips.

"Just let the liquid touch your lips, girls," she says. "Don't open your mouths. Just tip, don't sip, and release." She sets the glass back down. There is a purple smear where her lipstick has stained the glass. "Now you try!"

As I wait for someone else to go first, I look out the window, the only one our room has, and see that the thin men, too, are in a group session. They, too, have glasses filled with water and lemon wedges, and their leader, too, is lifting a glass to his lips. I scan their circle and spot my handkerchief-waving lover, staring at his glass of water as if, if he were to stare hard enough, it might shatter into nothing.

I wave discreetly while the rest of the thin girls focus on their glasses.

"Everything okay, Rose?" the group leader says.

I nod. Lift my glass. "Yes," I say. "I am!"

"Are you, darling?" Kat says. "Are you really okay? You seem a little, I don't know, wound up."

I say nothing.

"You sure you don't need a little something to help take the edge off? You don't want to just let loose? Lose control for a bit? Because you know I can help with that, baby." She licks her top lip and her tongue removes a layer of lipstick, pink peeking out from beneath the scarlet.

I ignore her. Turn away. Touch the rim of the glass to my lips, and, across the way, in the other window, my handkerchief waver does the same. Almost as if we're reflections of each other. Or like we are sitting across a candlelit table, a cheers (to love!), our first sip.

Heterosexuality! Me and my lover, a real live man!

"Well done, Rose!" Our group leader claps and claps. "You did it!"

I did. My lips make no mark on the glass. It looks untouched when I set it back down.

Back before I was admitted to the facility, walking down the sidewalk, sitting in the park, I'd see homeless people, cardboard signs gripped tight in calloused fingers. They always read: HUNGRY. I'd watch them from my bench, fresh espresso (zero calories) warming my palms, and I'd tell myself, *See, Rose, that's what real hunger looks like.* I'd tell myself, *See, Rose, you're hungry by choice.*

10

There's another envelope on my floor. I open it.

R—

I know I only just wrote, but I've been thinking about you lately. I hope this isn't intrusive, me writing you like this. If you want me to stop, maybe you could call me again? I won't pick up. Or I will, but I won't say anything unless you want me to. If you want me to, you could say the word *phalange*, or something. I'll know what it means. Or if you don't want me to say anything, you could maybe say *asthmatic*. I just chose those words. You can use different ones. I don't want our relationship to be on my terms. I think it probably has been, in the past, I mean. I really am trying to change, Rose. I hope you are, too.

I miss you very much, for what it's worth.

—M

I run my thumb over the handwriting, the grooves in the paper. *Phalange*, I think. *Phalange, phalange, phalange.* I close my eyes, put the letter away, and look out across the courtyard.

2003 (14 years old—Lily: 105 lbs, Rose: 99 lbs)

At school, Lily was good at doing almost everything, but to diet isn't to do, it's to refrain from doing. Refrain from eating. I was good at not doing. I was good at dieting. I ate a slice of apple for breakfast, half for lunch, and the rest for dinner. Lily ate the food from my plate.

Jemima and the other girls lasted two days on the diet, but I kept going, in love with, in awe of the new control I had over my body.

To be a twin is to relinquish power over the self. Lily and I had always been a single entity more than we were individuals. We were referred to as "the twins," and we referred to ourselves as "we" and "us" and "our," and we were always aware of what the other was doing and where and why. Lily and I played a constant game of controlling the other and ceding our control to the other. It was a game of self-protection and sister protection. A tiny, consensual war. But this diet was mine. Consumption was something I could dictate on my very own.

Each morning, I saw a difference: flatter stomach, leaner thighs. It felt like progress. If only that goalkeeper could see me now.

Jemima Gates said I looked hot, like a supermodel, and I swallowed her compliments with a hunger I barely recognized. "Look at you, babe!" she shrieked, a week after the start of my diet, when I showed her the gap between my jeans and my hips. "Guys, look at Rose! Look how skinny she's getting!"

She made the table watch as I pulled my waistband away from my body, an advertisement for the diet.

"I don't know how you're still doing it." She spooned yogurt into her mouth, licked the corners of her lips. She was trying a different diet by now. Plain Greek yogurt for breakfast, lunch, and dinner. I liked to watch her lick the stomach of the spoon. "I got so hangry."

Jemima Gates knew every new word before anyone else. I wrote them down and recited them like multiplication tables, etching them to memory. I wanted to learn her language. *Friggin'. Peace out. Muffin top. Catfight. Shit happens. Ride or die. Right on. Player hater. Hangry.*

As the other girls marveled at commitment to the diet that had made Kat Mitchells look the way she did, pixie-like, fragile, I sliced a sliver of apple, rested the fruit on my tongue. Skinny celebrity. Of course I was hungry. I was starving! What the girls didn't see as they eyed my new bones with envy, was me eyeing their lunches with the same.

Lily slid my lunch over to herself and took the cucumber sandwich we had packed together that morning, unwrapped the plastic, and bit into the bread with a crunch. She had already eaten her own.

"Speaking of," Jemima Gates said. "Hey, Lil. Don't you think you're looking a little, I dunno, bigger these days?"

The other girls giggled. I felt Lily's embarrassment, hot in my mouth, and kept my eyes locked on the empty table before me, refusing to acknowledge her blush. The truth was, she was looking a little bigger, her breasts swelling, her stomach folding like laundry when she sat, or was it my new smallness making her appear that way? I couldn't tell.

Humans desire most things in excess. We are creatures of consumption and products of capitalism, but weight is something we prefer to lack.

To me, Jemima said, "You're so pretty, babe." She took my wrist, flipped it, and leaned in. Her kiss lingered against the blue veins, my wiring. Her lips left a heart-shaped stencil, and I fought the desire to see if my mouth fit there.

Some things about the body can be controlled: One's fitness level. One's fingernail length.

Some things about the body cannot be controlled: One's height. One's blood type.

Some things about the body we have found ways to control: One's eye color. One's hair shade.

Some things about the body I learned to control: My sexuality. My appetite.

When Lily visits, she isn't alone. She is arm in arm with an unremarkable man. If he weren't called Phil, he would be called John, Mark, Joe. He is so boring that I wonder whether Lily is playing a prank. *This* is the man for whom she ended her celibacy? *This* is the man for whom she cast aside her morals? He looks like his favorite topic of conversation is the weather. Like his main love language would be reminding his beloveds to get their oil changed. Like he would refuse to rub in the sunscreen on his nose and like he would say, *Let's blow this popsicle stand*, as a funny bit before leaving a restaurant. The type of person who did these things did not cheat on his wife with his daughter's schoolteacher.

"You must be Rose," says the unremarkable man. He's more quiet than men usually are. "I've been so wanting to meet you. I've been nagging Lily for a while now. This might sound strange, but I sort of felt like I couldn't really get to know Lily without at least meeting you." He holds out his hand to shake, and I stare at the gesture. No one has tried to shake my hand in a long time. It is difficult to take me seriously.

"Hello," I say, accepting my new role as a sophisticate, a hand shaker. I remember to keep my fingers stiff, wrist straight, to squeeze but not squelch. "And that doesn't sound strange at all."

"Good grip," Phil says with a smile of approval. How I love to be loved!

"Yours, too," I say, because people like to be complimented.

"You know, though," Phil says, "in a way, I feel like I already know you. Lily talks about you all the time." He speaks softly, as if his tongue is wrapped in cotton. His smile reaches all the way to his eyes.

"Not all the time," says Lily, taking the spot at the foot of my bed. I check to make sure my pillow is covering the letters. It is. I can only imagine what she would do. Maybe shred them into tiny scraps right before my eyes!

"So," says Phil, choosing to stand, to lean against the wall like one of the smokers at school, too cool to stand unassisted. "Lily tells me you've been in here awhile now."

I wave my arms about, my very own palace. Welcome to my humble abode!

"I like what you've done with the place. You've really made it feel like home." He sounds so sincere that, when I look around to see what he must be seeing, I expect my room to be miraculously ornate, paved with photographs, maybe a decorative cushion or two. But, no. The walls, blank but for my tally chart and the hole I had poked in the wood.

"There's a hole in my wall."

"I can do something about that," says Phil. He looks at the hole, then back at me. "Only if you want me to, that is."

I gesture for him to go ahead, and Phil leans over my bed to inspect the puncture wound. "I'll be right back," he says.

When we're alone, Lily grimaces. "So?"

"So?"

"What do you think?"

"Of?"

"Phil. Obviously."

"Oh, Phil," I say. "He seems nice."

"He seems nice? That's it?"

"I only just met him, Lil! I'm not about to espouse my love for a stranger."

"Are you talking about me?" Phil says as he knocks his knuckles on my open door. "Or am I safe to come back in?"

"We are," I say. "But you are."

He proudly displays a roll of strapping tape, meant to keep the IV stuck in a thin arm. I move aside and he gets to work, peeling strips from the roll and biting them free, taping them over the gap in the wall. He covers the hole twice before stepping back to admire his work. "What do you think?"

"Better, I guess," I say.

"It's perfect," says Lily.

"Is that what you're reading?" Phil plucks the science anthology atop the pile of books that towers on my nightstand and opens the cover. "A science buff?"

"I like almost everything," I say, which is true. I don't make many distinctions.

"That's a relief." He lowers the book to smile. "I was afraid you wouldn't like me."

"Me too."

He laughs. "You're a hard case."

"That's what they tell me."

He laughs harder. Lily's gaze is switching between Phil and me. Phil and me. She's spectating our tiny tennis match.

"You know," he says after skimming a page, "I heard the other day that Johannes Kepler's mother was accused of witchcraft when he published his theory on orbits. He published it as fiction because he knew it'd be seen as heretic, but it didn't help."

I nod.

"It happened all the time, apparently," he says. Flipping the book in his hands. "Mothers stoned at the stake for the discoveries their sons made."

I look at Lily. She's watching Phil with what could only be called hunger.

"We owe them everything, don't we? Those mothers. Sacrificing themselves for science."

"Maybe they didn't do it voluntarily," I say, taking the book back and setting it into its place.

"That's a good point, Rose," says Phil, nodding, solemn. He settles into the chair in the corner of my room. Crosses his legs at the ankle. "I'm sure many of them didn't. Women are always taking the fall for men."

I smile. "I'm reading about animal behaviors right now."

"Fascinating," says Phil. "How are you enjoying it?"

"It's funny," I say. "I can tell you a human anecdote for almost every passage about an obscure animal behavior."

"We're all just animal," says Phil. "At heart, I think."

"I think so, too," I say. "Sometimes I think about what kind of animal I am."

"And what kind of animal do you think you are?"

"I'm not sure." I look at Lily. "But whichever animal I am, Lily must be that, too."

"I think we're different animals," says Lily. "Maybe similar animals, but not the same."

"Of course we're the same," I say with a laugh. "Don't be stupid, Lil. Look at us." And Phil is looking at us. He's frowning, his jaw set, calculating. He reaches for Lily's hand and the two lace fingers. I braid my left hand and my right.

"Well, I think . . ." Phil takes a pair of glasses out of his breast pocket and puts them on. They make him look like a professor and maybe I can see what Lily sees in him, after all. "I think you two are like a pair of swans. One black, one white. All beauty and grace, but with that twin synchrony."

I smile. Lily smiles, too.

"I think you're a bear," says Lily. "Strong but loving." She stands from the foot of my bed and lowers herself onto his lap. Her body is bigger than his, but he wraps his arms around her and takes the weight of her on his knee. Her skin is bright, her eyes dancing, and her joy tastes of butter, a slick coat of fat on my palate.

Jemima Gates was a fad diet guinea pig. She read about them in her mother's magazines and committed immediately. The Atkins Diet, the Baby Food Diet, the Lemon Detox Diet, the Cabbage Soup Diet. Once she tried an all-fat diet. At lunch, she'd gnaw through a stick of butter. Something about fighting fat with fat. We watched her swallow it with a smile.

She was already thin, Jemima Gates, but it was never enough. If she wasn't on some extreme diet, she was lost. She needed each meal dictated to her by some greater, more feminine power. *This will make you better*, the rules of every regime promised. *This will make you happy.*

"Anyway," says Phil, kissing Lily's bare shoulder with such affection I could pout, but I won't! We can only control our own joy. "We should get going. I have a little surprise planned for your sister."

Lily's smile widens. I have never seen her happiness so tangible. "A surprise?"

Phil winks at me, a conspiracy. I feel like part of his secret even though I know nothing of the surprise. "I'm sure I'll be seeing you again soon, Rose," he says. "It was so nice to meet you."

"Bye, baby sister," says Lily, standing to hug me. As she does, she hisses, "So?" in my ear. I like to be consulted on matters of importance.

"Approved," I whisper back.

When Phil shakes my hand, he lifts my knuckles to his lips and kisses them as light as a miracle.

...

In America, there's a divorce every thirteen seconds. That's 554 divorces over the running time of an average romantic comedy. How's that for love?

2004 (15 years old—Lily: 108 lbs, Rose: 95 lbs)

Lily was asked on a date, (our first date!) and I could taste the trace of ripening stone fruit at the back of my throat. Her excitement tasted of plums, but she said mine was more nectarine. Most of our other tastes matched up.

After finishing the Apple-a-Day Diet, I took it upon myself to read about weight loss on the internet. I learned about calorie tallying and tracking kilojoules. I learned about metabolism catalysts, and I learned that fasting can slow your metabolism to the point where your weight plateaus. It's important to eat intermittently, the internet told me, to keep the body working, to keep your digestion from falling dormant. I allowed myself two bites of every meal. Two spoonfuls of cornflakes for breakfast. Two bites of a sandwich at lunch. Two mouthfuls of macaroni at dinner. I kept a pack of Tic Tacs in my pocket, popped one any time my stomach growled.

We watched romantic comedy after romantic comedy in preparation for Lily's big night. Filled ourselves with Julia Roberts and Tom Hanks and Heath Ledger and Meg Ryan and Hugh Grant. One of the movies starred Kat Mitchells, who tried and failed to make the segue into acting. She played a straight girl in love with the high school quarterback, who doesn't date her until after the makeover montage. Until after she takes off her glasses, has her braces removed, straightens her hair, learns how to apply lipstick.

Lily, her eyes lit up with the reflection of those huge romances. The type of love she was seeking: Monogamy. I wanted to take her face in my hands. *I'm right here!*

After we exhausted the romance section of the video store, I held her hands, walked backward, a couple at an ice-skating rink, as Lily practiced teetering around the living room in a pair of our mother's heels.

The boy was Robbie Newton, and the girls at school told me he was hot. I didn't see it. There was something embarrassing about the way his chin shied away from the world, slunk back into his neck like a scolded child. I told Lily she was the luckiest girl on the planet.

The day of the big date, we got home from school, went straight to our parents' en suite, and stayed there for hours. Lily perched on the toilet as I crouched before her, smearing foundation, laughing when it made her skin glow a deep orange. Lily laughed, too, sighed, whined, "Can you stop messing around and do it good?" she kept saying. But I didn't want to rush our afternoon. We hadn't felt like ourselves in a while.

Eventually, I painted her face in a way she liked. A dusting of powder. A light rouge on the cheekbones. A gold smear on her eyelids. A red shout on her lips.

"I look like Julia Roberts," she said, when I finished swiping mascara through her lashes.

I stepped back, held her at arm's length. She didn't look like any famous actress. She looked like me, like us, in ten years. Grown-up and adult, and I knew we'd be beautiful.

Lily wanted to wear one of my skirts, one that was two sizes too big for me now, but when she zipped it closed it pinched her stomach in tight. A fold of skin slunk over the waistband.

"Is it too small?" I said.

"It fits."

She put on our mother's pussy-bow blouse and a pair of her own sandals because she'd never managed to perfect the stilettos. Then she sat on the stairs, waiting for seven p.m., which was the time Robbie promised to pull up in his new car. Or, new-old car. It was a shitty Corolla with rusted doors and a busted bumper, but owning something with an engine made him a hotter commodity than most of the other guys at our school.

Lily looked like a real woman, sitting, legs crossed at the knees, on our wooden staircase. I squatted beside her and tucked a strand of flat-ironed hair, still warm from its treatment, behind her ear.

"You look beautiful, Lil," I told her.

She blushed and I felt my own cheeks redden. We waited. Waited.

At eight p.m., she stood from her waiting spot, walked downstairs, opened the freezer door, and retrieved a pint of double chocolate chip. She took two spoons and led the way back to our room, sat on the foot of my bed. She opened the ice cream and took a mouthful. Then another. The other spoon, my spoon, lay untouched on the duvet. She had made her way through half the container, four hundred calories, when I decided to say something.

"Are you okay?" I said as she excavated more ice cream. "Lil?"

She said nothing, finished the container, licked the spoon, and then stood. She didn't even cry as she stripped the blouse, wriggled my skirt down her hips, which were embarking on a puberty I hadn't yet met, then wound her hair into a bun.

I sat on my bed, beneath my Kat Mitchells poster, cross-legged and weeping as Lily wiped layer after layer from her face. Then she pulled on a T-shirt, her own, and climbed into bed beside me. We hadn't slept together since we were much younger, and she took up more of the mattress now. The only way I could fit was to curl up tight into the arc of her body like a ball in a socket.

"It was Jemima, wasn't it?" she whispered into the crown of my head. "Was this whole thing a dare?"

"I don't know," I said.

"Don't you?"

"I don't!" I turned to face Lily, hoping that she might see my honesty somewhere on my face. She knew I was telling the truth. She could taste it.

"I know," she whispered. "I'm sorry, Rosie, I'm just. Nothing, I'm sorry."

"At least today was fun," I said. "It felt like—"

"Yeah, it did. And yeah, it was. Until."

"Yeah," I sighed. "Until."

"Have you ever thought about dating anyone?" Lily said.

"I'm not really into any of the guys at school."

"I said 'anyone.'"

"You mean, like, guys at different schools?"

Lily said nothing, just kissed my bare shoulder and slept.

I dream of eating. I often do. I dream of ordering a steak, the biggest one, and holding it in my palms, letting its blood seep through my fingers. I dream of biting it, chewing.

There are girls who do that, too. Girls who buy cartfuls of groceries, potato chips (10 per chip), chocolates (30–100, depending on size), candy (at least 10 apiece), breads (79 per slice) and cheeses (113 per slice), the most frightening stuff, and they sit at home and chew and spit and chew and spit and just the flavor satisfies them. They don't account for the calories in flavor. I account for every calorie. I count every calorie. I know the caloric value of every food, and I can spit those numbers out between my lips like watermelon seeds. I can calculate, add and subtract them, too. I can do all kinds of tricks, like tying the stem of a cherry with my tongue. I can tell you that a cherry has five calories but the skin only has one single calorie in it, so if you use your teeth to peel back the purpled epidermis to reveal the fruit's flesh, if you chew that thin, filmy layer, swallow, by that time you've expended more calories than you've consumed. Almost exercise. You then, of course, have to throw away the rest of that grotesque, flayed fruit. It contains too much.

In my dream, I chew the steak. I chew and chew until the meat is inedible as an eraser. I try to keep chewing, but this food doesn't want to be eaten.

I wake, shivering and nauseated, my fist pressed to my lips. My finger bleeding, my chin wet with blood. This is not the first time I have been carnivorous in the night. I've been self-cannibalizing for years. Stop eating and the body learns to eat itself.

Pressing my thumb to the wound, I flip my bedside light on and sit up. Across the courtyard, my lover's room is also aglow. He's been waiting for me all this time! Standing in the window, watching me sleep. It's a true love, ours.

He smiles, waves, then points at his bare chest, which looks like an X-ray, striped with ribs in a way that would alarm most, but not me. Then he starts forming shapes with his body. Angling his arms and legs. The shapes are letters, and they are difficult to make out, but I nod encouragingly, a supportive relationship.

He twists and morphs, stretches and contorts, as if he were made of dough. He reaches his arms up, a tall letter. *J* or *I*, followed by *R* or *K*. Eventually, I have *JRAM*, and I applaud his efforts.

I whisper, "Hi, Jram."

I spell my name for him. *R-O-S-E*; my limbs are thin as letters.

We smile at each other's titles. This is our silent love. It is so easy to be with a man! We blow good-night kisses and shut off our lights.

I barely think about the love letters beneath my head. I barely think about them all night long.

11

In the facility, genders are separated most of the time, including at meals. For many thin girls, their disorder is triggered by men. For some, it's their mother. And for most, it's nothing at all, or, not nothing, but everything. It's having to exist in this world, with this body that everyone can see. There is no privacy here!

I wonder whether Jram might take me to dinner one day. If we're ever released, he might take me to the fanciest restaurant in town. We would both sit, smiling, smuggling food under the napkins on our laps. Or perhaps we could go to dinner with Lily and Phil. A double date! Phil and I would talk about books. Lily and Jram would find a common love (of me?), and how we'd laugh. We'd laugh!

Today, lunch is Mexican themed. The nurses like to make our meals occasions; they think they can cure us with cultural appropriation. They slap straw sombreros atop our heads as we enter the dining hall. The meal is refried beans and rice. I use my sombrero as a trash can, scooping piles of food into its well. Sarah notices my trick, winks, removes her own hat, and joins in.

"I met Phil," I tell her as we work. "Lily's new boyfriend."

"And?"

"He seems . . ." I pause. It is important not to jump to conclusions. I won't fall headfirst into this relationship the way Lily did. It's true, he made a good first impression. Took interest in me, in what I was interested in. A feminist, probably, with the comment about women taking the fall for men, and he seemed genuinely fond of Lily, the way he let her sit on his lap, held her with such affection. His visit had me reassessing my former criticism. Maybe his encouragement of Lily's weight loss is simply a healthy form of support. Maybe her recent smoking habit is her own fault more than his. "He seems fine," I say to Sarah, who nods.

Kat, as usual, comes in to inhale her meal. "My plan is in action, bunnies," she says, a stage whisper. "All systems are go. Come by the supply closet sometime. I'll give you a good price."

"A good price?" I say.

"For what?" Sarah says.

Kat only winks, then picks up her empty plate and leaves, in search of a place to throw up. Only this time, when she leaves, she isn't alone. A choir of thin girls follows her, starry-eyed. They sit, eat a meal for the first time in days, weeks, months, then chase Kat out of the cafeteria. A bulk barf session. Imagine the smell. I take comfort in knowing they won't be able to keep their secret for long. There is nothing subtle about the stench of rotting vomit.

Animals love to follow one another. Their collective is often named for the verb they enact. A group of bees is a swarm. Crocodiles, a bask. A group of elephants, a parade. Flamingos, a stand. A family of hippopotami is a bloat. Lemurs make up a conspiracy. A leap of leopards. A crash of rhinoceroses. A knot of toads. Parrots are a pandemonium. Skunks are a stench. A group of thin girls, in recovery, we are surviving.

Sarah and I smile across the table from each other as we escape the meal in our own way. She isn't quite a Kat convert yet, but I'm clinging on with my fingernails. I see the way she yearns to be part of that new plurality. She watches them the way Lily always watched romantic comedies. With this great hunger.

"I'm having a love affair," I whisper, hoping to redirect Sarah's attention.

It works. Sarah turns away from Kat and her cronies, her attention back on me. Eyes fat. "In here?"

I nod.

"Wow." She stashes the last of her meal in her hat. "How?"

I smile in a way that I hope is coy.

"Wait, are you gay?" she says. "Hold on, are you *the* lesbian? From the supply closet?"

"Why would you ask that?"

"I don't know. Because we're only allowed to interact with other women in here. Who else could you be having an affair with?"

"Oh." I clear my throat. "I see. No. It's not a woman."

"Who, then?"

"Jram."

"Jam?"

"No, Jram."

"Jeromy?"

"Jram."

"I don't know what you're saying. I can't tell which word is coming out of your mouth."

"*J. R. A. M.* Jram."

"Jram. Weird name."

"I like it," I say, defensive. "I think it's German."

"German?"

"Yeah like, Jghchram," I say, from the throat.

"Oh yeah." She nods. "Probably German. Is he hot?"

"He's handsome," I say, smiling.

"He's in here?"

"On the other side," I say. "Obviously. The men's side."

"That's wonderful, darling."

I frown at her new pet name. It's wrong out of her mouth. Like an infant saying *fuck*. She pulls on her fingers, one after the other, as if a miracle could happen, and maybe that light cracking of knuckles finding air inside her *is* a miracle for Sarah, but to me it sounds like the ticking of a clock.

We leave the hall with hatfuls of carbohydrates. We wear them on our heads. One thin girl gets stopped at the exit, she's holding her hat like a purse, thoughtless. The nurse in charge of checking us out of the dining hall takes the girl by the arm, leads her away to be punished. The rest of us sneak away, unnoticed.

2004 (15 years old—Lily: 112 lbs, Rose: 94 lbs)

Jemima Gates introduced me to laxatives. Little blue capsules that promised to empty me. We clutched them in clenched fists in the school cafeteria. We cheersed them like champagne. We washed them down with Diet Coke, giggling. We were children, and shit was still funny.

There is nothing funny about laxatives in effect. The way they take the torso, grip the gut like a strong man's hands, wring your body out dry. The way they scrunch your insides into a balled-up bad draft. The way they grab and squeeze, a toothpaste tube being milked for its last dregs.

The sprint to the bathroom, the collapse, the cry. The way empty-ing yourself aches. The way it makes you feel bloodied and raw. The way giving birth might feel, as if you've pushed out more than you're meant to. After the first few times, there's flesh in there, with your waste.

I ignored the bloodied stool and flushed. This was the emptiness I craved.

On the way back to my room, my sombrero heavy with rice and beans, I knock on the supply closet door.

"Hello?" I hiss. "Anyone in there?"

I try the handle, but it stops, locked.

Freud believed all humans to be born bisexual, and that the libido was distributed between the sexes, either in a manifest or latent form.

Latency is easy. Stop eating and your appetite dwindles with your weight, only to be rediscovered, brought out of its latent slumber, by a sudden whiff of freshly baked bread. What Freud didn't address is that *latent* is a verb. You, too, can latent! I've been latenting parts of me my whole life!

2004 (15 years old—Lily: 115 lbs, Rose: 93 lbs)

Fiona and Freya, the girls who wanted so badly to be twins they wore matching outfits, as if similar cardigans could overcome their mismatched genetic codes. Freya wore foundation two shades too light, vampired herself in an attempt to be as pale as Fiona. Fiona ironed her curly hair so flat it hung around her face, her own personal rainfall.

The rumors were so repeated they became fact. Fiona and Freya were lesbians. People told stories of them spreading their legs and fitting themselves together, tessellating their bodies, cunt to cunt.

"Hey," Fiona said, taking the chair beside me in biology. It was one of the few classes Freya wasn't in with her. "Can I sit here?"

My jaw tensed, muscles ached. I swallowed. The stares from the class stuck to me.

What I wanted to say: *No.*

What I wanted to say: *Why are you doing this to me?*

What I wanted to say: *Why are you making me do this to you?*

What I said: "What makes you think you can talk to me, dyke?"

There was silence. And then Jemima Gates, perched upon her usual throne at the back of the class, laughed. And then everyone laughed. Fame!

Everyone except Fiona, who pinkened and closed her eyes. She left the class that day and switched to economics, never returned, never spoke to me again.

Lily doesn't visit after lunch, the way she usually does. She doesn't visit before dinner. She doesn't visit. I imagine her with Phil, at dinner, perhaps. Phil ordering something embarrassingly lavish, caviar and coq au vin, Lily ordering a side salad, undressed, and when the server set it down before her, she would gasp, she would say, *Oh, I can't possibly eat all of this*, the way us girls are taught to. I imagine her skipping out on dessert in favor of her hundredth cigarette of the day.

I can only control my own joy.

I mark another notch on my tally: 369 days. The wall, eaten away, bows to my touch. All that's left supporting this house is paper and paste.

I lie in bed with my phone. My fingers find Lily's number easily, as if that's all they were ever made for. She answers on the first ring, in silence. She isn't at dinner, isn't with Phil. She's home, and mine.

"You didn't visit."

"I know."

I wait.

"Phil thinks . . ." She pauses. "Phil thinks I should see less of you."

"Less of me?"

"He thinks you're bad for me."

"I'm bad?"

"He thinks that our relationship is unhealthy."

"Unhealthy? Where the hell did he get that from?" I think back to our meeting, Phil's and mine. It went so well. We charmed each other, didn't we? "What made him think that?"

"There was that animal thing," she says.

"I know," I say, recalling. "Swans. What's so unhealthy about swans?"

Lily says nothing. We sit in our moonlit quiet, as if our silence might preserve the phone's battery, until, at some point, I dissolve into sleep.

Given their size, swans have few natural predators. In England, the Crown owns all unmarked mute swans, and it is illegal to kill or injure one of the Queen's birds. In most other countries, the swan's main predator is man.

I wake around midnight, furious at Phil, taking Lily away from me. How dare he! Unhealthy? Me? I think of Phil, how he smiled, how he agreed (*Good point,* he'd said!), how he shook my hand and looked me in the eye. All that, a farce! I'd show him. Lily and I are family— no, closer, we're twins. We're a whisper away from being the same person. What would Phil know about sisterhood?

I yelp when a hangnail pulls too far. I've undressed my finger against its will. Protect my own peace. I divert my thought. Draw my blinds. But Jram's room is dark. Out my window, the leather sky is embroidered with stars. I love the night. It lets me feel small enough to mean almost nothing. I look for the constellations I know. The Southern Cross. Cancer. Hydra.

A binary star, I once read, is a system of two stars in which one revolves around the other. This is unexciting. It is simply a sisterhood.

So Phil misread the room. That's okay. I have plenty of time to convince him that I am Lily's most avid sporter, her most loyal watchdog, her best friend. Next time, I'll show him how Lily and I are not simply siblings, not like the girls at school who could forget about their older brothers, their younger sisters, for days on end, could go whole conversations without ever surfacing the name of their womb-mate. Lily and I were made for each other, I'll show him. How he'll apologize. How he'll accept me with open arms!

Sleep dawdles further away, almost out of sight, an outgoing tide. I yawn, stand, open my door, and peer out into the hall. Empty. I ease the door closed behind me and head toward the supply closet. Someone is in there, rustling, shifting. I press my ear to the door, attempt to discern voices, but no one is talking.

I try the handle, and it opens. Only, in the shadow of the closet there is no lesbian lovemaking, no solo masturbator riding a dildo, no. Instead, there is Kat, no top hat to cover her dry, bald scalp. She is crouched over a bag of potato chips. Mouth full. Her neck snaps up, and her eyes are wild on mine, a feral creature caught in the night.

"Get out," she seethes.

I swallow and apologize, back away from the room and let the door swing closed on its own. Oh, how every mighty does fall!

12

Lily doesn't come to see me for a week. I want to call her. I want to say, *Sister says, come visit me.* But Phil might see that as *unhealthy.* See what he has done? Lily has never gone a whole week without stopping in. A whole week of watching the other thin girls start to wear top hats and bow ties and pearls. I'm not sure how they're smuggling the costumes into the facility. Kat might be doing it, dressing her army as imitations of her. She's a celebrity, after all, and she probably has whole spools of strings to pull. A week of watching former anorectics, including Sarah, suddenly start to consume before rushing off to regurgitate. A week of watching Kat Mitchells become the facility's favorite thin girl. A week of watching Sarah watch Kat with her wide and adoring eyes. A week of feeling more termite than thin girl—I exist in the walls here now, watching the others change from the perimeter. The world is happening around me.

My chair in the dining hall starts to feel like home. I am a landmark of this room by now. I am the Egyptian pyramid of this cafeteria. Take my photograph! Here I am, sitting in the same chair, slumped over a full plate, stirring gluggy rice or pasta that still has its raw crunch.

You'd think that they'd try to woo us thin girls into eating with half-decent food, but instead they seem to have hired high schoolers taking their first home economics class. Not the good students, either.

I once read that George H. W. Bush banned broccoli in the White House because he didn't like it. If I were the president, I would ban food in the White House. The place would be so clean. Everything would smell fresh as linen. We would all drink sparkling water, my presidential staff and me, and we would sit around, insides bright and bubbling, discussing real world issues. We would solve the world's problems so quickly without breaking for every meal.

When I call Lily, on my slowly dying, battery-dwindling phone, she tells me she's sorry.

"I miss you," I say.

"I know."

"I know Phil doesn't want you to see me as often, but it's been a week." I breathe. See how healthy I am, Phil? See how reasonable and understanding? "You could just stop in for a minute?"

"I'll try, baby sister." Lily does sound sorry, her voice wilting, old vegetables. "I'm sorry. But I'm in love! I really am! Do I sound happy?"

"Happy?" I say. "I don't know."

"Don't be a brat." But I can hear the smile beneath the scold. "What about thin? Do I sound thin? I've lost about ten pounds. This diet's really working, and it helps that Phil's so supportive. He showed me this calorie-counting app. I can log my day's calories so I don't lose track of how much I've eaten. He's so great, Rosie. He took me away for the weekend. To the coast! We swam!"

As if swimming were a miracle. As if she's the first person to have ever swum.

What I want to say: *People swim every day, Lily.* I know exactly what he's doing. Phil. I know his game. Tricking me into liking him just for long enough to give Lily my approval, then pulling the rug. Taking her away from me. It's smart but futile. Lily can't live without me.

I say nothing. This is how to be mature. This is how to support your sister. Support, support, support! I can only control my own joy.

2004 (15 years old—Lily: 116 lbs, Rose: 90 lbs)

Without any conversation or agreement, Lily started to eat everything I wouldn't. She started eating breakfast enough for two, taking my packed lunch for herself, eating from my dinner plate while our parents were distracted. I wasn't sure if she was covering for me or just hungry. Her breasts were growing quickly. They began to hang heavy from her front. Sometimes, at dinner, they perched on the table's surface. I tried not to stare.

One night, I came down to the dinner table to find my meal already eaten, to find Lily leaning back in her chair, holding her distended stomach.

"Don't you get full?" I said. Trying to be gentle.

"No," said Lily. "I feel hungry. I feel hungry all the time."

In a way, I felt closer to her than ever, it was as if we were a single body, my hunger became hers. In a way, I felt further from her than ever. Loneliness occurs when we cannot see ourselves, our selves, in the ones we love.

The tongue-eating louse is a parasite that enters its host, a fish, through the gills. The female louse severs the blood vessels in the fish's tongue, causing the muscle to atrophy and fall off, and then attaches itself to the remaining nub, taking the tongue's former place and acting as a prosthetic. The fish can still eat with its parasitic tongue. The louse feeds mostly on the fish's mucus and blood left in the mouth area. Scientists have found that most fish infected with the louse are underweight.

Our parents didn't notice Lily's new hunger or my sudden lack thereof. They were too busy fighting. They had always argued. About money, about us, about themselves. Our father stayed late at the office, and even though we didn't know what that meant, our mother did.

"Am I not good enough for you?" she'd cry when he finally came home, too late, tie already loosened, only to be accosted in the foyer, slapped with whichever junk mail was piled nearest the door. "Am I not pretty enough for you? Am I too ugly? Too old? Too fat? Used up?"

He'd shake his head. "Not now, please, Mon. I'm exhausted. I need to sit."

"Really? What're you so tired from? Who is it this time? Tell me it wasn't the fucking mailman again, Bill. Don't be such a goddamn cliché."

Lily and I, pajama-clad, hiding behind the stairs, peering through the bars.

"I just want to eat dinner and go to bed. We can talk in the morning."

"No, we can talk right bloody now." Mum shoved her stockinged feet into heels and beckoned for us. "Girls, we're getting waffles," she said. "Get in the car."

It was always waffles. They took us to the diner down the road and tucked us into a red leather booth and used the menus, drink specials, dessert list, to make a flimsy wall between us. An attempt at healthy parenting. Then they'd hiss, venomous, about the men's numbers in my father's phone as Lily and I filled the grids of our waffles with syrup, poured the sweetness thick, until there were no more holes to be seen, until our plates were pooled with a layer of sucrose, enough to make us sick.

After I started dieting, though, Lily slid both plates over to herself. I ordered an orange juice and let myself drink half the glass. I tore open four sachets of zero-calorie sweetener, tipped my head back, baby bird, and poured the not-sugar down my throat.

Lily watched me consume before starting on the waffles. She waited until I wiped my mouth on the cheap napkin, then she sighed, then she ate. She fed herself because I wouldn't. We were an hourglass. Emptying the contents of one side only filled the other. We were only identical until we weren't.

I don't go back to the supply closet and I avoid Kat at all costs. For now she surely thinks that *I* am the supply closet lesbian. Tiptoeing around at night, sneaking into the cupboard when others are in bed. I want to tell her, *You're wrong.* I want to tell her, *I was just investigating.* But each time I think of confronting her, I picture her sneer, so familiar, it belonged to someone else before it was hers. It belonged to Jemima Gates.

...

Another thing Freud said is that humans have two basic drives. The first is aggression, or the fear of death. The second is procreation, or the desire to reproduce. If I do not fear death and cannot reproduce, does this make me less than human? This is something I would like to ask Freud.

Lily got her period. Woke one morning, climbed out of bed, and screamed at the sight of her murderous sheets.

"What?" I ran to her.

"Blood!"

"Your period," I said. Most girls already had them.

She tugged her pajama shorts down and, sure enough, her underwear was soaked red.

"Did you get yours?" she said to my crotch.

I pulled my duvet back to find pristine sheets. Pulled down my underwear to find only dry cotton. "No."

"Yes, well, you're becoming a woman" is what our mother said, at breakfast, when Lily declared the news. "Watch what you eat. Puberty is when you'll start gaining weight."

Lily wept. "I don't want to become anything."

"Don't be ridiculous," said Mum, sipping her coffee, black.

I put my arm around Lily, took the weight of her head on my shoulder. "It's okay," I hushed. "It's okay."

It was easy for me to say. I was stuck in a child's body, ungrowing, unchanging. I wasn't becoming anything at all.

Whenever I felt like I was going to break, I looked up at my Kat Mitchells poster, my own form of prayer. She smiled down at me, skinny.

She was biting her lip, hand on prepubescent hip. The poster excited me in a way I didn't understand. I found myself reaching beneath the covers, beneath my underwear. I watched Kat all the while, her wide eyes, stick legs. I had my first orgasm looking up at her airbrushed body. The collapse of it, a fleeting loss of control, frightening, exhilarating.

The line between wanting her and wanting to be her, indecipherable.

During Relaxation Hour, Kat taps me on the shoulder.

"Hi?" I say, setting my book down.

"*Animal Behaviors*, huh?"

"It's interesting," I say.

"I bet it is, baby," says Kat, shifting the beret on her head. "Animals are wild."

I can only picture the bald scalp beneath the felt. Kat, bingeing in the closet, feral as a marsupial on garbage day.

"Are you talking to me for a reason?" I say.

"I think we got off on the wrong foot," says Kat. "See, I think you're quite fabulous, Rose. I think you're just great."

I want to tell Kat Mitchells that she is a bad caricature of herself, but I won't. The only thing I can control is my own joy.

"I'd like to be friends," she says. "Think of all the fun we could have."

"Sure," I say. "I'll be your friend once you stop teaching Sarah to purge."

"She asked me, darling," says Kat. "She wanted it."

I pick up my book.

"Listen," she says. "It's healthier than starving. Don't you see how she's gained?"

I do not say, *Shut up*.

"Why do you hate me, baby? Let me ask you that, at least," says Kat. "Why do you despise me?"

Jemima Gates. The Apple-a-Day Diet. The poster above my bed.

"I don't," I say. "Just stay away from Sarah."

"She follows me," says Kat, hand to chest. "I never asked her to, believe it or not."

My eyes sting. I won't cry. "Everyone else loves you," I say, my voice barely there. "Every other girl in here loves you. Why do you have to take Sarah, too?"

"Everyone loves me?" Kat shakes her head. "No one loves me, darling. Your sister visits you almost every day. Have you ever seen my visitors' log? Have you ever seen a visitor in my room?"

I haven't.

"You think it's love, what I have?"

"Celebrity is a type of love," I tell her.

"It's not the type I want."

It's not the type she wants.

Birds, like gulls, that travel long distances to bring sustenance to their young, often swallow the food they've found on-site, then fly home. Back in the nest, the chick will peck at the red spot on their mother's beak, a pressure point that stimulates regurgitation, to make her throw up the meal. The chick consumes the barf. This is how they learn to eat.

13

2004 (15 years old—Lily: 119 lbs, Rose: 88 lbs)

"It's hurting you," Lily said as I inspected my laddered ribs in our mirror. I touched each one with the caress of a proud parent. She didn't understand. It was the first time we hadn't thought the same thoughts, felt the same feelings. Every time we talked, it was like keeping a phone conversation going while one of us was driving through a tunnel, the other riding in an elevator. There was so much static. Tears made her voice soggy. "Please just eat something."

I looked at Lily, hurting because of me. "I'll stop," I said. "Hey." I stroked the tears from her cheeks and wiped them on my own. War paint. "I'll stop. I won't diet anymore."

I didn't want to diet; I wanted to starve. I didn't want to be like Lily anymore. I wanted to be unrecognizable. To disappear. The truth was, if I were to evaporate into nothing, I would still exist. The better, sweeter, kinder version of me. Without me getting in the way, Lily could be both of us.

"I'm worried about her," I tell Sarah at dinner. She's looking around for Kat and only half listening to me. I talk anyway. "I'm worried she's taking this new relationship too seriously. She's stopped visiting."

"She's happy, darling," says Sarah, prodding at a pile of dry noodles that is masquerading as chow mein on the cafeteria menu. K-pop seeps through the hall's speakers. The nurses call it Asian night. We're all white, us thin girls, a cliché of our illness.

"She'll get over that honeymoon phase, baby," says Sarah. "She'll be back."

I scowl at her before quickly stocktaking the supervising nurses and pushing a heap of noodles onto my lap. I tuck the strands into my pockets, scanning for prying eyes all the while.

"She's never acted like this before. She's dieting! Have you heard of something called YourWeigh?"

Sarah perks up. "You mean the diet guide? I've heard it's incredible. Why? Do you have a copy?" Her eyes, hungry.

"No," I say. Sarah slumps.

"Maybe Kat does," she says.

"Kat?"

"In the supply closet, I mean."

I frown. I don't understand. But I don't feel like talking about Kat. She's boring! I'm bored! "So, what should I do?" I say. "Lily's always put me before her gross boyfriends, and now she hasn't got time for me."

"Maybe this one isn't gross," says Sarah. "Maybe he really is as great as she says."

"No," I say, a laugh. "No, no. She doesn't date great guys. I know Lily."

"Sure," Sarah says. She isn't mimicking my motions, isn't shoving noodles into pockets. "Sure you do. Or, I'm sure you used to." When my frown deepens, the offense tattooed, she holds up her hands in surrender. "I don't know. Maybe she's growing up, darling."

"Growing up?"

"Yeah," she says, lifting a forkful of noodles to her lips. The grease paints her mouth glossy. She swallows. "People grow up, fall in love, get married, move on. Things were always going to change between you two when Lily met someone."

"What about me?" I say, but Sarah has finished her meal. Is already carrying her empty plate away, blowing ridiculous over-the-shoulder kisses. Off to find Kat, to purge it all back up.

I stand from the table. My pasta-pockets sag, weighing me down like sandbags. Drop me in the ocean and I'll sink, quick as an anchor.

Back in my room, I send Lily a text: **Starving until I see you.**

I can only control my own joy.

2005 (16 years old—Lily: 130 lbs, Rose: 86 lbs)

Lily finished the year at the top of our class. She got a certificate that said her name, half mine, in an embarrassing cursive. When she stood onstage at our final assembly, people clapped. I wanted to join in with applause, I'm sure, but I was weak, my muscles eroding. By now, my diet consisted mostly of sugar-free mint gum to hide my mildewy breath.

On Christmas Day of 2005, Lily and I sat at the kitchen table, her eating soggy cereal that sounded like cellulite with every wet stir, me drinking warm water, a metabolism accelerant. I had always hated holidays, when everyone seemed to discard their regular emotional orbits in order to feel a collective feeling, be bound together by communal excitement for the upcoming celebration—they made me feel less human.

"Merry Christmas," Lily said, lifting her bowl, tilting it to drink the milk. I had done that, too, back when I ate cereal, ate anything at all. We'd race to lick our bowls clean, happy as puppies.

"Merry Christmas," I said to the ass of her bowl.

"Get ready for service, girls. Hurry up or the good seats will be gone," Mum shouted from her bedroom.

Dad wasn't coming to church. He and Mum had shouted into the night, something about his browser history, stomping, slamming, trying to scare Santa away, the ornaments on the tree trembling.

"Ah, that's the holiday spirit," said Lily, taking her bowl to the sink.

I didn't say anything. For once, I was grateful that my family didn't function like one. I thought of movie families, their tables laden with dishes, meats and potatoes, the heaviest foods, and sighed at the relief of knowing what our holiday meal would look like: takeout Chinese food in cardboard boxes that concealed how little I had eaten from them.

Our mother examined us before we left for church. Our matching white tunics, mine billowing like a bedsheet on the clothesline, Lily's clinging to her, claustrophobic as a wet shower curtain.

Mum told Lily she was getting a little big, then pointed at me. "Look how thin your sister is!"

I smiled. For the first time, the better twin.

Panda bears commonly give birth to twins. From birth, the mother panda will begin to evaluate her offspring, compare them to one another, force them to compete for her affections, nutrients, shelter. Eventually, she will ignore the weaker twin, leaving her vulnerable to predators, refusing her any milk, in favor of the stronger cub.

On the way back to my room, I try the door to the supply cupboard. It opens, but it's dark in there. I duck inside, close myself in. It smells so strongly of sick that it singes the back of my throat and I gag.

"Hi!"

"Kat?" I say.

"I knew you'd come."

"I can't see."

"I knew you couldn't resist."

"I'm not gay."

"What?"

There's a soft click, and a buttery-yellow lights the room. Kat, top hat, pearls, smiling. She gestures to the closet's shelves. Boxes of laxatives. A set of scales. Sugar-free gum. Cans of Diet Coke. Measuring tapes. Contraband.

"What is this?"

"Welcome to Kat's Korner." She gestures to a sign, written in crayon, taped to the wall behind her. "I'm Kat, and I'll be your server today. Can I get you started with an appetizer, perhaps a laxative or two? Only fifty apiece."

"What?"

"Or maybe this nice set of scales is more up your alley? Don't you want to know what you really weigh?"

"Kat this is—"

"I can offer you a measuring tape for an even hundred. Ipecac will cost you a cool ninety-nine. Or a simple plastic bag, perfect for purging, just twenty bucks, for the bulimic on a budget!"

"This isn't funny, Kat."

"Wow," she says. "A hard sell. I can offer you a spare key to the supply closet for some after-hours fun. If you have the key, you can binge or purge in secret, but it'll cost you."

"Is this where you've been purging?" I'm pinching my nose, and my voice is high. Just days ago, I'd sat, touched myself, listening to what I'd thought were the gasps of an orgasm.

"Okay," Kat says, holding her palms up. "I have one final offer."

I wait. She reaches to the back of a shelf, forages among the cleaning supplies, and pulls out a book. Pink. Hardcover.

"*YourWeigh*, by Lara Bax," she says. "The hottest diet guide out there right now. All yours for just eighty-five."

I take the book, the book that Lily is using to skinny herself for Phil.

"I knew you'd be interested in that one." Kat smiles. "No one leaves Kat's Korner empty-handed."

I open to the first page. *Do you hate your body? Want to lose some weight? Lara Bax's holistic health guide makes getting thin fun and easy! Find happiness today and join me on your weight-loss journey!*

"Why do they always say 'weight-loss journey'? Like losing weight is a trip to Paris, or something?"

"Okay, fine," says Kat. "Eighty."

I hand her the book. "I thought the rumor was that girls were fooling around in here."

"Sadly, no," she says. Then smiles. "But we can change that."

I swallow. Kat's eyes dance.

My phone buzzes with a text from Lily: **Don't be an idiot. Eat your meals. Be there tomorrow.**

"And look!" says Kat, leafing through the pages quickly. "Look at this!" She opens the book, baring its innards, holds it out for me to see. "A celebrity appearance!" The page she is pointing to is titled

LOSE WEIGHT BUT FIND YOURSELF, and, beneath the terrible title, is a pair of pictures of Kat Mitchells. One from her late teens, when she, to the paparazzi's delight, gained 20 lbs and made the mistake of wearing the new weight in public. The other looks as if it could have been taken today. Her cheeks concave, her eyes wide, her collarbones growing out of her chest like eaves. They are captioned with the words: *BEFORE* and *AFTER*. As if Kat's new figure is all thanks to this fad diet. "It's me!" Kat says, as if I mightn't have been able to tell.

"No thanks," I say to Kat, backing out of the closet. "No thank you."

I go back to my room. I can only control my own joy.

During the nineteenth century, German psychiatrist Baron Albert von Schrenck-Notzing prescribed men who were experiencing homosexual feelings a few field trips to the brothel and intensive alcohol consumption. Women experiencing the same feelings were simply referred back to their husbands.

I dress up for Jram. This is what women do for the men they love: they wear dresses and high heels and lipstick. Look how feminine I can be! Sexuality is a choice, and I am making it right now! See how much estrogen is coursing through my veins?

I don't have any dresses at the facility, but I take the sheet off my bed and wrap it around my body, tug one of its corners over my shoulder and tie it to itself. I feel like a Grecian goddess. I stand on my toes and smile. I use ketchup to paint my lips red, careful not to let any touch my tongue. I pace my room, smiling at him, for him, and he applauds and applauds from across the courtyard.

14

The next day, I manage to slip my breakfast waffle into the waistband of my leggings, cover it with my sweater. Not even a single mouthful. Back in my room, when a nurse hands me my morning CalSip, I show her my finger, still bloodied from my carnivorous night, and empty the CalSip onto my mattress while she's off getting a Band-Aid. Cover it with my comforter. Not even a single sip. What do I have to eat for, if I don't have Lily?

My anorexia smiles her most seductive smile.

2006 (17 years old—Lily: 140 lbs, Rose: 84 lbs)

Jemima decided that the popular girls needed nose piercings. Puncture our skin to pledge our loyalty. We swarmed into the only parlor that would pierce underagers and slapped cash on the counter.

"Who's first?" The man who would be piercing us looked like Santa if Santa were from Florida and into hentai porn.

"Me," said Jemima. "Nose. Left nostril. A hoop." *Confidence*, she had told us on the way to the mall, *is key*.

He gestured to a stool and Jemima sat. When he shot the gun into her nose, she barely winced, and when he held up a mirror to let her see the piercing, she smiled. It looked so natural, as if she'd been born with it.

"Rose?" she said. "You next."

I looked at Lily. I had always copied her. At restaurants, I ordered my meals after she did. At clothing stores, I spoke to the salesperson after she did. At salons, I got my hair cut after she did. All I had to say was, *The exact same, please.*

"You're not backing out, are you?" said Jemima, and it was a threat.

"Nose," I said to Florida Santa. "Left nostril. A hoop."

I bit my tongue when the needle punctured me through. Lily grimaced at the pain. Santa positioned the mirror to show me my new nose: a loop of silver, like a price tag. I looked like Jemima.

"You next, big girl?" Santa said to Lily.

She perched on the stool, reluctant.

"What do you want?" He used his sleeve to wipe the sweat that decorated his upper lip.

"The exact same, please?" she said, looking at me. "Right?"

When he held the mirror for Lily to see, I crouched beside her, looked at her reflection. The piercing looked new and raw and sore. The swelling on my nose had already retreated. The redness paled. For the first time, it was Lily who looked like me.

There's another letter on the floor of my room.

> R—
>
> It wasn't until after I sent that last letter that I realized my mistake. I said that you could choose the code words, but if you choose them, I won't know the code, will I? You could say *asparagus* or something, and I wouldn't know if that meant *talk* or *be quiet* or *jump off a building*, would I? I'm an idiot.
>
> I hope recovery is going okay. If anyone can come back from this, it's you, Rose. Once, you told me that Lily was better than you at everything, and that you didn't see a reason for yourself to exist. But you're not like Lily. You're like you. And the world is so much better with a Rose in it.
>
> Call me? But only if you want to.
>
> —M

I want to call and I want to say *asparagus*. I want us to repeat *asparagus* back to each other until the word blurs into meaningless sound. *Asparagus asparagus asparagusaspa ragusa sparag usas para gusa spar agus asp a rag us.*

Calories are measured by a bomb calorimeter, a small chamber in which food is burned to heat water. The calorie count is determined based on how hot the food burns, how much it raises the water's temperature. The calorie itself weighs nothing at all; it's a measurement of energy. The most frightening things are the things we cannot see.

2006 (17 years old—Lily: 143 lbs, Rose: 83 lbs)

One day, after school, I was walking with Jemima and the girls in our usual paper-doll chain, ponytails swinging unabashedly behind us, people moved the hell out of our way. You've never felt power unless you've been a popular girl. Boys stared, girls gawked, even the teachers wanted to be us. People fucking cowered.

We were synchronous that day, step-step, swish-swish, our arms linked, move or be flattened. Striding down the hall, gorgeous, superior, when I caught a glimpse of Lily, lip-locked with a senior in an empty science lab, leaning up against the granite counter, kissing with fury. His hands grabbed her flesh so hard they looked like they'd leave prints; like pressing palms into wet concrete, his mark would be there long after he left her.

I rubbed my chin, the scratch of his almost-beard itchy against our skin.

My pace barely wavered. I was afraid to cause a glitch in the programmed-perfect life of the popular girls, but Jemima noticed the falter.

"What's up, babe?" she said.

"Nothing," I said. "Cramps."

I never got my period, but the rest of the girls had them, or at least pretended to, so I did, too. I pretended.

"Such a bitch, right?" said Jemima, dropping our linked arms and catching hold of my hand. She lifted my arm to her lips and kissed the white flesh of my wrist. Her lip gloss left a little pink heart. It felt like a tattoo.

After the popular girls dispersed at the gate, catching one another's air kisses, vying for Jemima's last goodbye, which I won, I wondered the whole way home whether I had just witnessed Lily's first kiss. The way she had her arms vined around his torso, her pelvis tilted against his groin, made me think she'd done it many times before. Times she'd never told me about. My body ached.

Boys loved Lily, I knew that. They loved her breasts, which swelled like a liquid with every step, her laugh that was true and deep. They loved the way her ass spread, a cushion, when she sat. They loved the way she wasn't one of us, Jemima's girls.

Boys didn't love me, understandably. My figure looked just like theirs. I didn't care.

When Lily got home that day, I confronted her.

"You never told me you had a boyfriend," I said. She was still shedding her coat, and she paused, the jacket halfway off.

"You never asked."

"We tell each other everything."

"Do we?"

She shrugged the coat free and hung it on a hook. Her T-shirt bunched around the waistband of her jeans.

"You're acting weird," I said.

"Am I?"

"Yeah. Different. Not like yourself."

"Maybe I'm changing," she said. "Growing up."

"Are you saying I'm immature?"

"I'm saying we don't have to be the same, Rose."

"Are you dating boys because you feel like you don't have me anymore?"

"What?"

"Are you replacing me with them?"

"Rose—"

"Because I have Jemima now?"

Lily sighed. "It's okay for us to be different, Rose. You've been looking for a way to fit in for such a long time and now look at you. It really seems like you've found yourself."

"But I don't want to be myself," I said, reaching for her hand. Her fingers were always warm, but now they had a comfy layer on them. "I've never wanted that."

She nodded. Her smile was not the happy kind.

Pigs root the ground for a number of reasons. For comfort, to cool off, to find food. I think they do it for another reason, too. Pigs are smart creatures, third after humans and chimpanzees, but they can't look up. Something to do with their anatomical structure; no pig can look directly up at the sky. I think they know there must be something else to the world, pigs. Something they're not seeing. I think they're looking for it—what's up there—they're just looking in the wrong place.

15

Lily finally visits, and I feel relief. Now I can go back to two CalSips. Now I can go back to surviving.

She has one of her students in tow, which is unusual. Many in-patients have only a single regular visitor, and many have none at all. Eating disorders are not social illnesses. We've lied to those who loved us. We've thrashed, shoved, isolated ourselves from anyone who pushed us to eat; we live on a lonely island, and there's no food source here in our secluded paradise.

My visitors' log has only one name scrawled over and over again, like a naughty child had written lines: *Lily Winters, Lily Winters, Lily Winters.*

The child clutching Lily's hand is called Diamond, and she looks like a child. As in, if someone were to ask me to imagine a child, I would picture Diamond's face.

Diamond has large dark eyes, such a deep brown they seem to have their own echo. She keeps pushing bangs out of them. Big-eyed people must experience more object-in-eye issues. I ask Diamond if she often gets things in her eye.

"You're, like, really skinny," Diamond says in response.

"Yeah?" I say. "Well, your name is Diamond." It doesn't do the intended damage.

"Are you on a diet?"

I don't dignify her with a response.

Lily tells me that Diamond is Phil's daughter, and I nod because I already guessed it. She tells me that she offered to bring Diamond home from school since she, after all, is Diamond's teacher. I'm considering telling Lily about Jram when she takes a cigarette from her purse. "Diamond's mother is so thin," says Lily, as if that were explanation enough for her new habit. "Just a few more pounds."

"Lil, you're not really meant to smoke in here."

She lights up and inhales, swallows the smoke, then coughs. "This is different," she says. "It's for my health. I'm starving. I'm *controlling my own joy*," she says.

I want to tell her, *So eat something*, but the hypocrisy twists my tongue.

She makes it about halfway through the cigarette before giving up and extinguishing it on my windowsill.

"I need some advice," Lily says, and I gesture for her to go on.

"I know Phil's not going to leave his wife," Lily says. "And I don't necessarily want him to leave her; I mean, they have a kid. I just, you know, it'd be nice to have the conversation. It'd be nice to at least know that he was thinking about it."

"About it?"

"About leaving her for me."

"Oh, about leaving her. Do you think you should be talking about this right now? With, you know, her here?" I tilt my head toward Diamond, who is sitting on my floor squashing termites with her fingers.

"She's five. She doesn't understand any of it," says Lily. "It's fine."

"I'm five and a half," says Diamond, not bothering to look up from her bug massacre.

"What was the question?" I say.

"I just wish he'd float the idea of leaving her so I could tell him not to."

"Right."

"That doesn't make me crazy, right? That's normal, isn't it?"

"Sleeping with a married man?"

"Don't be a bitch, Rose." Lily watches her hands as she speaks, twisting her decorative rings around her knuckles. She's lost weight. The rings twirl with a new looseness, spin on her fingers like an abacus. "You know what I mean."

"Do I think it's normal that you don't want your lover to leave his wife so much that he actually leaves her, but you do want him to want to leave his wife enough to have the conversation with you about it?"

"You're oversimplifying it."

"Am I?"

A nurse arrives with my afternoon CalSip and leaves again.

"Can you not be so judgmental for just a minute?" says Lily. "Please. I'm asking for your advice here."

"Well, I think you're asking the wrong question."

"What?"

"I think you should ask me whether I approve of the affair in the first place."

"I know you don't approve of it," she says "Obviously. It tastes like I'm sucking on a bar of soap, idiot." She pokes out her tongue as if I could see the lather of an impossible taste: the bubbles of disappointment. "But it's happening whether you approve of it or not." She shrugs. "So, tell me, should I talk to him about leaving his wife?"

I sigh. "But you don't want him to leave his wife," I say.

"No," she says. "But I want him to want to."

"What?"

"I want him to want to."

"No," I say, "I heard you. It's just ridiculous. Consider the outcomes, Lil. If you bring it up, then either he agrees with you and leaves his wife or he disagrees with you, thinks you're becoming too attached, and ends things, right?"

Lily lights a new cigarette, and I watch her inhale easily. She's a natural by now. "Maybe I do want him to leave her."

"That's going to give you cancer," I say.

"It's not permanent, baby sister. Just a few more pounds." She smiles. "This YourWeigh diet really works, you know. Yesterday, Phil told me I was beautiful."

"Why are you doing this for him? Why him? Because he's charming? So what!"

"I love him," she says, and it's true, she does. I can taste it, feel it. The taste, something almond-based, vanilla-laced, a sweet comfort.

The feeling? It feels as if my heart is growing branches, a tree in my chest, growing each day, reaching sunward.

"And anyway, I'm not doing it for him, I'm doing it for me," she says, but her cheeks are touched red and I can taste the lie, sour. She clears her throat. "No one has ever called me beautiful before."

"You *are* beautiful."

Lily rolls her eyes. "You know what I mean. Skinny."

People often think us thin girls are starving to be pretty, and maybe it started that way for many of us, but we know we don't look good. I was never one of those body dysmorphic types who saw an inflated version of herself in the mirror. No. I saw the bones. I saw an inside-out girl—skeleton worn over her skin, like a jacket.

It was hard to explain the specific *why* of it. Why I was doing this to myself. People always asked, *Why are you doing this to yourself?*

The truth is, I didn't believe I was doing it. When my lips refused to budge, rusted gates, it was not me holding them closed. I was on the sidelines with my family, the doctors. I was helping them cheer, joining in the mantra: *Eat! Eat! Eat!*

The truth is, even if there was a *why* at the beginning, there's a point where any form of reason is lost.

The truth is, why I was doing it didn't matter; what mattered was that I couldn't stop.

I can't remember when, exactly, the paranoia started. I must have been very thin, because it was when people would comment, would let their eyes widen, let their hands float up to their open mouths. *Look how much weight you've lost*, they would say. At first, I believed them. It was later that I became suspicious. The way calling to the absence of something only reminds us of the existence of it. For example, if I were to compliment you on your hairless stomach, the immediate image in your mind is a hairy one.

Another, similar trick, is to call attention to something so accepted as indisputable fact that it is rarely named aloud for the redundancy of it. Like, if I were to point out your two arms (*Look at both your arms!*), you would imagine that I had noticed something abnormal about them. That's the way I felt when someone would say, *Look how thin you are!* It was so obvious I became skeptical. How thin was I?

In 1892, neurologist Graeme M. Hammond recommended that anyone experiencing homosexuality should ride those urges away on a bicycle. He reasoned that the desires were rooted in nervous exhaustion and that extensive biking would help restore heterosexuality.

I rode my bike to school each day, even though walking or taking the bus was cooler. I rode and rode and rode.

Lily puts out her second cigarette. She's smoked all the way to the yellowed butt this time. I am so tired of tasting the love she is feeling.

What I don't say: *This man doesn't care about you like I do.*

What I don't say: *Why are you hurting yourself like this?*

What I don't say: *You are worthy of a true love.*

What I don't say: *You have to be the healthy one.*

What I say: "Lily."

Lily crosses her arms. They flatten her chest, and I want to touch. To feel what it is to have breasts, large and soft, hanging from me. I want to feel what Lily feels. It would be so much easier if we were one.

"What?" Her voice is a challenge. "Go on, say whatever you need to say."

I say nothing. I don't need to. She already knows, so I only stand, watching my thinning sister reach for the hand of her married lover's daughter. There's a buzzing sound, a humming, and Lily takes her purse, digs around for her phone.

The screen is alight with notifications. Fifteen text messages. All from Phil.

"That's a lot," I say. "Is everything okay?"

She opens the messages, each one its own essay. She frowns as she reads.

"Yeah, I'm fine. Phil just likes to know where I am. He worries if I don't reply to his messages." She types as she talks. "I should go," she says.

"Lil."

But Lily, suddenly restless, stressed, zips her jacket and beckons Diamond up off the floor. She's nervous, bitter.

"Just be careful," I say. "Take care of yourself. Maybe try to cut back on the smoking. Protect your own peace."

She laughs, melody-less. "*You're* giving *me* health advice," she says.

When she tries to hug me with her new corroding body, I stand still, feeling punched, and I'm not sure whether the feeling is concern or betrayal. She's so much thinner. Of course she should be allowed to diet. People diet every day.

I can't help but feel that Lily has taken something from me.

Crocodiles have been known to swallow stones to make themselves feel fuller. The stones also add weight to the beasts, helping them swim lower in the water, making them less visible to their prey.

If I dropped Lily in a lake, she would float, empty but for cigarette smoke, visible to everyone, predators and prey alike.

Some nights, I broke. I'd lie in bed, praying for sleep, knowing that the only thing keeping me from the looming binge was unconsciousness. But a hungry gut is a night watchdog. She growls as the sky darkens, howls at the winking moon.

I'd grimace my way down the hall and ease the refrigerator open with bated breath.

Then I was animal. I pulled toppings off slices of week-old pizza and swallowed without chewing. I took tubs of ice cream from the freezer and scooped with my hands, anesthetised my throat with the chill, clawed until my fingers ached, my teeth stung, my mind, numb.

Still, I ate. How I ate! How could I have an eating disorder if I was capable of this? If, in the night, I could gulp down calories enough to feed a family?

I drank cream from the carton, gnawed on hunks of cheese. I went to the trash can and rescued the pizza crust I'd tossed. Dusted off old coffee grounds and potato peelings and ate. I only stopped when my stomach, a balloon too inflated, threatened to burst.

Then I closed the refrigerator, my mind high on nutrition, and bent myself over the sink, deep-throated my fingers, brought everything back up before my body could digest. Like a scene rewound, see how this eater uneats.

It is so dark tonight. Screams score my wait for Jram. Nurses storm the rooms of girls who have lost weight since their last weigh-in and thread tubes around their ears, into their noses, down their throats. The tube is attached to a bag of translucent yellow sludge, so much like lard in appearance that one had to laugh at the cruelty of it. The formula, apparently nutritious, oozes through the tubes, into the body; they feed us this way, unconsensually.

This is the way they keep us corporeal. Just as you feel that helium haze in the brain, that too-light-for-this-life, that near-weightlessness that makes your fingertips hum like a caffeine overdose, blood turned bee, veins vibrating, every organ gutted of its substance, that purgatory between living and dead, that's when they come. The nurses, to anchor us to this earth.

They set the machines at a constant clip, and we can do nothing but watch as the fat seeps into us, slow and definite as a change in the weather. Some girls try to tear the tubes from their throats, but that only results in a nurse spending the night, eyes alert, watching us sleep.

Tonight, it's Kat. I can tell by her rasping yelps. It's the first time she's lost weight, and her screams last well into the night.

Tomorrow, I will teach her how to maintain her weight like the rest of us. I don't like her, Kat, but no girl deserves to be filled like that.

2006 (17 years old—Lily: 158 lbs, Rose: 80 lbs)

Our mother left. Packed a single shopping bag with clothes and shoes and money and moved out one day while we were at school, while Dad was at work.

Lily and I got home to find the note:

Jim: Fuck you. Rose: Eat something. Lily: Look after Rose. It's for the
best. Mum.

Lily shredded the page before Dad could see it.

"It'll be hard enough for him as it is," she said.

Dad got home while I was doing my nightly sit-ups—an even hundred before bed to tone the stomach. When he saw her car gone, their room ransacked, us alone, he took a beer from the fridge, cracked the can open, and sat on the couch. Football.

"Dad," said Lily. But he only kicked his slacks down his legs, sat in his underwear.

I reached the halfway point—fifty to go. He took the remote and turned the volume up higher than we were allowed it.

"Dad!" Lily, shouting to be heard.

He picked up his phone.

Thank god, I thought, we thought. *He's going to ring her. Tell her to come home.*

But instead, "I'll order a pizza, yeah, girls?" He looked at me, curling and unfurling on the floor, then frowned. "Maybe two."

One night, my mind was droopy with hunger and sleep, and I didn't notice that Lily wasn't in her bed when I got up and tiptoed to the kitchen to binge. Our house was old and wooden and had a way of cracking and groaning with every step, its own way of making us feel heavy.

"Lil?" I yawned when I reached the kitchen. She was wedged into the refrigerator, her face lit only by the fridge's blue glow, her body keeping the door from swinging shut, scooping shredded cheese, forcing handfuls between her lips.

She startled when I said her name and she tossed the bag of cheese back onto its shelf.

"I was just . . ." But Lily didn't bother to finish the sentence. "Why are you out here?"

"Water," I said, stepping past her, both of us light on our feet to keep from waking the house.

"Remember when we used to come out here for midnight snacks?" said Lily.

I nodded. As kids we'd hide our Halloween candy from our parents, a pile in the always-vacant bread box, a handful in the gap between the microwave and the counter, and we'd set our alarms for eleven p.m. and tiptoe into the kitchen, find our candy too quickly, and eat it long before midnight reared its head. Sometimes we'd nod off in the kitchen, slumped over on the linoleum, heads resting against the fridge's gentle hum.

"Sure," I said. "When we were kids." We were in our senior year now, and I felt like an old woman, so weathered and exhausted.

"It was like two years ago," said Lily.

"Yeah," I said. "Kids. We were kids."

"It's weird that one of those times would have been our last time and I didn't even know it."

"What?"

"Like, if I knew the last time we'd done it would have been the last ever, our last midnight snack, I would have made a better effort to remember it, you know?"

"Not really," I yawned. "I'm gonna go back to—"

"I'm not going to ask why," said Lily, a new confidence in her voice. "Because I don't think you even know why. But I just want you to know"—she swallowed—"that you're putting me through this, too."

"What?"

"You hating your body is you hating my body, so yeah."

"I don't hate your body."

"Well," said Lily. "At one point, not so long ago, we had exactly the same body. And you've done almost everything you can to destroy it."

I looked at my sister. She had grown big. I didn't hate bigness, and I didn't think she looked bad. She looked unhappy a lot of the time, sure, like when she caught her reflection and one of her hands darted to her stomach as if she'd discovered a sudden pregnancy, or when she saw photographs of herself and immediately averted her eyes, flipped the photo facedown. But her body didn't look bad. She just looked like Lily, my sister, who I loved.

"I don't hate your body," I said to Lily. "I love you."

"Do you understand how that's hard for me to believe?"

I nodded. Swallowed.

"This isn't just affecting you."

"Okay," I whispered. I knew she was right. Lily frowned almost all the time now, and even my teachers at school had pulled me aside to have a word about dieting. There was nothing I could do. I wasn't in control anymore.

Lily's sadness was soap in my mouth, and I spat the lather into the sink. I had no way of knowing whether her feelings were calorie-free.

"What're you two doing up?" Dad, who had taken to sleeping in front of the television since Mum left, muted the set and stood, the room's only light coming from the open fridge, the silent TV. "It's way past your bedtime."

"I was hungry," said Lily.

"How about I fix us a snack?" he said. "We could have a midnight picnic. Junk night."

Lily started to forage around in the fridge, a can of whipped cream, a bottle of chocolate sauce. Dad got a pint of ice cream from the freezer, vanilla bean. I got a packet of pink wafers from the pantry. Each movement, the gathering of ingredients, the collation of foods on the counter, it all felt weighed down with the significance of tradition.

Lily scooped three scoops into Dad's bowl, then just one into her own.

"Give yourself another, girlie," he said. "You're a growing girl."

Lily was so used to our mother's constant criticism, the judgmental looks at her full plate, her full stomach. She rolled another scoop.

"Rose?" Dad said.

"No thank you," I said. "I'm just out here for a glass of water."

"No ice cream?"

"No thank you."

"It'll make you feel better," he said, his tone teasing.

"I don't need to feel better," I said. "Nothing's wrong."

When I left them to their feast, they were laughing. I could hear their wounds healing over without me.

• • •

As Kat screams from the room over, I show Jram how to pre-eat. He picks it up quickly. We alternate bites out of our air sandwiches: a romantic meal for two. A man and a woman, sharing a meal, a relationship.

When we're done, he pulls his shirt over his head. I shouldn't be so surprised. We've been seeing each other awhile now, after all. Still, I hold my palm against the glass, meaning *stop*, but it must come across as a lustful yearning, because he only reaches for his fly.

Jram's naked body is skeletal. I can see all of his bones, and I feel embarrassed. Like witnessing a building's scaffolding stages, his foundations are on show. He strokes his flaccid penis at me, and how strange that a body so emaciated can spare a chubby cock. It grows and grows as I watch his show. It fattens and bloats and I only sigh.

I say, "Please stop, Jram. Please stop," but he doesn't. I tighten the knot of my robe and finger its fabric and watch as his body swells and inflates until, eventually, he gives up. He doesn't say my name or wave a lilac handkerchief. It's my fault, of course. He took me to dinner, albeit a hypothetical one, and I've read enough romance novels to know what a dinner date means. Nothing ever really survives.

In 1830, Sylvester Graham, a Presbyterian minister, spread word that people were gaining weight from having too much sex. He was a vegetarian, Graham was, and believed that optimal health could be achieved through a diet of abstinence, vegetables, and whole-grain bread. He later invented the graham cracker, one of which contains about sixty calories.

He had no way of knowing that a typical dose of ejaculate contains less than a single calorie, about the same nutritional value as a can of Diet Coke. I could survive on semen. I could!

I take the letters from under my mattress and open the envelopes, one by one. It's too dark to read, but the words are so purposefully written, their shapes etched into the paper. I trace each one with my finger, whisper love letters aloud to myself.

I set them in a stack on my nightstand and see a termite scuttling away. I pluck the bug. It's tiny and its little legs flail. I set it on my tongue and swallow. The calories will be worth the results. I wish to be as empty as this house. Nothing more than skin, puddled on the floor.

16

On Garden Day, we're allowed to walk in the courtyard. It's a beautiful morning. The sun stings my tired eyes, parched from a night of fearing for Lily's health, listening to Kat's screams, recalling Jram's aroused and emaciated figure.

2006 (17 years old—Lily: 165 lbs, Rose: 79 lbs)

When concerned teachers confronted my father about my not-eating, he didn't speak to me about it. He and Lily had grown close via their midnight meals, their cocktails in front of some cop show that played consistently on channel four. I was invited to both events, but the calories. I shook my head—*Too tired*, I was always telling them. Instead, he sent me to a therapist.

Her name was Paula, and she was in her fifties, smelled of lavender, and always had a hyphen of red lipstick dashed across her two front teeth. She called me Rosey Posey and hugged me so tight to her chest I thought I might get stuck there, between her breasts.

One day, Paula asked me to bring Lily along to my session. She held up ink blots and asked both Lily and me to write our answers to the Rorschach test on separate sheets of paper. When the test was over, our answers were different for every single shape. I saw fleas where Lily saw stars. I saw an apple core where Lily saw a kissing couple.

"Interesting," said Paula, licking her top teeth but somehow missing the lipstick that resided there. "Very interesting." She sifted through our answers and then frowned. She held up a new ink blot. "Rose, can you write down what you think Lily sees here?"

The image was of a feminine mouth. I wrote the word *mountains*.

"What do you see in this blot, Lily?" asked Paula.

"Mountains," said Lily. We went through the rest of the ink blots this way. Me guessing every image on Lily's behalf. I didn't miss a single answer.

"Very interesting," said Paula. "Very, very interesting."

"What's interesting?" said Lily.

"Well," said Paula. "Every set of twins I've run this test on has seen the same shapes as each other."

Lily and I said nothing. This was not interesting to us.

"But twins also usually share sexuality."

"Share sexuality?" I said.

"Yes," said Paula. "You know, if one's gay, usually they're both gay."

"But . . ." I said. Only before I could correct Paula, Lily's hand gripped mine, and that meant I should stop talking.

What I was going to say: *Lily and I do share the same sexuality.*

What I was going to say: *Both Lily and I are normal.*

I didn't go back to Paula after that day. Dad couldn't afford weekly therapy appointments, and, as he said, I wasn't even eating more than I had been before therapy, anyway.

In seminary school, in order to become an ordained priest, one has to complete a Rorschach test. Ink blots are held before the seminarian, and he is asked to interpret the shape. This test, the seminarian's answers, are meant to determine whether or not the potential priest is at risk of same-sex attraction.

The garden is gorgeous but so carefully cultivated, manicured, that it feels more like walking through art than nature. Ivy climbs our brick prison, dressing the walls in a layer of leaves and vines. The body, too, grows a layer of insulation if it isn't cared for. My arms are warmed by a coarse coat of my own hair.

The plants wind around and around a wooden pergola's ceilings, aiming to suffocate, they don't know that the wood is already dead, killed and crafted into such a pretty roof.

White flowers hang low and are only just waking as we walk our morning walk. We brush them aside to keep to the path. There's a rose garden. Roses of every color, reds and pinks, whites and yellows, some sunset gradients and garish greens. Even a pocket of pitch-black roses grows at the center of the garden like a pupil to an eye. Reminding us of our surveillance.

I once read about a man who had the same depersonalization disorder as the university professor. His life was ruined by a set of plastic fruit. One Christmas, when he was middle-aged with a job and a wife and two children, they all went to his parents' house for dinner. Hungry, the man took an apple from the fruit bowl on the counter and bit into it—only to find that it was plastic. The bowl had been there all his life, and he had never tried to eat a piece.

He turned to his wife, who was wearing an apron and red lipstick, and taking the ham from the oven; a movie wife. His children were sitting on the floor, stacking blocks, being too entirely childlike. His wife and kids were actors, his life a lie. In the fleeting pivot from familiar to alien, the sudden and complete unraveling of recognition, he attacked his family. Kept attacking them. The man pled guilty but refused to plea insanity; he was sorry for his actions and certain of his mind. Bodies are fickle, we know, but we refuse to believe that our minds might fail us, because without them, we are just hopeless meat.

Oftentimes, on Garden Day, I pause my exercise to pluck a petal or leaf from a plant, just to test whether it's synthetic. But the flowers always fall apart in my hands, their colors bruised from my grip, and the garden is either real, or a very convincing replica of real. Some twisted simulacrum made just for us thin girls.

Kat is sitting on a bench when I arrive. She's not wearing her hat, and her scattering of hair is awry. She's still, her legs and arms crossed, all limb and appendage, pointed and angular as an asterisk.

"Hi," I say, slowing my power walk to greet her.

She looks up, her eyes wet and empty. Her lips bare, her complexion so pale it looks overexposed.

"I can teach you how to maintain," I say, marching on the spot. We're not allowed to run. One foot on the ground at all times is the rule. "So they never do that to you again."

"You've been injected with it, too?" Kat's voice trembles like it's walking a beam. The act dropped.

I nod. "It's important not to lose or they'll force you to gain. But if you can figure out how to maintain, then they'll leave you alone, mostly."

"How?"

"Walk with me." I gesture to the path. "I need to walk."

She nods and stands. "I gained this morning," she whispers. "The stuff they put into me. I gained overnight." She skipped to keep up with me. "What is that stuff?"

I shrug. "We don't know. Something. Calories. But we all gained, too. All you have to do now is maintain the weight you are today and they'll never do it again."

"How do you?"

"How do I what?"

"Maintain?"

"Oh." We pass a nurse, who nods at my march, my adherence to the rules. Once we're out of earshot, I say, "Weights."

"Weights?"

"I'll show you at tomorrow's weigh-in."

Kat asks more things, but I have my eye trained on Jram's window. We're about to pass it, and I suck in my stomach, aiming for two-dimensionality, try to relax my expression into something serene, carefree. Last night, the way he had shown me his whole self, the way he had stroked himself for me. Jram had ruined our fairy tale, but I had imposed that fairy tale upon our relationship. I hadn't considered that my fairy-tale projection was met with one of a sordid affair from him. One of lust, raw, animalistic sex. An affair doesn't sound so bad. It's so boring in this place.

Time moves like traffic here, doesn't it?

Jram's room is empty. His bed unmade. His desk piled with books. His closet open, clothes strewn about. We keep walking.

"I'm having a love affair," I say.

"In the supply closet?"

My cheeks warm, and I swallow.

"No," I say. "With a man."

"A man?"

"Jram."

"Who?"

"Jram."

"Jerome?"

"Jram."

"Really weird name," she says.

"We're in love," I tell her. "We'll probably get married."

"Sure," says Kat. "Sure you will, Slim."

I can hear the doubt in her tone. I want to shout at her. Shake her. *I am not a lesbian*, I want to cry. *I am nothing, nothing like you.*

In the 1960s, psychologist I. Oswald thought that homosexuality could be cured by overdosing on it. He gave gay men nausea-inducing drugs and sat them in small rooms, where they were surrounded by glasses of urine and videos of men having sex with other men, playing at full volume on a loop.

Kat hops over a worm carcass, splayed and tragic on the path, and is immediately reprimanded by a nurse, who tells her to keep one foot on the ground at all times. She rolls her eyes and falls back into our march.

"Why are there so many worms?" Kat scrunches her nose. "It's grotesque. You'd think they could pay someone to deal with that!"

"The rain," I say. I tell her what I know about worms, which is a decent amount. The previous occupant of my room left a book about insects on the shelf. It was the only book I had for the first month, until I found a second book on linguistics, a third on mental health conditions, and then a fourth on animal behaviors. But the first month, the month in which no one came to visit, I had only my insects book, called *Insects*. My father didn't understand, or didn't know how to care. Even Lily didn't visit for those first weeks, maybe too afraid I might infect her with my illness, the way I always had.

Growing up, I was always the one getting sick first. I got a cold and then Lily did. I got the flu and then Lily did. I got lice and then Lily did. I got chicken pox and then Lily did. I'm the weak one, the one who succumbs to any illness that approaches, hand outstretched. I take the hand of any offering stranger without asking questions. I'm a sucker for affection.

"Worms," I tell Kat, "absorb rain through their skin. Like sponges. Usually soil has a combination of air and water, which keeps the worms hydrated and lets them breathe. But, when it rains, the pores in the soil fill with water instead of air and the worms can't breathe. Instead of taking in air, they just keep absorbing water."

Kat grimaces, shudders, and I know she's thinking of the IV last night, the way the bag of lard emptied into her body, filling her, filling her, a worm caught out in the rain.

I go on. "So the worms have to crawl to the surface to breathe."

Kat's eyes, wide, her palm pressed to her mouth in horror. I'm enjoying horrifying her.

"Then what?" she says.

"Worms can't control how much they absorb. Any bit of moisture that touches them, they consume it, so, if they're out in the rain for too long, they just bloat and swell, filling up with rain, and then, pop."

"Pop?"

"They explode."

"Time's up, ladies," shouts a nurse.

There are tears in Kat Mitchells's eyes. I should feel bad about lying to her, skewing the end of the fact into fiction, but I like that I've had an effect on her. Made her drop her little performance, even if just briefly.

"Back inside!'" shouts the nurse.

One week. Seven days. One hundred and sixty-eight hours until we're allowed outside again.

• • •

When I get back to my room, there's a missed call on my cell from a number that isn't Lily's. I press to call back.

"Bright," says Phil's voice.

"Phil?"

"Yes."

"Phil Bright?"

"Yes."

"It's Rose."

"I know," he says. "I called you."

"I know," I say. "I called you back."

There's a silence.

"So, why did you call me?"

"I just wanted to apologize," says Phil. "For changing your relationship with Lily. I know it must be hard."

The nerve! "You haven't changed anything," I say. I hope I sound smug. I think about British people and hope that it might inflect my tone.

"Well, okay, sure, but I know she's spending less time with you now. Less time at the facility. Visiting, I mean. I just, you know, I really think that Lily should focus on herself for a change. Should focus on her own health, physical, mental, spiritual, all of it. I can help her with that. I can help her grow and change, but I can't help her if she has you influencing her the way you do."

"The way I do?"

"Yes." He sighs. "You two are so connected, it's difficult to help Lily when she has you in the other ear."

"She doesn't need help."

"She's not well." I could laugh. Lily? She's always been the well one!

"You're not well."

"What?"

"Listen, Phil," I say. "Lily and I are forever. You're a brief interruption in the lifetime of my relationship with her. Men come and go, the way they always have, always will, but I am Lily's forever. You think you've changed our relationship? You couldn't change our relationship in a million years. And the joke's on you, Phil. Lily's been visiting me even though you told her not to. She was here just yesterday. That's right. You're nothing." I hang up the phone, panting, exhausted from all of the confrontation.

17

At lunch, the nurse who spoons undercooked, swampy rice onto our plates and claims it's a risotto also hands us a pamphlet. I open mine as I carry my tray to a crowded table. We work better in herds, us thin girls; we use the buddy system. One is more likely to get away with hiding her food if she is sandwiched between other girls.

"A dance," says a girl whose name I don't know. "We're seriously going to be allowed to dance?" Her voice spills over, yellow with glee.

The pamphlet announces a social. An evening of dancing, fruit punch, music, and snacks. It announces that we will be allowed to interact with the men from the ward across the courtyard. I read the words so closely I accidentally swallow a mouthful of rice. I keep reading as I scoop the rest of the meal into my palm and drop it down my underwear. It sags like a dirty diaper.

"Hey," Kat says, taking the seat across from me. "This means you'll get to see Jerome! How fabulous. It'll be a ball!"

"Jram," I say. This could be it, the night Jram and I profess our love for each other. Cold suddenly, I pull the hood of my sweatshirt over my head and tighten the drawstrings, a cave around my face.

"Who's Jerome?" says a thin girl.

"Jram."

"Germ?"

"*Jram*, with a *J*."

"Jerm?"

"*J. R. A. M.* Jram."

"Oh, Jram," says a thin girl. "Jram. Never heard that before."

"Who is he?" asks another thin girl.

"Rose's lover," says Sarah, beside me, peeling her fingernails off in slim crescents. "He's German, darling."

I blush and feel my groin warm with excitement, reheating the rice that resides there.

"Lover?" The thin girls lean in. It's usually so dull in here. We can find a speck of excitement in anything that isn't just another meal-time. "You have a lover? But how?"

I smile, my face still humid with embarrassment. "He lives across the courtyard from me. We've been spending nights together."

"Wow," say the thin girls, chins in palms, eyes slick with lust. "Ro-mantic," they whisper.

"You could meet people, too," I say, feeling maternal and impor-tant. "You could all meet people at the dance."

"Thin men, darling?" says Kat, her lip raised in disapproval. "No offense," she assures me, the way people do when something is irre-futably offensive. "But, like, thin men? Really?"

"That's really sexist," says Sarah.

I smile at their disagreement. I want them to disagree forever. I want them to throw chairs! Chip each other's rotting teeth with cutlery hurled like spears. Claw at each other's eyes with those gag-trigger fingers.

"Women can't be sexist against men," says someone.

"Of course they can, baby," says Sarah.

"It's just, girls are meant to, like, diet and be thin," says a thin girl. "Men aren't. So how did those thin men even get that way?"

I tune out. My moment of fame is over. I waddle back to my room with a crotch full of rice and await Lily's visit.

2006 (17 years old—Lily: 174 lbs, Rose: 78 lbs)

Lily was doing the grocery shopping with Mum gone. She'd buy candy and chips, chocolates and crackers and cheese. She ate and ate. She grew and grew.

Jemima Gates told Lily she shouldn't sit with us, the popular girls, because you had to be thin to be popular. Lily took the news well, lifted both her packed lunch and mine, left the cafeteria, her head high. I wanted to say something, to stand up for Lily, but instead of doing those things, I didn't. I sat in my hunger, curled up in it comfortably. Complicity is so easy. I let everything wash over me like some useless seaside shell, hollow of any creature, picked up, carried by the waves. There was nothing left to me.

I got home after school to find Lily, standing at the stove, stirring yet another edible thing, dinner, she was the mother now, and weeping huge wet tears into the pot. Her overwhelming sadness tasted of seawater, noncommittally salty, watery, weak.

"Lil?" I said, standing at the door to the kitchen, too afraid to enter.

She sniffed. Her T-shirt was too short for her, the hem bunched around her navel. Her mole was visible above the waistband of her pants, bigger, stretched to twice its size, like a tree's rings growing as its trunk does.

"Lil," I tried again, but she kept stirring, lifted a wooden spoon to her lips, and lowered it back into the pot.

I held my breath as I approached, vision perennially blurred by now. There were two of her. I reached for one and my fingers fell through bare air.

On the next reach, I found the real Lily. Ran my fingers through her hair, which was different from mine by now—hers still healthy and full. I braided the familiar strands carefully, mourning what I had lost.

"Lil, I'm sorry," I said as I plaited, my fingers cold, clumsy. "I should've said something to Jemima. I'm sorry."

She lifted the spoon to her lips again, inhaled at the heat. It was macaroni and cheese. Smell the boiling fat.

"You know, Rosie," she said, her voice suede, "I would forgive almost anything if only you'd just eat something." I dropped her hair and stepped away. Went to bed hungry. Lay there, stomach twisting, looking up at my poster of young Kat Mitchells. Compared my wrist to her wrist. My ankle to her ankle.

• • •

She's without Diamond, this time, and when she walks through my door I think, for a tiny moment, that she's a nurse. She's thinner. Her frame too lean, her breasts too small, her arms too linear. I inhale and hold the air in my mouth, like a pet, a possession, I keep it safe.

It is so strange to see change. It is so much easier to see something stay the same. Like those long summers when the sky is so persistently blue it seems stuck that way. Like parents, stagnant characters in their roles as caregivers. Like the family house, with worn couches and an old television and photos on the walls. These things, comforting until they shift. Like when the summer sky applauds with unexpected thunder, or overhearing your parents at war, or returning home from a vacation and everything seems just slightly askew.

Lily is always the same, reliably herself, until she isn't.

Like when she started eating and her body ballooned. Like when Mum left, and she became the mother. Like how she's started dieting and, all of a sudden, she seems like me.

She's wearing sunglasses and she doesn't take them off, even when she's in my room, sitting beside me.

"Why are you wearing those sunglasses?"

"What?"

"Sunglasses." I point.

She reaches for them, takes them by the frame, hesitant. "Don't freak out," she says.

"What?"

Beneath her disguise, Lily's face is bruised. Her left eye is at the center of a purple ring. Her cheek is cut. And now that I'm inspecting her appearance, I notice that her lip, too, is swollen and split like a sausage overcooked.

I swallow. "What happened?"

"Listen," she says, "I don't want you to panic, okay?"

I say nothing.

"Phil and I, we, well, our relationship is . . . It's not . . . I mean . . ."

I wait.

"I mean he's, well, *we*, we're into BDSM."

"Like bondage?"

"Sure." Lily laughs a little, then winces, reaches for her torn lip. "I guess."

"You're hurt. Really hurt." I can only think of my phone call with Phil. How I told him about Lily's illicit visits.

"No!" she says. "I know, that's not what I was saying. I mean, we were having sex and he was using a, well, a riding crop, and I moved when I wasn't meant to, and he wasn't expecting it and he acciden-tally, well . . ." She gestures to her mauled face. "This is a onetime thing. We're usually more careful."

"He whipped you?"

"I agreed to it! It was all consensual. This was just an accident. Please don't freak out." Her cheeks, red, her eyes, awash. My jaw aches with the sour aftertaste of a lie.

What I want to say: *This was no accident.*

What I say: "Are you sure it was an accident?"

"Don't be ridiculous, baby sister. Of course it was. Phil would never."

I reach for Lily's eye, brush the bruise with my thumb.

"I'm worried about you," I say.

"Don't be." She smiles. "I'm happy! But I do have to go. I'm see-ing Phil tonight. His wife's out of town." She winks and then gasps. Her eye.

"Are you sure you're okay, Lil?"

Lily nods, smiles. There are tears like weather in her eyes. "He's my forever," she says.

"I'm here," I say. "I'm forever."

And so the time has come. I need to get out of here. To protect Lily from Phil, from herself. If I ever want to complete my list, my catalogue of reasons to live, then she must be happy, healthy, well. And, while she is with Phil, she can't be any of those things. He is a bad man!

It's the first time Lily has ever really needed me to keep her safe, and I can only do that from the outside. But to be released means gaining weight, and the thought makes my breath quicken, shallow and rapid as fast running footsteps. I close my eyes, hold my breath, count, and release.

Of course, there's the other thing, too. The letters. I'm not ready to stop receiving them. I like to be the recipient of love letters, the way I could read them with a tear welling in the corner of my eye, the way I could press the page to my chest like an Elizabethan girl, overwhelmed with the romance of her suitor's cursive. I swallow the selfish thought deep. They have no calories, thoughts, ideas, memories, and you can store them in your stomach!

Thought Diversion is what our group leader would say.

I turn on my bedside light. Jram's room is dark, so I flicker my light, on and off, on and off. Eventually, his room winks awake. I'm already topless. This time, he strokes himself until he paints his window white, and the reward rolls down the glass like bird shit. I smile myself to sleep, feeling woman again.

2006 (17 years old—Lily: 180 lbs, Rose: 77 lbs)

I lied to Lily. To everyone. Dieting is acceptable until it isn't, and then people start to fear for you and fear you, which is when the lying begins.

I always said: *I already ate.*

I always said: *I'm not hungry.*

I always said: *I'm not feeling well.*

I always said: *I'm a celiac.*

I always said: *Herbal tea is fine, no milk.*

I always said: *I don't actually like cake.*

I always said: *I'm on a cleanse.*

I always said: *I have a stomachache.*

I always said: *I'm vegan now.*

I always said: *I'm allergic to nuts.*

I always said: *I'm about to work out.*

I always said: *I ate earlier.*

I always said: *Just a coffee for me.*
I always said: *I had a huge breakfast.*
I always said: *I'm on the Atkins.*
I always said: *I'm saving myself for dinner.*
I always said: *I'm full!*

Lies are so much lighter than the truth. The truth paces, grounded, heavy. Lies? Helium filled! Watch as they float away! Lily didn't believe me, of course. Not even once. To us, lies taste like gin, bitter and citric, and as I explained my way out of eating she would pucker her lips and close her eyes and sigh and sigh and sigh.

Termites don't sleep. They are so hungry that they forgo rest in order to keep chewing, keep swallowing, keep feeding and feeding and feeding. Termites have a life span of two years, and they do not sleep during their lives. They'd rather eat those 730 days away.

18

I hand the group leader my journal.

"Here," I say. "I'm done."

"What do you mean you're done?"

"I wrote about it. The start of the diet, the losing weight, the bingeing and purging. It's all in here."

She flips through the pages, not reading, barely glancing at all my hard work.

"So," she says. "What was it?"

"What was it?"

"That made you this way? Why are you here, Rose."

"Because I started dieting and I couldn't stop. It really was a helpful exercise, thank you."

"Why couldn't you stop?"

"I just couldn't."

The nurse hands the journal page to me. It's heavy. Have my words made it heavier?

"You're not done," she says. "Keep writing."

"I've run out of stuff to write. It's getting boring. I'm just writing about dieting and dieting and dieting."

"People don't just diet, Rose. They diet for a reason. Here's what I want you to do. Stop writing *about* your eating. Just write about you. Anything that comes to mind."

2007 (18 years old—Lily: 187 lbs, Rose: 75 lbs)

Our father lost his job. He told us it was because his department was cut, but he told us with his flammable breath and Lily and I exchanged a look. He had not stopped drinking since our mother left. He hadn't smiled in just as long. It confused me to see him so upset. I had always thought that the root of his sadness was Mum, the way she accused him of infidelity, shouted, screamed, the way she rolled her eyes at his very existence. But now he was small and sad, and it was clear he had loved her. Or, if not love, then something else. Family.

He decided not to look for a new job for a while—he *deserved a break*—so our eighteenth birthday was a stingy affair with a banner that had once read: IT's A GIRL! And now read: IT's 2 GIRL!S BIRTHDAYS!

Jemima Gates asked if I wanted to pick a dress from her mother's closet. I did. We went back to her place after school on the night of the party, just the two of us, the first time we'd ever really been alone together without the rest of the popular pack. Her attention made me feel royal.

She took her T-shirt over her head, her breasts were bigger than mine, which were flat as they had always been. Then she wriggled out of her jeans. Her underwear was made of an intricate lace. It was like watching an adult undress. I gawked.

"Jeez," said Jemima. "Stare much?"

"Ego much?" I said, barely missing a beat. I had learned how to please Jemima. The best path to her approval was a tightrope be-tween compliment and critique, tribute and tease. I never dropped a step.

We twirled in dresses two sizes too big but so glamorous we'd forgive the extra fabric.

"So, your sister will be there?"

"Of course she will be," I said, cinching a white gown around my waist with my fingers. "She's my twin. It's her birthday, too."

"I don't get people who use family as an excuse to have to be close to someone," said Jemima, whose parents mostly ignored her. "Es-pecially you. You don't like your parents, so you don't hang out with them. Your mum got it. She left, see? You know you can ditch Lily, too, right?"

"No," I said, "I can't."

And when I said it, Jemima's expression fell, and I realized what she wanted. She wanted me. She wanted family.

"Did you know," I started, "that mother cuckoo birds lay their eggs in the nests of other birds? They don't care for their young. They just ditch them and go. They let the other mother bird raise their chicks."

Jemima frowned. "How do you know all the stuff you know?"

"I read."

"Well, I think you're brilliant," she said, and I felt it. She smiled as she took a silver necklace from a jewelry stand and draped it over my neck as if I were being crowned queen of somewhere wonderful. "You can keep this," she said.

"My parents are one thing. But it's different for me and Lily," I said, fingering the necklace. "Lily is, like, it's like, we're the same, so it's different."

"Not really," said Jemima, fixing my gown's strap and stepping back, smiling. "Have you looked at yourself lately? You're not anything like her anymore."

The remark made me recoil, a jab to the gut, but, looking in the mirror, bones in a ball gown, I smiled.

"Whatever," Jemima continued. "Isn't she dating that Tyler Marks guy now? Will he be there? He got kind of hot over summer."

The dress surrounded me like a lampshade. I didn't look pretty, but I did look so, so thin.

The party was a disaster. Defrosted hors d'oeuvres circled the room like flies over a bloody carcass, and the crowd was a bag of odds and ends: old neighbors, acquaintances, some of Lily's exes, the popular girls, our father.

Lily wore a flash of red lipstick and a matching dress that licked her body, thigh to breast. She stood in the kitchen with her latest boyfriend, Tyler, and two of Tyler's friends. She didn't tend to have girlfriends, but Lily knew how to exist at the center of a ring of boys.

"Lil," I shouted from the door of the kitchen. I was tipsy on vodka and ice water. Jemima suggested a lime wedge to take the edge off, but those five citrus calories would put me over my day's quota. I beckoned and Lily excused herself from the boys, who were already chugging bourbon, a masculinity show.

"Hey." She smiled. "What's up? You okay?" She inspected my eyes, and I knew she knew I'd been drinking. And she knew I knew she knew, too. This had always been the way.

"Let me get you a drink," I said.

"No, that's okay, but thank you. How are you?" she said. "You look beautiful. I like that necklace."

"Thanks. It's Jemima's. I'm okay. How are you?"

"I'm okay."

We watched each other. Wary. Like looking in a fun house mirror and not knowing where, exactly, the self stopped and the reflection began.

"Babe," slurred Tyler from over Lily's shoulder. "I did ten seconds!"

"Proud of you, babe," Lily shouted, but she was still looking at me. We were acting like acquaintances except I could taste the heat from her blush and the rosiness was transferring to my own cheeks.

"Do you want to go talk somewhere?" I said.

Lily turned and checked on Tyler, who had started the drinking contest anew, and then back to me. She nodded. "Okay."

I took her hand, so like mine, like leading myself to our bedroom. We sat on our old piano stool, side by side. Before they gave up on us, our parents had arranged weekly piano lessons, and we had sat, just like this, sharing the stool and sharing the keys, me on the low notes, Lily on the high.

I pressed a key, a low blurt rang through the room and ricocheted off the walls and then seeped like a leak into the floors.

"What's up?" said Lily.

"How are you?" I tried again.

"Good," said Lily. "How are you?"

I pressed another key, frustrated. It was like talking to a distant relative. A stranger. Someone who barely knew the language.

"You're dressed up," I said.

"Thanks."

"Red," I said, but I had wanted to tell her she looked beautiful.

"What?"

"You're wearing red."

She nodded. "Oh. Yeah. I am. Yeah."

"How's Tyler?" I tried.

Lily shrugged. "I don't think he's the one."

I laughed. She laughed.

"That's probably good," I said, and Lily pressed a high note. I waited until it bled into silence. "Jemima said something earlier, something about how he's cute, about how she's going to make a move tonight."

Lily chuckled. "I'm not worried. He's not into skinny—I mean, well, he's not into Jemima."

I swallowed. "Lily," I said.

She turned to face me, and I her.

"I don't know," I finally said.

"I don't know, either."

I nodded. She nodded.

"Sometimes it seems like the only thing we can talk about anymore is my dieting," I whispered. I could hear my words tilting, italicized with alcohol. I hadn't even finished a single drink, but my body felt made of liquor.

"Sometimes it seems like that's all you are anymore, Rosie," said Lily. "But you could be so much more than that."

"You mean I could be you."

Lily shrugged. "You couldn't keep being me forever."

I downed the rest of my drink. Stood, let the vertigo cyclone through me, and left Lily sitting alone. She shifted into the center of the stool before I even left the room.

I've never known how to be me, but I've always known how not to be. The best way to not be yourself is to be someone else. I could be Lily, I could be Jemima, I could be Kat Mitchells. I've always morphed to fit my container, like a liquid. Look at all the forms I can take! Like the Celaenia excavata, a spider that uses camouflage as a defense mechanism. The spider is mainly hunted by birds; its back looks like a pile of bird droppings, and all it has to do to deter its predators is keep still. No bird wants to eat its own shit.

The night traipsed on and I got drunker. Tyler had long since blacked out and so Lily shook her body against a number of men who held their erections tight against her ass. Everyone was Lily's orbit, and she was the sun, crucial and bright. I stumbled toward her.

"Jason," Lily said, pushing a man's body away from her and toward me. "This is my twin, Rose."

"Twin?" said Jason. "Man, I must be fucked up."

"You guys should dance," said Lily. "Dance," she said again.

I did, jolting my body, flailing my arms wide. I felt good. I felt better than I had in a long time. I smiled up at the swirling ceiling and twirled.

"You want another drink, babe?" Jason whispered in my ear and his breath was hot and smoky. I nodded. I did. I wanted so many more drinks.

He came back with a can, some premixed cocktail. I squinted at the nutrition information on the back, but my eyes were doing acrobatics and the can was kaleidoscoping.

"Just drink," Lily shouted, reaching over to crack the can open. I nodded, tipped the drink to my lips, and swallowed. I finished the whole can before I realized what I'd done. I reached for my stomach and felt the swell of it, convex against my palm.

I ran from the dance floor, from Jason and Lily, their eddying bodies, into the kitchen, and I purged the sixty-calorie vodka soda into the faux–champagne bucket before fainting on the linoleum. My head hit the floor, blood spread quick as a spilled drink. The party, Lily would later tell me, had stopped soon after my demise.

The next day, when I was vulnerable and soft as a newborn, the way a hangover tends to bruise, Lily told me she wouldn't eat until I did.

"It's my last resort," she said. "I don't know what else to do."

A final effort to help me be well. A hunger strike, protesting my very personhood.

"Don't," I whispered, delighting in the nausea that made me feel as if I could never eat again. "You're being ridiculous."

"I'm so scared for you," she said. "I have to do something. This is all I can think of."

She stuck to her fast for three days, a valiant effort, before passing out in the shower and splitting her scalp wide open on the ledge that held our shampoo. I whispered her awake, wrapped her sweet bloody head in her towel, and her big naked body in mine.

When she finally woke, my mouth stung with cold. I was used to tasting her emotions by now, and my palate was refined, a Lily connoisseur. This chill on my tongue was fear, and it was as cold as I had ever felt.

"What happened?" she said. "Did you pass out? Are you okay?"

"No, *you* passed out," I said. "Your stupid hunger strike. You have to eat something, Lil."

"Did you eat?" she said. "Have you eaten?"

I said nothing.

"Then I won't." And her tone was final.

My gums were numb from cold.

"Okay, okay," I said. My teeth clacked together like a wind-up toy as I promised her I would seek recovery. I promised and promised and promised. And I meant it, but even as I swore my oath I was tucking my fingers under my rib cage, seeing how far I could bury myself in myself.

"Look," I say to Kat at the morning's weigh-in. I hold my hand open, showing her the black disks in my palm, and then I thread each weight onto a string, knot the string into a loop, and use it to ponytail my hair. "See?"

"Where do you get them from?" Kat says, reaching to touch my weighted hairdo.

"Shower curtains," I whisper, although we're alone in her room.

"Do you have extras?" she asks, and from my pocket I pull two weights I took, yesterday, from a new curtain.

"Quick," I say. "We've only got five minutes until weigh-in." Being late to weigh-in results in a body search. The nurses haven't found the weights in our hair during a search yet, but they've discovered our other tricks. Holding balls of rolled bread in our mouths, packing bras with socks like self-conscious pre-teens, chugging water until it sloshes, tidal, inside us.

"Why do you only use them to maintain?" says Kat. "Why don't you use them to gain, darling, to get out of here?" She says the words easily, and I feel myself blush, as if caught out in a lie. I feel exposed. But, of course, it's a natural question, it just seems uncanny given my formulation of that very plan just last night.

I watch my shoes to keep my rosiness from her, to keep suspicions at bay.

If I'm really going to do this, I can't tell any of the others. I don't want them to follow me. I won't be responsible for their discharge from this place that is meant to help them survive. Won't be responsible for their death by starvation on the outside. "Because we do want to recover in the end. We're just maintaining until we learn how to gain. How to be okay with gaining."

"Why are you being so nice to me all of a sudden?" Kat asks.

I shrug. "You remind me of someone I used to know."

She nods. Smiles. "She must've been just fabulous."

"How do you want to be loved?" I say.

"Entirely," she says.

I nod. Me too.

"I wasn't always this way, you know, darling." Kat sighs. "I remember being happy. I remember being healthy. There really was a time when I was worthy of love. The world made me like this. The way I am now. You did."

"Me?"

"You. My fans. The media. They watched my figure so closely. No one should be that aware of their own body."

I nod. I know. "The group leader tells us, *Your body is only your own.*"

Kat blinks. "Do you really believe that?"

I say nothing.

"Do you really think you'll ever be okay with gaining?" Her voice is so hopeful.

I take Kat's hand and we start off toward the weigh stations. "I hope so," I say. "Don't you?"

Sometimes I wake in the morning, brighter than usual, and I think, *Today, I will eat.* I think, *Others eat every day, every meal.* I think, *I'll just do it. I'll eat today.* Sometimes the feeling lasts as long as it takes for a dream to disappear from the mind. Sometimes all the way until breakfast, when the nurses ladle soupy scrambled eggs onto my plate. My new resolution ripples like water in the wind.

I can eat this, I tell myself. *I can eat this?* I ask myself.

I can't.

We're never allowed to know our weights, of course. We're too fragile to bear that knowledge. The screen that calculates our worth is always turned toward the nurse in charge. She tells us only: gained X pounds, lost X pounds, or maintained. It's okay, it doesn't matter that they don't tell us. Us thin girls measure ourselves in different ways. We measure in hands, like horses. How close are our fingers to circling our thighs? Are our biceps still slight enough to be clutched in a single fist? Can we grip our waists with fingers clasped like a lover's? We can!

There is an envelope waiting in my room.

> R—
>
> I won't contact you again. I'm so sorry if these letters have been harmful in any way. I know I'll never be able to apologize enough for how I was, but I really have been trying to change. I miss you and I love you. Maybe I'll see you again one day.
>
> —M

● ● ●

We heard from Mum just twice a year after she moved out. A Christmas card and a birthday card. One for us to share. *Happy birthday, girls. You must be getting big, I'd imagine. Mum.*

She friended us on Facebook, which might have been a virtual olive branch, but it felt like a renunciation of her motherhood. *We can still be friends* is what that notification felt like.

Her Facebook was active. Photos of a new family, complete with children, two little blond girls with tiny button noses and clear skin. She posted photos of them together, smiling, a family portrait, one girl on her knee and one on her new partner's. They went overseas, to Disneyland, to the Eiffel Tower, to Rome. *Happy Family at the Colosseum*, said her caption. They were at the Colosseum. They did look happy. I wasn't mad at her for leaving us behind. She deserved a chance at happiness. A life without the buts.

Lily let me keep them, the cards, tucked into my pillowcase, as if I had the kind of mother who hushed me to sleep at night.

19

The group leader is showing us how to greet our food.

"Eat it?" says Sarah, eyeing up her banana nervously.

"Greet it," says the group leader, holding an orange at eye level.

"*Greet* it?" says Kat, who managed to happily gain a half pound at the weigh-in.

"Yes, *greet* it, like this," says the leader. "Hello, orange."

Us thin girls look at one another, our fruit still on the surface of the table.

"Do we have to, darling?" says Kat. "It seems a little—"

"Yes," says the group leader. "Part of having a healthy relationship with food is learning to converse with it. Interact with your meals."

"Interact with meals?" I say.

"Yes," says the leader. "Think about your relationships in life—"

"With humans or fruit?" says Sarah. Then she stops to crack her knuckles, right on three p.m.

"With humans," says the leader. "You would always greet a person, wouldn't you? If you wanted to have a healthy relationship with them."

"Of course," I say, and I'm rewarded with a smile. "Greet people," I say.

"Exactly, Rose," says the leader. "And you want a healthy relationship with food, don't you?"

"I do," I say. "I do, that's for sure!"

"Good girl!" says the leader. "So then, you must greet your food."

I take my peach, hold its fuzzy face in my palms, and lift it to meet my eye. I hold it tight in my fist, and its shape gives. It's so hard not to feel powerful.

I have to at least give the illusion of improving, recovering, if I'm ever going to con my way out of this place. And so, despite the hungry eyes watching me, I clear my throat, look at my peach, and say, "Hello, peach."

"Yes!" the leader leaps from her seat, a standing ovation, and I grin up at her, feeling triumphant. She kisses the crown of my head, and I smile and whisper, "Hello, peach. Hello, peach." It isn't so hard, having a healthy relationship with food.

As the other girls greet their fruit, I hold mine tight. Then too tight. My nails break the peach's thin skin, my fingers sink into its guts, and then I'm squeezing and the fruit is destroyed and I'm gripping its pit with all of my might.

"This is an unhealthy relationship," says the group leader, and she is pointing at me.

Dad wore his sadness like sunscreen, you couldn't see it, but the odor of it wafted off him in waves. His loneliness was selfish—maybe all loneliness is.

It's easy to be consumed by one's suffering. *How can I possibly live this day?* is how it feels. *How can I possibly pretend everything, anything, is normal?* That's what it feels like, too, to smile in the presence of others, to have a conversation, to shower. Pretending. *Here I am*, you lie to the world, a bad actor in a B-grade indie film: *Here I am, human and everything.*

Dad wasn't good at pretending so he stopped. Stopped smiling in the presence of others, having conversations, showering. He seemed smaller.

"We should set him up," said Lily.

"Set him up?"

"Like on a date." She was gesturing with her whole body, the way she tended to. "Imagine!" she said, her eyes too wide, smile too wide, too wide, too wide. "Imagine being able to introduce people to *both* our dads. Two dads! Like a celebrity family, Rosie. Like Neil Patrick Harris and his husband!"

"I don't think he's gay," I said. "He was married to Mum all those years. You think all that was a lie?"

"Well. Not a lie, exactly."

"Then what?"

Lily was quiet. She raked her fingers through her hair. "You know how we used to go to Sunday school and everyone believed in god, so we believed in god as well?" She spoke quickly. "And how it wasn't until we looked around at other options, other ideas, until more and more people around us seemed to be atheists, how it wasn't really until then that we even questioned our beliefs, that we realized that maybe we didn't believe in god at all, we'd just been surrounded by that idea for so long that it felt like the truth? Like a fact?"

I waited.

"Well, I think it's like that. Kind of."

"Being gay is like not believing in god?"

"No. No, just like. Like being a certain way because the people around you are that way even if you're not *really* that way. I'm not explaining it well. I just think it's much easier to be like the people around you."

The dance is tomorrow night, and us thin girls are allowed to take a bus into town to buy new dresses to wear. Clothes shopping is triggering for many thin girls, so the facility has closed down a shop for us, and they have asked the staff to cover all mirrors.

We are allowed to try on clothing in sizes ten and up, so that nothing can be too small, and we are not allowed to comment on one another's choices. A girls' day out!

That morning, I had carefully gained a pound. I stuffed socks into my bra and filled my cheeks with air, an imitation of health. I'd also added an extra weight, hoping to raise my number, but when the nurse said the word: *gained*, a smile strung across her face, a congratulatory banner, I had to keep from crying.

Back in my bedroom, I unwound my ponytail, slipped the shower curtain weights from the string, and tucked them beneath my mattress. I imagined my sister's bruised face, whispered, "Lily needs me," and "Lily needs me," and "Lily needs me." And it was a chant and I could do this. I would gain on alternate days, just a pound or half of one, I decided, to keep from being too obvious. I would be released in a matter of days. Lily needs me.

We pull dresses from hangers and inspect their sizes. They needn't have taken away the small ones, for us thin girls always choose clothing that saturates us. We like to feel like stick-figure girls beneath baggy layers. With so much excess fabric swathed around our bodies, it's hard to tell whether there's a body beneath there at all.

Sarah chooses a dress that is tiered as a sport stadium, and when she spins, like a movie girl, air catches under the skirt and fills the fabric and it almost looks as if she is an average teenager, filling out dresses on a shopping day.

Kat opts for a silver suit, so oversized it makes her look childish.

I choose a charcoal sack-like number that flows all the way to the floor. It's made of satin, and when I move, I feel like molten metal, my body soldered from steel.

"Did I look stupid in it?" Sarah asks as we line up to make our purchases.

"You looked gorgeous, darling," I say. "I mean, Sarah."

"I gained a pound," I tell Lily when she comes to visit. "This morning, a whole pound."

She's smoking as I talk, her cigarette noncommittally out the window, its tip spewing ash onto the sill. I watch the embers fall, sometimes caught by the faintest breath of air that sends them skyward, lighter than dust.

"That's great, baby sister," says Lily, but her voice slouches. "I lost three." She stubs her cigarette on the glass pane, leaving a ring of black, and tosses the butt into the garden beneath my room. "Look at us." She wiggles her finger between our bodies. "We're gonna be identical again in no time."

I inhale, count, exhale. "Lily," I start. "Your dieting—"

"No," she says. "Don't say anything. It's not forever, Rosie. I'm much happier now; I really am." She folds her hands. "Let's just have a nice visit, okay?"

Her bruises are fading; they're an expired green now. I sigh, nod. Soon. I will be discharged soon, helping her in the real world. Feeding her. Saving her. Bringing her back to me. So, instead of protesting further, I open my closet. "Look," I say. I take the hanger and hold the dress out to Lily, who looks it up and down.

"Try it on for me!" she says, and her excitement spreads like a smell. I smile at her, thinking of Jram, and how we will soon meet in person. How we will fall in love under the dining hall's temporary disco ball, slow dancing and kissing until our tongues are tied tight together, a knot of muscle, inextricable from each other.

I unbutton my cardigan and Lily hisses through her teeth, she whispers, "Your ribs, Rose." And I think I detect a lick of desire in her tone. A wanting, which frightens me. I dress myself quickly.

"Beautiful, baby sister," says Lily when I smooth the gown down my body, swish its hem about my ankles. "You look beautiful."

"Beautiful enough to make a man fall in love?"

She raises a brow. "A man?" she says. "Which man?"

"Oh." I shrug. "Just a guy I've been seeing."

"What!" Lily reaches for my hand and pulls me toward her, winding me in like a fish until we're nose to identical nose. "Who is he?"

"His name," I pick at my cuticles, "is Jram."

"Did you say Sam?"

"Jram."

"Jram?"

"That's it. Jram."

"What is that, Greek?"

I shrug. "Maybe? I think it's sexy."

"How'd you two meet?"

"He lives here," I say. "In the facility, like me."

"He's sick?"

"What?"

"I mean," says Lily, correcting. "I mean, he has an eating disorder, too?"

"Yes."

"Hm." Lily sucks her lip into her mouth and begins to chew. I let her feast on herself. "Well," she says finally. "I'm not sure that it's such a good idea to see another, you know, another."

"Another?"

"Someone with an eating disorder."

"Why?"

"Just . . ." Lily kneads my knuckles with her thumb. "I just worry that you two might, you know, sort of, um, enable each other?"

"Since when has enabling each other been a bad thing in a relationship?"

"You know what I meant, Rosie. I meant enable each other in the other way, in the bad way, as in, he might encourage you to stop eating again, and vice versa. You know? I just think it might be unhealthy."

"He wants the best for me," I say. She's looking at me with sympathy—no, with pity. Her eyebrows crowd together, stitched into a single row. She thinks my love is ridiculous. She thinks I am unworthy of love.

"And anyway." My mouth is moving ahead of my mind, rolling downhill quickly, and I can't catch up. "Who are you to give me dating advice? To talk to me about unhealthy relationships? You're dieting for a man you barely know. You're letting him hit you. Why would I take relationship counseling from a homewrecker who got herself addicted to smoking for some guy?"

Lily seems to swallow her lip whole. She stands and tucks her hair behind her ears. I can tell she wants to shout, to retaliate. But she won't. Instead, she retreats from my room, letting the door close too loudly behind her.

Our sisterhood is made up of disagreement and forgiveness. The disagreements are by choice; the forgiveness runs through our veins.

We know we can push the other, shove her as far from us as we can, and we know she will pull herself back, reeled in by a strand of DNA.

We visited Mum only once after she left. The invitation to her fiftieth birthday party came in the mail, pink and rose-scented with a curly font that said *CELEBRATE*.

She lived in a townhouse that was attached to about ten other identical townhouses. There was a doormat that said FAMILY, and it was the only point of difference between this house and its neighbors.

Mum opened the door with a flourish but stopped dead upon seeing us standing there, on the porch of her new life. She dropped the door-knob and visibly winced. She had her hair done up in a spidery bun, and her makeup was too heavy, as if painted at a carnival. She'd put on weight, maybe 40 pounds, maybe even 60. She looked good.

"You came!" she cried, in a voice too high for itself. "Ted!" she shouted over her shoulder. "Ted, come here! Look who came!"

A short, bearded man came hopping over, his hands clasped and wringing together. "Girls, you made it!" His excitement was genuine, his eyes glinting, cheeks high and stretched in a smile. It was clear who had sent the invitation. "I'm so glad you made it! We're so glad!" All of the exclamation was making me dizzy. I held Lily's shoulder.

"Where's your father?" said Mum, peering around us as if he might have been crouching behind our backs, waiting to jump out—*Surprise!*

"He couldn't make it," said Lily.

"Couldn't make it," I echoed.

"A shame," said Mum, looking unashamed.

"Come in, girls," said Ted, taking my arm, taking Lily's, guid-ing us into the house. "You're every bit as gorgeous as I imagined. Come in. Come in and sit, sit." He lowered us onto a pair of stools at the kitchen island, set a champagne flute before each of us. "Cheers!" he said. "Mingle!" he said, before backing away. "Make yourselves comfortable!" he called as he was absorbed into the crowd. Some-where in the commute from the front door to the kitchen, our mother had found a way to disappear. We were not comfortable.

No one came to speak to us. Lily chugged her glass of champagne

and then mine and then another that she found, half-empty and decorated with a crescent of old lipstick. About an hour into the night, our
mother came over wearing a tight smile.

"Girls." She nodded, as if to an acquaintance in the office.

"Hey, Mum," said Lily. "So, how're things?"

"Good!" said Mum. "Good, thanks. Things are good. How're things
with you?"

"Good," we said with symmetry.

"Good, great," said Mum. "Great, great. Anyway, I was just coming over for a refill." She leaned between Lily and me to take a pair
of champagne glasses, then clinked them together with a giggle.
"Cheers!" she said. "Oh, and there are snacks over there, Lily," she
said, already retreating. "Don't snooze on the wontons!"

It's the last thing she ever said to us. *Don't snooze on the wontons.*

"She seems happy," said Lily, a wonton in hand.

"How can she be happy when Dad is, well . . ."

"She doesn't have to suffer with him," said Lily.

"She could," I said. "At least a little."

"No," said Lily, a shake of her head. "She's choosing happiness. Dad
is making the choice to be sad."

"No, he isn't. Why would anyone choose to be sad?"

Lily shrugged. "Things are complicated."

"Wow, Lily," I said. "Profound."

"I just mean that he could be dating. He could get himself a boyfriend, get married, do the happy family thing. He could, if he really
wanted to."

"If he's gay, that is. We don't know."

Lily cleared her throat and stood, gestured to the door. "Yes, well,"
she said. "Like I said, things are complicated."

We left our mother's party, unnoticed.

2007 (18 years old—Lily: 191 lbs, Rose: 73 lbs)

Jemima Gates started bringing me to the mall instead of her other
popular friends. Being friends with Jemima Gates made it easier to be

human. Her requirements for personality traits in a best friend were so specific and comprehensive that there was no room for any ad-libbing, no room for any Old Rose to show through. Even in private, it helped if I imagined that Jemima was watching me. Alone in my bedroom, I'd flip my hair. I'd roll my eyes at cheesy moments on tele-vision shows, raise my eyebrows at Lily's raised fork. In the back seat of the car, I'd look out the window like a girl from the movies. It was all performative, but I was sure that if I performed Jemima for long enough, the wind might change. I crossed my fingers for a southerly. I'd never felt more normal in my life.

Lily would watch with a furrowed brow as Jemima shoulder-tapped me during lunch and bent over my shoulder, slim and flimsy as a designer scarf, she whispered invitations in my ear, her lips tacky against my lobes, her cherry gloss sifting up my nose.

Jemima and I rushed past the food court, breaths held, so afraid of caving, and dipped into stores for grown women to try on dresses we would never buy. Admired our thinness in velvet-curtained changing rooms. She looked good in everything, moved like a liquid. Jemima's body, which, like mine, had changed lately, her fad diets taking their toll on her chest, her ass. Now, she craned her neck to inspect every angle of herself, all straight lines and sharp angles, it made my own body hurt. And I couldn't tell whether it was the sting of jealousy or want.

"Stare much?"

"Ego much?" It was our little routine, now.

I counted my day's calories. Popped a Tic Tac, my drug of choice. Their calories kept me conscious when my body threatened to close up shop. Sometimes I could last on one an hour—that's a twenty-four-calorie day. Not bad!

The shop assistants would ooh and aah, thinking we had money to spend. People often mistook our lean figures for wealthy ones. The wealthy are so often thin, are so careful about what they eat, as if they want to be mistaken for hungry. Only some forms of excess are fashionable.

"I love your arms," said Jemima, as we examined our bodies in the changing room. "They're so tiny. And your collarbones!" She ran her fingertips down the ramp of them, loving the parts of me I couldn't. I clenched my teeth to keep from trembling.

I would have invited Lily along if we had been speaking. But every time Lily talked to me those days, it was only as an attempt to force some sort of food on me, so I stopped talking to her at all, meeting her questions with silence, her greetings with mere nods.

We went days without speaking, weeks, and the silence felt permanent. I replaced her companionship with Jemima. She replaced mine with a series of boys.

Sometimes I locked myself in the bathroom and ran the shower as I spoke to the mirror.

"Hi," I would say, facing one way. Then I'd turn to face the other way. "Hi," I'd say. "How are you?" "Good, how are you?" I'd say. "I miss you." And I'd say, "I miss you, too." And it was good to hear the words from Lily's face, in Lily's voice.

During one of our window-shopping excursions, Jemima got caught stealing a snakeskin purse from Gucci. We were taken to mall prison, which was a supply closet with a gate that rolled down as if the jail were just a shut store. A moustached man asked us for our names and our addresses. Jemima said her name was Lindsay Lohan, and the mall cop scribbled it down without an accent of suspicion. I said my name was Lily Winters, because those syllables were all I could muster, like a game of word association, her name was more familiar to me than my own. I hardly introduced myself, but I talked to Lily a million times a day. The problem was that we shared an address, and I reeled that off, too, the world's worst criminal.

When I presented my father with the shoplifting ticket, he sighed. My punishment was no dessert for a week. He seemed to have forgotten that I had a problem. Forgotten that I wasn't naturally thin. Forgotten that Lily and I were supposed to be identical. He seemed to forget almost everything but for the exact number of cans of cheap beer in the fridge—that he knew by heart.

He had picked up a new accounting job and was working long days and going out for longer nights. He would stop home between work and bar, usually, just to remind us he existed, and then disappear again, sometimes until the morning.

Did I miss my mother? Not really; she'd never been much of one. Did I resent my father? Not really; we all deal with pain in different ways. Eating, starving, drinking. When the pain is too much for the mind, we take it out on the body.

Long after I had been released from mall jail and banished to bed by my father, Lily got home from school and headed straight for our room and sat on the foot of my bed as I pretended to sleep. She knew, of course, by the taste in her mouth that I was faking it. The flavors of each other dulled when we were unconscious and dreaming.

"Rosie," she said. "I'm worried about you, you know. You're not being yourself."

I said nothing.

"Are you . . ." Lily swallowed, which was my move, not hers. "You're not, like . . ."

I already knew what the question would be. Like the world's most pointless future teller, I always knew what Lily was going to say an instant before she said it.

"You're not in love with Jemima Gates, are you?" she whispered, her eyes on my duvet.

"What?"

"No one would judge you," she went on. "For being, you know, like, into girls, I mean. I wouldn't care." She wiped her eyes. "And if what you're doing, the starving thing, is, like, a punishment, you know, you don't have to punish yourself for being gay."

I laughed a cold laugh in the hopes of hiding my hot cheeks, then swallowed her sadness, sour as a winter plum, and said, "You're just bitter because I'm the better one now."

"The better one?" said Lily.

"You know exactly what I mean." I turned away from her. "You can't have two things without comparing them."

20

The group leader is teaching us how to confront our food, but none of us thin girls are paying much attention. We're all hazy with romantic daydreams of slow dances and tongue kisses. The dance!

"Come on, girls," says the leader in her lowest, slowest vocal fry. "Let's focus."

We each hold a single slice of bread, one of the scariest foods. Girls are taught to avoid carbohydrates more than anything. More than strangers on the streets, more than men who let wandering fingers linger on bare shoulders, more than bosses with bulging crotches and office doors that lock.

"Take your bread," says our leader, "And give it a pair of eyes. Just like this." She lifts her slice and jabs her index finger through the bread, one, two, a couple of holes, side by side. "See?" she says. "Confrontation is much easier when you can look them in the eye."

We look at one another with superior smirks. Tonight is our night, and we are women. Women going to balls did not make faces from bread!

"Do we have to?" says Sarah, whose face is already painted in heavy layers of foundation despite the morning hour. It's too much makeup. Kat did it. She's been doing girls' faces all day.

"Yes," says the group leader. "Anyone who fails to complete the activity will be uninvited to tonight's dance."

We poke holes in the bread.

"Now," says the leader, "lift your bread to meet your eye."

We do. She smiles at our obedience. We stare our bread straight in the eyes. Unafraid, then afraid.

"Now I want you to confront your food," says the leader.

"Confront?" Kat says, her face still bare.

"Yes, confront," says the leader. "Like this." She brings the bread closer to her face, closer, closer, and us thin girls hold our breath, for we are sure she is going to take a bite. But then the bread stops, nose to nose with the leader. And the leader says, "Bread. We need to talk."

She breaks eye contact with the slice to turn to the group of us. We sit, silent, unmoving.

Smell the yeast, the bakedness of it. Calories smell like hunger, and my stomach writhes like churning waters, but I need to get out of this facility. I have a greater plan.

"Bread," I say to my slice's eye holes. "We need to talk." Saliva thickens, lips chap, I fear my mouth, my tongue, that it might attempt to eat. I drop the bread and look at the leader, who is nodding at me, grinning, applauding. As the others confront their bread, I ball mine into a fist.

At my worst, I wouldn't use lip balm for fear of accidentally ingesting a lick of it. I quit taking any pills except diet ones, suspecting pharmacies of sneaking calories into their drugs. I couldn't even brush my teeth in case toothpaste had nutritional content.

I couldn't concentrate at school, and my grades plummeted. We went to a school where they had decided to stop using the word *fail*. After all, it was a public school; we didn't need any further discouragement from education.

Instead of letter grades they used *thriving, arriving, striving*. They equated to A, B, and C. If we ever failed an assignment—that is, if we didn't make an *arriving*—we were allowed to repeat the project until we did. The change in terminology did not affect grades in any way. I achieved *striving*s in every class while Lily, fully nourished and without the distraction of friends, was *thriving*. Calling something another thing does not make it so. The signifier is not the sign. A duck is not a cat. I was not Lily.

• • •

We get report cards at the facility. Mine says:

FINISHING MEALS: *Working Toward.*
COOPERATING WITH NURSES: *Working Toward.*
POSITIVE ATTITUDE: *Working Toward.*

I don't know what the grade above *working toward* is.

Instead of *anorectics*, they call us *survivors*; they say we are *surviving* as if calling it that will make it be, as if we're not all actively *working toward* dying.

A doctor visits as I'm wiping a layer of dust from my desk.

Dust, says my linguistics book, *is a contronym.*

Contronyms are words that have two or more contradictory meanings. For example, *dust* refers to both the noun and the verb. One, the particles of matter; the other, to discard of those same particles. Another example is the word *fast*, which can mean both to move quickly, to run fast, or to remain still, stuck fast. *Fast* can also mean to quit eating. For me, to fast is to move backward. To deteriorate. This means that the word *fast* is a three-way contronym.

"Rose, hi," says the doctor. His name is Dr. Windham, and he is fat. "You've been gaining. Haven't you?"

I nod.

"That's great, honey. Keep this up and we'll be talking about a discharge date in no time. How does that sound?"

I smile up at him.

"Good girl," he says with a tap of my nose. "See you later, alligator."

2007 (18 years old—Lily: 192 lbs, Rose: 72 lbs)

Jemima Gates was suspended from school for the shoplifting incident. I was excused because I came clean. It wasn't that I had turned Jemima in; the store had surveillance cameras and Jemima, tiny and miniskirt-clad, stolen purse peeking out from her backpack, was framed in perfect, headshot lighting. Still, she was disappointed in my weakness.

"I thought you were cool, Rose," she hissed over the phone. Both of our cell phones had been confiscated, as suggested by the school, but not before we arranged midnight landline check-ins.

"I *am* cool."

"You told!"

"They already knew."

"You still told."

I said nothing.

She sighed. "Well," she said, "you know you're going to have to make it up to me."

I held my breath.

"Aren't you going to ask how?" she whispered.

"How?"

"Meet me in two hours on the school field," she said. "Bring rags."

"Bags?"

"Rags. Like cloth."

"How many?"

"As many as you can," she hissed. "Gotta go."

Jemima stood, dramatic in the center of our school's shadowed field when I arrived with a laundry sack of old dishrags slung over my shoulder. She chuckled when I approached. The question itched like cheap fabric against my tongue, but I wouldn't ask. I was proving I could be cool, which meant not needing to know what we were doing here.

"You came," she said, and her eyes shone with the moon, which was full tonight, and held captive in the green of Jemima's irises. "Here," she said. "We've gotta be quick."

She took a rag from my sack and dunked it in a bucket that sat at her feet, then she set the cloth carefully on the ground, shaped into an arc. "You gonna make me do all the work?" she said.

I took a rag, dipped it, and the smell of gasoline hijacked my breath.

"Oh god," I said, the smell catching in my throat like an unwelcome fly. I coughed.

"Shut the fuck up," said Jemima. "And give that to me." She took the rag and laid it down, its nose touching the end of the first. We worked quickly, making a circle from the cloth, and, when the loop's ends met, Jemima took a cigarette from her pocket, a lighter from her other, and lit the tip. She inhaled, sighed, and offered me a drag. I accepted. Breathing in, letting the smoke fill me. I smiled as I exhaled.

"You look so pretty in the moonlight," Jemima said, taking the cigarette from my lips.

I shrugged. Then she leaned in and kissed me. Her lips were soft, and I wanted to keep them. She stepped away again. Winked. Then, seemingly, forgot.

She paced the circle, flicking her lighter, and every time the flame sparked, her teeth shone aglow. "Ready?" she said. Then she bent over, flicked the lighter, and pressed the flame to a saturated rag. The fire was immediate, moved so quickly that even Jemima jumped back. Without a word, we turned and sprinted. Flames soared behind us, cracking like bones, the heat so fierce that even we, the least insulated girls in the world, felt hot.

Sappho, an Archaic Greek poet from the island of Lesbos, wrote about her love for women. The majority of her work is lost to time, but one fragment reads, *When I look on you a moment, then I can speak no more, but my tongue falls silent, and at once a delicate flame courses beneath my skin, and with my eyes I see nothing, and my ears hum, and a wet sweat bathes me and a trembling seizes me all over.*

Jemima and I, we held each other's hands and ran from the fire, silent and aflame, unseeing in the night, ears ringing electric, sweating and shivering, we ran.

At school the next day, the field was a scorched brown, brittle and dead. The area was cordoned off by yellow tape.

...

When an anglerfish finds a mate, he fuses with her, their bodies morph into one. A shared circulatory system. Their hearts beating in time.

Isn't that all love is, anyway?

I read the last page of *Animal Behaviors* very slowly. I pause after each word, and after every punctuation mark, I take a long, slow breath. Still, the end comes. I close the cover and open my suitcase and stare into its hollowness. It's time to start packing. To go back to life. The suitcase is small. Me-sized, I think, quickly calculating its mass. I step inside, sit, curl, tuck, squeeze. I lie on my side, fetal, and reach for the lid. I tug the case closed and all goes dark, quiet.

Something I will never tell is that I like living in the facility. There's comfort in its structure. So long as I keep skipping meals but drinking my CalSips, I will stay alive. I will maintain my weight. My body will not grow. Everything, my life, in here, is paused.

Boredom is the emptiest emotion; there's no weight to it. I'm just waiting out my life.

The thought of existing outside of the facility's schedule makes my teeth ache. In here, food is served in the dining hall, the same space every day. Out there, food is everywhere, and you never know when someone might offer you a slice of their cake.

I breathe into my tiny space. Finger the fabric that lines the bag. There is a ridge, an embroidered name. I trace the letters, and they're not mine, they're hers. Lily's. I push the suitcase open and blink into the bright, unravel my limbs, climb back into the world.

Lily needs me. So I start packing, folding clothes, stacking books, ready to be discharged from the facility. I take the letters from under my mattress and swallow. Then I take one, hold it to my chest, and tear it down the middle, again, again. I shred my letters into little strips of themselves, then I put them in the trash can, cover them with an empty CalSip box. Lily needs me! My lungs ache. I swallow and continue packing. The books on animal behaviors and linguistics, and the one on insects, which, ironically, is now nude, its cover eaten away by termites.

Animals, unlike humans, are not capable of evil. They kill to eat, they fight to protect, they chase to mark territory, they survive. No animal has any sense of morality, and so they cannot act immorally. Humans are capable of evil because we created it. We burdened ourselves with right and wrong, with good and evil. And it is in knowing this evil that we can be.

21

Us thin girls stand, rattling around in our too-big dresses, nursing glasses of ice water with cocktail umbrellas, and swaying to some bad '60s disco, waiting for the boys to arrive. The long dining hall tables are pushed up against the walls, covered in cheap plastic tablecloths and offering glasses of water and punch and sliced fruit. Streamers in clearance colors, browns and grays, hang limp from the ceilings, and there are pockets of half-inflated balloons, not full enough to distract us from how each one contains someone's expired breath, clinging to the room's corners. The disco ball, though, sends silver diamonds twisting, twirling about the floor, the walls, and that is enough to get us girls giddy.

My breath keeps catching in my throat.

"How are you feeling?" asks Sarah, her basset hound eyes agape. "About meeting Jram and everything?"

I stir my water with the umbrella, letting the tinkle of ice on glass, both light and clear, translucent and empty, ring. Such reminders of emptiness make me calm. How am I feeling? I am feeling like soda, shaken and opened, all of my fizz is rising up my throat.

"They're here, ladies," says Kat, and she's staring at the far door of our dining hall. My back straightens itself without my command, and I close my eyes, hold my breath, count, release. I do it over and over, waiting for Jram to approach.

"Eope?" says a low voice, which I know, immediately, is Jram's. The word is beautiful. Ee-oh-pee. I wonder whether it's a greeting in his native tongue, Greek or German, and I turn to face him, utterly charmed from the first stretched syllable.

"Jram," I say, and he frowns.

"Eope," he says.

"Hello to you, too?" I guess.

"Hi," he says, in an accent that is not a foreign one, not even at all. "It's so nice to finally meet you in person, Eope." He pauses. "Your name is Eope, right?"

"Oh," I say, understanding the confusion. But I don't want to ruin our romance, so I nod. "Yes," I say. "Okay. I am Eope. And you're Jram?"

"Sure," he says. "Okay. I mean yes."

We reach for each other, hands meeting between our bodies, our fingers entwining, and we have made a little limb swing bridge. We smile from shore to shore, and our bridge sways between us. "Hello, Jram," I say.

"Hi, Eope," says Jram.

"It's nice to meet you, Jram," I say.

"It's nice to meet *you*, Eope," he says.

These are the times I wish most to be Lily. Lily who knows how to interact, how to talk about the menial as if it is interesting, how to ease into a conversation like climbing into a hot bath, aah, she is so easy to be around.

"Um," I say. "I liked your penis the other night."

"Oh, okay," says Jram, his cheeks searing. "Thank you."

"For liking it or for telling you?"

"I don't really know."

"Okay." My hands are slippery in his, or his in mine, and I don't know how to end this swing-bridge grip. "I like your handkerchief, too."

"Oh, thank you," he says. "Um, which one?"

"The purple one," I say. "The lilac one."

"Okay, thanks," he says.

We stand, our bridge slowing to a stop.

"But it's nice that you have more than one," I say. "Handkerchief, I mean. You have handker*chiefs*. Plural."

He nods. "Sure," he says. "I think I have about five or maybe six of them."

"Handkerchiefs?"

"Yeah," he says. "Five or six handkerchiefs, probably."

"I sometimes think they should be called handkerchieves."

"With a *v*?"

I nod. "Like *thief* and *thieves*. *Knife* and *knives*, you know?"

"Sure, that would make sense."

I keep my mouth closed through a yawn, and it makes my eyes water. I don't want Jram to think I'm crying about his handkerchief collection. Or that I'm bored. "Um," I say, smiling, demonstrating how not-crying I am. "Here's something. I bet *handkerchief* is probably the only word with the letters *ndk* all in a row."

Jram says nothing.

"Don't you think so?"

"Probably," says Jram, looking over my shoulder, around the room. He wants to leave, I know it. He wants to go talk to some other thin girl. He's not interested in my conversation about penises and handkerchiefs and linguistics. I follow his gaze, and it's fixed on Kat.

Desperate, I say, "Let's dance," so that I won't have to think up any more topics, and, thankfully, Jram nods.

He sets his hands on the juts of my hips and then withdraws them quickly. "That's not a trigger for you, is it? Me touching you like that?"

I shake my head. "You can put your hands there," I say. "It's okay."

He replaces his hands, and his fingers are warm on my bones. I say, "Your fingers are warm on my bones."

"What?"

"Oh, nothing," I say.

"Are you sure?'

"Yeah."

"Okay."

We sway, and I let my fingers trace the ladder of his spine, each rung prominent through his skin, and the thinness might have been off-putting if only it weren't so familiar. Like dancing with myself.

"There are fruit slices over there, Jram," I say to Jram, who ignores me and rests his forehead against mine. When our faces are this close, his eyes merge into one, a big cyclops eye, and I smile and he must take the smile to be more about my affection for him than my appreciation of his cyclops eye situation because he tilts his mouth toward mine. I let him press chapped lips against my red-painted mouth, and the kiss is dry and brief, like a tap on the shoulder when a kind stranger notices you've dropped your wallet: nice but impersonal. Heterosexuality!

Behind Jram, Kat is surrounded by men but standing at the center of them, alone, watching us, watching me, her eyes shadowed with eye shadow and maybe a touch of jealousy.

"Do you remember having sex?" says Jram, when the song ends. I tear my stare away from Kat.

"With you?" I say.

"No," says Jram. "We haven't—"

"Yeah, I know," I say. "That's why I was confused."

"Oh, I meant just, like . . ." Jram scratches his chin, and the sound is a relaxing static. "I meant just sex in general."

"Um." I look at Jram, who seems to be remembering sex, and then I nod. This is my first lie to Jram. The first mislaid brick in the foundation of our relationship. "Sure," I say. "I remember having sex." I will go on to regret the lie, and wish I had disclosed my virginity, but it's important to have things in common, and so I let him believe me a deflowered woman.

"Do you want to?" says Jram.

"Want to?"

"Have sex?"

"Oh," I say. "Sure, yeah, someday." It's true. I do want to have sex someday.

"What about today?" says Jram. "Do you want to have sex today?"

"Like right now?"

"Sure, like, nowish."

I swallow and nod, not wanting to upset, wanting only to please, to be liked, to be loved. "Sure," I say. "I want to. But we can't."

"Why not?"

"Where would we go?"

"To the bathroom," says Jram. "We would go to the bathroom."

"But escorts," I say, thankful for the excuse. We can't have sex in the bathroom because all bathroom trips are escorted by nurses.

"I don't get escorted," says Jram. "I'm on recovery privileges." I scan Jram's bones, my eyes trained to see the extent of thinness, a specialty X-ray. He is too thin to be on recovery privileges. His hip bones make a bridge of pubis, and his rib cage is prominent as an insect's thorax. I wonder which trick he's using to fool the scales. His hair is long, but it isn't long enough to tie into a weighted ponytail.

"Oh, cool," I say. "That's nice, congratulations."

"Thanks, Eope," says Jram, looking proud. "So, bathroom?"

"I still need an escort."

"Then tell the nurse you're going to your bedroom," says Jram. "To change shoes or something." Jram has thought this plan through, I realize. While I have been imagining our love, our old age together, he has been planning this bathroom affair. Still, I nod, and lift the hem of my dress.

"See you soon," I say, and I go to ask a nurse for permission to change my shoes.

It's not that I don't want to have sex with Jram, because I've always wondered what it's like. Sex. It's more that I don't want Jram to know my virgin status. Don't want Jram to find out that I am a twenty-four-year-old virgin. It isn't by choice, of course; most men just aren't into us thin girls. And even when we do get invited on a date by some man mistaking us for models, those evenings are just hopeless consumption events. Men take you out for dinner, dessert, a drink. It's when we make excuses, when the fear hijacks our eyes, it's then that the men know something is up. When the ovation in their jeans slackens into surrender.

"Excuse me." I clutch my fingers behind my back as I speak to a nurse. "Could I please go change shoes in my room? I'll just be a second. These ones are hurting my toes."

The nurse nods. "Five minutes," she says. "I'm timing."

I thank her and leave the cafeteria to go lose my virginity. On the way out, I make eye contact with Kat, wiggle my eyebrows in the way she does.

I don't even really agree with the concept of virginity. Is there any other instance in life where one takes on a title for having *not* done something? I collect a few examples in my mouth, but they turn sour. Off. If you haven't had sex, you're a virgin. If you don't drink, you're sober. If you don't eat, you're anorectic.

In the 1930s, a dieting trend emerged in the media. Slimming soaps, which professed to wash away extra weight by simply working up a lather in the shower. See all those women, in the midst of the depression, still desperately scouring their skin, scrubbing themselves skinny.

2007 (18 years old—Lily: 193 lbs, Rose: 71 lbs)

Jemima was still grounded. Her parents heard of the fire from afar, somewhere European and pretend-sounding, their fairy-tale life, and they put Jemima under house arrest, paid the maid overtime to keep watch outside her bedroom door. I was spending my afternoons with the television. I watched the cooking channel compulsively.

People obsessed with food either become chefs or anorectics. I watched shows about making elaborate cakes and cooking school shows and game shows that made two food trucks compete to see which one could churn the most meals out of its tiny van kitchen. Something about watching food on a screen comforted me. It reminded me of my hunger, almost satisfied a desire to taste. Food at a safe distance.

I was sucking a Tic Tac, watching a speed cooking show, a gossip magazine opened to a page about Kat Mitchells's eating disorder recovery open on my lap, pictures of her before and after body, when I heard my voice.

"Hey, Rosie."

I turned to find Lily, greeting me. We hadn't spoken in a long time and had taken to treating each other like shadows of ourselves. Something to be acknowledged and then ignored.

She was with a boy. Robbie Newton. The same one who had stood her up all those years ago. I frowned at her, communicating my distaste, even as I said, "Hey, Lil. Hey, Robbie."

"Mind if we join you?"

I did mind, but I could taste a light chill that made my teeth ache with cold, and it was clear that Lily did not want to be alone with this boy. Was *afraid* of being alone with him, even, and the extent of that fear was proven by how she was willing to lay down her pride and speak to me, be around me, for the first time in months.

"Sure," I said, scooting to one end of the couch.

"How's it going, Rosie?" said Robbie, his chin as absent as ever.

"Rose," Lily and I both corrected him at once. I had never let anyone other than her call me Rosie. We refused to exchange glances. Refused to acknowledge how good it felt to connect on our own little frequency again.

"I'm fine," I added. "What's up?"

"So you made that fire, huh?"

I shrugged.

"Are you and Jemima Gates, like, a thing?"

I snorted.

"Hey," said Robbie, hands up in surrender. "I didn't start the rumor."

"There's a rumor that Jemima and I are together?" I said, turning on him. "Did you know about this, Lily?"

Lily shrugged. I felt the lemony lie bleed into my mouth.

"Whatever," I said.

"Have you, like, made out?" said Robbie.

"Shut up, Robbie," said Lily.

I looked at her, then back at Robbie, said nothing, settled into the couch, arms crossed, tried to focus on the show.

"People are taking bets, you know," said Robbie. "About you two."

I said nothing.

"My money's on lesbians."

"Fuck off," Lily and I said, at once. Or maybe just one of us said it.

"Maybe you should go home, Rob," said Lily.

"Babe," said Robbie.

"Babe?" I asked.

Lily gave me a look that said not now. Then she stood, tried to pull Robbie off the couch, but he wouldn't move, a slimy grin painted on his face.

"I mean it," said Lily. "You need to leave."

"Oh, don't be like that, babe," he said. "I was just having some fun."

"I don't care what you were doing," said Lily.

"Jeez," he said. "What's got you all riled up? You a dyke, too? It a twin thing?"

"You heard her, asshole. Get the fuck out of our house," I said, pushing his back, hoping to lever him from the couch, but he was heavy.

"Or what?" he said.

"Or we'll hex you," I said, looking at Lily, who nodded.

Robbie laughed.

Lily and I took each other's hands. It was a trick we hadn't done since a number of Halloweens ago, when we went as witches and threatened to hex everyone who wouldn't give us candy. We pressed our palms together, and to any outsider we looked like a single girl looking at her reflection, or we used to, now we were too dissimilar, but our minds still worked the same.

Lily started speaking in gibberish, and I followed, saying the same sounds she was, a barely audible moment later. I heard her before anyone else in the world could, it seemed, and the result was Lily's voice having an almost echo. We chanted louder, louder, until our voices strained.

"Okay, stop," said Robbie. "Stop, stop, jeez." He was pretending not to be afraid, but his cheeks were pale, and we smiled as we continued. "Okay, shit, I'll go," he said, but we didn't stop our song until he was gone and the front door was safely shut.

We released hands and sank back onto the couch. I turned up the volume and we watched the cooking show together. It had been a long time since we had acted as one, and it felt good to fall back into our most natural roles.

"Hi," I say when I arrive in the bathroom to find Jram, pants open, penis pointing at me. Choosing me. I try to feel flattered among the nerves.

"Did you know that there's a type of penguin who press their bellies together and dance before they mate?" I say, making small talk.

"Put your mouth on it," says Jram, and he means his penis, and he doesn't seem surprised when I shake my head. I'm not about to risk those milky calories. "Fine," he says. "Then give me your hand."

I do. Jram in the bathroom is different from Jram in the dining hall. No. Jram with his penis in his hand is different from Jram without it. He's more assertive, more like the other men I know.

His penis feels like any other limb. A finger or an arm. Only its skin doesn't fit as well. When I move my hand, the skin moves with it. I ask him if I'm doing okay, and he tells me my grip is limp. I tighten my hold, and he winces. I let go.

"That's enough," I say, hoping that my insecurity might come across as sexy aggression. It works, because he takes me by the shoulders, twists me abruptly, and shoves my stomach against the sink. I double over the porcelain, and my cheek slaps against the wall. It is only then, with my face pressed against the cold, hard tile, that I realize we could have gone to my bedroom instead.

Jram lifts my dress and shifts my underwear to the side. Then there is a rough jabbing between my legs. I know there's no chance of entry long before Jram gives up. I'm dry and uninviting. Unwanting. He might as well have been trying to stick it in my ear.

He eventually sighs and stops trying.

"Well, see you back out there, Eope," he says, tucking his dick into his pants and smiling. Penis-less Jram is back. He is human again. He waves, a wiggly-fingered wave, and lets the bathroom door swing closed behind him.

Alone, I fix the hem of my skirt and long for a mirror. I feel exerted. Like I should be flushed, hair distressed. I try to force some reflection out of the tiled walls, but my only echo is blurred motion in the varnished surface. There's makeup smeared where my face had been—mine. Lipstick instead of lips. Mascara instead of eyes. My cosmetic doppelgänger. I give up and go back to the dance, feeling hardly any more woman than before.

22

Jram's room is dark for eight nights in a row. I stay up late, later than I have in a long time, there's not much to stay up for in here. But tonight, over a week since our moment of passion in the bathroom, I look out across the courtyard, crossing my fingers for a flicker. Nothing. I wonder whether I'm the only girl in the world to have ever been broken up with via light. No, via darkness.

More than once, I empty my trash can onto the carpet, hoping that one shred of one letter might have been saved, a snippet of a past love, but the nurses empty them every morning, and mine is so hollow it looks starved.

Our group leader is showing us how to flatter our food.

"Did you say *fatter*?" says Sarah.

"No, I said *fatter*," says the group leader. "I mean *flatter*. I said *flatter*. *Flatter*."

"With an *l*?" I say.

"No," says the group leader. "With an *f*."

"Obviously," says Sarah. "Rose meant *f*, *l*, *a*—"

"Yes," says the group leader. "Flatter. *Flatter*. Compliment. Praise."

Sarah winks at me, and I smile at our tiny rebellion.

"So," says the group leader, "flattering our foods. Can anyone tell me why flattering our foods is important?"

"It isn't," Kat whispers under her breath.

"Nobody?" says the group leader. "Well, flattery is an important part of friendship. It's a love language: words of affirmation, and we're learning to become friends with our food."

I lift the tomato from the table in front of me and examine its surface. Not even one blemish.

"Studies show," says the group leader, "that plants actually grow quicker and are healthier when they're spoken to kindly. A group of scientists did an experiment, and the gardeners who complimented their plants each day ended up with bigger, better plants than those who said nothing at all."

I press my thumb against the tomato's skin, and the flesh is soft as an infant's thigh.

I once read about the study that the group leader is referencing. She's nearly right. The scientists divided a group of sixty pea plants into three groups. The group that was complimented by growers performed equally as well as the group that was actively insulted by growers. It was the group that was left to grow in silence that didn't perform as well. Plants don't care what you say to them, so long as you're there. Living beings don't care how you treat them. We just don't want to be alone.

"This shows," says the group leader, "that our food likes being spoken to. Likes being flattered. So, in order to befriend our food, we should compliment it." The group leader looks around, collecting the room in her gaze. "So," she says. "Take your food items from the table."

We do.

"And now say something kind to it. Tell the food what you like about it."

There is a scramble of uncertainty. A rumble of mumbling. Finally, one of the thin girls, maybe called Laura or Lisa, says to her avocado, "Your thick skin is, uh, it's admirable."

"Yes!" says the group leader.

My grip breaks through the tomato's thin epidermis and finds a slippery wetness inside. My thumb is coated in its sticky juices.

"You," Kat says to her carrot, "look like a penis." And it does!

2007 (18 years old—Lily: 195 lbs, Rose: 71 lbs)

When I told Jemima of the rumors about us, she shrugged.

"All boys have lesbian fantasies," she said. We were in her bedroom, and I was watching her stand before a mirror, clutch her waist with her hands, a belt made of her long fingers, straining to touch fingertip to fingertip. "It's because we're the hottest girls in school."

I wanted to hold her waist like that. Wanted to feel what it was to hold a body that wasn't my own.

"You think so?" I said. "You think that's all it is?"

Jemima turned away from the mirror to face me. "What do you mean?"

I swallowed. Shrugged. "I don't know. Nothing, probably." I picked up a magazine from her nightstand, and the cover story was about Kat Mitchells. *CHILD STAR FLAUNTS NEW CURVES IN CROATIA.*

"Here," she said. "I have an idea. Come here."

I stood, obedient, from the foot of her bed. The everyday vertigo swallowed me for only a second. I had grown used to staving off fainting multiple times a day.

She took a yellow measuring tape from her desk and held it out to me. "Hold this," she said, letting her fingers linger on my palm. I smiled at the touch, the highlight of my day every day. I lived for the brief moments she'd let her body whisper against mine.

Jemima lifted her blouse over her head. Unzipped her skirt and let it fall. I'd seen her so many times by now, after all the window-shopping, but this time she watched me, eyes wide, as she undressed. I looked her in the eye, too afraid to let my gaze wander.

She reached behind her back and unclasped her bra. Then ran a finger around the elastic of her underwear. Out of the haze of my peripherals, I saw the fabric fall.

"What are you doing?" I said, my voice a husk of itself.

"Measure me," she said, holding her arms out wide, legs spread.

I swallowed and stepped toward her, measuring tape slick with my sweat. My hands trembled as I strung the tape around her chest, across her hardened nipples, pink and puckered, and pulled the rope tight.

I told her the number, and Jemima nodded. "My hips," she said.

I let the tape fall to her waist, then lower. She was clean shaven, which didn't surprise me. She was so good at knowing what to do with her body, what was expected from a girl our age. I pressed my thumb against the top of her pubis, the skin pebbled with the heads of dark hairs not yet surfaced. She shivered, or I did, and I waited for the tape to stop quaking before I read her the digit.

"Do the rumors bother you?" Jemima said in response to the measurement. "I can tell Joel to put a stop to them."

Joel Banff was on the rugby team, and his ears curled into themselves like roses in the morning, scrummed into submission. He was Jemima's boyfriend. Her boyfriend. She had a boyfriend who was a boy. Joel Banff was at the bottom of our class. An idiot!

I stepped away from her nudity and dropped the tape on her bed. "They don't bother me," I said, bothered. "Rumors are rumors."

Jemima smiled and went back to examining her bones in the mirror. What I minded more than the rumors was that rumors were all they were. I wanted to tell Jemima that we could just be together in secret. That I wasn't gay, I just wanted her. Just her. Just one girl. That other than her, I was probably, no, I *was*, straight. We could kiss without anyone knowing! I'd do anything for her.

"You okay, babe?"

The looming confession was heavy on my tongue, the weight of honesty, like a doctor with a popsicle stick telling me to open up and say *ah*.

"Do you think I've lost weight again?" she said, stroking her pelvis. "My hips look kind of different."

"Yeah," I said. "They look good." And that was enough honesty for the day.

After breakfast, on the day I trick the scales into thinking I'm heavy enough to be released, I pass the supply closet and, as I do, there is a loud gasp. I stop and look at the closed door. I try the handle, unlocked, open the door into the dark. There are two people in there.

One is Kat. I'm sure of it. I can make out the tall rectangle of a top hat, even in this overwhelming shadow. The other . . . I swallow.

"Sarah?"

They're crouched on the floor like something primate, buckets on the ground at their feet, hands buried in their mouths. The smell hits before I see it. The spiced scent of sick. The buckets are filled with chunky liquid.

The two bodies are still, statues. Sarah looks up at me, tears in her eyes. Kat retches. I slam the door closed and go back to my room. I can't wait to get out of this rotten place.

Honeybees drink flower nectar and barf it back up as honey. We buy it in bulk, eat that sick off the blunt blade of a butter knife, spread it on toast. Some thin girls like to drop a dollop in a cup of herbal tea during a fast to keep them vertical. It's a sugar boost, that vomit.

We encourage their disorder, too. Buzzy little bulimics.

Dr. Windham glows an iridescent red when he tells me I can be released in two days if I keep improving. I'm wearing four layers of clothing. Four pairs of leggings. Four shirts. Trying to give myself some breadth.

"I'm proud of you, sugar," he says. "Honestly, when girls have been in here as long as you, we usually give up hope that they'll ever really recover." He scratches the bald summit of his head. "But you're doing great."

I smile and he says, "We'll miss you in here, you know."

Dr. Windham might be in love with me.

I'm still smiling when there's a knock at the door and Lily's voice says, "Knock, knock, it's me!" She is already in the room when she says, "Am I interrupting something, Doctor?" She says his name in italics, and I frown at her finger, which is slowly coiling its way around and around a strand of brunette. There's something different about her hair, something that makes it look less like human hair and more like a woman from a shampoo commercials' hair. She's got highlights. Her boring brown, identical to mine, has new streaks of honey slashed through it at curated intervals, just enough to make it look like the sun is always shining on her, just enough to ruin my whole life.

"You got highlights," I say.

"Hi, Dr. Windham!" Lily is the sun today. "Hi! How are you?"

"Why did you get stupid highlights?"

"You look great," she says to my doctor with a smile. I know this Lily. This is flirting Lily, seducing Lily, alluring Lily. She transforms into a lighter version of herself.

"Lily!" says Dr. Windham, who calls healthy people their real names instead of food nouns. "Look at you! You've lost so much weight! Congratulations. You two are like two peas!"

Lily grins and hooks her arm through mine. I seethe at the hypocrisy.

"Oh, I've only lost a little," says Lily, ducking her head underneath his compliment and smiling. The scab on her lip strains. She's almost healed from Phil's abuse. "It's this health guide I'm following. It's called *YourWeigh*."

"It's working for you; you look great," says Dr. Windham, heterosexually. "Like a supermodel! Stunning."

I look at him, his ruddy cheeks, scrunched eyes. I could have growled for all of my building anger.

"I was just telling my favorite cupcake that she can be released in a couple of days if she's got someone to care for her while she's in remission."

"Of course I'll be caring for her," says Lily. Our former fight forgotten overnight, as they always are; our cruelness dissolves at dusk. Each day is a new chance, a chance to be a more graceful sibling. We both know it isn't how the world works, of course, but our twinship has always functioned that way. We will never stop forgiving and that knowledge is comforting.

"You'll come home with me, won't you, Rosie?"

"I don't know." I shrug. "I might." I cross my arms.

"She will," Lily tells Dr. Windham. "She's just being silly. She'll come live with me until we get her back on her feet." She turns to me, all luminous with pride. "Baby sister, I can't believe you gained enough to come home! Look at you! You're glowing!"

I am. I smeared the grease from this morning's bacon on my cheeks.

On the ceiling, my termite colony is at work, marching its procession, off to devour their next meal. I say, "There are termites in here, Dr. Windham. This place is being eaten alive."

"Anywho," says Lily, ignoring me again. "How can I thank you, Dr. Windham. Really, how?" And her voice is slick as a proposition. I wince at the obviousness of it. I miss Jram, our silent love, so elegant in its distant silence, separated by glass and garden.

"Oh no," says Dr. Windham, who actually blushes. "I'm just doing my job," he says. "And anyway, I'd imagine that Rose's sudden improvement has more to do with the new Intellectual Eating program we've recently implemented than anything I've done."

"Intellectual Eating?" says Lily.

"That's right. It's all about teaching the girls how to think about food, develop a healthy relationship with eating and such, to help them act normally." He refuses me any eye contact.

"That's great!" says Lily. "That sounds great, Rosie. Is that what's been helping you?"

"This morning I had to compliment a tomato," I say. And the two of them laugh as if I'd made a joke.

"Lily, could I have a word in the hall?" says Dr. Windham. "I want to ask you something." He wants to ask Lily on a date, I know it. His affection for me forgotten. He can have the better, healthier, happier version. Who would ever choose the worse of two options?

But Lily frowns. She clears her throat, crosses her arms, checks her phone. Eleven texts from Phil. I watch her swallow, the gulp of it, as she reaches for her eye. Its bruise has faded pastel. "No, sorry, Dr. Windham," she says, clearing her throat. There's a new tremble to her voice, as if it's walking a beam.

When the doctor leaves, I turn on Lily. "Why did you change your hair?"

"You don't like it?"

"Did Phil make you do that?"

"He doesn't *make* me do anything."

"Just because he doesn't explicitly tell you, 'Lily, I am command-
ing you to dye your hair,' doesn't mean he's not manipulating you into
changing yourself for him."

"He's not manipulating me."

"How would you know?"

She raises her eyebrow at me, which means I'm being immature.
Immature, shmimmature. I cross my arms. "Why wouldn't you go talk
to my doctor in the hall?"

"Can you just—"

"Is it because of Phil?"

She sighs. "He's the jealous type."

"He's literally married to another woman," I say. "All these reasons keep accumulating against him, Lil. Against Phil. But it's like
you can't see them. It's like you can only see the stuff that supports
the opinion you've already decided to have of him. The gifts. The
vacations. But the dieting, the hitting, all the changes he's making
to you. Opinions are meant to change as the facts do, Lily. And your
hair looks tie-dyed."

Jram's room is dark, and I sit on my bed, wrapped in the night, watching his window, waiting for a lightness.

There is a light tapping sound, innocent as rain, and I don't look
up as Sarah opens my door, sets a hand on my shoulder, and then
climbs into my bed. She curls her body around mine. Her breath is a
whispered song against the nape of my neck, and I like lying there,
beside her beautiful arrangement of bones, but her touch is so cold,
her body clatters, and this is how it must feel to lie with the dead.

23

I promise to write letters to the girls, the same way every discharged thin girl does, and then I forget to ask for anyone's names, the same way every discharged thin girl does. Kat tries to meet my eye, but we're not friends and I want her to know it. I kiss Sarah's cheek and tell her to contact me as soon as she gets out, and then I don't give her my phone number, and she doesn't give me hers. We are all so good at deceit!

As we pack my room into boxes, Lily and I, I wish for Jram to see me moving out. Cured of my illness and of him. Good riddance!

The day before graduation, Jemima invited me to stay at her place. A sleepover. Her parents were in Europe and she'd been hearing noises in the night.

We lay, side by side on her bed, and smoked.

"I feel like I'm waiting for something to happen," she said.

"Like what?"

"Don't you feel like you're waiting for something?"

"To happen?"

"Don't worry about it." She took a long drag from her cigarette. "The best part of my olds being gone"—she exhaled— "is I ran out of food a week ago."

"Do you have money?"

"Of course I do. I just want to see how long I can go without it."

"It?"

"Eating. Like you do."

Like me. I took the cigarette and inhaled a long drag, breathed deep, until my lungs swelled with smoke.

"How long can you go?" she said, rolling onto her stomach, chin in hand, to look at me. She was wearing only her underwear. Nudity was something she did around me often and you'd think I would be desensitized to it and you'd think wrong.

I shrugged. A long time. "I don't know."

"Do you get tired?"

"I'm always tired."

"How do you get the energy to do anything? Homework? Sex?"

I spluttered on the smoke, a rare occurrence. I could make it through a pack a day by then.

"Oh," she said. "You're still a virgin."

I extinguished the cigarette. "You know I am."

"Why?" she said. "Someone would fuck you, you know."

I looked around, looked around at not her.

"Is it because you're gay?"

I said nothing.

"Is it?"

I stretched and stood. "I should go home."

"No!" She reached for my hand, pulled. "You promised you'd stay."

"I don't really feel like it anymore, sorry."

"Wait," she said, pulling me closer, closer. She flipped my arm, kissed my wrist, let her glossed lips stick to my skin. I waited for her to be done with the ritual, but she wasn't. She kissed her way, slowly, up my arm, to my shoulder. I swallowed. She kissed the curve of my neck, my chin, jaw, ear. She sucked on the swoop of my earlobe, and a moan came from me.

"What're you doing?"

"Stay," she whispered against my cheek, before continuing with the kissing.

Then her mouth was wet against mine. Her tongue, quick to part my lips, find my tongue, tickle it with hers.

"What's happening?" I said, pulling back.

"No one should leave high school a virgin."

"That's what this is?" I said, pushing, standing. "Is that all this is, Jemima?"

She leaned back, head against the wall. "Isn't that enough?"

Her underwear was wet at the crotch. A diamond-shaped patch of desire on the gray cotton. I wanted to touch it. Taste. Instead, I took my coat from her nightstand and shrugged it on, itchy with need.

"No," I said. And I left Jemima Gates to deal with the noises in the night, alone.

It is so strange to walk out the facility doors, past the administration desk, and into the parking lot. I squint into the sunlight and the breeze feels like a lover's fingers against my skin. I breathe deep and the air is bigger out here. I look up and the sky stretches so far, my stomach tips askew at the size of it.

"Wow," I say.

Lily frowns at me. "Don't be dramatic," she says. "It wasn't like it was a prison in there."

I say nothing, just inhale the air, which is so fresh it almost hurts.

PART TWO

24

There's a line in *Alice's Adventures in Wonderland* that reads: "How funny it'll seem to come out among the people that walk with their heads downwards!"

It's so cold out here, outside. There are so many people. None of them thin. None of them me. I walk with my head downward.

"Eat something!" a stranger shouts upon seeing my body. It's hard to know if he's looking out for me or being cruel, and it doesn't matter because the two intentions are not mutually exclusive.

Lily's apartment is on the third floor of a skinny building, small, with only a single bedroom, water-stained wallpaper, peeling linoleum. She's turned her couch into a bed, smaller than a twin, the perfect size for me. The house is dirty. The kitchen floor sparkles in a way that isn't the clean way, and clothes are strewn about the furniture like trash after a storm. Half-smoked cigarettes litter her carpet. There are all of these hanging plants and all of them are dead. I pace the room politely, giving myself the grand tour, but there isn't much to see. I poke at a plant, and it rustles at me, its leaves so dry they're yellow and crisp. They've hardened in their hunger.

"They're dead," says Lily. I wasn't going to point it out, but I'm glad she knows what she's done. I leave them to their passing and join Lily in the kitchen.

YourWeigh by Lara Bax is the centerpiece of the counter. I sit on a stool and take the familiar book, flip it over. A woman, long, black hair, too-wide eyes, smiles at me from above the bar code.

"Lara Bax," I say. "Sounds like a laxative."

"Ignore that," says Lily. "I should've put it away. Sorry."

I frown. Open the cover.

"It's nothing," Lily says.

"This is the diet you're following?"

"Kind of. Not really. It's, well, Phil gave it to me."

"Phil gave you a diet book?"

"Drop it."

I do. The book clatters to the table.

What I want to say: *What kind of man gifts you a diet book?*

What I do say: nothing.

It is important to support the ones we love.

We sit in quiet for a moment, waiting for the tension to ease, slacken like a stretched muscle. Usually, this would be the time to change the subject. To talk about the last time either of us called our father or about how some high school acquaintance is pregnant or married or divorced. But the woman, Lara Bax, stares at me, daring me, and it is very difficult to be mature all of the time.

"Why would Phil give you a diet book, Lil?"

"It's not a diet book." Lily's cheeks scorch. "It's *his* book. And anyway, it's a holistic health guide."

"It's his?"

"He owns YourWeigh with his wife."

"His wife?"

"Lara Bax." Lily points at the woman. Phil's wife.

I stare at Lara Bax, and then at Lily, and then at Lara Bax. "You . . ." I pause. "Lily, you're doing Phil's wife's diet?"

"It's not a diet!" She's flushed and, as a result, my face warms. "It's a holistic health guide!"

"What even is holistic health?"

"Like, self-love." She throws her hands up, frustrated. "I don't know. Just leave it."

"Phil doesn't think you love yourself?"

"Rose."

"What?"

She closes her eyes and does deep breaths. "I really am so proud of you. You know that, don't you?"

"Sure."

Lily goes to the pantry, takes a granola bar from a shelf, and unwraps it. I feel relieved. Relieved that she's eating. But, when she takes a bite, I hear the squeak of rubber against teeth.

"What is that?" I say.

"Oh, it's just a diet bar."

"A diet bar."

"It has zero calories, but it fills you up."

"Zero calories?" I watch her chew. Once upon a time, Lily would have been aware of what she was doing. Discussing caloric value with a recovering anorectic. She would have been more sensitive than to bring up something as triggering as dieting around me, the best dieter in the world. But I recognize this new Lily, too, the way she holds a palm against her stomach to reassure herself of her size. The way she has started wearing clothing that drowns her body in fabric. She's stuck in that spiral, the one I know so well, that selfish starving spiral that keeps you inside yourself.

"Want to try?" She holds the bar out to me, its end wet with her saliva. I take it and squint at the nutritional content. SkinnyBar by Lara Bax. Zero calories. It looks like chocolate but smells like trees; damp soil, rotting leaves.

"Try it," she says. "You might like it."

I nibble a corner, and the bar has the texture of an eraser. Rubber crumbles on my tongue. It tastes of muted dirt. Of kissing the earth.

The cotton ball diet was one that stormed the modeling industry in 2013. Girls dunked cotton balls in juice and swallowed them whole. They expanded in the gut, made the models feel full. Imagine those catwalks, thin bodies prancing, fluffy on the inside.

"This is disgusting." I spit the mouthful into my hand, where it fizzes and bubbles, a science experiment in my palm. I lick my gums, slippery. There are grains of something stuck between my teeth. "Are you sure they're actually edible?"

"It's not that bad." She takes the bar back, defensive. "They grow on you. And they're really working. I've lost, like, thirty pounds by now."

She's right. Her sweater looks like an old skin, ready to be shed. It's so baggy it nearly reaches her knees. I recognize myself. The way, back when I was shrinking, my clothes seemed to grow, as if replaced each night with the same garment, just a single size up. She chews and chews the bad bar, and I make a promise to myself. To her. I am going to help her! I will save her. This is why I am here. This is why I am back in the real world.

"Are those bars a part of your new diet? From the book? This book?" I pick the diet guide back up, leaf through it, open to a random page, and read. "'Your weight is not your worth, but weighing less might be worth it.'" I close the book. "Jesus fucking Christ, Lily."

"I know. But I'm going to quit as soon as I hit my goal weight. God, I just . . . I just hate that he's with that skinny bitch over me, you know?"

I say nothing. Feel my eating disorder's cold, thin fingers wind their way around my throat, tighten their grip. She always means to choke.

She's an abusive lover, anorexia is.

She stands next to you before the mirror, combs your hair into silk, and points at your reflection with a manicured finger. *Fat*, she whispers into your ear.

She takes the apple you've picked from the bowl, presses her lips to your mouth in its place, tangles her tongue with yours. *You don't need that.* She winks and drops the fruit to the floor.

Don't go out to dinner with your friends, she whines from the bed, naked and splayed. *Stay home, with me.*

She runs acrylic nails down your cheeks, then forces the tips between your lips, reaches deep into your throat, tugs your tonsils until you are empty of everything but her.

• • •

"Look at her," Lily says, taking her phone, opening Instagram, which is already on Lara Bax's page. I wonder how much time Lily spends searching that woman's name, scrutinizing her waist, squinting at this stranger's smile.

She's pretty. Thin in a way that looks healthy. Has many thousands of followers, and each post has many thousands of views, likes, hundreds of comments. In one photo, Lara Bax is sitting in a kayak, bikini-wearing and beautiful, looking over her shoulder. *Stay fit to stay thin!* says the caption. In another, she's sitting at a desk, grinning up at the camera, Sharpie in hand, autographing her own diet guide, scribbling her signature across her own face. *#LaraBaxDiet #YourWeigh.* In another, her arms around her husband, his chin resting on her head. The caption: *Love.*

"See how thin?" Lily is looking over my shoulder, frowning at the feed.

What I want to say: *Losing weight won't make him want you more.*

What I want to say: *Losing weight doesn't make anyone want you more.*

But it is important to support the ones we love. All I can say: "Be careful, Lil."

"I will be. I promise, baby sister. Now. Are you hungry?" she asks when she swallows the last of the eraser bar. "I think I have some cereal."

"No."

"Sure?"

"Sure."

A photograph of Lara Bax holding five of the bars in various flavors, splaying them like a poker hand. The caption: *Tag ten friends in the comments to be in the draw to win a month's supply of SkinnyBars!* There are over two hundred thousand comments, each tagging ten people. That's two million people newly aware of this diet. I click on one of the commenters and am taken to her page. The girl is maybe twelve. The first photo, her and her dog. The second, she is holding a trophy, beaming after winning a soccer match. The third, a photo of her reflection in a mirror. She's wearing scarlet lipstick, so much mascara that her eyelashes have turned spider. She's facing the camera, pouting, but her body is turned profile, her stomach so sucked in that her ribs look like protrusions.

I set the phone on the counter and take a pillow into my lap. It smells of Lily, floral and honey. I inhale the scent until it seeps into my brain.

Lily has a shelf full of children's books in the living room. One is called *Der süße Brei*. I find a German dictionary and sit on the floor, back against the wall, and translate: *Sweet Porridge*. A German fairy tale by the Brothers Grimm.

I sit with the story, plucking each word from its passage like flowers from a garden and finding the direct translation. It takes a long time. I love things that take a long time. Things that steal my mind away from the hunger and lower the day to its navy end, easy as a shoehorn.

The story is about a young girl who lives with her mother. They're poor, and they don't have enough food. They're hungry.

One day, the girl goes into the forest to seek out some berries to eat, and instead finds an old woman. The woman gives her a magical pot, and when the girl says, "Cook, little pot, cook!" it starts making a sweet porridge and continues cooking until the girl commands, "Stop, little pot!" Then the porridge would stop accumulating and the pot would be still. The girl brings the pot home and she and her mother eat.

Only, one day, when the girl goes out without her mother to look for any food that isn't porridge, the mother becomes hungry. She commands, "Cook, little pot, cook!" as she's seen her daughter do, and the pot cooks, and the mother eats the porridge with a great hunger.

When she's full, she wants the pot to stop making porridge, but it won't. It keeps cooking and cooking and cooking, the porridge overflows, filling the kitchen, filling the house. The porridge flows out onto the street, filling the town, the city, the world.

When the little girl returns home, she has to wade through a wall of porridge to eventually announce, "Stop, little pot!" The pot finally stops.

And from then on, anyone who wants to visit the girl and her mother have to eat their way through a wall of porridge to find the right house.

25

On Monday morning, we have to go to school. I'm not allowed to exist on my own yet, not to be trusted with my own life, and so I rebecome Lily's shadow, I follow her to school.

Lily's students are much smaller than I expected them to be. Of course, I've met Diamond before, and she is small, but I didn't realize that she was the rule rather than the exception. Their flock of heads barely reaches my hip. To walk between a crowd of them is like wading through long grass. I feel like a monster come to invade a city and I consider knocking down a miniature desk with one mighty blow. How can Lily live with feeling so big?

I didn't want to come to school, but I'm also grateful for the structure. The world's freedom frightens me. I've grown accustomed to having breakfast, a doctor visit, group sessions, lunch, free time, then dinner and bed. I like being told what to do. I am so good at following instructions. Talented at the art of obedience.

"Listen up, team," says Lily, who is different when standing before her class. Taller, brighter, her expression open wide as a new day. She claps her hands to settle the room, a magic trick.

"Listen, kids," she says. "This, here, is my sister, Rose. She'll be helping me out for a while. Can everyone say hello to Rose?"

The chorus, they sing!

"Great. Now, Rose is going to sit at the back of the classroom, and she's going to watch. But she's very smart, Miss Rose is, so if you need any help with your spelling words, you can ask her instead of me if you'd like."

Wide eyes are in awe of me. So smart I can help them spell.

Diamond waves from her seat beside the window, and I wave back, the uneasy start to our relationship apparently forgotten. Diamond mouths, *Hi, Rose.*

Hi, Diamond, I mouth back.

I sip on a CalSip as Lily teaches spelling and I also read a story, not a Grimm fairy tale, but a different book. A collection of stories simply called *WE*, with no blurb nor explanation, no acknowledgments page, contents page, or dedication. It launches into its tale immediately:

WE LOSE OUR VIRGINITIES: *We make pacts to lose our virginities to-gether by taking a nail file and slicing, a whisper of a line, through our palms, bisecting the juncture where heart meets head. The wounds open wide, baring all, the salacious whores, and love and intellect will never again interact without that slim scar to remind us of pain.*

The next boys to walk in, says our favorite brave idiot, the very next boys to walk into the bar will be the ones to whom we will gift our flowers.

Luckily, the next boys who walk into the bar, who step out of the day's sunshine and into the pub's cool gloom, are identical. Not so much boys as mere silhouettes of them, and this is just fine, for shad-ows mean nothing at all, really. Shadows are only the interruption of light.

We take the boys by their hands and we lead them out into the summer. We are delighted by the conditions; it is perfect weather for growth. We lead the boys, walking in twos, a little march of pairs like we are parading, a fitting celebration for such an occasion.

The garden to which we take the boys is unimpressive. Mostly grass, but what grass, so green, so lush, it is the richest grass in the world. This grass drinks champagne, this grass feeds on caviar and sunshine, and this grass can speak fluent French, can order coq au vin in flawless French.

The boys say, Why are we here? and we only smile secret smiles and we each find a patch of earth, ungrassed. We slip our toes from stilettos and bury our feet. Stand in the soil. We say to the boys, each of them, respectively, we say, Now bury us! Bury our bodies in earth!

The boys laugh because they think we are joking but sex is no joke, not to us, we have been warned about gifting our flowers from birth. We have been spat at, sneered at, we have been called slut skank hoe whore hooker and we have been warned of the terrible diseases, the most terrible of all, of course, being fertilization. It is so important not to give birth until one is allowed to give birth.

But now, we know, it is time. Bury us, we tell the boys, we are so ready to grow.

The boys shrug, their sex drive higher than their suspicions, and they cup their palms into bad little shovels and they begin to scoop, the world's worst machinery, they scoop tiny piles of soil around our feet, ankles, calves. The day is fiery, and the work is slow. The boys are sweating, and we are hot. We are buried up to our knees when our favorite brave idiot says, Enough! She says, Stop!

But they don't, the boys, they don't, and we have already begun to bloom. Sugars run up and down our trunks, groin to lip and back again, xylem and phloem, we are so sweet with our own made-in-house syrup. Leaves are sprouting from our biceps; buds are forming on our fingertips.

The boys watch in wonder. This is not what they were taught in health class, that's for sure. This is what we were taught in poetry. The words of men have made us this way. Fruit grows heavy from our limbs. Pears and apples. The boys are so amazed, but we have been compared to fruit all our lives.

It is when the buds break, split open wide like crude exhibitionists, bear their innards for all to see, it is then that the boys' erections return. They want so badly to taste our sap, they want so much to finger our florets, fuck our flowers. But we don't want them anymore. We shake our heads, but our leaves only rustle, as if disrupted by a light breeze.

We try to push the boys away, but fruit only falls from our fingertips. We say nothing as they prepare themselves for penetration. We

*cannot speak, for our mouths have hardened with bark and our bodies
are wood and we can only wait. We wait as our limbs grow, gnarled
and knobbed, our arms branch off into twigs. We grow into one another, the way close-standing trees do. Our branches wind, twirl,
twist around sister branches and we are entwined and all of our arm-
linking was training for this. Now, we are helixed as genetics and we
are together and one. We are the strongest jungle.*

*By the time we feel phalluses against us, we are only flora. All
of us, together, this small and lush forest, we have made this garden
beautiful.*

*But, already, we can feel the termites moving in, scuttling up our
thighs, torsos, necks. We can feel their sharp little teeth beginning to
gnaw, chew, feast on our parts. Even the strongest trees can be destroyed from within, even the most fertile flesh will rot. These bodies
cannot last.*

From the first sentence, it is clear that Lily wrote the story. The
words feel like my own, like someone scraped them, letter by letter,
from my tongue while I slept. Their arrangement is familiar as a childhood song.

Diamond shoulder-taps me out of my thoughts, and I smile at her.
"Hello, Diamond," I say. "How are you today?"

"I'm good."

"Well," I say. "You are well."

"Well what?" says Diamond.

"You're doing well, not good."

"I *am* doing good."

I shake my head. "Superman does good," I tell her. "*You* are doing
well."

"What?"

"If you say you're doing good, it means you're doing good things.
If you say you're doing well, it means you're fine."

"I am doing good," says Diamond. "Good things, I mean. Look."

She hands me a drawing of three people, smiling, holding hands. "It's good," she assures me.

"It is," I tell her. It isn't. Each character's fingers reach all the way to their shoes. Impossible. "Is that your mother and your father and you?" I point to the drawings in turn.

"No," says Diamond. "Silly. It's me and Daddy and Miss Winters. See? You can tell because she's fat. Not like Mummy. She's skinny." Lily's body, in the picture, is a ball on sticks.

"Miss Winters? Your teacher?" I look up at Lily, crouched beside a boy who is coloring with a fist so clenched I'm surprised the crayon doesn't combust into a blue dust.

"Yeah," says Diamond. "She's special friends with Daddy. I'm giving it to Mum for her birthday."

"That's nice," I say. "Here," I tell her. "Let's draw something different."

"Why?"

"Well . . ." I find a piece of bright pink card and a red marker. "Because this one's just drawn on white paper, but wouldn't your mum prefer this nice pink card?"

Diamond looks upset. "Pink used to be my favorite color," she says. "But now I don't like it."

"Why's that?"

"Just seems like everything's pink these days," she says, rocking back in her chair. I half expect to see a stick of straw between her lips, a tattoo on her bicep. "Too much pink around here."

"Okay," I say, looking around, finding a yellow piece of cardboard. "What about this one instead?"

Diamond closes her eyes, perhaps trying to channel her mother, then slowly nods. "I think she would like yellow," she says, solemn and measured. Diamond knows what she wants. She is logical and reasonable even though her name is Diamond and even though she is five years old. I feel underdeveloped. "I definitely think yellow," she says.

"Here," I say, offering Diamond my chair and opting to crouch on the floor instead. "Do you have a pet?"

"Yes. Jingles."

"Jingles?"

"Our dog, Jingles." Diamond laughs, as if it's ridiculous that I don't know more about her family pet.

"Does your mother like Jingles?"

"We love Jingles. I'm five and a half."

"That's a great age." I take the lid from the red marker and hand it to Diamond. "Why don't you draw Jingles?"

"Yeah!" Diamond is already scratching away at the card, her tongue peering out from the corner of her lips in concentration, other drawing forgotten. I carefully fold the page and tuck it into my breast pocket.

In the summer before Lily left for college, she woke me one night by pressing her hand over my mouth. I snapped awake and she held a finger to her lips.

"What?" I hissed into the dark.

She shushed me and gestured to her ear. Listen. A clatter and a bump. A masculine voice. A laugh. I sat up. She eased the door of our bedroom open, peered out into the hall.

"What is it?" I whispered. "Who's there?"

She closed the door again, quiet.

"What's happening?" I said.

"It's just Dad," she said.

"Is he with someone?"

"It's nothing."

"Does he have someone over?"

"Go back to sleep, Rosie."

In the morning, he hummed "Sweet Caroline" as he dropped bread into the toaster. He smiled for the first time since our mother left. This was the first and only time he would bring someone, a lover, into our house. He would later use this night, this simple one-night stand that brought him such fleeting joy, to blame himself for everything that was to come.

. . .

"Who was here last night, Dad?" I asked, filling a mug with warm water.

"Toast?" he said.

When the bell rings for the end of the day, Diamond runs up to me with her drawing of Jingles, panting and wild, and says, "Quick, hurry, before my mum gets here, can you write *happy birthday*?"

"How about I help you write it?" I say. "So that your mum will know it's from you?"

"I can't," says Diamond. "I don't know how to spell it."

"I'll help," I tell her. "Start with an *H*."

We are up to the *h* in birthday when my light is eclipsed. I look up. A lean woman, with long, disheveled black hair and big round glasses that make her eyes gape wide, is standing over me. She looks familiar, and I wonder whether she might be a celebrity.

"Hello?" I say. "Do I know you?"

"Oh, hello, dear," says the woman, ignoring my query.

"Mummy!" says Diamond, shielding her page. "Don't look yet!"

"Add a *y*," I tell Diamond. Then, "Oops, you've done the *d* around the wrong way. It says *Happy birthbay*. Just switch that *b* into a *d*."

And then, to the woman, I say, "I hear a happy birthday is in order?"

"Oh yes," she says with a rasped chuckle and a shake of her head, which makes the many thin chains circling her neck jangle and chime. She is shiny, this woman. "Silly, isn't it? Time. So arbitrary and con- trived at the same time."

I find myself nodding with her. Agreeing with her. Believing her. "Totally," I say. "It doesn't really mean anything. I don't believe in the linearity of time." And suddenly, it's true. I don't.

She crouches to join me at Diamond's level. "I'm Lara Bax," she says. Of course she is! If she is Diamond's mother, then she is also Phil's wife, which means she is also the woman Lily is competing with. She looks older than her photograph on the book jacket, but not less beautiful. I glance at Lily, who is collecting homework and waving goodbye to her students. She can be such an idiot.

I consider telling Lara Bax that her name sounds like a laxative brand and then decide against it. For some reason, I want to impress this woman. The *woman* to Lily's *other*. There's something about her, the way she stands, her shoulders thrust back, her neck elongated, reaching. The way her sweater falls from her shoulder, baring her clavicle. She smells like the color magenta might, floral and musty all at once. Women are witches, all of them, enchanted and enchanting. Each one has her own magic, and Lara Bax's is all-consuming. I introduce myself. "Rose Winters. I'm Lily's sister."

"I can tell," says Lara Bax. "I mean, your energy is entirely different. Opposite, really. Green versus red. But your eyes."

I nod. "We get that a lot. The eyes thing, not the energy thing."

"Twins, aren't you?" says Lara Bax. "You're just a moment younger."

I nod, in awe. Lily and I haven't been recognized as related in a long time. I want so badly to hate this woman who refuses to be hated. "Yes," I whisper. "We are, and I am. How?"

"Oh"—she shrugs—"I'm a seer."

"A sear? Like cooking?"

"No, I'm a seer. I see."

"Oh, a *seer*. I see."

She smiles. "Was that a joke?"

"I don't think it was meant to be," I say.

Lara Bax only nods. Her earrings, tiny crystals, pirouette beneath her earlobes, send little light rays dancing about the ceiling. This woman can create light. Can carry brightness around like an accessory.

"Mum, I'm done now. Happy birthday, I made this for you. It's Jingles."

Diamond hands the page to Lara Bax and promptly curls herself around her mother's thin leg, which is dressed in a brightly patterned legging.

"I love it, Diamond, thank you, dear," says Lara Bax, stroking the crown of Diamond's head with ringed fingers. My scalp itches, and I want that jeweled hand to touch me, too.

"Are you training to be a teacher?" says Lara Bax.

"Oh no," I say. "No, I'm just recovering from . . ." I swallow. "A long-term illness. I don't have a job right now."

"You should come to one of my YourWeigh evenings," says Lara Bax. "I hold them twice a week. They're all about learning to love yourself. Finding your worth and sharing it with the world."

"What?"

"I have an instinct about you. We are meant to spend time together. Let me help you find your peace. Here, sign up for my mailing list. You'll get exclusive Lara Bax offers right to your inbox."

I laugh at the advertisement. Lara Bax doesn't. She has no idea that she has, in the last moment, become nothing more than a commercial for herself.

"I don't have an email," I say. "I've been protecting my own peace."

"Ah." She nods, as sage as her daughter. "It's smart to log off every once in a while. Go off-grid. Reconnect with reality."

"What?"

"But that can't last forever, hon. Internet is reality now. Reality is the internet. If you're not online, then you hardly exist. Here, give me your phone. I'll make you an account."

"I only have a flip phone."

Lara Bax frowns, then sets her purse, a burlap bag, on a table, starts to sift through its contents. She retrieves a rectangular box and hands it to me.

"Here," she says. "For you."

I open the box. The phone looks like something from space. "Why are you giving this to me?" I say, running my fingers over the screen.

"How else would you become a YourWeigh woman?" She presses to turn the phone on and a start-up tune rings out. "Anyway, it's one I got sent for free. I'm an ambassador for the brand, and I already promoted it on my Insta. It's all yours."

As she tells me all of this, she tap-tap-taps the screen. "What's your name again?" she says.

"Rose."

"Rose Winters?"

I nod. She passes the phone over. It's light in my hand.

"RoseWinters11 is your email. I've already added you to the Lara Bax mailing list. I also downloaded Instagram and made you a profile. You're following me. I have a YourWeigh session tomorrow night. Will you come? Learn to love yourself?"

I nod, nod, nod. "That sounds wonderful," I say. And it does! To love oneself.

2008 (19 years old—Lily: 200 lbs, Rose: 70 lbs)

My first and last job, before I was admitted to the facility, was as a receptionist.

Lily graduated high school with top grades and went off to college. I was going to live at home, with Dad, and work until I had enough money for a place of my own.

"Don't go," I pleaded as she filled out her dorm application. "Please don't go."

"I'm going," said Lily. "I can't put my life on hold for you anymore."

"Please," I said. "I need you. Lil, I'm sick. I need you. I'm sick!" It was the first time I'd admitted to it, and she closed her eyes upon the confession.

"I know, Rosie."

"No," I said. "No, you don't. I sometimes go for days without eating a single thing. When I do eat, when I finally eat something, I usually pull on my tongue until I throw it all up. I don't even fit kids' clothes. Lily, I'm starving."

Lily kept her eyes shut the whole time, seeing a child dive into a too-deep pool and looking away to keep from seeing the mess.

"Lily!" I yelled at her twitching eyelids. "Lily! Lily!"

"Do you understand what you're asking me to do?"

"If you're gone, I won't eat. Not even a little bit. I'll starve to death without you here. You're the only one who makes me eat anything, Lil. Without you, there's no one to care."

"You can make yourself eat, Rose."

"I can't. I'll starve," I said. "I'll die. And it'll be your fault."

She finally opened her eyes, reached for me, lifted my knuckles to her lips, kissed each one, one, two, three, then she dropped my hand and walked away from me, me, me, the drowning child.

She went.

Everyone in our grade dispersed like leaves in the wind, off to find their real lives. Even Jemima Gates got into some fancy liberal arts school that accepted students based on their attitudes rather than their grades. Jemima's attitude was a million-dollar donation paid by her grandmother's Absolute Abs fortune. She moved to the other end of the country.

I overcame mediocre grades with my thin frame and scored a gig behind the front desk of the *CHIC* magazine headquarters.

I fielded calls and sent company-wide emails about the arrival of food trucks. I checked models in to see casting directors, sent hopeful interns to job interviews, and signed for packages. Mostly, I read. I read every women's magazine, cover to cover. I read about every fad diet. Soup diets, smoothie diets, celery diets, cigarette diets.

One diet, started by Instagram guru CLEANTEEN19, claimed to cure cancer. CLEANTEEN19 herself had been diagnosed with leukemia, and, through a regime of spinach-based smoothies and fruit juices, she had cured herself of the cancer. Her diet handbook was only $200 plus shipping and handling. She had accumulated three million followers in just a year of Instagramming.

It was later discovered that CLEANTEEN19 had diagnosed herself with leukemia, and then cured her perfectly healthy self with her homemade meal plan. No one received refunds.

I read about workout routines that promised to make you better in bed. About which lingerie you should wear based on your horoscope. About how to match your furniture to your most flattering lipstick shade.

I read about Kat Mitchells, whose drastic weight loss made the front page of *CHIC* despite her dwindling relevance. *CHILD STAR BARES BONES IN BERMUDA.*

I was lonely. Lonely!

Sometimes I thumbed Jemima's number into my phone before hanging up again. We had stayed in contact for a bit. Late-night phone calls. She talked about all her new friends. Cool types. Artists with ironic moustaches and nicotine addictions who wrote music and smoked pot and boasted about their insomnia. Something had shifted after she kissed me, after I left her room that night. After a while, she stopped picking up. After a little while longer, I stopped calling.

I slept during my shifts. Since it was a fashion office, no one questioned my insistence on wearing large dark sunglasses to work, heavy moons over my eyes. I was tall and thin and pretty enough that they thought it was a fashion statement, a personal style, and so I wore my glasses and slept through many hours of my day, my mind wilting with hunger, my tongue lolling in my mouth.

I was well rested, but I was unhappy. It wasn't that my work was unfulfilling. I never wanted to be filled. But it's difficult to feel any kind of hope when you're raising a void inside yourself, supporting its growth like a pregnancy.

The job was boring, but the people were not. The models were thin and violent-looking. They walked with a scary rigidity, a forward pressure, like if they were to stop they might melt into the ground, their layers liquefying, until they became nothing more than a puddle.

The editors, all men, were always a little aroused. Their sneers were puppeteered by their penises. Their low drawls always suggestive of sex. The writers, mostly women, were tired and frustrated. They looked like rusted cogs, coming to work with liters of coffee to rewrite the same article on mind-blowing blow jobs, day in, day in, day in.

The reason I could get away with sleeping through the working day at my receptionist job was because, in all my years of working there, I had never once taken a lunch break. My lunch was a Tic Tac, once an hour, on the hour. No matter the time, if anyone needed me, I was at my desk. All they had to do was wake me.

At the end of each day, I went home. Dad would get in an hour later, order dinner for one, sit on the couch. When I heard his key in the door, I'd retreat to my bedroom. We didn't understand each other, didn't understand how to be around each other without Lily to mediate. Talking to him was like talking to an instruction manual, the prescriptive steps (*How are you?* Good. How are you? *Good.*). We danced around each other like this, in silence, not wanting to ask or be asked. We were luxuriating in our own separate miseries, and we wanted it to stay that way.

I grew. I grew thinner. I grew sicker.

Hi, YourWeigh Woman!

Welcome to the YourWeigh community. My name is Lara Bax, and I'll be your guide, your guru, your friend throughout your journey. I founded YourWeigh just a year ago, but already it has grown into a powerful movement, with nearly a million online followers, all of them strong, beautiful women like you! We are so excited you've decided to join us.

YourWeigh isn't just a weight-loss program. It is a holistic health experience dedicated to helping each brave woman find self-acceptance, self-love, and peace.

To get started on your journey, why not come to a YourWeigh session? The evenings are held twice weekly in my personal home. It is important to me that you feel welcomed into my growing family. Your first YourWeigh session is free, my little gift to you for taking the first step to loving yourself. Click here to be redirected to my website, where you'll find details about the sessions.

If you're a faraway YourWeigh woman and can't make it in person, I livestream each session on my Instagram, and you can watch for free from your own home! Click here to add me on Insta!

If you're here for Lara Bax products, click here to be redirected to my online store, where you can purchase SkinnyTea, SkinnyBars, Skinny-Gurt, and more! All of my products are zero calorie but full delicious!

If you're a first-time buyer, you can use the code NEWWOMAN when you check out for 10 percent off your entire order!

Well, that's about it for now. It's my pleasure to have you in my YourWeigh family. I thank you, your body thanks you, and your soul thanks you.

xoxo,

Lara Bax

26

After school, we sit on my bed, the couch, Lily crunching on a zero-calorie SkinnyBar in the hope that Phil might be wooed by a slightly thinner version of her. The logic of exclusive deals and designer brands: *Maybe he'll want me more if there's less of me!*

Lily also seems to have forgotten that I'm meant to drink two Cal-Sips a day, or forgotten that she's meant to be looking after me. She isn't making me eat real food, so I'm surviving on one CalSip, three hundred calories. Not enough to maintain. There's a hum in my head. I see through a haze, like looking at the road ahead on a hot summer day, waves wafting up from the asphalt like a mirage.

I ask Lily if she ever goes to the YourWeigh meetings.

"No," she says. "That would be too weird. Being in her house, you know? Why?"

"I think I want to go to one," I say. "She invited me today."

Lily wipes a brown crumb, so like soil, from her mouth, before speaking. "I don't think that's such a good idea, Rosie."

"Would it be too awkward? For you, I mean?"

"No, it's not that. It's just, I don't think you should be signing up for YourWeigh any time soon. Give yourself some time to focus on your recovery. Just relax."

"But you said it was about wellness."

"What?"

"You said YourWeigh was about wellness. Holistic health. I want to be well."

"Sure." Lily nods. "Yeah. And it is! About wellness, I mean."

"But?"

"You were right," said Lily. "It's the awkward thing. It'd be too awkward for me." My tongue, citric.

"Lil."

"End of discussion, Rose."

She rubs her finger across her front teeth. "Slippery," she says, referring to the strange texture left by the bar. She's taunting me, waiting for me to criticize her diet, but I don't. And even if I did, the bubbly taste of my disapproval would have become lost in her lather.

The next story in Lily's *WE* collection:

WE GET PREGNANT: *Secondly, we grow too big. Too big for our house, our legs poking out of windows, our arms out of doors, and our mountainous stomachs have popped the roof off like a soda lid and our navels are the ceiling now.*

We receive phone calls inviting us to the ocean (a beach day!), but, of course, we can no longer fit in the sea. We are too big for open waters. Our friends say, Oh, come on, you're not even that big. And we say, If we bellied into the ocean, like a toddler fallen into a puddle, the water would splash out, tidal wave spill, we would flood cities. Our friends say, Oh, please, you've just got to get your summer beach body! And we stroke our expectant bulges and we say, Go without us this time.

That all happens secondly, but firstly we vomit. Everything inside us leaves for good, like mothers packing bags in the night or boyfriends upon spying a broken condom. Every liquid leaves us, stampeding through lips that fight to remain locked, we groan our goodbyes and wipe tears from our eyes and sob into the toilet bowl and the only response is the echo of our own woes, ricocheting off porcelain and fading like retreating footsteps. Soon we are left to our own silence.

Then we are hungry. Our stomachs are empty as churches; the space is so open that gut grumbles sound holy. We eat everything. Eggs, shells and all, and the crunch sounds like walking on gravel but the yolks slip down our throats like fine silk. We claw butter from wax paper and fill our mouths with fat. We chug milk like partygoers;

we squirt mustard straight down into the void. The hunger, though, is eternal. And it isn't even ours.

Later, we feel movement. Intestines turned snake, old machines spluttering to life, everything inside writhes. We feel concerned that we will give birth to something slimier than human. Worm children, slug babies. Their fathers, after all, seemed unhuman, inhumane.

Don't worry, says our leader as we fold into contractions. Our insides, clenched fists. These babies are their fathers' babies, violent and heartless. They want us dead.

We weep and wail, scratch at our stomachs, wanting to excavate, wanting to extricate. To exorcise. One of us, the leader, tells us all to lie down, and we do, in rows so we feel like categories.

She apologizes as she stomps, a beast invading a village, she uses our bloated bellies as stepping-stones she is hoping to crush.

Once our leader is exhausted, the movement inside us has slowed, sure, but a good huntsman ensures death. An extra bullet or a bat to the skull, we stand, cradling our aching guts, and we shove one another, apologizing and apologizing all the while, we shove and punch and push. This is how we get our revenge. We didn't ask for these babies and these babies will not be born.

The *we* in the stories feels so familiar. Like I'm part of the character. Like the character is part of me.

Lily prepares for a date with Phil. She says things like "Do I look fat in this?" and "Does this one make my arms look huge?" My hatred for Phil burns slow, grows brighter with every insecurity. She's never worn much makeup, but now her bathroom counter is blooming with pots of lotion and bottles of foundation and tubes of mascara and palettes of shadows and pencils in every shade. She puts so many layers on her skin, I expect her head to loll forward, front-heavy from all the new weight.

"I've been dressing wrong," she explains, leafing through her closet. "My whole life."

"What do you mean?"

"Phil taught me about dressing for my body type," she says. "How to flatter my figure with the clothes I wear. I'm an apple."

"An apple?"

"An apple," she says. It's as if we're reading a children's book together, one of those ones that runs through the alphabet. "There are apples and pears and strawberries and a couple of other types, too."

"Bananas?"

"Not really."

"I'm not following."

She sighs. "Well, I'm an apple because I don't have a defined waist, see? I'm bigger around the middle, but I've got these nice legs, see?" She held up a leg. If someone were to take a photograph of us right now, it might look as if my sister were about to kick me.

"Nice," I say. "It is nice."

"Thank you," says Lily. "So I'm meant to draw attention to my legs and away from my middle."

"Like rerouting traffic."

"More like an illusion."

"Give me an example."

Lily pulls out a pair of shiny black jeans. They look as if they are made from trash bags. "Skinny jeans," she says. "See!"

"They're so shiny."

"Thank you." She pulls a large beige poncho from its hanger. "And this!"

"Oh!" I say. "Look at that."

"A tunic," she says, pronouncing it like *tyu-nic*. Like those people who say *tyu-na* or *tyu-lip*. Those people who usually think they're better than the rest of us, the *too-na* and *too-lip* people. "So, it's beige," Lily is saying, "which means that attention will be drawn away from this area and toward the shimmer of the jeans."

"And what does this have to do with apples?"

"That's the shape I am?"

"You don't look like an apple to me."

"Well, I am."

"What's the best shape to be?"

"That's not really what this is about. You can't really compare them."

"So what you're saying is—"

"Don't."

"It's like apples to oranges?"

"Shut up."

The first use of a form of the phrase *apples to oranges* was in John Ray's proverb collection released in 1670. In his book, the meaning of the proverb was the same, but the wording was *apples to oysters*, which makes much more sense.

"Phil bought me this dress," Lily says, holding up a tiny black slip. "It's the perfect dress for an apple, and, Rose, look, it's designer!"

I take the coat hanger and let the satin drool over my forearm. The tag still dangling from its label tells me that the piece was over a thousand dollars and it's a size small. "Lil, this is a small," I say.

"It's a goal dress!"

"A goal dress?"

"I'll fit it once I reach my goal weight."

I hate him.

Lily chooses to wear a silver dress that dips deep below her cleavage, which is still abundant despite the diet, and embarrassing to me in the way a sibling's sex appeal always is. She wears heels that make her feet look wrong and a lipstick so wholeheartedly red I can't see the rest of her face without the awful scarlet distraction looming in my peripherals.

There's a bruise on her arm, half-hidden beneath a cap sleeve. "What's that?" I say.

She tugs the sleeve farther down her bicep.

"Did Phil do that?"

"It's nothing. No, he didn't."

"If he didn't do it, then why are you hiding it?"

"Because." Lily throws up her hands. "I'm sick and tired of this third degree!"

"Fine," I say, backing off.

"Can I wear your necklace?" she says, pointing at my chest.

I finger the silver chain that Jemima Gates gave me back in high school. It was one of the first wearable items that I owned and Lily didn't.

"Don't be weird about it, Rosie. It'll look so good with this dress." She's already behind me, her fingers working against the nape of my neck. "I want to look nice for Phil." When she pulls the chain away, I feel bare, and I replace the metal with my own hands.

"You're obsessed with him," I say.

"Why do you have to be like this?"

"Like what?"

"Cruel."

She fastens the chain around her own neck, and it looks different there, decorating a chest without having to climb a mountainous clavicle or settle in the hollow between ribs.

"How do I look?" she says, on her way out the door.

I look up from my book, her book, only long enough to say, "Terrible. Yuck."

She smiles her way into the night. Sometimes it feels like she smiles no matter what I do. The only thing I can control is my own joy.

The "evil twin" trope might grow out of the Zurvanite branch of Zoroastrianism, whose creation story goes as follows: In the beginning, God, Zurvan, existed alone. Desiring family, offspring that would "create heaven and hell and everything in between," Zurvan executed the first of many sacrifices. The sacrifices were fruitless until the very moment that Zurvan began to doubt their worth, and, in that moment, a set of twins was conceived: Ohrmuzd, born of the sacrifice, and Ahriman, born of the doubt. Upon realizing that the offspring would be twins, Zurvan resolved to grant sovereignty to the firstborn. Ohrmuzd, still a fetus, learned of this promise and informed his brother. Ahriman then proceeded to tear open the womb in order to emerge first and rule.

The twins are considered to be opposites. One good, one evil. A distinction that is made in Zurvanite writings, though, is that both twins are capable of good, but that Ahriman chose, chooses, is still choosing, to be evil.

Lily's apartment is so quiet without her here. I'm surrounded by her dead plants. Ungrateful creatures. If I could survive on nothing but sunlight, I'd live forever. I fill a glass with water and soak each pot, watch the gray soil brown. There's no point—I'm feeding a dead thing.

In Lily's bedroom, splayed across her mattress, body-like, is a contraption made of leather. There seems to be a muzzle attached. A spiked dog collar. I back away slowly. I imagine Lily's date, her new strange and violent lovemaking. A carousel of chains and leather. Things darken. As a Thought Diversion, I pick up the phone, scroll through the numbers Lily has saved in its memory.

"Dad?" I say, when the dial tone becomes a rasping breath.

"Who?"

"Rose," I say.

"Rose?"

"Your daughter."

"Right, right."

I hold the phone tight. "I'm out of the facility. I was discharged."

"The what?"

"The clinic you checked me into, remember?"

"Right, right." His words bleed into one another, ink smeared on the page.

"Are you doing okay, Dad?"

"I'm doing fine, Lil."

"Rose," I whisper.

"Righto."

"Are you dating anyone?"

"What?"

"I said are you dating anyone?"

"No, no. I don't think so. No."

"You can, though. You know that, right?"

"I don't think so, kiddo. I don't think so."

There is a long silence. Then I hang up, listen to the beep of the severed call for a long time. After a while, it becomes music, a lullaby. I sleep. In my dreams, Phil Bright, who looks a lot like Dr. Windham, but is my father, is twirling me beneath one arm, twirling Lily beneath the other.

I wake to a dull thumping, which is normal for me. Hollow bodies echo, and my heart is beating its persistent percussion against all odds. Only, as I learn how to be awake, the way I have to every morning, and my senses settle into place, I realize that this sound, this drumming, is an external one. It's not yet morning—no, it's still the middle of the night, the way nights always are.

Then the steady drumming filling Lily's apartment is punctuated with a moan, and the realization comes, sudden as a sneeze.

Without thinking, because I can't, because my tongue tastes of gin, and Lily's moans are like sirens, too deep in my ears, I charge toward her bedroom and shove the door open and stand, watching the new, collapsed version of my sister gyrating atop a sweaty stomach.

A hand extends into the air, his, and makes a loud, meaty thwack when it slaps Lily, hard and cruel, across the cheek. "Don't!" I cry, clutching my own cheek, stinging from the smack.

The bodies still, then they turn.

I should leave, but I'm stuck watching this terrible thing. Like craning your neck to see the collateral of a car accident or ogling a fainted body, I can't look away. Or maybe, maybe it has more to do with how, in the navy shadows of Lily's bedroom, slick with someone's sweat, it looks like me up there, having sex with that man.

"Get out!" Lily's scream is nasal. She heaves herself off Phil's silhouette and stampedes. "Oh my god. Get out, you crazy bitch!"

She marches toward me. Her stomach doesn't seem to fit her anymore, and her breasts swing low and sad, half-empty. My necklace looms above them, and it's the only item of clothing she is still wearing.

She doesn't look like me, exactly. I don't have the loose skin, and no part of me wobbles or shakes. I'm tight all over, my skin clings to me, an abused pet, hanging on for dear life, pleading, begging me not to mistreat it the way I do every other part of me.

Lily's new body isn't like mine, but it's closer than her old, bigger body. Now we're like one of those holographic images, tilt it one way to see Lily, tilt it the other to see me, and right now she's somewhere in the middle, a blurry distorted picture, on her way to becoming one or the other. She hisses into my face, showering me with saliva, and then I am looking at the closed door.

27

I am awake, coffee in hand, watching the door to Lily's bedroom, when I start to hear movement. I have been holding my body in a natural-looking position for a long time, waiting for this moment. One leg is crossed over the other, and the dangling foot has long been numb. I take a breath, count, release. The door finally whispers open.

"Fuck," Lily hisses when she sees me sitting, waiting. "I thought you'd still be asleep."

I smile.

"Rose, you remember Phil? Phil, you know Rose."

"Rose, so nice to see you again," says Phil, his grin wide, his teeth so bleached they look luminous. "You look just as lovely as ever."

His hair seems grayer than before, or more silver, perhaps dyed that way, because every strand is the same metallic shade. The result is eerie. Hair sculpted from steel. He reaches to shake my hand, and I stare at it, the palm that I had watched slap my sister across the face just hours ago. I've never been so close to a weapon. I look at Lily, expecting her cheek to be shadowed with bruise, but she's smiling, her eyes on Phil and adoring.

Phil drops his hand. "I'm sorry you had to see that last night, Rose," he says. "We should've gone back to my place. I'm so embarrassed." He is smiling. He is never not smiling.

I say nothing.

"I hope you can forgive me." He looks at Lily. "Well, us," he says. His eyes are this hard blue.

I smile. It is important to support the ones we love. "Hello, Phil," I say. "Nice to see you." I reach to shake his hand. He frowns at my outstretched fingers. Frowns at me. I smile. I smile. I can play his game. I am a seasoned game player and I can beat him at this duel.

Lily watches our civilized battle, a bewildered audience.

Phil clears his throat and takes my handshake, his grip too tight to not be compensating for something. We pump our arms twice and release. "Always a pleasure," he says.

"It's all mine," I say. "The pleasure."

"We're so proud of you," Phil says, and he's saying it to me. "Everything you've been through. You're so strong. And, if I might say so, you really do look beautiful." When he compliments me, my tongue sings sour because Lily feels betrayed, or jealous, the two are hard to differentiate. I can see myself, my reflection, in Lily's living room window. I look like I'm meant to be dead. A beautiful, beautiful carcass.

It's quiet. Lily claps her hands. "Okay," she says. "Great. Phil, you'd probably better be getting home before. Well. What time does she get back?"

"Do you mean his wife?" I say. "Lara Bax?"

Phil clears his throat again.

I say, "Does she know you're here?"

"Rose," says Lily.

Phil coughs, and Lily flinches.

"Do you have an open marriage?" I say.

Phil tenses his jaw and his cheek shifts. He does it again. Again.

"That's enough," says Lily.

I smile. "I'm just getting to know him better, Lil. I'm just making small talk. Just shooting the shit."

"I'd better be going."

I nod. "Back to your wife," I say. "Lara Bax. I met her, you know."

Phil's smile falters and I feel energized. I could run a marathon! I could run laps around this chump all day long!

"She invited me to one of her YourWeigh sessions. She said she thought we were meant to spend time together."

"Is that right?"

"Yes," I smile. "Do you think I should take her up on that offer?

Imagine all the talking we could do. Imagine all the things we could discuss."

"Rose," Lily nearly shouts. "It's okay, Phil. Rose isn't going to the session. She's not saying anything to Lara."

Phil looks between Lily and me, and his hand, at his side, it's clenched into a tight ball. Lily is looking at it. He notices our gazes, fixed on his fist, and loosens his grip. "Okay, then," he says, wiping his hand on his slacks. "Okay, then. I'll see you later, Lily," he says, but he won't meet her eye. "Nice to see you again, Rose. I'm sure we'll meet again soon."

Have you ever fought and won? This feeling is why war exists.

Hi YourWeigh Woman,

It's Tuesday, and you know what that means! I'll be hosting a Your-Weigh session tonight! Tonight, we're all about getting offline and getting back in touch with ourselves. It can be hard, in this day and age, to keep from comparing yourself to others, so tonight we'll be focusing on finding ourselves, understanding ourselves, and loving ourselves, and I'd love for you to join us! Click here to reserve your spot at the class, or here to watch the event live on my Instagram. Follow me while you're at it!

As a little thanks for being such a loyal member of my YourWeigh family, I'd like to extend an exclusive offer of two-for-the-price-of-one Lara Bax SkinnyGurt packs until five p.m.! That's right, that's sixty SkinnyGurts for the price of thirty! Get in quick, while the offer lasts!

See you tonight, my strong, beautiful woman.

xoxo,

Lara Bax

Lily eats a tub of Lara Bax SkinnyGurt for breakfast. It smells overwhelmingly of sunscreen.

I say, "Is that sunscreen?"

"Zero-cal yogurt."

"Are we going to talk about last night?" I say. "About Phil slapping you, I mean?"

"No," says Lily. "No, we are not."

"Lily," I say.

"Rose."

"He *slapped* you."

"Stop being so close-minded."

"About abuse?"

"About sex!" she says. "What do you even know about sex, anyway?"

I think of Jram in the bathroom. I think of Lily sitting atop Phil in bed last night. I don't know much about sex, but what I do know is that it certainly isn't all it's cracked up to be.

"Watching you hurt yourself like that is triggering for me," I say. "Watching you harm yourself makes me want to harm myself, too. I don't want to relapse, Lil."

"I'm not ending things with Phil," says Lily. "I can't put my life on pause for you anymore, Rosie. And it's not harming me! BDSM is a widely practiced culture. It dates all the way back to the early 1800s. There's nothing wrong with what we're doing, so I need you to stop judging me for it."

"But—"

"You know I'd do anything for you, Rosie, but not this. It's the best relationship I've been in for a long time."

I say nothing. I stroke my stomach. "So what you're saying is that you wouldn't do *anything* for me."

"Jesus Christ," says Lily, tossing the empty yogurt container in the trash. "I've got to get ready for school." She takes a CalSip from the fridge and tosses it to me. "Drink this."

I catch it, nod, and Lily leaves to get ready. As soon as I hear the shower running, I empty the contents of the CalSip into the sink. It's white and thick as ice cream. I've always starved my revenge. She always surrenders. Lily can't live without me.

Freud coined the terms *sadism* and *masochism* in his Three Papers on Sexual Theory. He saw sadism to be a distortion of masculine aggression and masochism to be a form of sadism against the self. The desire to inflict and receive pain during sex, he claimed, can be ascribed to incomplete or aberrant psychological development in one's childhood.

Practicers of BDSM reject the theory, arguing that Freud, a psychologist, was primarily researching unhealthy cases of sadomasochism, and that, in consensual situations, BDSM could be healthy.

The question, then, is whether Lily's situation is consensual, or whether she is responding to some long-standing trauma. My stomach aches. And it aches with the suspicion that I might be that trauma.

2010 (21 years old—Lily: 202 lbs, Rose: 69 lbs)

Every time Lily came home to visit, she was a little different. It wasn't an unfamiliar difference, more of an exaggeration of herself. She was becoming more like Lily, Lily-like, with every semester. Each one of her traits, the parts that made her Lily instead of me, seemed to grow, bloom, flourish, as if she were only watering, only tending to the parts that helped to differentiate herself from me.

I resented her for it. The way she was leaning away, growing toward the sun, a plant trying to free itself from its stake. I was the stake.

Of course, I knew my sickness had been the first distance between us, but Lily, now almost unrecognizable, more confident, more opinionated, louder and more outgoing, she was growing and learning and changing while I was stuck in my life, a starving receptionist with nothing to do and nowhere to go. Lily was making friends at college, learning, sleeping with boys, bringing them home to meet her emaciated twin.

"You said you were identical," the boys would say, eyeing up my angles.

"We were," I told them.

Initially, Lily had a type. Boys with bad facial hair and a liberal outlook. She swooned when they smoked their blunts and tucked too-long hair behind their ears, maybe unveiled some bad tattoo of a quirky food item—taco, avocado—or a roman numeral, talked about the environment as if it were their true love and then dropped cigarette butts on the street. Most of them played the acoustic guitar despite not knowing how. Most of them acted as if they were doing Lily some sort of favor by dating her. *Look how much of a feminist I am*, their proud smirks announced. *I support women so much I'll even date a fat one!*

I hated them all.

WE BLEED: *The blood comes slowly and slowly and then so quickly so fast so all at once that we're all just sitting in our own personal blood pools like some fancy spa day:* We'll take a blood spa, thanks.

I've heard it's good for the skin, says our leader, and we all nod with her, for we've heard similar genres of the same story. Feeling productive now, given that we are not simply sitting in pools of death, but that we are, in actual fact, undergoing a rigorous homemade skin treatment, we smile at one another as we sit, our underwear stained scarlet and the pools continuing to grow.

Eventually, when the blood is up around our waists and we can't see the lower halves of our bodies when we look down, we decide to start cleaning. We don't have any sanitary products, of course—we haven't needed tampons for months—but we do have a number of absorbent materials in the house. Towels, for one. Cotton balls, for two. Socks, for three.

We find everything we own, we empty drawers, we ransack cupboards. Our leader says, How about this whole-grain loaf, and we all say, Yes, yes, bread is very absorbent, after all, consider eggs and soldiers.

We have thrown everything we own into the blood pool, but still, the blood flows. The pool laps at our breasts and, had everything been different and nothing the same, this might be our first attempt at breastfeeding.

The problem is that we are absorbing the red at the same pace as we are bleeding, and so the mess seems to stagnate. Like bailing water from a leaking boat, we can keep up, but there is no way to plug the flow.

*Then there is a knock on our door and we stop our frantic cleaning
and drop whichever absorbent object we are holding and we watch the
door tiptoe open. Hello, says a voice, anyone home?*

It's us, we say, we're home, who is it?

*It's your neighbors, say two women who look only vaguely famil-
iar. We are from the apartment beneath yours, they say, and our roof
is raining red.*

We nod. Gesture around ourselves by way of explanation.

It's a bloodbath in here, says one of the women.

*Yes, says our leader, it is a spa day. Blood has incredible healing,
antiaging qualities.*

The women share a look and they say, Can we join you?

*We nod, nod nod nod, Of course, we say, of course. And our leader
says, But it'll cost you a hundred dollars to come in. After all, this
blood belongs to us.*

*The women laugh and they say, A hundred bucks, it's a bargain,
and they each hand us a bill and we usher them inside.*

*The women remove their clothing and lower themselves into the
red. They say, This is great, and then they say, Why is there a loaf of
whole-grain floating in it?*

*It's to eat, we tell them. And suddenly it is. Suddenly what we feel
is empty. Does an unhaunted house ever miss its ghosts?*

2010 (21 years old—Lily: 210 lbs, Rose: 68 lbs)

Something changed in Lily's third year of college. It was hard to pin-
point, exactly, what was different, but her shift in romantic interests
was drastic. Suddenly she was bringing home strays. Overt racists.
Blatant misogynists. As if she took the hand of any old passerby and
dragged him back to her dorm room. As if she wanted to be treated
badly. Her weight skyrocketed. She had a hole in her stomach—her
appetite, a well never filled.

Spring break, when she arrived with the first of the terrible boys,
Lance, I opened the door and sucked my tongue to keep from gasp-
ing. She had grown. The wood of the wraparound porch winced under

her weight. When she shifted, the boards creaked. She was beautiful, of course. She always was, but her light had darkened, her smile fell flat.

"Hi," I said, but my voice sounded wrong, and Lily knew immediately. She held her arms around herself, a barrier.

Lance took a cigarette from behind his ear.

"You can't smoke here," hissed Lily, trying to snatch the cigarette. "My dad." But he held on tight, lifted it to his lips. I was accustomed to people wanting to smoke around me. As if I triggered the habit in them.

"You two ever had sex with the same guy?"

"What? No," said Lily.

"Want to?"

"What?" I said. "What did you say?"

"A threesome." He exhaled a dawdling strand of smoke and winked at me. "I bet you'd be into it, huh? Skinny girls are always so freaky." Lance, it turned out, was not a boy but a ridiculous caricature of one.

"Jesus Christ," said Lily. "You should just go."

Dad hadn't even arrived home from work yet.

"You gave me a ride, sugar tits," said Lance. "How'm I meant to get back to the dorm?"

"Sugar tits." I snorted. "Scram, man. You heard her."

Lance went. Lily took my hands and lifted them to her cheeks. The feel was familiar. I used to have the exact same cheeks. Lily's face hadn't gained the weight her body had, like it was protesting the change, insisting that Lily return to her former self.

"I'm so sorry," said Lily. "About him. What a dick. I didn't realize."

"Why are you dating him?"

She ignored my question, but her cheeks warmed beneath my palms. "Are you okay?" she asked.

I laughed. "It's fine," I said. "I'm fine. I'm not some fragile fucking flower, Lil." As I spoke, I ran my fingers over my décolletage. I liked to hook them under my collarbone, hang myself on myself.

"I know," Lily said, barely glancing at my jutting bone. "I know that. He just, that threesome thing. And I just, I mean, you haven't . . . you know . . . yet . . . have you?" All of her trailing ellipses dizzied me. I held her arm for support.

"Spit it out, Lil," I said.

"I mean you haven't . . . done *it*?"

"You're having the sex talk with me?" I laughed. Of course I hadn't lost my virginity. I was hungry and ugly.

"I didn't mean to—"

"Just stop," I said. I didn't know why she was worrying about sex when I was clearly under seventy pounds. A child's weight. A skeleton!

I bent to pick up Lance's discarded cigarette, smoke still lifting from its tip. I took a drag. The smoke tasted light as air until it didn't. Until it coated my throat in an oil slick. I swallowed and swallowed to flush the pollution. "I've done things that'd make you blush," I said. She didn't believe me. She could taste the lemony lie, in the way we could always taste each other's business. But she needn't know just how extravagant the lie really was.

I unbuttoned my shirt, an oversized denim from my father's closet, and spread the lapels wide. *Look*, I didn't say. *Look at me.*

She frowned at my body. "You look terrible," she said. But she didn't beg to help. She didn't offer to make me a salad with barely any calories. She didn't even ask how much I weighed. She only wrinkled her nose and looked away.

"Thank you," I said. "Thank you so much."

"What do you want me to say, Rose? I can't keep babying you. I've got my own shit going on."

Her own shit? I hugged the fabric back across my body and swallowed. What if Lily had given up on me?

Back in the facility, the group leader told us that, while we couldn't control people, we could learn to better understand them and therefore predict their actions. The illusion of control without any of the harm. We played *The Type of Person Who.*

"For example," the group leader said, as we sat in a circle. "Rachel is the type of person who twiddles her thumbs as she listens." She nodded at a thin girl, nondescript but undeniably thumb-twiddling. "What type of person twiddles their thumbs?"

The rest of us, watching Rachel's thumbs chase one another, cat and mouse, we clasped our fingers, began to rotate our thumbs, too. "The type of person who jiggles their leg?" says one.

"The type of person who picks at their fingernails?"

"The type of person who wears cardigans until they get holes in their elbows!"

"The type of person who embroiders their initials on their handkerchief."

"The type of person who apologizes after speaking."

Rachel looked at the table, nodding at each answer.

"Another example," said the group leader. "Rose is the type of person who wears gray, head to toe." She gestured to my outfit. A walking raincloud. "Can anyone tell me what type of person wears gray head to toe?"

There was quiet. Then Sarah, who was brand-new, raised her hand. "The type of person who wears gray head to toe is the type of person who plays the victim."

Diamond and I sit and stare at each other. She picks her nose, youthfully unaware of how inappropriate. What do you do with a child?

"Where are Dad and Miss Winters?" she says, wiping her finger on her pants.

Lily and Phil are going to a sex store. "New toys!" Lily said as she tried on every shirt in her wardrobe. Her body is the weather these days, always changing. Sometimes marred with old gray bruises, other times reddened with a fresh wound.

She showed me each outfit as I watered her plants. I'd taken to watering them each day, knowing they were dead, feeding them anyway. I wasn't ready to give up on them.

"It's a way out of town, the store, but we won't be long. He knows what he wants."

"Whips and chains."

"We're more nuanced than that, Rosie."

The intricacies of bondage. I'm babysitting Diamond for the afternoon.

"Is there anything to eat?" Diamond looks at the kitchen. "Do you have nuggets?"

"No."

"Chips?"

"Let's do something different."

But she's hungry. She is so used to being fed. I cannot feed her. Her eyes are fixated on the refrigerator, a predator and its prey. I wonder whether her hunger is a product of her attention. Thought Diversion. "Come with me," I say, taking her by the hand. Hers is much smaller than mine, the entire thing the length of one of my fingers.

The only room in the apartment, aside from Lily's room (which I can't take Diamond into for the obvious reason that her father commits adultery in there with her schoolteacher once a week, a bad porn film premise) is the bathroom.

"Look!" I say, hoping my excitement might mask the fact that I had taken her to the bathroom.

"What?"

"Look!" I gesture around us. Look at it all.

"The toilet," says Diamond. "What's so exciting about a toilet?" What is so exciting about a toilet? I tear off a single square of toilet paper and drop it into the shallow well. It turns transparent and begins to dissolve. Diamond is not impressed. I reach for the handle and flush. Ta-da! A disappearing act!

"No offense, but you're just flushing the toilet."

"Magic! It disappeared," I tell her. "See?"

"Into the pipes," says Diamond. "It didn't really disappear."

I give up on the toilet. The truth is, there is nothing exciting about a toilet. "What about this?" I say, opening the medicine cabinet with a flourish.

"Makeup!" says Diamond.

"Exactly," I tell her. "Makeup."

"Makeovers?" she says. "I want pink lipstick like Barbie."

"That's exactly what I'm going to do," I say. "That's exactly why I brought you in here. Makeup." A different magic act, a quick change.

She closes the toilet, filled with new, fresh water, and sits on the lid. I take Lily's makeup bag and crouch before her. "I want to look like you," she says. I reach for my cheek and she reaches for the other. Two hands on my face, one big, one small.

"Like me?"

"Like you."

I check my reflection. No one wants to look like this! I look like old roadkill. "I look like old roadkill."

"Yes," says Diamond, solemn, a nod.

I take a container of powder from the bag. It's too pale for Diamond. Perfect. I dust a layer onto her complexion, then another, then another. She looks very ill. I take a palette of eye shadow, a monochromatic spectrum. Every color between black and white is here, every shade of gray displayed in a neat row. I roll the brush in charcoal and color Diamond's cheeks until the pink convex curves contour into hollows of themselves. The result: death.

"Where's Dad?" says Diamond.

"Shopping," I say.

"I hate shopping," says Diamond.

"That's why you're here with me." I use a black pencil to color around her eyes and then smear the lines into bruises.

"Dad hates shopping, too. He tells Mum that."

"He likes this kind of shopping."

"Dad puts me on his shoulders."

"What?"

"He puts me on his shoulders. He calls me his scarf."

"His scarf?"

"Because I put my legs around his neck to hold on."

His scarf. To be someone's scarf.

"That's nice. I'm all done."

Diamond climbs off her toilet throne and looks in the mirror, frowns, then starts to laugh. "It's so ugly!" Our reflections, mine next to hers, mother and daughter. For a twinge of a moment, I might feel maternal.

Diamond soon tires of the novelty and rubs at her face, complains about the itch of cosmetics. She paws at her eyes until she looks punched. I use a makeup wipe to clean the rest while she sits still, glad to return to normal, to health. I wouldn't know how to raise a girl like me.

When Lily and Phil arrive home, Diamond is asleep, her face so clean it's glowing.

"How was she?" says Phil, running his fingers through his daughter's hair. I wince, imagining the pain that hand could inflict on something so small.

"Fine," I say.

Lily is carrying a black shopping bag. Weapons. She looks different. I squint at her. "What's different?"

"I got a tan!" She reaches an arm to show me her new shade. "I was looking so pale!"

"We've been this color our whole lives."

"But don't I look better?" She lifts a leg for me to inspect, uses Phil's shoulder for balance. "A good tan can take off ten pounds, right, babe?"

"That's right." Phil nods. "That's right, hon." But he's not looking at Lily. He crouches beside Diamond, eyes only for her. "Did she eat?" he asks, a whisper, afraid to wake her. Is it possible that someone so violent with one can be so gentle with another? The type of person who can hit their beloved during intercourse is not the type of person who can be a good father.

"There's no food here. All Lily has in the house is your wife's diet stuff."

"Diamond loves that stuff. She eats it all the time."

"You're teaching her to diet?" I say.

"Just to be mindful. YourWeigh is all about mindfulness."

Lily smiles up at him. As if what he's saying is true. As if what he's saying is brilliant. The type of person who will starve herself for a man is the type of person who will let that same man beat her bloody in the bedroom.

In a half moment, I imagine stealing Diamond. Running away to a home in the woods. Letting her eat what she hungered for. Never making a comment about her body. Never criticizing my own. It's a fantasy. So far from possible. I would make a terrible mother, but I would know how to be a good one.

I only received one call at the *CHIC* offices that was meant for me. It was Dad. He sounded old, tired, his voice dusty from neglect.

"Yes?" I said.

"It's your father."

"I know."

"Did Lily call?" he said, his voice quiet, as if he were far away from the phone.

"Lil?"

"Did she call?" He cleared his throat, trying to cough up the cobwebs.

"Did she call me?" I frowned. "No?"

"Oh, I see." He cleared his throat again. "She said she would. I guess she hasn't yet. I thought she might want to be the one to tell you."

"Tell me what?"

"Your mother."

"Mum?"

"She had an accident."

"What?"

"She didn't make it."

"Through what?" My world, it eddied.

"The accident."

"What happened?"

"Drunk driver," he said. "Drunk. Drunk driver."

"A car crash?"

"He hit her."

"He hit her?"

"The drunk driver."

"Who was it?" I was having trouble understanding him. He was speaking in a strange font.

"The driver?"

"Yes."

"I'd better go, Lil."

"Rose," I said.

"Right. I'd better. I'll get your sister to call."

"Dad?"

"Mm?"

"Are you okay?"

"Righto. I'll see you."

The driver had been Dad's age, Dad's build, had the same number of prior DUIs as he did, but it wasn't him. He didn't do it. Still, he kept saying *sorry. Sorry*, he rasped, a wheeze, a last breath. *Sorry, sorry, sorry.*

You didn't do it. Lily shushed him as he sobbed at the funeral, scrunched into himself, like he wanted to ball himself so small he might vanish.

He opened his eyes and I understood him, maybe for the first time. He didn't kill her, but he didn't let her live, either.

We sat at the back, wearing black, trying to blend in. Mum's newer family, Ted and his kids, were front and center; after all, they'd organized the event, paid for the coffin, the cremation, the ceremony. We let them cry louder. We watched as they mourned the mother we'd lost long before they had. They each stood up, walked slowly, weighed down by the sodden heft of grief, to the podium, where they clasped their hands and choked out their final memories of their mother. Ours. *Don't snooze on the wontons.*

When the funeral was over, we slipped out the back like the last of the night's stars.

28

Lily is spending the evening with Phil. I imagine them playing with their new paraphernalia. Lily choking on some terrible gag. I clutch my own throat and relearn how to breathe. My hunger is humming. Every organ aches, my mind is a blur, and I've started to separate from myself. I'm my own shadow now, hovering just outside of my body. This is a late stage of starvation, and it frightens me, but I won't eat until Lily learns. This is the only way I can help her.

"Look at this," says Lily. She steps out of her room, shrouded in the night's shadow, and her silhouette is that of an hourglass. I frown at the unfamiliar shape.

"It's called a Waist Tamer," she says, running her hands over the corset, which cinches her body into a bow tie. Her new figure. "It's a new Lara Bax product. It's not even for sale yet. Phil gave it to me. Look, Rose."

I am looking.

She looks a little ill. Her skin has yellowed; her eyes sag like they've lost their elastic.

"Don't I look thin?"

"Can you breathe?" I imagine her organs beneath that rubber tube, clutched into a bouquet of themselves.

"Kind of," she says. "Mostly," she says. When she leaves, the house is so silent I can hear my blood, can hear the way it crawls through my veins.

I water the plants. They are dead. They keep being dead.

Hi YourWeigh woman!

Lara Bax here! I was just thinking about you! Unhappiness is lonely, isn't it? Sadness can be so isolating. Have you ever had the thought, if only x, then I'd be happy? If only I were thinner, if only I were prettier, if only I were more popular. Social media has a way of making everyone feel inadequate. We've all been there, YourWeigh woman! But I'm telling you now that you don't have to be sad, and you don't have to be alone! YourWeigh is a path to joy, and I've paved it just for you! The key to happiness is learning to accept you for you, and I can help you get there. Come to my YourWeigh session tonight and learn to love yourself. Click here for more details, and sign up now to receive tonight's session, if it's your first session, absolutely free! As an added bonus, tonight's newcomers will receive my brand-new merch, a YOURWEIGH: THE WAY TO YOU T-shirt and a cute calorie-tracking notebook, on the house!

Happily,

Lara Bax xoxo

2010 (21 years old—Lily: 215 lbs, Rose: 67 lbs)

Even Lance wasn't as bad as the next guy Lily dated. It was like she was hooked on assholes. Addicted to the hurt they brought.

Lance was an idiot, but the next guy, Tony, was scary. Lily didn't want him to meet our father, but she did want to introduce him to me, so we went to a coffee shop a little way from our house, and I ordered a black coffee because it was the only thing keeping me on my feet at that point.

Coffee was discovered by a goat, tells a popular legend. An Abyssinian goatherd, Kaldi, found his goats frolicking and dancing around, more energetic than ever before. Upon investigation, Kaldi found them to be eating the red berries and shiny leaves from a specific tree in their pasture. Kaldi tried the berries for himself and found that he, too, became energized and excited. They had discovered coffee, an incredible plant, one that creates energy in the consumer without any

calories. One could, theoretically, live off black coffee, and be energized enough to exist as she whittles away into nothing at all.

Lily ordered a hot chocolate, and Tony ordered a latte, to which he
immediately added the contents of a number of mini whiskey bottles.
He stirred them in with his finger.

"Babe," said Lily.

"What?" he said. "Hair of the dog. Want some?" He held out a
mini, but Lily gave him a look. "Oh yeah." He snorted. "That's right.
No booze for you."

"What?" I said.

"Nothing," said Lily.

"So," he said as he swirled his pinkie around and around. "You're
twins, right?"

Lily nodded. "I know we don't look much alike nowadays," she
said. "But we're actually identical."

"Looks like you got the good deal in the womb." Tony winked at
Lily, and I watched her cheeks darken. "Didn't leave much for your
sister."

"Looks like you got a good deal in the womb, too," I said to Tony,
eyeing up the pregnant beer gut he was hiding beneath a stupid slo-
gan T-shirt that said: IF FOUND, PLEASE RETURN TO THE NEAREST PUB.

"Rose, don't," said Lily, but Tony set a hand on her shoulder, and
she flinched, only a tiny tic of a motion, but I saw it, and I didn't like
how his knuckles whitened, how it looked as if he were attempting to
wring Lily's bones of something. Tony raised an eyebrow at me, and
I glared.

"So your sister's got a mouth, does she, Lilypad?" he said. "Interesting."

"She just gets nervous," said Lily, and I could taste her fear, cold
and watery.

"I'm not nervous," I said. "Lilypad."

Tony laughed. "So," he said, taking a sip of his spiked drink. I could
smell the whiskey from across the table, and it smelled like poison.
"You're Rose," he said. "Anorexia, huh?"

I snorted at his lack of anything. "You sure know how to pick them, Lil."

"Tony, baby, come on," said Lily. "Leave her. She's having a hard time right now."

"Hey." Tony's knuckles, which had faded back to their dull peach shade, tensed on Lily's arm again. "Rose and I are having a conversation," he said. "Don't be rude."

I stared at him, drinking liquor at eight a.m., grabbing my sister until she winced, and I stood. "Actually, I think we're done here," I said. I turned to Lily. "I hate him." And then I left, but not before Lily's frightened gaze begged me to stay.

Lara Bax's house is large and eerie. It's painted in pastel colors like an oversized dollhouse, its yard is a suspicious green, its fence an unnerving white. This suburbia looks pretend. A dollhouse. I knock on the door and my knuckles clap against the wood and the sound seems to echo around the silent perfect cul-de-sac. I check over my shoulder, half expecting to see Lily, furious at my disobedience. "I can only control my own joy," I tell the closed door. "I am learning to love myself."

"Rose Winters," Lara Bax says when she opens the door. "You came!"

A small, furry dog, who I assume is Jingles, yaps at me until Lara Bax picks it up, strokes between its ears, and then releases it back into the house. "Sorry about Jingles," she says. Lara Bax wears a skirt that plays around her ankles and a tiny bra that shows almost all of her torso, including a scar the shape of a smile that stretches from hip to navel. She has a tattoo, an elephant wearing a top hat, his trunk standing up, separating her breasts. She is too cool for this dollhouse in the suburbs!

"I like it," I say.

"What's that, hon?" says Lara Bax. And I realize that I haven't told her what it is I like. It seems so glaringly obvious to me, that what I am commenting on is the elephant tattoo that covers half of her stomach in its thick black detail.

"Oh, nothing. Your tattoo, I meant."

"Lilian," says Lara Bax. "I call her Lilian."

"My sister's called Lily," I say.

"Yes, Miss Winters." Lara Bax's tone chills, darkens. "Diamond's teacher."

I wonder how much she knows about the affair.

"Come inside, Rose." Lara Bax rests her hand on my back—it's warm—and she guides me into the house. "Can I get you anything?"

"Anything?"

"Water, juice, tea, kombucha—"

Afraid she is going to go on listing and insisting on calories, I say, "Water is fine, thank you."

2010 (21 years old—Lily: 221 lbs, Rose: 66 lbs)

Reception at the *CHIC* offices was always slow on Fridays, and, one Friday, just an hour before I could clock out and go home to continue my eternal nap, there was a rap on my desk. I startled out of my sleep and looked up to find Jemima Gates, thin as ever, hair dyed dark and cut into a terrible helmet around her sunken face. She was smiling down at me, her teeth browned, her eyes yellowed, discolored as an old photograph.

"Jemima?" I said, when my slurry mind recognized her, all cheekbones and jawline, sharp angles, straight lines. Her eyebrows were so dark they looked like crevices in her skin.

"I need a tampon," she said so loudly I blushed. She drummed her acrylics on my desk, ta-ta-ta-ta, the percussion of her very own theme song. Jemima Gates was the sort of girl with signature behaviors—things that made her, her, separated her from the herd. The way she punctuated her sentences with a wink, how she smoothed her eyebrows with her index fingers. I couldn't have pointed to my eyebrow if I wanted to, unfamiliar with the geography of my own face. I'd never been close with my body.

"What?"

"Tampon."

I rummaged through my bottom drawer, where the office management made me keep tampons for this very purpose, and slapped a regular into her palm, raised my eyebrows.

"Why are you here?" I said.

"Aren't you going to ask me what it's for?" she stormed. "The tampon?" Her voice was so fierce and flat and defiant it felt like my own.

"No," I said.

"Why?"

"Um, because I know what tampons are for," I said, although I'd never used one.

"Not this one," she said. "Not this tampon."

"No, really, I attended health class."

"No, you didn't," she snorted. "And anyway, this trick wasn't taught in fucking health class."

I sat back in my office chair and crossed my arms over my chest, swiveled on the chair's axle and let its wheels roll across the fake wood floor. "Fine," I said. "I'll bite. What's it for?"

Jemima smirked and beckoned for me to follow her. I looked around at the reception area, wondering whether I should put up a sign and deciding not to. I might have been trying to get fired. It was a terrible job and I would have much preferred to lie home on the couch, deep in a hungry slumber all day every day.

I followed her into the women's bathroom, where she quickly lifted her leather skirt to reveal that she wasn't wearing any underwear. Then, she took a flask out of her purse, unscrewed the top, and held the tampon to the bottle's lips as she tipped it upside down. Liquid spilled out of the flask, splashed onto the bathroom tile, but the tampon caught most of it, growing, swelling. The smell of cheap whiskey caught in my throat like a lost bug and I coughed.

Jemima set the flask down and bent into a bad plié before shoving the tampon, too roughly, inside herself. "There," she said, spreading her hands in a ta-da!

I shrugged. I was unimpressed. I had no energy to be impressed those days. I didn't even have a CalSip keeping me going. Back then I had only a carton of Tic Tacs, and I took them like pills, one an hour, and another every time I almost blacked out, just to keep myself half-conscious.

"Wanna try?" she said. "It gets you pretty drunk pretty quick."

"No thanks."

"Oh, come on. No calories, I promise. I learned it from my model friends."

"None?"

She made a circle with her thumb and index finger. Zero.

"Fine," I said, and went to retrieve another tampon from my desk.

Once we were both plugged with whiskey, we sat on the fire exit steps, her smoking, me not, both smiling as our limbs became listless, our minds twirling into a vertigo abyss. She showed me how a wispy fur grew over every one of her limbs. I showed her how the corners of my mouth were perpetually split, even though I never remembered smiling so wide. We were children, comparing bruises, a contest of injuries, marveling at how our bodies could take such severe blows and keep living. These were just some of the symptoms of our shared sickness.

After a while I stopped asking why she came back, why she was at my work, and we settled into past versions of ourselves easily.

"I missed you, Jemima," I told her. She grinned, took my hand, flipped my arm, and kissed the inside of my wrist, her lips chapped and rough against my skin.

"I go by Mim now," she said.

"Jim?"

"Mim. With an *M*."

"Mim?"

"Yeah. Jemima. Mim."

"Mim. People don't usually use the middle section of their name as the nickname."

"What?"

"Like someone called Andrew would go by Andy or Drew. The start or the end of the word. He wouldn't go by Ndr. Probably. Right?" And then she kissed me, really kissed me, and her tongue tasted of silence.

• • •

Water glass in hand, Lara Bax points me toward a room labeled YOURWEIGH, and tells me to join the group. I open the door to find a large space filled with women. The room is a bad advertisement for the spiritual. Black feathers hang, heavy as plumage, from the ceiling. Stand on your tiptoes and one might tickle your scalp. A crystal ball in the corner, shining a slow orange glow, but there's the electrical cord, and it's plugged into an outlet. Is the divine allowed to run on electricity? Old, hardcover books line the room. Titles like *Be Your You* and *Fearless Female* and *Light Your Peace* and *Dream of Hope*. From the titles, I cannot determine what even one of them might be about.

I join the circle of women all sitting on the floor, cross-legged and eager as children in class, their diet books open on their laps, and they look so young and afraid sitting there like that, just waiting for something to happen to them.

The women, in their circle, are talking about Lara Bax with such an open adoration it's almost religious, worshipping, their mouths wide in prayer.

"So," I say to the room, from outside of the circle, interrupting their odes to the leader. "What exactly do you do here?"

"We mostly just support one another," says a woman with wild red hair. "We learn to love ourselves, love each other. Lara Bax is amazing; you're really going to love her. She's so empowering."

There's a poster on the wall. An advertisement for YourWeigh. Lara Bax is standing, wearing too-big pants, and pulling the waistband away from herself to show how much room is left. I presume they're a pair of her own old pants, and I presume she's showing us how much smaller her waistline has become since starting the diet, but nowhere on the page does it say that. It only says: YOURWEIGH: WAY MORE YOU. SIGN UP TODAY.

"Good evening, my lovelies," says Lara Bax, entering the room through a back door, the world's least impressive miracle. Her words are projected as if through a microphone; I search her person for a cord that might suggest she's wired up, but there's nothing. Her voice, a natural megaphone. "We have a new face here today," she says, smiling in my direction. "Wonderful. Everyone is welcome," she says. "Join the circle and we will begin."

Lara Bax paces the perimeter of our ring, then stands, arms outstretched and sacrificial in the center of the circle. "Who wants to love themselves?" she shouts up into the air. "Who wants to find self-love?"

There is a cheer. The circle applauds, Lara Bax is spot lit.

"Who wants to find their worth within?" she cries. "Who wants to be happy in their body? Who wants to embrace their physical form?"

I want to love myself! Of course I do! What else is there to do?

"Do you?" says Lara Bax, pointing at a woman, who nods, eager as a child. "Do you!" Lara Bax shouts at another.

"I do!" the chosen woman calls.

Lara Bax stands before me. She reaches out a hand, sets her palm flat on my shoulder. "Do you, Rose? Do you want to love yourself?"

"Yes!" I cry up into the feathered ceiling. "I do!" The woman beside me takes my hand, squeezes my fingers so hard I know exactly where I am. Back in my body. Here on this planet.

"I do!" the woman screams at me.

"I do, too!" I scream back. Our open mouths each consuming the other's words.

I once read about a cult started by an ex-marine-turned-trapeze-artist who thought that the world was going to end when the clocks struck midnight of the year 2000, and the only survivors would be clones. He dedicated his life to cloning in the hope that he might save the human race, and, in 1999, he eventually succeeded in cloning a person.

People joined his movement by the hundreds. New Year's Eve was approaching, and everyone wanted to be cloned. It cost thousands of dollars just to add one's name to his wait list.

Over ten thousand people had joined his cause by the time his cloning experiment was debunked. He had used the identical twins from his circus and called one of them a clone. He spent the money on a state-of-the-art bomb shelter for his backyard. No one's sign-up fees were refunded.

Lara Bax asks us women to take selfies and then share them with the rest of the room, pointing out our favorite parts about ourselves. She wants us to upload our selfies to Instagram with the hashtags #LaraBax and #YourWeigh.

"I want you to look at that photo, really look at it, and I want you to learn to love it. Learn to love yourself! Weight gain is usually to do with a lack of self-love. Depression? Lack of self-love. Even physical illnesses, the flu, asthma, even"—she pauses—"some cancers result from a lack of self-love. So look at that selfie, girls. Love that selfie! Love yourself! And, if you use the hashtags, you can go in to win three free group sessions, a month's supply of SkinnyTea, and an extra copy of my YourWeigh holistic health guide to give to a friend!"

The women lift their phones, tilt their chins, turn and twist, finding their angles. I want to join in, but I'm distracted by an icy cold on my gums. I run my tongue over the chill, and it, too, is freezing. The taste is so strong that Lily must be close. Closer than she can possibly be.

"Rose," says Lara Bax. "Are you going to take a photo?"

"I have to pee," I say, standing, retreating from the reading room. The chill in my mouth grows colder. Colder. My teeth start to chatter like a cheap toy, and I hold my arms around myself. Marco Polo. Sister Missed-Her. The bathroom door is ajar, a light on. I knock.

Lily's voice calls, "Occupied!"

My whole body is ice. I push the door wide, and there is Lily, back pressed up against a floor-length mirror, which is shattered, the glass turned spiderweb with cracks. I can only imagine the force with which Lily's body hit it. I wince. The way the Waist Tamer is the only thing she is wearing. The way her legs are wrapped around Phil Bright's waist, their bodies folded together, origami, both of them naked, wet with sweat, moaning like wild creatures.

Lily cries out in orgasm or terror.

"We have to stop meeting like this," I say.

Then, before Lily can respond, before she can even remove Phil's dick from herself, I am gliding down Lara Bax's pastel-colored hallway, head light, helium-filled, out into this symmetrical suburbia, away, into the evening, alone.

I watch from up here, I watch as I walk, my body is so small, so small down there.

2011 (22 years old—Lily: 230 lbs, Rose: 65 lbs)

Jemima, who was Mim now, ate, vomited, and flushed. That was her latest method of thinness. She liked flavors too much to quit food, she told me. And she was addicted to chewing, she said. But she hated the feeling of any weight in her gut, and she was a talented purger. She didn't even need to use fingers; just a single unsanitary thought was enough to fold her over the toilet bowl.

"Don't start," she said, as we sat outside the office, smoking lazily, faces to the sun in the hopes of feeling some kind of warmth. "It's not worth it."

"Purging?"

"My throat hurts all the time. My mouth always tastes of sick. And, because I purge so often, because my body is so used to it, sometimes food comes up even when I don't want it to."

"Why don't you stop?" When I realized what I'd said, I laughed. "Sorry," I said. "That was stupid."

"It's kind of like porn, you know?"

I shook my head.

"Like, right before you watch, it's exciting. And while you're masturbating to it, it's great. But afterward, after you've come, and the porn stars suddenly look hideous and the sex becomes feral and the sounds are too loud and too awful. You know?"

I didn't. I nodded.

She smiled. She loved to be understood. "Who are you?" she said, running a fingertip down my cheek like a tear.

"Who am I? What do you mean?"

"I want to know you. I'm trying to know you. You're hard to know. I mean, it's hard to know who you are."

I felt the blush rising, filling me. I couldn't answer the question. I didn't know, either. Instead, I redirected. "Who are *you*?" I said, but it wasn't the same thing. She was so Jemima Gates, there was no question about it. Like someone pretending not to recognize George Clooney. Everyone knows George Clooney is George Clooney. Jemima Gates was Jemima Gates.

In 1903, Horace Fletcher's diet gained traction after he lost forty pounds by simply chewing his food more than normal. He called it Fletcherizing, the act of chewing each bite until it became a liquid and then swallowing it in sips. The diet was followed by celebrities, including John D. Rockefeller and Mark Twain. Fletcher became a millionaire off its prominence.

His advertisement: *Nature will castigate those who don't masticate!*

Mim was a part-time model, but she didn't need to be. Her grandmother's '90s workout, *Absolute Abs: A Workout for Women*, paid serious royalties. Women everywhere had the *Absolute Abs* VHS, wore neon-colored leotards in front of their television sets as they watched Mim's grandmother squeeze a hundred crunches and a hundred push-ups and a hundred bicycles into just fifteen minutes. "Get abs like these in just thirty days or your money back!" she said at the start of the video. She knew no one could keep up with her for thirty days. She was selling an unreachable dream.

We were fast friends, this new Mim and me. Which is to say, we fasted together. Every day, as soon as five o'clock seeped in, she appeared at my desk, dinged the bell like a customer, and held her palm out flat for a tampon. I would take two from the drawer, one for me, one for her, and we'd store ourselves in the bathroom's disability stall, dousing the tampons in whichever liquor she'd siphoned into her flask that day.

Once we were happy and drunk, she'd take me dancing. It was

early evening, but she knew places that were good and dirty in the daytime. Strip clubs and sports bars, mostly, where men became their most feral selves given one of two vices, naked women or ball sports. We took to the floor even when the place was empty, and she twirled me, I held her, she rocked me, I pressed against her, she kissed me, I kissed her.

We danced until a manager saw us as the centerpiece of his bar, entertaining the men, spiking sales, and he would turn the music up as loud as it would go. We wound around and around each other, Mim and me, climbing plants, clinging and weaving and spinning, twisting, binding ourselves together like neighboring ivy. We were one on the dance floor. A *we* and an *us*.

We tired quickly, of course, given our malnourishment. As soon as the liquor haze sharpened into reality, we grew bored of the tacky floor sticking to our stilettos, the men whose gazes were Velcroed to our very fabrics. Mim's helmet of dark hair stuck to her wet-hot face like a cartoon and mine, long and scraggly, matted. We leaned against each other on our clumsy limp home, delirious with the slow burn of hunger and dancing. When I caught sight of us in shop windows, I could hardly tell who was who.

After work, one day, Mim brought me to her support group. "Come," she told me as we both slipped vodka-wet tampons inside ourselves during lunch. "You'll love it, babe. It's such a community feel. You know?"

I didn't know. At that point, I was almost entirely alone. My father barely noticed me, his diminishing daughter. My twin was at university, earning friends and learning how to be human. I didn't have any people of my own.

I agreed to go to the support group, despite not knowing what, exactly, was being supported, because I missed belonging to something, someone. Twins were not made to be alone.

Mim's group wasn't so much a group as it was two girls who also had severe eating disorders and clung onto Mim like lint. We met at a coffee shop and ordered peppermint tea in the hopes of taking a shit.

The girls turned when Mim and I walked in. They were stick-figure thin and hunched over the table like a couple of scarecrows on a coffee date. They waved us over, grinning, manic.

"Mim!" said one, her eyes bulging like bubble wrap against her shrunken face. "And Rose Winters? Hey, girl, it's been a while."

My judgment eased into recognition. Lauren, Mim's lead minion from high school, looked terrible, a neglected tire, shrunken, flattened, a dead version of the preppy girl I had known.

"Lauren," I said. "Wow, hi."

"Lin," said Lauren. "I go by Lin now."

I nodded and turned to the second girl, said, "Hi, I'm Rose."

Her eyes were closed and she was slumped in her chair, but I could see the slow rise and fall of her thorax-like rib cage.

"That's Flee," said Mim. "She's mid-fast. Excuse her."

"Last night I was so hungry, and I really thought I was gonna cave," said Lauren. No, Lin. It seemed that she was talking to me. "But then I looked at Mim's latest campaign, that beach photo shoot," she winked at Mim. "And I didn't do it. I just took one of my mum's sleeping pills and . . ." She clicked her fingers to show suddenness. "Out like a light. I wasn't even hungry when I woke up."

"I had a hard week, too," said Flee, suddenly wide awake. Her voice was just the outline of one. Weak and perforated. "My parents wanted to check me into some kind of crazy clinic, so I ran away from home. Ended up at this gross women's shelter. It's disgusting, so dirty, but, like, there's a bed and there aren't any rules. No one watches what I eat, and you should see the food they serve. Powdered mashed potatoes and sausages every night. It's easy to keep ana in there."

"Keep ana?" I whispered.

"Anorexic," said Mim. "Slang."

"Wait," I turned to Mim, frowning, confused. "This is a pro-anorexia meeting?"

Mim shrugged. "Is that okay?"

I didn't realize that I had bitten through my tongue until I was swallowing my own blood. It almost tasted nutritious. I looked at Mim, so beautiful and angular as architecture, standing in the shadowy light, and I swallowed and said, "I guess." After all, I didn't want to get better. I didn't want to gain weight. Maybe these were my people. I looked around at the dying girls, killing themselves with restraint, and I settled back into my chair, surrounded by birds of a feather, fasting together.

Penguins are said not to flock, but rather to huddle. In the coldest months, they starve, surviving on only their own body fat. They scrum like rugby players to warm themselves and those around them. They rotate, giving each bird a turn on the outside of the circle where the wind is cold and rough, and then a turn on the inside, where there is shelter and warmth. This is nice to think about.

In warmer weather, penguins hunt for food. They're famished after a winter-long fast. Their huddle disperses, like strangers disembarking a bus, like their relationship was always one of convenience alone, and they head for the ocean to eat. A waddle of penguins standing on the shore will only wait for so long. When one becomes impatient or hungry enough, he will shove a friend into the water to test for predators. Only once he knows it's safe in there will he join his brother. This is less nice, and also less surprising.

I leave Lara Bax's cookie-cutter neighborhood, start off back to Lily's place. She's all I have and hers is the only place I have. There is nowhere else for me to go.

People go places, I know that. People go places to eat and to drink, to be around other people who go to places. Look here, at all of these people in this restaurant, sipping lattes made by liberal arts students who seem to be using foam as a creative outlet. Two girls, poised over their tiny table, phones carefully positioned in the air, a bird's-eye view, their cameras flash, capture their coffee in a frame, and only then do the two sit, ritual over, and lift their mugs to drink.

I am so hungry, not even a canister of Tic Tacs to keep me lucid, and the world looks like a film. Like I'm sitting in the back row of the theater, alone, watching this old-timey classic, see how the actors look more human than humans. Act more human than humans. They never go to the bathroom! Never burp midsentence. Never stub a toe. Imagine being so good at your job! Being human!

This restaurant, so fancy it's called itself a bistro. I laugh. It is full of diners. Families and friends tucked into booths, menus in hand, smiling. Happy to be eating together. To be sharing such an animal necessity. It's beautiful, what humans have done with the biological need to eat. Unlike other animals, who claw others apart in order to fill their stomachs, who chase and kill, who scavenge and battle and plunder. Not humans. We smile around tables, cutlery politely in hand, napkins over laps. We share bites from forks, order an appetizer to sample, and we laugh, we tell stories, we bond over a meal. Something so human and so beautiful in masking how animal we are at the heart of it all.

I swallow rising bile.

Here, a fast-food hole-in-the-wall. People queueing down the block. The air is heavy as cream, and I inhale. There are cooks in the back, pulling baskets out of fryers so hot the oil is applauding. What a supportive environment! A couple take their cone of fresh fries and the boy lifts one, blows the heat from it, and sets it between his girlfriend's teeth. Her eyes roll. That is how much she likes that greasy stick of potato. Or that is how much she likes her boyfriend.

A man, beard shaggy as a wet dog, ragged sweats, torn sweater. He sits on the sidewalk and holds a cardboard sign that says only: PLEASE. When I walk past, I try not to make eye contact, but he looks up, his eyes so blue. "Hungry," he whispers.

I puke in the gutter, but my sick is just liquid neon, this fluorescent warning sign: YOU'VE GONE TOO FAR! ROAD END! TURN AROUND! GO BACK! PROTECT YOUR OWN PEACE!

I wipe my mouth on my sleeve and continue.

29

2011 (22 years old: Lily 238 lbs, Rose 64 lbs)

One Saturday, I was sitting in bed staring at the ceiling, the way I always seemed to be. I was so well acquainted with it, the ugly white stucco that belonged in the '70s, the mottled texture that looked like something edible, ice cream or frosting, something that hovered between liquid and solid, awkward like a friend of a friend at a party. I often imagined dipping my finger into it, the texture of cream, licking it clean.

I was doing just this, my head a-twirl, when I heard a thwack. The source of the sound: a blackbird splayed against my window. It hung, almost comically, for a moment, before falling.

I made my way downstairs, past my father, who hadn't been sober since the funeral, who was passed out and snoring on the couch, beer still upright in hand.

The bird was a handful of feathers, unmoving, but when I crouched beside it, an eye opened, wild and afraid. Have you ever seen yourself in an animal? I have never been so familiar to me as when I saw that feebled creature.

"Hi," I said. "I'm Rose."

Its eye, suspicious, helpless.

"I'm going to try to help, okay?"

I cupped my palms around the bird's body and lifted it, nearly weightless, so fragile it barely existed.

"I'm going to carry you inside now, okay?"

Asking permission for each action seemed like the only way to level the imbalance of vulnerability. After each question, I waited, watched the bird's eye, until I was certain that consent had been given.

"Okay, this is my house," I told the bird. "That's Dad."

My father, perhaps roused by some flicker of parenting past, blinked awake.

"What're you doing down here?" He rubbed his eye with his empty hand and then took a swig of beer.

"It's my house, too, isn't it?"

"Sure, sure." He paused to scratch his chin, the stubble sounding like static. "What's the time?"

"Noon. It's Saturday. Lily will be home from college in a minute." The bird, still held in my concave hands, let out a small chirp. Dad didn't seem to notice.

"We got some food in the house?"

"Don't think so."

"Your sister can go to the store," he said. "Will you tell her to pick up some beers?" He was in denial about his drinking, and he thought that if he ordered his booze in tangent to groceries, the two balanced each other out. Health and harm.

"You could tell her."

He chuckled as if I'd said something funny.

"Dad, what do birds eat?"

"Birds?"

"Yeah, birds."

"Worms. That's how it goes, isn't it? Early worm gets the, I mean, bird."

"What if the bird is sick?"

"What?"

I closed the distance between us, the expanse of the living room, and lowered my hands for him to see. The bird, both eyes wide now, gurgled a little.

"Who's this?" he said.

"I just found her. She flew into my window."

"Flew inside it?"

"No, like, she crashed into the glass and fell."

"She doesn't look too good."

"No."

"Her wing broken?"

"Don't know. What should I do?"

"Don't know."

We sat in quiet, staring at the crumpled creature. She looked back at us, expectant, the question in her gaze: *Why aren't you helping me? Why aren't you saving my life?*

The world's worst paramedics, one starving, one drunk, we were still huddled over the bird when Lily arrived home.

"What've you got?" was the first thing she said, hanging her coat, tossing her keys on the counter. She loomed over us, my father and the bird and me. "That thing's too far gone," she said.

"What?" I said. "What do you mean?"

"I mean it'd be kindest just to kill her."

"No." I stood, brought the bird into my chest. "What do you mean too far gone? She's going to be okay. You want to just kill her? We can't just kill her. Look at her!"

"Yes, we can," said Lily. "She's as good as dead."

"Help me make something for her to eat."

"She's dead, Rose. Let her go."

But I couldn't. I took my winter scarf and wound it into a nest, then I set her in it, covered her trembling body with one end to keep her warm, and went into the garden to dig. In just minutes, I'd found two fat worms. They thrashed in my pinched fingers as I dangled them over the bird. She watched them writhe, interested, her beak opening and closing with want, but she didn't seem able to reach for her meal.

"Lil!" I called. "Come help!"

Lily appeared on the stoop and watched me try to lower a worm into the bird's waiting mouth.

"Even if you feed her that, she's going to die."

"Can you just help?" I held the struggling bug out to her. "If you hold the worm for her, I'll hold her beak open."

Lily wouldn't. Her counteroffer was to knock the bird on the head with our father's hammer. Something about her was different. She was sharper. Meaner. "Are you still dating Tony?" I said, looking for something to blame, like asking a toddler if she'd had her afternoon nap. At his name, Lily's expression softened. Her hands found her stomach, cradled it, almost affectionate.

"Yes," she said, so quiet she mightn't have said it at all.

"Why?"

She didn't respond. The bird didn't eat. I shut her in the laundry room, the warmest room of the house, overnight. I kissed the tip of her beak. I promised her recovery. The next morning, when I went to check on her, she was dead.

It's not until I walk past a grocery store that I realize what being alone means. I haven't been alone, really alone, since before I was admitted.

The store is one of the expensive ones. Organic vegetables and food from other countries that woo every white person into thinking they're cultured. Kimchi and kombucha, acai berries and goji berries and chia, matcha, quinoa, kale.

It has been a long time since I've been to a supermarket. I am always afraid that, confronted with so much food, my body might hijack my mind, might force me to take packets of snacks, pull the plastic open, gorge myself right there in the candy aisle. So I keep my eyes trained to the ground as I take armloads of chips and chocolates, a loaf of bread, a tub of peanut butter. These are the things I've seen Lily binge on. These are the things she will not resist.

When I pay, the cashier eyes me up. I can see the accusation in her eyes. *You are not going to eat any of this.*

"It's not for me, obviously," I tell her suspicious stare. I leave, panting but proud. See how I can shop for groceries! See how adult I can be!

When I get back to Lily's place, I empty the cupboards of Lara

Bax products, toss them in the trash, and squirt dish detergent over the top, untouchable. Then I restock the pantry with the new snacks, so appetizing, so enticing. I dust my hands at the job well done.

Next, I take the landline from its hammock on the wall and tap Mim's cell number. I'm barely me now. I'm watching myself from a distance. These actions cannot have consequences! The phone rings once, twice, and for a third time before I hang up. What would I even say to her? To Mim? Thank you for the letters? Then the phone, still cradled in my hands, starts to ring. I stab the off button and hang it back on the wall. The floor seems to be moving, like standing on a carousel. I close my eyes. I count the things that are real: Lily's apartment, the phone, the dying plants. But when it comes to the intangible, I'm not so sure. The memory of the grocery store? The bathroom at Lara Bax's? I check the cupboards and, sure enough, real groceries. The ones I had just bought. Reality, I think, isn't any more real than fantasy. Reality is just a collective fantasy. Nothing is real and nothing isn't real.

I am tired. I am hungry. I am hungry! I sit, I cry, I swallow. My pulse, too slow, like an instant replay of a pulse, the referees searching for errors. It's slower than a clock. I let it rock me to sleep.

The very idea of anorexia is contradictory. Us thin girls indulge in deprivation. We feel fullest when starving. Our own slow deaths give us life. By renouncing our bodies, we hope to find our identities. We yearn to be visible as we annihilate ourselves.

Lily wakes me with both hands around my biceps, shaking and shaking, shouting my name.

"What?" I say.

"Fucking Christ, Rose, I thought you were dead."

"Dead?"

"You look like a dead person sitting there like that."

I wipe crusted drool from my chin and squint at my sister, who is blurred as a bad photograph. I rub fists against my eyes, hard, and don't stop until my vision whitens.

"What time is it?"

"Nearly midnight," says Lily.

"Where've you been?"

"Where've *you* been?" says Lily.

We're both in trouble.

"You went to a YourWeigh meeting," says Lily.

"You had sex with Phil in his wife's house while his wife was there."

An impasse. We watch each other's faces, which is to say, we watch our own faces.

"Let's just forget about tonight," says Lily, running her fingers through my hair. "I don't have the energy for a fight."

She doesn't? Can't she feel how sparse my hair has become? Can't she see how I've grown even thinner? How I need her help?

"He told me he loves me," Lily says, aglow and buttery. "It's the first time he's said it back. He cried, Rose. He actually cried."

"Yes, well, so do infants."

"No, but he's a man, like, oh my god, he is *such* a man."

"Because he's a dick, you mean?"

"He told me he's decided to leave her. Lara Bax, I mean. For me! Apparently, she's been just terrible to him since her social media stuff took off."

"You mean he's leaving her because she's successful?"

"She's barely been paying him any attention and they haven't had sex in weeks."

"He told you that?"

"Rose, he told me he thinks I'm the one. The one!"

I swallow. "He hurts you."

"Not really. I mean, yeah, he does, but it's in our contract. I agreed to it."

"Contract?" I blink. My sister, who? "Do you like feeling abused?"

Lily snorts. "Do you?"

What I want to do: take Lily's new skinny shoulders and shake her until whichever ball bearing has come loose in her mind pinballs back into place.

What I do: fill a glass with water and begin to fill the flowerpots.

One, I notice, has a small green sprout growing hopeful from the darkened soil. It is so important to support the ones we love. I sit beside my sister and take her hand in mine.

"Lily," I say. "I understand that you want to be loved. But this is an abusive relationship."

"How would you know?"

"He's manipulative. He's controlling. He's making you diet. He's making you wear makeup and get your hair done and get a tan! He's a liar and a cheater. He *hits* you."

She shrugs her cardigan, *my* cardigan, off her shoulders and folds it over the back of a chair. It lies dead. She hasn't stretched it, because it fits her just fine. Her body is shrinking so quickly.

"Show me your back," I say.

"What?"

"Take your shirt off. Show me your back."

She crosses her arms. "No."

"Show me."

"No."

I stand, vertigo swarms. I grab Lily's shirt by the hem.

"Stop," Lily says, trying to writhe free, but I've already lifted the T-shirt enough to glimpse gashes, crisscrossed over her skin, the blood now dried a dark brown. "Stop," Lily says again.

Silent, I unclasp the corset that is binding Lily's body and drop it to the floor. I go to the kitchen, run the faucet until the water warms, and wet a dish towel.

"Come here," I say.

Lily does.

"Take off your shirt," I say.

Lily does. The plane of her back is slashed with red. I dab at the shredded skin gently, pressing the towel against each laceration, cleaning her body. Lily hisses through her teeth at the sting. Once most of the blood has been cleared, I notice that her mole, the mark that has separated us our whole lives, is gone. Taken off by a shard of glass. I run my fingers over its old land, and Lily shivers.

"Question for a question?" says Lily.

We haven't played the game in years. I nod.

"Why now?" she says. "Why have you decided to save me now?"

The question has such an obvious answer, I squint at her. "What do you mean?" I say. "You're in an obviously abusive relationship, Lil. You've lost, like, half your body weight."

"I've been in worse pain than this, you know. Things have been worse than this."

"What?"

"You're recognizing your pain in me, I think," she says. "Now that I'm losing weight, you're recognizing it, because that's how you always dealt with your pain. But you had no idea before; you've never known when I'm hurting."

"You mean at high school?"

She shrugs. "Your question."

"What?"

"You get to ask a question."

"Right. Okay. Why Phil? I mean really. You don't get to just tell me you love him. You're smarter than that."

Lily sighs. "I mean, I know there are parts of our relationship that aren't ideal. I'm not an idiot, Rosie. I know it'd be better if he weren't married, for example. I know it'd be better if I were more into his, you know, his kinks."

"Violence isn't a—"

"Can I just answer the question, please?"

"Sorry."

"It feels really good to be loved, Rosie. In the way he loves me, I mean. It's so complete. Does that make sense? He's all I think about. He's, our relationship is, it's everything. It's nice to be consumed like that, you know? Nice to have something so all-consuming. It's like, this sounds stupid, but it's like something I can drown in. Does that make sense?"

It does. I drop the bloodied towel into the sink, retreat to my bed, close my eyes, and let the fatigue in. I know how to live underwater.

• • •

Weeds compete with flowers and grasses and vegetables for resources. They can also be allelopathic to neighboring plants, hindering their growth further. As a result, the more desirable plants lose valuable phosphorous, nitrogen, and potassium, leaving them weak, and, sometimes, dead.

30

2012 (23 years old—Lily: 251 lbs, Rose: 63 lbs)

The pro-ana girls gave me a nickname. Riz.

"It sounds thinner, don't you think?" said Lin, stirring her over-priced green tea.

"What does that mean?" I said. I had taken French in high school and I wasn't sure how being named Rice was thinner than being named Rose.

"You can just hear it in the sounds of the letters," said Lin. "None of us are allowed an *o* in our names. Too fat."

"Okay," I said. "I guess. Riz."

"Yeah, see, it suits you." Lin's teeth were yellowed, her gums browned, the inside of her mouth, autumn. "Just like Lin suits me. Mim suits her. Flee. Thin girls need thin names."

I nodded. "Sure," I said. We paused to watch a group of four girls sit down at the table beside ours. They had a single plate of cake to share and, before touching it, they took turns photographing it from above, twisting the plate, shifting the cutlery. Once documented, they took turns mining the slice, each with their own fork.

"It's so good," one said.

"We're so bad," said another.

"I'd better get back on that treadmill," said a third.

The women spent a long time on each mouthful, savoring. We watched their sin, hungry. Watching others eat had a way of reaffirming our hunger. We loved it.

The girls left the last bite, the way women do, and each took a turn describing how full the quartered cake had made them, the way women do. A ritual. Then they stood, hugged, promised to see one another again soon. Us pro-ana girls, we stared at that last bite. We each, in turn, imagined plucking it between our fingers and swallowing. I looked at Mim who looked at Flee who looked at Lin who looked at me. We looked back at the mouthful of cake. Finally, a server came to clear the table. He bussed the plate and tipped it into a trash can without giving that last morsel a second glance. Free from temptation, we returned our attention to one another.

"Anyone got any new tips or tricks?" said Flee. "I've plateaued, but I've got like five pounds to go before I reach my goal weight."

"Tips or tricks," I said.

"Tips and tricks," said Mim. "You'll have to contribute at some point."

"Tips and tricks for?"

"Staying thin," said Mim, lighting a cigarette despite the coffee shop's NO SMOKING sign. "Getting thinner."

"Ah," I said. "I'm not sure that I have any tricks."

"For example, last week I shared with the group that I went to a psychiatrist and got a prescription for Prozac. It stunts the appetite."

"Prozac?"

She unclasped her purse and foraged around inside, took out numerous canisters of pills before finding the one she was looking for. "Prozac," she said. "Prescribed as an antidepressant. Weight loss is a side effect."

"Are you sure you should be—"

"Take it." She slipped the bottle into my hand. "I can get more. That's the kind of thing I'm talking about. We just share information. It's cool. So, what do you do when you're hungry? Or if you feel faint?"

"A Tic Tac. I eat a Tic Tac."

"There you go!" Mim clapped my back and her bones rattled against mine. "That's a good one. Take notes, ladies."

"I broke last week, and I ate so much of the shelter's powdered mashed potato that I got my period for the first time in two years," said Flee. She slumped over the table. Distraught at her body's display of recovery.

"But that's a good thing," I said. "You're getting better."

Flee's glare was immediate.

"Be supportive or fucking leave," said Mim, turning to me with embering eyes. I backed off.

That was the problem with us thin girls. We would agree to anything. Support any cause just because it asked us to. We hadn't learned how to be ourselves because we were born with voices in our heads. Voices that told us what to do and when. Voices that told us what others wanted, what the world wanted, that kept us from being selves.

What I had not learned yet: unconditional support is not the same as unconditional love, even if it might look similar.

Elvis Presley was said to be a fan of the sleeping beauty diet. This involved sedating oneself for long periods of time. You can't eat if you're unconscious.

Lily and I are woken by a phone call in the night. Lily stumbles out of her bedroom just as I am sitting up on the couch. She takes her cell phone off its charger and rasps, "Hello?" But the ringing continues.

"Is it your cell?" she says. But no one has my number.

Eventually, our eyes settle on the landline, hanging on the wall like some ignored insect. Lily grimaces, says, "I don't think I've ever answered that."

I'm certain it's Mim, returning my call. My teeth feel cold. We let the phone fall silent. Sigh into the quiet. I check the clock: six a.m. Not the middle of the night, after all. I yawn and the ringing starts up again.

"What?" says Lily, taking the phone off the wall and holding it away from her ear, suspicious of its intent. There's a mumbling on the other end and Lily's expression falls. "Yes? Oh. Okay," she says. "Thank you." She hangs up and stares at the phone, as if it might continue talking from its cradle.

"What is it?" I say. "What happened?"

Lily blinks her way over to the couch and falls onto the cushion beside me.

"Ah," she says, pulling her lip into her mouth, chewing. "Your friend," she says. "Your friend from the center?"

"Jram?"

"What?"

"Who are you talking about?" I say. "Which friend?"

"Kat?" says Lily.

"What about her?"

"She died last night." Lily is looking, examining, waiting.

"Oh."

"She wasn't eating," says Lily. "She was, ah, she was somehow cheating the weighing system and the nurses thought she was gaining weight, but I guess she was actually losing it. The nurses wanted you to know. They said you were close."

"Oh," I say. Then, "I have to go."

I walk to the facility slowly, body trembling, hands numb with cold despite the rising sun. I vomit behind a bus stop, but all that comes out is a glob of yellow. It's too yellow, too bright to have been inside this shadow of a body. I pause to think, *I just coughed up my last bit of hope.*

Kat Mitchells. Gone. No one ever survives.

I laugh. The melodrama!

2012 (23 years old—Lily: 264 lbs, Rose: 62 lbs)

Flee fainted at her job as a grocery store cashier. Split her face open on the register. She was hospitalized for dehydration, and the doctor kept her in for malnourishment.

When Mim and I arrived at the hospital, Lin was already there, lying beside Flee, both fitting easily on the thin hospital bed.

"Hi," Mim whispered. "Is she okay?"

Lin opened her eyes. "Hey," she said. "She's asleep. A stitch in her lip and a pretty bad concussion, the doctors think. And she's way, way underweight. She's scared they're going to check her in."

"Check her in?" I said.

"To a facility," Mim said. "Recovery."

Lin shuddered at the thought.

I looked at Flee, lying still and nearly dead. Tubes threaded through her nose and throat, more in her arms, her hand. I wanted to turn and run and never stop running. I wanted to run until my skin became translucent, until my bones ground into the road, until I was only a pile of dust and the wind could sweep me away, weightless.

Dr. Oliver Di Pietro developed the KE Diet, which involves having a feeding tube inserted through the nose, down the esophagus, and surviving for ten days on a solution of proteins, fats, and micronutrients, which is pumped through the tube. Laxatives are given to patients to ease constipation.

One night, the same night, I would later learn, that Lily ended things with Tony, I got a shooting pain in my stomach. An electric shock that woke me from even the dark depths of a sedative-induced coma. I yelped awake, my hands pressed to my stomach, and groaned.

I took my phone from the nightstand and called Lily. "Are you okay?" I said.

She was crying. I could taste the tears.

"Are you okay?"

She wouldn't answer, so I waited, listened to her breath until it deepened. I finally hung up the phone to go to the bathroom, and there, between my legs, blood.

Mim reached for Lin's hand and I watched their fingers entwine. She climbed up onto the bed, her head at Flee's feet, and then patted the spot beside her. I followed, slipping myself, a puzzle piece, into this strange jigsaw of thin girls in bed. I took Flee's fingers. We lay, head to toe to head to toe, and cried long into the night. Eventually,

Lin nodded off, snoring lightly into our tangle of limbs. A knot of girls.

"Want to hear a joke?" I said to Mim, wanting to relieve her tears.

"Sure."

"Okay, so a piece of string walks into a bar—"

"Oh, I don't really like this kind of joke," said Mim. "Tell it anyway."

"Okay, so a piece of string walks into a bar and orders a drink. The bartender says, 'We don't serve string in here.' So the string—"

"This is so stupid."

"What?"

"This talking fucking string joke." She wrapped her pinkie in a strand of hair and pulled tight. I watched as her finger purpled and bulged.

"It's actually funny once you get to the—"

"Okay, keep going."

"So the string goes away from the bar and messes up his hair."

"Hair?"

"Yes."

"It's a fucking string." She released her finger and it returned to its usual color slowly. "String doesn't have hair."

"Just—"

"Okay, sorry."

"I don't have to tell it."

"No, I'm sorry, babe. I'm sorry. Keep going."

"Okay, are you sure? Okay, and so his hair is all messed up and when he comes back to the bar he orders another drink and the bartender goes, 'Hey aren't you that string from before?' and the string goes, 'No I'm a frayed knot.'"

Mim didn't laugh. She wound a new strand of hair around the same finger. "I don't really get it," she said.

"That's okay," I said. "I think I want to get better."

Mim rolled her eyes. "You don't want to recover, Riz, you fucking idiot. You don't. Or you would have."

"I think I do," I whispered. "I just don't know how."

"Yeah? Well, go turn yourself in, then. Go get help. I'll watch from the sidelines like your cheerleading girlfriend."

"Girlfriend?" I said, and if Lily were there she would have said that my hope tasted fresh as spring apples.

"Calm your tits," said Mim. "I meant platonically. Christ."

I stood. "Even if I don't get help. Even if I stay like this, I'm not going to end up like Flee. I'm not dying of this, Mim." And I meant it. I didn't want to die. "I'm gonna be late for work," I said. "I'm not coming back." And I meant that, too. Even if it meant leaving Mim.

It was that day, when I got home from the *CHIC* offices, that Lily was waiting with my father. An intervention. And I let them intervene.

When a banana matures, it secretes ethylene gas, a substance that accelerates the ripening of any surrounding fruit, spreads toward them, seeps through their skin, catalyzes their rot. A murder suicide.

31

2012 (23 years old—Lily: 269 lbs, Rose: 61 lbs)

It was Lily who eventually convinced my father, who didn't know how to deal with my disorder or didn't care or else was so hopelessly inattentive that he hadn't noticed how I tucked every dinner up my sweater sleeves to later flush down the toilet, that my thinness was no longer merely dieting, but a bigger problem.

I came home from the hospital where Flee was being kept and where Mim and Lin had set up their camp of support to find Lily already sitting in the kitchen, only it wasn't a weekend, and she should have been back at university, in class.

"What?" I said, staring at her, unable to read her for the first time in my life as she sat next to Dad, the pair of them looking at me.

"Rose," she said.

"What?" I said, cruel with hunger.

"Baby sister," said Lily, and my mouth tasted of seawater, which meant she'd been crying. I had become a connoisseur of my sister's emotions from a young age. I tasted everything she went through. It was only a matter of refining the palate. "Rose, you need help."

"What?"

Lily looked to our father, on her left, who kept his mouth shut except when he needed to take a long swig of Budweiser. Then she sighed. "You have a problem, an eating problem. You need help."

"What is this, some kind of intervention?" I looked only at Lily, who had known about me, my problem, for so long. "Why now?"

"We've found a facility," Lily continued without answering. But she must have felt it, the hospital, Flee's sickness, or a change in me, maybe. Maybe she tasted that the time to intervene was now, when I was softened, vulnerable. "It's not a fancy place, but it's only a half hour from here and it's within our price range."

"Wait," I said, shrinking into a chair. "Wait, wait. Wait. You're sending me away?"

"We're trying to help."

"By sending me away?"

"Well, you're not getting better here."

My father burped, but, to his credit, he did cover his mouth with his palm. Then he said, "We just want you to be happy."

"I'd be happy if you didn't send me away," I said.

Lily threw her arms in the air, as if trying to get rid of her hands. "How are you meant to get better here?"

"I will," I said. "I'll eat."

"You won't," said Lily. She knew I was bluffing. She could taste the citric. "You've been battling this for years now. People like you don't just get better. Don't just start eating."

"I can."

"You can't."

"I can try."

"You won't."

I sighed. "So, what? You've already made the decision? You're sending me away and that's that? Well, guess what? I'm an adult. I don't have to do anything." It wasn't me talking. It was her, the thing inside me had taken over. Seized control, made me so thin and angry.

Lily looked at my father, then she said, "Well, if you don't go to the facility, you can't live here anymore."

"What?" I stood, but vertigo shoved me back into my seat with a heavy hand.

"Right, Dad?" said Lily.

He nodded. "That's right."

I crossed my arms. Swallowed empty saliva. "Are you fucking serious?"

"We only want you to be healthy, girlie," said my father.

Lily crouched on the floor, her hands on my knees, tried to look me in the eye. It once felt like looking in the mirror, to look into my sister's eyes. But now I was insect-like, all angles, and she was heavy and soft. We were opposites. "Baby sister," she said, her voice gentle as a breeze, "I am so worried about you."

I swallowed spiked tears, held my breath, counted, released. There was a new taste on my tongue. An awful, frightening taste. Like chewing on ice, my throat flooded cold, and the taste was terror, and it was my sister's. My own twin feared me. Flee, I realized, had no one to be afraid for her, to care about her, to intervene even when she was on the precipice of death. I still had one person. I still had Lily. I whispered, "Okay." I nodded. "Okay. I'll do it."

I had decided to recover before. I'd made the decision so many times, the way alcoholics decide to quit drinking, or how smokers decide that this one would be their last. My first days in the facility were lonely, but I was focused, determined, to get better. I would be normal again. I would live again.

The other thin girls watched me from a distance at first. Seeing how I spooned food into my mouth at mealtimes. Amazed by my eager participation in group sessions. When we were asked to shake hands with our foods, I thrust my arm out, took my banana by its head, and shook.

I was doing well. Eating well. I had never felt so hungry, or, I had never felt so empty. Every night, I lay in bed, wanting Mim, missing Mim. Her snorting laugh, her snide insults, the way she walked head-first. I felt homesick, not for my house, with my father, who barely cared, but for Mim, who felt more like a place I belonged than any place I'd ever been.

It wasn't a breakup, of course. There can't be a breakup if there was never a relationship. But the hole in my stomach, my sad, wet heart, the way I could eat, mechanical, machine, the food no longer disgusted me, it just was.

Something felt broken. Me. I did.

Things changed at my first weigh-in. I'd gained two kilograms, and I managed to smile my way out of the room, down the hall, and back to my bedroom before I forced my fingers down my throat and threw up everything I had consumed into my trash can. The cleaners, of course, noticed, and told the nurses. That night was my first intravenous intake. I thrashed my way through it, and, the next day, the thin girls accepted me as one of their own. One of them handed me my own collection of shower curtain weights and a ball of twine. I was welcomed in with open arms, and it was nice to feel like part of a community again. Being alone is a lot of responsibility.

The thin girls welcome me when I arrive at the facility to ask about Kat. They cheer like I'm a celebrity at a parade. They have no idea I faked my recovery, and, if they find out that I cheated, they'd respect me, and they'd want to know how. If they believe I've recovered, they'd respect me, and they'd want to know how. They are all so generous! Too generous! They are one another's best support systems and worst enablers. This is their toxic friendship. Interdependent and cannibalistic.

"Rose," they cry. "Rose, it's you. Rose, you came back. Rose, you remembered us." Their thin arms reach for me like sirens at sea. I am pulled into their huddle and drowned in their bones. Their hugs are sharp and I let them hold me, let them hold on to the hope that they, too, might be allowed back into the world one day.

"You look great," they say. "Not any bigger at all," they manage to splutter before the nurses hush them. No body talk is allowed in the common room, or anywhere within the facility's white space. They are all meant to act as if they don't have any bodies at all. Treat one another like incorporeal beings. A bunch of spirits collected in a room. Protect your own peace.

"Kat," I whisper, when their clamoring quiets down. "What happened?"

Their eyes fall to the floor, tongues lick dry lips, they swallow. It's a relief to call the thin girls a *they* instead of a *we*, to exclude myself from their plurality.

"She was using extra weights," one of the girls whispers, and when I look up, it's Sarah, her cheeks gaunt as a corpse. "More than she needed just to maintain. The nurses thought she was gaining. They cut back her CalSips. She was zeroing out."

Zeroing out is the point thin girls get to, the goal, when they can survive on no calories at all. When air is all they consume. They become plants, hoping to photosynthesize, living off only the light.

"Sarah?"

Sarah smiles. "I missed you."

"Sarah, you look—"

"You too," says Sarah. She reaches for my hand, and hers is all bones. When our fingers entwine, I lose track of whose are whose. We are identical. I swallow. I look at Sarah, too thin, a dead girl. I swallow. This is not what I want.

A tiny funeral: the girls begin to compliment Kat, like tossing flowers on a grave, they decorate the dead with their words. "She was so good," they say. "So smart and funny." They say, "She seemed to be getting better for a while!" And "She seemed happy." "She had such a pretty smile," they say.

Humans are not the only species to romanticize the dead. Elephants, too, touch passed peers with their trunks, have been seen spreading leaves over bodies, a shroud of foliage and shrubbery. They stand over the corpse for days, weeping together, remembering only the good.

"I taught her," I eventually say. "About the weights."

"Oh." The thin girls rest knuckles on my back. They stroke, up and down my laddered spine, vertebra by vertebra, running a stick along a xylophone. "It's not your fault," they whisper. "Any one of us could've done it," they say. "We all taught one another that trick."

One thin girl, a middle-aged woman who has been in the facility for many years, says, "I taught you the trick back when you were new. I will take that burden."

I barely recognize her.

"We all would have done it," say the girls.

"I was the one who suggested we use the weights to gain weight, rather than just maintain," says Sarah, a whisper. "We've been doing it together. Zeroing out."

I hold her fingers. A collection of toothpicks. There's a silence as the room looks at Sarah. "It wasn't your fault." The support resumes. "Was not your fault," the girls say. "It was everyone's fault. Our fault. We. Us. Don't feel so bad."

And I do feel better, even though I know I shouldn't. It's no wonder being part of a community is so popular: no one ever has to take the full blame when your existence is part of a plural. With the thin girls offering to remove my guilt, I feel supported, lighter, like I just might be able to continue to live with the fraction of responsibility I am left to bear.

Statistically speaking, queer women are twice as likely to develop an eating disorder as straight women. We think we can exorcise desire by famine. We think we can starve that sin out.

Statistically speaking, identical twins are 33 percent more likely to develop an eating disorder than single-born children. There has never been a time when we haven't been compared to another.

Dear YourWeigh Woman,

Thank you for joining me at a YourWeigh session last night, and congratulations on taking the first step toward loving yourself! I hope you left feeling lighter, happier, and, most important, at peace!

You have now used your first free session, but, for today only, I'm offering 50 percent off your second session! You're already well on your way to loving yourself, you strong, beautiful woman, so don't quit now! Reserve a seat at the next YourWeigh evening here.

As a bonus offer, just for you, use the code SKINNYME at checkout to receive a 10 percent discount on SkinnyTea, my favorite appetite suppressant and a solution to bloated stomachs, for today only!

This tea is my bestseller because of its immediate results. One cup can cleanse your body of toxins in a matter of hours! Click <u>here</u> to try it today. You'll love yourself for it.

Be kind to yourself today. You deserve it!

xoxo,

Lara Bax

2013 (24 years old—Lily: 277 lbs, Rose: 60 lbs)

I had already been an inpatient for months when Sarah was checked in to the facility. She was still acne-ridden, potholed as a rural road, and the youngest of us by far. *Seventeen*, the nurses had whispered, and we had overheard. They tutted, and we wept. Seventeen was so young to be fighting this food fight.

Sarah didn't speak for days. In group sessions she sat on the floor in the corner instead of at the communal table; she clutched her legs to her chest as if we might steal her most precious commodities: her gnarled and knobbly knees.

"Why don't you come sit up here with us, Sarah?" the group leader tried. "We're learning to flirt with our food."

Sarah's eyes only seethed.

"Okay," said the group leader with a shrug. "Stay down there if you want. But feel free to join us at any time. The only thing you can control is your own joy. Now, girls." She turned to us. "Try winking at your food."

My food of the day had been an orange. The pucker of its pedicel made me gag. I hadn't liked oranges even before I grew to fear them. I hated their bitter, leathery exterior. Didn't trust them. What did they have to hide with that gross skin? As the other thin girls seduced their food, I took my orange and crouched next to Sarah.

"Look," I said, taking a pen from my pocket, one I had been using to underline difficult words in my *Insects* book, and drew a pair of eyes above the fruit's hole. I drew a nose, eyebrows, ears, even. "Look," I said again, sticking my finger into what was now the orange's mouth. Sarah smirked. I took the slight break from her fury as a win.

That night, she was forced to drink her first CalSip. I heard her shouting, retching, slapping skin, the nurse's, and I knocked on her door. "Hello?" I said.

"Get out," she hissed.

"I'll help her," I said to the nurse, who eyed me suspiciously, but also cradled the already blooming hit spot on her cheek. Sarah had broken skin and a little drool of blood dripped from the nurse's chin. "I'll make sure she drinks it while you go sort that out," I said. "You can trust me."

The nurse nodded and said, "I'll be back in two minutes and it had better be finished. The whole thing. You hear?"

I nodded. Sarah smirked and kept her lips so closed they might as well have been sewn. "You drink half and I'll drink half," I told her when the nurse closed the door behind her.

"What?"

"Drink half of it and I'll drink the other half."

Sarah stared at my bones, glaringly obvious, overhanging cliffs. "Why would you do that for me?" she said.

"Because I want to get better," I said. "And I want you to get better."

"Why?"

I had never told anyone about Flee. About Mim and the pro-ana girls. Just remembering those days in the café, sharing starving techniques, left my gut ripe with nausea. But something about Sarah was desperate. If she had been Lily, I would have been able to taste her despair, a clinical fizz on the tongue like a pill dissolving. "I watched a girl nearly die," I said. "I watched a girl starve herself almost to death not too long ago. She was admitted to the hospital. Her organs started to shut down and she was all alone. Do you want that?"

"No," said Sarah, her voice falling flat.

"No one visited her," I said. "In the hospital. The nurses wanted to call her family, but there was no one to call. She didn't have a family anymore. She didn't have friends. She had no one. She was nearly dead, and no one even cared. Do you want that?" My voice creaked and broke. I wiped wet from my eyes and answered my own question. "No," I whispered.

"I don't," Sarah barely managed. "I don't."

"Good," I said, clearing my throat of a swollen ache. "Now drink half before the nurse comes back. If you don't finish the CalSip, they'll just inject the calories intravenously."

Sarah swallowed, inhaled, chugged her share of the drink, before passing it to me. I squeezed my eyes shut as I finished the rest, trying to think of anything but the extra calories.

"There," I said, passing the empty container back to her. "Tomorrow you do three-quarters and I'll do a quarter."

"No fair," said Sarah.

"Then do the whole thing yourself," I said.

"No," she said. "Sorry, I just . . . Okay. Thank you. Thank you."

I dropped a handful of shower curtain weights into her hand. "Tie these into your hair," I said. "For when you next get weighed. They'll help you maintain."

Sarah looked up at me, her eyes aglow, as if she were looking at something divine. "What's your name?"

"Riz," I said. "I mean Rose," I said. And I left her playing with the weights, my stomach distended.

I wave goodbye to the thin girls, and Sarah walks me out.

"You have to stop," I whisper when she hugs me goodbye. "Don't do this to yourself."

"I'll stop when you do," she whispers back. We separate and stare at each other. One girl and her reflection.

"I'll stop," I say. "I'll stop. We're not going to end up like Kat. I can stop. I'll do it." I mean it. "I'll do it."

Sarah nods. "We'll do it," she says.

When I kiss her cheek, it tastes of bare bone. The only options that exist for us thin girls. Die or be let go. Die or let go.

In the garden, where I spent so many morning walks, I catch sight of the thin men pacing the track that circles the perimeter. I take the metal bars that keep the garden private, or that keep thin people inside, pull a handful of ivy aside. Jram is walking with another thin man. He is talking animatedly. Gesturing wildly. He is talking about the most exciting thing in the world.

"Jram!" I shout, plunging my hand through the bars, through the ivy, waving. "Jram!"

He frowns at the dismembered arm poking through the fence. His expression is one of recognition that becomes one of dread. The pause in his monologue is fleeting. He returns to his conversation and walks past my now-limp arm as if he hasn't seen me at all.

There is only one thing left to do. I walk to Lara Bax's house.

"I want to get better," I tell no one. The confession is frightening. *No*, I shout down to my body from where I am floating, my place in the heavens. *You have no idea what you're doing!*

Dr. Matthew Anderson's Prayer Diet insists that one might pray themselves into losing weight. There is a prayer for weight loss, a prayer for resisting cravings, a prayer for keeping the shed weight off. God counts calories, too.

Every hour, someone in the world dies as the direct result of an eating disorder. The way I swallowed Tic Tacs on the o'clock. This tiny tribute to those who starved themselves into nothing at all.

32

Despite walking slowly, I'm panting, my body aching, when I arrive at Lara Bax's house. I knock, try to catch my breath. Lara Bax greets me with a hug. A patterned silk scarf tickles my cheek.

"You left last night," she says. "I was worried about you!"

"I had to," I say. "Sorry."

"Are you okay, Rose?" Lara Bax frowns. "Your aura, it's wilting."

"Wilting."

"Would you like to come in?"

I nod.

"Would you like a SkinnyGurt?"

I shake my head. I can't eat until Lily lets me.

"Would you like a glass of water?"

I nod. I need to sit.

Lara Bax leads me to the kitchen, points to a bar stool, fills a glass from the faucet. I take it from her and sip. The water is good.

"Are you sure you don't want a snack? You look . . . well, you're shivering. It might be your blood pressure."

I shake my head again.

"You don't eat well, do you, Rose?"

I say nothing.

"Are you punishing yourself for something? Are you punishing your body?"

I say nothing.

"Have you tried going gluten-free?"

I could laugh. "That's not the problem," I say instead.

What I want to say: *Your diet is dangerous.*

What I want to say: *You are the problem.*

But something keeps me from confronting Lara Bax, from telling her what she is, what she's doing to people like me. I had a whole speech prepared, one I'd recited and recited on the walk here, keeping myself conscious with the repetition. I was going to tell her about the harm her little faux-feminist Ponzi scheme was inflicting on the world, all the hashtags and the promotions and the zero-calorie everything and the diet facading as self-love. But being here, in her house, her hand covering mine with such tenderness, she looks so human in person.

"Is your husband home?" I say, redirecting.

"No. He's at work. Why?"

"I need to talk to you. It's about him. Phil."

"He's having an affair," says Lara. "Yes. I suspected."

"Yes."

"I suspected," she repeats.

"With my sister. With Lily."

"I suspected that, too."

"He hits her."

Lara Bax nods. "Yes," she says. "He can be . . . well, he has a temper." That's what we say when a man habitually inflicts physical harm on others. *A temper*, we say. *A bit of a temper.*

"Does he hit you?"

Lara Bax smiles. She tightens the knot of her scarf. "Let's not make this about me," she says, taking the empty glass from my grip and setting it in the sink. "This is about you. It's so important that you learn to love yourself."

I want to tug on the silk around her neck. I'm certain that, if I did, I'd find bruises in the very shape of Phil's fingers.

"I'd like to read your chart," says Lara Bax.

"What?"

"Your chart," she says, clarifying nothing.

"When were you born?"

• • •

Whoever was meant to be born first wasn't ready to be in the world yet. The smaller of the two bodies twisted herself sideways in the womb, blocked the exit, then moved to the side, letting the bigger baby pass. I'm sure that was Lily, barging into the world headfirst. Once she had taken her turn, I was left upside down. It's called a breech, which always struck me as funny. As if I'd broken a contract with my mother by flipping around in the womb. I took a long time to emerge. I didn't want to be here, in the world. I wasn't ready.

"You're a cancer," Lara Bax says.

"That's really rude."

"No," says Lara Bax. "Your sun sign."

"Oh, a Cancer," I say. "Yeah."

"It means you're sensitive and nurturing. Deeply emotional. Committed to your relationships."

"Sure."

"Your moon is in Gemini," Lara Bax says, her eyes skimming the chart quickly, her nose scrunching just slightly.

"Is that bad?"

"None of this makes you inherently bad," says Lara Bax. "Astrology is a way of better understanding yourself. It doesn't have to dictate anything you do, or anything you are."

"Okay, I get it." I pause. "But it's a bit bad?"

Lara Bax laughs. "There is no bad," she says. "That word means nothing here. Your moon being in Gemini means you're often emotionally unsettled. It also means you want to create. You love creating meaning, significance. Art."

"Art?"

"Do you draw?"

"No," I say. "Not at all. Not even a bit."

"Write?"

"No."

"Well, maybe you just haven't found your creative side yet. Let's work on that. Why don't you paint something right there?" Lara Bax points at a blank wall.

"But I've never—"

Lara Bax has already found a number of tubes of paint. Brushes. Even a palette.

"I've never painted." But, even looking at that wall. At the colors Lara Bax has set up. At the brushes, all brand-new and lined in a row along the kitchen counter. I do want to paint. My fingertips itch. I want to make something big and important. "Okay," I say. "Okay, I'll do it."

I haven't seen Mim since that night. The night we all slept in a weeping lasso around sick Flee. I was checked into the facility the next day and stayed for over a year.

Still, I think about her. Every time I see a thin girl with dark, cropped hair. Every time I hear someone with a voice that purrs like oiled cogs, smoothed by cigarettes. I think about her every time I open an old magazine, hoping Mim might be in there, brooding out from its centerfold. I think about Mim as I masturbate, the way she would mew, feline and sensual, with every small pleasure.

It's Mim that I think of as I paint, then Kat, and Sarah, and Lily, but I don't paint Mim, and I don't paint Kat, or Sarah, or Lily.

What I paint is a pile of birds, dead crows, bodies upon bodies, a mountain of feathered carcasses, eyes black with death. I climb a stepladder to add a bird to the top of the pile, and my eyes haze, my mind whirs, I fall, and, when my body hits the ground, it mightn't make any sound at all.

WE DIET: *We have been hungry since we were children. Our mothers taught us hunger from such a young age. Us girls were taught to eat only enough to blur the edge of hunger's angry tone. Us girls were taught to fill our stomachs with water, water water water, there is so much liquid in all of us, pick us up and shake well and we will slosh about obediently.*

Today, we seem to be taking up more space than usual. We are filling our room like a gas, our bodies are pressed to bodies and our skin is wet with sweat, slipping against other skin, and those of us on the edge are pressed against the cold of the wall like climbing lizards and we are too big, we cry.

We decide to stay inside. We decide to stay in our house so that no one will know, no one will see us taking up all of this space, too much space for women, that's for sure.

Our favorite brave idiot says, But how will we eat? Our favorite brave idiot says, There is not enough food in this house.

We shake our heads, she is so sweet and so lovely, and we say, We will not eat. We will not eat until our bodies begin to eat themselves.

Only, when our stomachs do begin to protest their emptiness, they shout their cravings so loudly the skies could be rolling with thunder and we would have no way of knowing, and we open the refrigerator and stare at its contents. We say, Perhaps we should finish this food so there is no more temptation. We say, Yes, yes, we must finish this food before we can start our diets. We say, And anyway, it's 10:34 in the morning, which is no time to start a diet. We will start our diet at noon, we say. Noon is when we will start our hunger.

Then we sit, eat condiments with spoons, suck mayonnaise from fingers. We sprinkle shredded cheese into our mouths from great heights. The pantry, too, says our favorite brave idiot. We must also finish the food in the pantry. She makes a paste from flour and water and spoons the solution between her lips until they gum together for good.

She weeps and sobs and the rest of us lower our cans, which we had been chewing open, tooth to metal, trying to pierce the seal and swallow tomato paste or garbanzo beans, foods that had been in our possession for years and years. Our favorite brave idiot tries to tell us something, but her mouth has been glued shut and she can only cry and cry and hum and hum.

Then we have an idea. Calories can only be ingested orally, of *course. So we take the bowl of paste from our favorite brave idiot's hands and we take handfuls of her special paste and we smear the stuff over our lips, cover our mouths in cement and wait until the glue sets. Once it does, then we, too, cry and cry, hum and hum. We are so hungry. We have no mouths.*

33

Faces halo above me.

I whisper, "Am I broken?" and lights flash blue and red and blue red blue red, and I say, "I'm not okay."

Lily's voice, Mim's, Lara Bax's, and every stranger in the world is talking, strange tongues I don't understand, and I can only say, "No, no, no, I am not okay. I am broken. Not okay." Outside, things move fast. Inside, things move slow. Thoughts crawl, but life sprints so quickly I'm dizzy from it.

Termites and Jram and Lily and Kat Mitchells and yogurt and Diamond and birds and Sarah and Mim and paint and Phil Bright and Instagram and Lara Bax saying *skinny, skinny, skinny.*

The word *intravenous* eventually wakes me. I've been conditioned to fear the sound of its syllables, for at the facility it meant an invasion of calories.

My mind is syrupy and slow. My limbs can't move, or won't, body heavy as concrete blocks or tied down. I think of how the word *bound* is a contronym, meaning both tied down and headed somewhere. Then I think about how I have more important things to think about. Things like, *What happened?*

"Can you hear us, Rose?" says a voice coming from somewhere in my hazy peripherals. Searching for it is flailing underwater. I try to speak, to answer the anonymous call, but can emit only a dry grate.

"Water," I say. But I didn't say it and am not able to, and so it must have been Lily. Lily is here, here, in the hospital. I try to reach for her, but my arms are either still bound or full of sand. Instead, I let my tongue trace my teeth, and there is the undeniable chill of ice, sharp, filling my mouth. Either Lily is afraid or I am drinking ice water or I am afraid or Lily is drinking ice water or both or everything.

Her fear or the drink makes me shiver, and someone says, "She moved."

"Can you hear us, Rose?" says Lily again. "Can you hear us?" she whispers, her lips against my earlobe.

The final story from *WE*:

WE ARE ABUSED: *We started dating them when we were young, so shut your damn mouths. They were sexy and gentle back then. Their bodies were perfect as lakes and their voices still cushioned with puberty. They whispered our names and asked permission to touch, then they trailed pillowed fingertips all over our flesh, too light to scratch an itch. We knew they would grow into men and we waited and they did but we were wrong. Things changed like this:*

- Their words: *Their wet lips started chapping started crusting started to scratch our fragile philtrum with every kiss. That new roughness seeped into them, spongelike, they absorbed their new jagged edges until their words were honed to a point. They were terrible critics and their new violent voices called us ugly called us awful. They called us bitches they called us sluts. They called us words that can only be written in a series of asterisks and pound signs, exclamation points and ampersands. Their new vocabularies tore through us like terrible winds, typhoons, tornados, tsunamis, our cheeks were slashed and burned and red and raw from the gusts they blew over us and we curled into corners, cuddled our knees and one another. We whispered about sticks and stones until we forgot their weaponed words.*
- Their touches: *They became artists overnight. Masters of color. Their fingertips hardened into tools and they worked with a violent passion. We were their canvases and they splashed us*

reds and purples, blues and browns. They coated our coats in color and we were beautifully beaten. Our lips grew bruised as grown women, as if we'd started drinking merlot by the gallon. But gin, neat, was a much better mask for our fresh pains, and we sucked it down with lime, those citrus teeth biting us better. They sat with us and watched for dusk, one strong hand in one weak, a romantic date, and as the sun fell below the corrugated horizon, we braced ourselves for the battle of night. Like were-wolves, they turned with the light.

- Their emotions: *They became feral so fast. Have you ever seen those clowns at the carnival? Openmouthed, heads swiveling on necks, they turned and turned back again. But when they turned back to us, their faces turned evil, and they were not ours anymore. Those clown men swallowed us whole. We are stuck inside.*

When I wake for a second time, I feel more myself. I understand why when I turn to see the IV, full of that telltale yellow gunk. The calories. I sigh.

"Rose?" says Lily.

"Lil," I say.

"Hi, Rose," says a deep voice. It's Phil. I could groan.

"Why is he here?"

"Did you stop drinking your CalSips?"

"What?"

"Have you been drinking your CalSips?" Her voice is hard. Her anger, searing my tongue. "Have you been throwing your CalSips away?"

I try to swallow, but my throat is too dry; it sticks.

"Rose," says Lily.

"I had to," I say. "I had to. You were hurting and you wouldn't leave him. I had to do something. But I'm done with that now, I swear, Lil. I want to get better," I say. "I've decided. I want to recover." And I mean it. I do!

"Dishonesty is a symptom of anorexia," says Phil. I could hit him.

I could stand from this bed, wrench the needle from my arm, spike his terrible eyes.

"Shut up," I say instead. "Shut up, shut up, shut up."

Phil clears his throat. "Are you going to let her speak to me like that, honey? Are you going to let her abuse me like that?"

"Me?" I could laugh. "Me? Abuse? Have you seen what you did to my sister? Her back? Have you seen the blood?"

"Enough," says Lily. She turns on me, her eyes ferocious. "You can treat yourself like shit, abuse your own body, but you can't treat me like that anymore, Rose. That food you bought? All that junk food you filled the cupboards with? You don't want to help me. The only reason you want me to be healthy again is so you can keep being the sick one. You think I don't notice how you starve me into submission? How you stop eating to control me? Stop eating so I'll forgive you? That's not how forgiveness works. That isn't how a relationship works, Rose." She's crying as she talks. Her tears, salty on my tongue. "There's only one abusive relationship here." Her voice, laced with anger. "And it's not between me and Phil."

I am deep underwater.

"You told Lara about us. Phil has a daughter, Rose. You could have ruined his life. Mine, too. Do you just not care? Do you just not care about me? Are you the only person you care about?"

I say nothing. Am I the only person I care about?

"It doesn't matter anyway," she says. "Your plan backfired. Phil and I can be together now. I mean really together. We're thinking about moving in."

I swallow.

"I give you everything," she says. "I give you everything, Rose."

"I was trying to help."

"Your relationship is unhealthy," says Phil.

I close my eyes. I'm tired.

"I can't do this anymore, baby sister. I'm tired." She takes Phil's hand and leaves. The door slams behind them. My heart monitor's beep is steady. I watch the calories drip from the plastic sack, through the rubber tube, into my arm. I can feel my body swelling. Thought

Diversion. I take my phone from the nightstand and call the only number I know by heart.

Siblicide is the process in which sibling rivalry among a litter of animals results in death. The spotted hyena, for example, begins to act aggressively toward its siblings just moments after birth. The behavior establishes and maintains a hierarchy among the littermates. In the instance of food scarcity, a hyena pup might resort to killing and eating its sibling in order to decrease competition for food and attention.

34

Mim is holding my hand when I wake. Mim! She's made a bed out of hospital chairs, three of them, and is stretched out over the seats, asleep, clutching my hand with both of hers. I don't want to wake her, so instead I watch her, the rise and dip of her breath, the tiny tics in her eyelids. With my free hand, I reach out to touch her cheek, needing to be sure she is real and alive. She wakes with the touch and smiles. "Can I help you?"

"Mim?" I say.

She smiles wider. "Haven't heard that in a while."

Then she stands and arches her back, which snaps and cracks. "You look really shitty, Riz. You're a ghost. You look like a fucking Olsen twin in public."

I nod. I know. "You don't look shitty," I say. "You actually look really, um, really—"

"Fat?" she says at the same time as I say, "Healthy?"

"You look *good*," I say.

She closes her eyes, nods. "I mean, objectively I know that's true. It's what everyone keeps telling me, but fuck." She pushes my legs over to make room for herself to sit. I'm relieved to note that my limbs can't be as heavy as they feel if Mim can move them so easily. "Let me tell you," she says, her hand still resting on the mound of my knee. "It gets easier, babe—a little, maybe, but not much."

I sniff and realize I'm crying.

"I wrote letters," says Mim. "To the facility you were in."

"I know."

"You got them?"

I nod. "Sorry I didn't . . . I mean, sorry for not . . ." I swallow.

"Shut up," says Mim, so gently. She tucks a strand of hair behind my ears. "You look just the fucking same," she whispers, a soft smile touches her lips.

"I'm crying," I tell her. She nods. "Your hair," I say.

"Was hideous," she snorts. "Like a helmet. God. I thought it was so edgy. Idiot."

"You're beautiful," I say, and my whole face spikes with heat.

"You still do that?"

"What?"

"Blush." She touches my cheek with the back of her finger as if feeling for a fever. "Just like back in school. Cute," she says.

I sniff again. "Why am I crying?" I say.

She shrugs.

"I'm so glad you called," she says. "I've thought about you every day. Every day since you left."

There's a silence, and Mim uses it to reach behind me, puff my pillows. I feel mothered, looked after. Then she settles back down beside me and uses the heels of her hands to flatten her eyebrows. The gesture reminds me so much of Jemima Gates, of Mim, of her, her self, she is still so herself.

"What happened to you? And the other girls after I left."

Mim sighs. "Flee got discharged, and we kept at it," she says, and she runs her fingers up and down my blanketed leg as she talks. Mim pauses to clear her throat, maybe of tears. "I didn't even fucking consider quitting my bullshit until Lin."

"Lin?"

"Lauren," says Mim.

"No, I know who she is. I mean what happened?"

Mim says nothing.

"She died? Lauren died?"

"She was hospitalized," says Mim. "But it was too late."

"Lauren," I say. "From school. Lauren. Lin."

Mim nods, wipes tears from her eyes, rubs her running nose, and then wipes her fingers on my blanket before going back to stroking my leg. I don't care about the snot, so long as she keeps touching me.

"That was six months ago. And then something sort of snapped. I was there. In the hospital. She was still breathing, but, god, her breath was so slow, and she couldn't move. She started making this, this rattling sound. I called the nurse, but it was . . ."

She takes a quaking breath.

I lift her hand to my lips. Kiss her fingers. Turn her wrist over and kiss the network of veins there.

"So I moved in with my grandmother," Mim says. "Since I knew she'd force-feed me. I finally pulled my shit together. I came out to her. To everyone, actually. My parents cut me off. Fucking homo-phobes." She sighs. "Ah, it was probably a good thing. So I went back to school."

I swallow. "You came out?"

"As bi, yeah."

"Bi," I say. Nodding. "Bisexual," I say. "Bisexual," I try, lengthen-ing the word, rolling it like dough, adding a syllable between the last vowels.

"Don't be weird, babe."

"Sorry."

Mim shrugs. "So, I was controlling my eating because I couldn't control my sexuality. Not exactly revolutionary."

I swallow, and the saliva hurts.

"So, you went back to school? University?"

"Art history." She nods, smiles, her eyes piqued with a light. "I love it. It's important to have something you love. I don't mean a person; I mean something within yourself. You know, Lin's death probably stopped me from dying, but I kept me living. At some point, I think I realized that the thing you live for should be yourself."

"I'm so happy for you, Mim." I mean it. "You really do look, you know, you look like a person," I say. "Like a real human woman."

"Thank you?" says Mim, dusting imaginary dust off her knees. "I do pride myself on being especially human." She looks at me, shakes her head, smiles. "But tell me about you. I caught the weird end of some pretty screwy stuff in your life, huh? You said something on the phone. A fight with Lily?"

I tell her about the facility and about Sarah and about Jram, whom she calls a jackass. I tell her about Lily's new diet and Lara Bax and the affair with Phil. About Phil. The abuse, emotional and physical. I tell her about painting and fainting and ending up here. And, lastly, I tell her about Kat.

"Kat Mitchells? Like, *the* Kat Mitchells? Holy shit. What was she like?"

When I say nothing, Mim sighs. "You know that's not your fault, right?" she says. "You can't take the weight of that, babe. It'll crush you. Kat did what Kat did. It was the disorder, her own mind. It was her that did it."

"I helped," I say. "If this were court, I'd be an accessory. To murder, Mim."

"Well, I'm the judge and I say 'not guilty.'" Mim slams her fist into her hand, a firm gavel. "You are free of any burden," she says. Then she reaches for my hand. I let her familiar fingers curl into mine, and we link, she and me, like LEGO. "No, but seriously," she says. "You think I didn't try taking the full blame for Lin? Flee, too? You, even? I took all of that blame, babe. I was so full of blame I was going to burst with it. I had your lives on my hands. And then Lily told me what you did. You got out. You were so fucking strong. You just, like, after Flee was in the hospital, you just said you weren't coming back. Just like that. It was that easy. I called to tell you about Lin and your sister picked up and she told me you'd checked yourself into rehab. You made the call and you got out." She shakes her head. "And I realized, you checking yourself in, deciding to recover, it made me realize, that it was my decision. On my own. I was the only one that could fix me. Not the group. Not the girls, friends, family, whatever. No. It was me. And I told myself, 'Mim,' I said, 'Mim, if Riz can make that call, then you can, too. And Lin could have, too. We've gotta do it for ourselves. We're the only ones who can. I mean, you're the only one who can.'"

I nod.

"So, Lily's dating an asshole, huh?" Mim has her pinkie finger hooked around mine, and I stare at the little lock.

"She's obsessed with him," I say. "I've never seen her like this."

She shakes her head. "God, I was such a bitch to her at school."

I say nothing.

"Ouch," says Mim. "I'm sorry, babe. I really am. I know I've been awful. But I'm different now. Trying to be. I've changed. I'm chang-ing. Eating disorders are the real bitches. They take over. They change you."

I say more nothing.

"So, what're you doing about Lily? The guy? The diet? The abuse?"

My breath quickens as Mim lists the responsibilities I've taken on. At all the work I have left to do. Life is a burden!

"I told his wife," I say. "But now he's just officially with Lily. I don't know what else to do."

"We have to help her," says Mim.

"You just talked about how we couldn't help anyone. About how we can only help ourselves."

"That's to get better," says Mim. "Sounds to me like Lily doesn't even know she has a problem. You can't get better until you know you have a problem. Everyone knows that."

I nod.

"So, we help," says Mim. "We get Lily to see the light about this Phil guy, and we get this whole fucking diet thing shut down."

"Lara Bax's YourWeigh Holistic Health Program?"

"Jesus. Who is this Lara Bax bitch?"

"She's actually not that bad," I say. "I mean, she isn't as bad as she seems. She's this social media celebrity, and her whole self-love thing is a farce. But she's actually kind of a nice person? I think she genu-inely wants to help."

"Well, she's not fucking helping Lily, is she?"

There is a loud beep. The bag is empty. I am full. I wish Mim would leave so I could go into the bathroom and make myself vomit.

Reject everything they made me consume. No. *Get out of my head!* I tell the urges. *This brain is mine!*

"Listen," says Mim. "I'll help you with Lily. On one condition."

I look up at her.

"You have to recover."

PART THREE

35

They release me two days later, feeling better, more myself, a single self, with an impressive arsenal of painkillers, a cast on my arm, a sling, and a wheelchair that I don't really need. The hospital lets me take a bunch of CalSips, but I still don't have any clothes because I am too afraid of Lily's anger to go over and collect my things. Mim takes me to her house, which she shares with her grandmother, Grace Green, of Absolute Abs fame.

"She's kind of crazy," Mim warns me, tapping her steering wheel along to a song I have never heard, but immediately like given Mim's fondness for it. "But I love her," she says. "And I think you'll like her. It's tough to say. She's one of those love-her-or-hate-her types."

Mim keeps talking, and I realize she's nervous. I lean over and kiss her cheek, hoping to calm her, but she glances at me, laughs an uneasy laugh, and taps her steering wheel a little harder, a little out of time. I've never seen her nervous before. Old Mim seemed incapable of any emotion but for bitter snark.

Grace Green's cottage is like something out of a storybook. A perfect place on the sea. White and fenced, moated by rose gardens. Mim pulls into the driveway and sits back in her seat. "I just haven't ever brought anyone home to her before. Anyone from, you know, like, those days. She doesn't know about the, well, you know, our, ah, little club. I mean," she says.

"You don't have to tell her about that. You can just tell her about us."

"Us? I guess. You mean just, like, tell her you're a friend? Which you are. It's not like we're . . . It's just . . . I don't know."

I inhale, count, exhale. Then I ease myself out of the car.

"Jemima Gates, where have you been?" Grace Green still looks like her '90s self. Her hair chopped into a pixie cut that matches Mim's new style, her smile wide, her body athletic. She's wearing an all-white suit. "And who is this poor beaten-up soul?"

"This is Rose," says Mim, pushing me forward. "Rose, this is Grace."

I hold out my good hand to shake but Grace pulls me into a hug. Her arms are strong, and I feel that if she squeezed just a little tighter, my bones might shatter in her grip. I hiss when she presses against my ribs. She leaps back, apologizing.

"It's okay," I assure her. "They're just bruised. And it's so nice to meet you, Mrs. Green," I say. "Or Ms.? Um, my mum did your workout pretty religiously. She never made it thirty days, though."

Grace smirks. "No one ever did," she says. "That was the trick of it. After day one, you're in too much pain to do a second day. And if you manage two days in a row, no way can you do a third. That, girls"— she smiles—"is called *business*."

I laugh. Mim is too busy watching, glancing between Grace and me and Grace again, to have caught the joke.

"And good god, call me Grace," she says. "Call me Grace. Jemima does."

"Thank you for having me at your home, Grace," I say. "I won't overstay my welcome."

"No, you won't," says Grace. "That would be impossible, given that your welcome is infinite."

I duck my head and whisper a thanks as Grace leads us into the cottage. White wooden floors and white-painted walls. The rafters hang low, and the windows are huge. The space inside is bright, but not in the sterile, clinical way that the facility had been bright, not in the way that forces a wince, that makes one feel weaker than they are. This brightness feels illuminating. Like a blank page. The start of something.

"You have a beautiful home," I say.

"This old thing?" Grace says, smiling. "What can I get you girls for lunch?" she says. Then, "Trick question. I've already got bread in the oven. Freshly baked. I'm making French rolls. Ham and cheese on fresh baguette."

I swallow. "I've got these." I hold up my bag of CalSips.

Grace hums and nods. "Ah," she says. "You're one of *those*. Jemima was, too, but we soon fixed her, didn't we, Jemmy?"

"Jemmy," I repeat.

"Shut up," Jemima says to me. "Don't you start calling me that."

"Jemmy will show you where to put your things. And why are you still wearing that awful hospital gown? Get changed. Jemima, give Rose something to wear."

The guest bedroom is nautical themed. The duvet is striped blue and white, and a large wooden anchor hangs on one wall. Seashells decorate most surfaces, and a little sailor teddy bear sits between the pillows.

"This is you," says Mim, setting my bags on the floor. I look at her. Her pixie cut makes her face look younger. Her eyes wider. She has a splatter of freckles sprinkling her nose and a crescent-shaped scar beneath her eyebrow like a shadow. She is so human in a way she hadn't been back before the facility, when she was more of an idea than a person, a character. Almost animated. If I had forced old Mim into this seaside cottage, she would have stood out like a terrible blemish, all dressed in black, eyeliner so heavy it looked like a villain's mask, frame so thin she could snap at any moment. I wonder if I look like a blemish here, too.

"Thank you," I whisper.

"For what?" She snorts.

"I think you might be saving my life," I say, and then descend into my humiliated redness. "Sorry," I say. "That was so stupid."

Mim looks away, clears her throat. "I'll just go get you some, ah, something to wear."

She leaves the room, giving me time to return to my natural hue, and I sit on the foot of the bed. The mattress dips under my weight. I sigh, rub my temples in slow, small circles. If only, I think, now and usually, I could twist off an ear like loosening a bolt. Swing my face back on its hinges. I could rewire my brain myself.

When Mim returns, sees me sitting there, fantasizing my self-surgery, she stops in the door, cocks her head. Then she waves as if I hadn't seen her in a long time, a swooping, over-the-head wave, like a father wanting to be found in a crowd. I smile, wave back.

She holds out a pair of white underwear and a dress. I frown at the outfit choice. "My pants wouldn't stay up on you," Mim explains. "It's a T-shirt dress," she says. "It's meant to be baggy, and it definitely will be on you."

I nod and take it from her. She doesn't leave, doesn't avert her eyes. So, I stand, lift the hospital gown, one-handed, watching her all the while. My ribs protest partway, and, when I gasp, she takes the hem of the gown and gentles it over my head. When I step out of my old underwear, she clears her throat, but lets her eyes wander down my neck, chest, stomach, and then settle between my legs.

Her gaze isn't that of a doctor or a nurse, inspecting my weight. It isn't Lily's terrified stare of unrecognition. It isn't women in public whose eyes glare with some putrid potion of pity and jealousy and wonderment. Mim's eyes are wanting and bare. To feel wanted.

I step closer to her, and then I am wrapped in her arms. "I have to apologize to you," she whispers into my hair. I shake my head. My nudity presses against her jeans. She steps into me until I have to step away. She holds my body as she lowers me onto the bed and then lowers herself until she is hovering above me.

We stay that way, her body above mine, and I feel safe there, beneath her. As if she were the lid to my container.

"You're like my lid," I say.

"What?" she says.

"Lid," I say.

"I don't get it."

"Sorry." I blink to break the eye contact. "Nothing."

Mim smirks her signature smirk and climbs off me. "I love that blush," she says.

I shrug.

"Rose," she says. "I owe you an apology."

I say nothing.

"That diet, back in school. I was an idiot. I can't believe I, I just can't help but think that, I'm just . . ." She wipes at her eyes and turns to me, tears glaze her cheeks, she sniffs. "I'm as bad as this Lara Bax person. I'm worse. I am so, so sorry, Rose."

I laugh and tuck my hand into hers, her fingers weave between mine. "As if this could all be your fault." She looks at me, trusting, and I lift her arm, flip it, and kiss the soft underside of her wrist. "Ego much?" I say.

She dries her eyes on her arm, the one not stamped with my kiss. "I mean it, Rose. I've been wanting to say this for a long time. The things I did, the way I was, I was so unhappy. And I was confused. I was having these feelings for girls, for you, and I was afraid, and I know none of this is an excuse. I just, I couldn't control myself, so instead I controlled you, you girls, all of you, it's terrible. Looking back, I just . . . The point is, Rose, that even if I can explain why I acted the way I did, even if there were reasons for it, it doesn't change the fact that it hurt you. It doesn't make it hurt you less."

"Understanding it makes it hurt less." She looks at me, unblinking. "I forgive you."

"You shouldn't. You should hate me."

"But I love you."

"But I hurt you."

"But you loved me."

"I still love you."

We look at each other, puffed from the emotional duel. We wouldn't reach the conversation's conclusion today, but I'd think back on this moment many times throughout my life. I'd think back to here, lying on this bed with Mim, trying to understand what had happened between us, what was happening between us. When I was older, wrinkles reaching like fingers from the corners of my eyes, the skin around my mouth parenthesized with the echoes of smiles past, I would wake one morning, early, and, before my eyes coaxed themselves into opening for the day, I'd roll onto my side and see Mim there, still asleep and peaceful, and I'd feel happy. I'd feel, not heavy, but full. And I'd imagine, the way we do, all of the ways in which my life might not be this exact life. All the ways in which things might've gone even just slightly differently, had I not kissed that soccer player at the pool during Sister Missed-Her, had I not given that banana a blow job in the cafeteria, had Lily not met Phil, had I never called Mim from the facility, had I not fallen at Lara Bax's house, had I not fought with Lily at the hospital . . . All these years in the future, I'd feel so grateful that, despite so many mistakes, my life seemed to be the best possible outcome of itself. I'd feel grateful for forgiveness, that harm does not necessarily beget grudge, or hate, or resentment. Sometimes we hurt the ones we love the most. Forgiveness, that magical elixir, can turn any stewing emotion into love—add two drops to the brew and see what can become!

But, for now, many years before that morning, that morning when I would kiss my wife's eyelids awake, for now I only tuck my head into the crook of her neck and smell her, salty from the sea air and her own sweat, and I feel so at home here, with my body beside hers.

"Did you just smell me?" She snorts a laugh. "Come on, little one," she says, standing, and pulling me with her. "Time for lunch."

I ache my way to my feet, her hand in mine all the while. I would still go anywhere for Mim. Even to lunch.

36

I sip my CalSip as Mim and Grace eat crusty baguette rolls filled with slices of ham and sharp cheddar. I watch Mim eat, tear the bread with her teeth, carnivorous, chew, swallow, all while talking to Grace, seemingly unaffected by the calories she's consuming.

"You know," says Grace, pointing at my drink and breaking my Mim gaze, "those things aren't food."

"I know," I say, sipping. "They're awful."

"So why keep drinking them?"

"They're safe," I say. "They're what I know."

Grace nods. "Safe is often boring," she says. "And sometimes what you know isn't what's best for you."

I sip. Swallow.

"For dinner, I'm making grilled fish, spinach, and baby potatoes. A light meal. Will you try some?"

I sigh. Talking about dinner at lunch. The thought of three meals a day makes my stomach tilt. Imagine being an eater! The food would be nonstop. Eating until you have to eat again.

"If you're just going to keep drinking those things, you might as well have stayed in the hospital," says Grace. "Drinking those is not recovering. You can't recover from an eating disorder unless you *eat.*"

My expression must shut down, the way I know it does when people try to preach recovery to me. Healthy people do it all the time. Doctors. Lily. Even my parents back before they gave up. Mim must see the change because she sets a soft hand on my shoulder. "Grace was sick, too," she says. "Orthorexia and excessive exercising."

"Why do you think I started Absolute Abs?" says Grace. "I was obsessed. I was only eating organic vegetables. Breakfast, lunch, and dinner. I ate so many tomatoes I'm surprised I didn't turn into one." She finishes her sandwich and wipes her mouth with a napkin. "And I was doing six workouts a day. One before every meal, and another one after. I was obsessed with sweating out double the calories I ate, like I thought it would cut me in half or something." She chuckles and shakes her head, as if the memory were almost fond. "I don't know where I found the energy."

"How'd you recover?" I say.

"I had an accident. I was running, on my twentieth mile of the day, and I'd probably eaten a handful of snap peas, maybe a couple of grapes. I was running on fumes." She closed her eyes. "I ran in front of a car. The driver braked, but he couldn't stop in time. He hit me. I rolled over his windshield. Broken hip, ribs, collarbones, both arms, a leg. I was in the hospital for weeks, and my eating was monitored, which probably helped, but beyond that, I was kind of shocked back to life, I think. I couldn't believe I had survived. I couldn't believe how my body was healing itself, so resilient. I hadn't been respecting myself, my body, any of it. And I promised myself that once my body was better, I would be, too."

I nodded. I understood. "I don't think I really know what ortho-rexia is," I say.

"Oh." Grace smiles. "Of course you don't. Us orthos are way down the bottom of the ED food chain. You anorectics take the cake." She snorts at the irony of the expression. Mim-like in her laugh that gets caught somewhere in her sinuses. "It goes anorectics, bulimics, like our Jemmy here was, then bingers, then restrictors, then maybe orthorexics, picas, and, below them, even, are the overeaters."

"Orthorexics are pretty common," says Mim. "Those Instagram diets. Eating clean and everything. None of it is normal, babe."

"I don't think that's an eating disorder," I say. "That's more like a lifestyle."

Mim snorts her inherited snort. "Said just like an Insta-dieter. There's a difference between eating healthy and the kind of green smoothie diets those girls are on. They're all disordered eaters. I don't think there's one girl left in the world who isn't fucked up about food. Sorry, Grace. I meant *messed* up. How are we meant to be normal about eating when we're taught to count calories before we learn long division? None of it is normal."

I sniff. "You said pica?" I turn to Grace. "What's pica?"

"Eating the inedible," Mim jumps in while Grace picks at a fallen piece of cheese on her plate. "Like what your sister is doing with those zero-calorie things. If they don't have calories, I'm pretty sure they're not food. Actually, I've been thinking about this. Like, if we can make a case, if we can accuse Lara Bax of encouraging, instigating, even, disordered eating, then she'll be shut down for sure."

"But—"

"I'll join," says Mim. "I'll join this YourWeigh thing. This Lara person knows you, but she doesn't know me. So I'll join and document it. Get some quotes. Maybe some footage. We'll make a strong case, and we'll win. Lily will be out of there in no time."

I close my eyes, suddenly exhausted. "I don't think— "

"I'm not going to sit here and do nothing," she says, her hand covering mine. "Not this time."

"I just—"

Mim squeezes my fingers, and it's an embrace. "It's not going to stop Lily from dating that guy, but at least it might stop her from eating that zero-calorie shit all the time."

I swallow. "Okay. Thank you," I say. "Thank you," I say again. And I feel lighter in the realization that Lily might be saved. Nearly weightless.

There's an animal called a collared pika that survives on a diet of flowers. They spend their summers collecting up to thirty times their body weight in flora, then nibble on petals as the weather cools down.

"Hello?" says Mim.

"Hello?"

She waves. "Hi," she says, a smile. She holds out her hand to shake. "I'm Mim. Nice to meet you. Where'd you go?"

"Where'd I go?"

"You were somewhere, up there, in your head."

"Tired," I say, and I am! I yawn.

"Bed," says Mim.

There's a news article about Kat Mitchells's death. Then another one and another one. *TROUBLED child star Kat Mitchells STARVES herself to DEATH,* say the articles. They show photographs of her, a stew of them. Smiling onstage, drunk in a club, a mug shot, one of her at her highest weight in a bikini, another at her lowest, also in a bikini, kissing a woman, kissing another, the photograph I had on my bedroom wall, and a final photo of the facility. From the outside, it almost looks like a resort. Each photograph is captioned in the same way, as if there were a formula for it. *Kat Mitchells, skinny onstage! Kat Mitchells, curvy in the club! Kat Mitchells looking newly busty in Barbados! Kat Mitchells is all bones in the Bahamas!* Name + body-related adjective + location = caption.

At the bottom of each article: *If you have an eating disorder, you can get help. Visit www.eatingdisorderhelp.com for more information.*

Nowhere in the article: *Stop commenting on women's bodies.*

37

Days pass easily in that white cottage by the sea. Each morning, I wake and take a long, slow walk along the sand, sometimes with Mim, sometimes alone. The beach smells of morning no matter the time of day, and the salt of the ocean spray paints my skin in a new, tighter layer. The wind blows like shaken laundry. I like to walk barefoot, and sometimes a shell cuts my skin, and it hurts, and sometimes the sand is loose and it slips out from underneath me a little, but this all feels important, and, even when these things happen, I keep walking.

After my walk, I sit on the porch with a mug of coffee, watching the waves harass the shore with an awful persistence. The sun rises above the mountains slowly, and then, all at once, there it is, proudly announcing its rotundity, fearlessly taking up space. Day.

I only stand when I hear movement in the kitchen, which means breakfast. Sometimes I have a CalSip, sometimes I stick to coffee, sometimes I have a grape or even a handful. Grace and Mim usually eat toast with butter, two foods I can't fathom ever eating, but some days, when they aren't so hungry, they make a fruit salad, and I have a bowl of it, and it feels so normal to eat what others are eating.

Tasting is difficult. I don't do it well. It's as if I've forgotten how. I remember liking foods as a kid. Getting excited about pizza night and salivating over candy in October. I remember disliking foods, too. Wincing about broccoli and scrunching my nose at mayonnaise. Tasting is different now. Like trying to hear a coveted whispered secret on a crowded dance floor. Things I know are low calorie make me happy, heavier foods are frightening, and it is difficult to find taste beneath all of the calories shouting their values like eager learners in math class. I think, though, that I definitely like strawberries. The way their flesh sweetens with every moment in the mouth.

After breakfast, Mim goes to classes while I tidy Grace's house, do the laundry, make the beds, weed the garden, hose sea salt from the house's exterior and the fence. Cleaning is how I know to earn my keep. It's more difficult than it had been in the facility, since I'm one-handed now, the other arm still stuck in a sling, but I've become accustomed to the impediment. The way we do. Humans are so resilient; we can live through almost anything, adjust to such drastic change.

Once I'm done with my chores, Grace and I sit down for lunch. She caters to me, calorie-wise, so we usually eat cold vegetables. Carrots and celery, cucumbers and tomatoes, all sliced into sticks. Grace dips hers in hummus and pesto, ranch dressing and oils. I eat mine naked, but sometimes, if I'm feeling good, brave, I will drizzle a sprinkle of fat-free dressing over a mouthful before I chew, and the flavor is welcome on my virgin palate.

The fairy godmother trope was likely born from Cinderella. A character who appears out of nowhere to help the protagonist overcome an obstacle. But in the original story, Cinderella's godmother was truly her godmother. She did not appear—poof!—a magic trick. She was there all along and stepped forward when needed most. In life, there are godmothers everywhere. Strangers who step forward—poof!—when they're needed most.

When Mim gets home from her afternoon YourWeigh meeting, she tells me about the session and I copy down any quotes that might hold up in a lawsuit. Mim is in full-swing detective mode. I feel less confident that we're on track to take down Lara Bax's whole operation, but I don't let on. Mim's excitement is effervescent, and I love watching her new energy rise.

The problems with our plan are obvious to me. There are countless diets just like this one in the world, and none of them have been shut down for causing harm. Neither Mim nor I have any understanding of the law nor how to go about using it. We keep referring to things as *evidence* without really knowing what *evidence* means. Still, it feels as if we are doing something, really *doing* something, and it feels good. I understand why those men push airplanes down runways with their bare hands. Why activists chain themselves to old trees and scream, *TAKE ME INSTEAD*—it feels good to do something.

I think of Lily as we toil, of the other women who are following Lara Bax's unattainable diet. I think of how healthy they could all be because of me, millions of them, and it feels good. I realize that I like to help. That I want to help people. It's the first time I've ever had a goal, an aspiration, something to live toward.

We prepare dinner together each night, us girls. I do the vegetables, Mim does the proteins, and Grace does the carbs. I make vegetables I feel unafraid of, starting out with undressed salads that the other two can load up with extra calories if they want to, and raw vegetable sticks, and boiled greens on the colder nights. Mim makes chicken or fish, tofu or eggs, lighter proteins that I have a better chance of taking a bite of. Grace bakes fresh breads that make the house smell of heaven, and buttered mashed potatoes, oily fries, and piles of spiced rice. I'm not ready for Grace's part yet. Even Mim eats those foods sparingly.

We eat together, around the dining table, and the other two agree to keep their eyes on their own plates during the meal. I am tired of being monitored, watched like a villain about to commit some terrible crime.

Maybe it's the house, or the beach, or Mim, or Grace, maybe it's Kat's death or Lily's anger, or my own injury. Something about this time, this decision to recover, is different. I could hide the food, escape the calories, if I wanted to, but I don't, so I don't.

We sip herbal tea around the fireplace into the night. Mim and Grace sometimes nibble on dark chocolate, and, smelling the cocoa in the air, I remember that I had definitely liked chocolate in the past.

One night, Mim lets me press the pad of my thumb against a square of her chocolate and then stamp the taste onto my tongue. The flavor is familiar and delicious and terrifying; I resist the urge to spit it into the fire. Mim watches me and whispers, "It's okay. Look at you. Nothing happened. Nothing changed. It's okay." She hushes me until the urge subsides.

It is sacred time, our evenings around the fireplace, and we are not allowed to speak of food or of Lara Bax or our plan. These are the rules, and they are good rules. We enforce them together, gently steering one another away from the forbidden conversation points if we ever veer too close. Instead, we talk about our lives. Grace tells us of her great losses, greater loves. Her husband, who left her after Mim's mother was born. Her wife, who left her because she wouldn't, couldn't, stop exercising.

Mim speaks about her friends who died, and then smiles her way through the ones who lived. I mostly listen, because I haven't lived yet. Not a life outside of food or my disorder. And I can't talk about those things here. My silence makes me want to live, to have stories and memories, to have wants and desires. Hobbies and interests. Things to be passionate about and to want to talk about. The only time I speak up is when we talk of art, Mim about its history, Grace about her love of collecting it, me about all the things I want to create. When we bid one another good night, it is because our eyes are already halfway closed.

"No more chores." Grace stops me from picking up the mop on a brisk, windy morning. The seaside brings wind with it. The air here has no sense of personal space, and it is always moving, always pressing itself against you, winding its way around you. It has a way of making you feel touched and unalone. I vow to always live by the sea, where I can watch the waves thrash the sand, abuse the rocks with such an enraged persistence, smooth the craggy cliffs, slowly, wave by wave by day, month, year, into smooth sheets of rock that look stronger, and that seem to console and embrace the water, rather than remain its victim.

"I have a different idea for you today," Grace says, putting the mop back into its cupboard.

"But the floors," I say. "It's Tuesday, isn't it? Floor day."

"You are dangerously interested in routine," says Grace. "And in habit. It's no wonder you caught on to that diet so quickly." I had told her about the Apple-a-Day Diet, which she had thought would absolutely catch on were it to be publicized and commercialized. The media loved a fad diet, she told us, when she spoke of the rise of Absolute Abs. Two almonds every hour to keep belly fat at bay or a liter of water before every meal as a natural appetite suppressant, licorice teas that induced diarrhea and miracle pills that swelled in the stomach. Women rushed to each new diet and jumped on board as if what they were mounting were a lifeboat, come to save them from their own fatness. They would spend millions on trainers and surgery, because excess is gorgeous unless the excess is you. Grace was treated as a goddess. Women begged her for tips; everyone wanted the miracle solution to their own bodies.

"But just because something is routine doesn't mean it has to be your forever. Routines can, and should, be broken. Or you'd be doing the same thing your whole life, wouldn't you?"

I say nothing. I feel boring.

"Here," says Grace, leading me by the hand. Hers is very thin and frail, which shocks me, given how strongly she speaks, how proudly, confidently she holds herself. "Come with me." She leads me to the garage, which has no cars in it. Grace doesn't own one, and Mim says her bag-of-trash car doesn't deserve a home or a roof.

"The door doesn't even work." Grace laughs, knocking her knuckles against the garage door and enjoying the echo. "I never got it wired up! It's a room with no purpose."

I feel sorry for the room. Unable to function as itself. "Look," says Grace, pointing to a stack of canvases in one corner, a pile of supplies in the other. "I haven't made it into a studio because I'm a weak old girl, but here is everything you need."

"You got me this?" I look around. "Why? I mean, thank you. But why?"

"You need to create," she says. "I've heard you talk about art. About painting. You did that painting for the woman, the one with the child and the elephant tattoo. Laura? Art is important to you. It makes you happy."

I'm not sure how everyone knows this about me, but I do feel a great joy at seeing the paints, the brushes, the canvases white with possibility. "Lara," I say. And it is all I can say.

"That's right. Lara. Now, I want a painting for every wall," says Grace. "It's too white in here! And no more chores until you've covered the house."

"Grace," I say.

"Rose," says Grace.

"No," I say. "I mean—"

"Be quiet," says Grace. "And get to work! Chop chop! I want you started before lunch. Which, by the way, is grilled vegetables today."

I look at her. *Grilled* means oil.

"I'm using avocado oil," she says.

"I'll have to watch," I say. "I'll have to watch you cook them."

And she nods. She understands. She understands that if I don't watch how much oil she puts on, I would imagine she'd used butter, lard, and had ladled the stuff into my food, packed it full of so much fat I would balloon with a single bite.

"I'll call you when I start," she says. Then—"Too-da-loo"—she leaves me to work.

I choose the biggest canvas. An enormous square. It is taller than me, and its size is loud, an announcement. "Hi," I say to it. "Hello. I only have one arm," I tell it, waving my slinged wing. "See?"

The canvas says nothing, not least because it is an object.

"It's just that this whole painting thing might be more difficult with one arm," I explain. "I don't want you to think it's your fault."

I think of Lily's book, *WE*. The way I feel so connected to it in a way I only ever feel aligned with things that have something to do with Lily. The words are powerful, and they are good. I want to talk to her about it, about where the ideas came from, about whether they came from her life, and I suspect they did, a suspicion that makes bile bubble inside me. Lily always told me everything, she talked about her life, filled our relationship with herself, her words, her experiences, until I was pushed to the side, taking up only the sliver of space that remained, but, I am growing to realize, Lily mightn't have really told me anything at all.

With the book in my mind, the first story I had read, about the *we* losing their virginities, becoming a garden, I take the blue, the yellow, and a dash of white, and pool them together until they make something organic-looking, grassy. I start to gesture across the canvas, thinking of Lily's story, the *we*, and thinking of Lily, of us.

When Grace leans in through the doorway, I'm too involved in my motions to stop. "I'm going to start grilling," she says, hushed. I only nod and keep painting, keep moving, keep dreaming.

She returns with the vegetables soon after and pulls a folding chair over from the storage side of the garage. She sits, the plate on her lap, and every so often stands to pop a disk of zucchini between my lips, a wedge of eggplant, a slice of bell pepper. I taste the oil in the vegetables, but the flavor is warm and the texture is soft and I swallow each one that is fed to me, working all the while.

38

That night, when Mim gets home from her YourWeigh meeting, she finds me and Grace, sitting, looking at the painting, which I finished over a half hour ago. We're watching it dry, how the colors settle into themselves.

"That," says Mim, and then nothing else. As if the very thought has left her.

We all watch the painting. I'm not sure if it's good, or if I like it, but something about it makes it watchable, makes me want to keep seeing it. The colors are vibrant, screaming pinks and greens, blues and oranges. The shapes suggest vegetation, gardens, flowers, trees. The lines, angles, suggest violence, the arches, curves, bring a gentleness. Everything is at once feminine and soft, strong and powerful.

Grace is the first to stand, groaning as she does so. Her orthorexia had done a number on her joints. Like a mistreated dog, her body has grown old before she has.

"You are so afraid to take up space," she says. "In life, you don't want to take up any. But look at what happens when you do." She stretches, and her back creaks like an old hinge. "I'm going to make dinner. You girls are off cooking duty tonight. Rose has done a hard day's work."

I go to change, and Mim follows me to the bedroom. My muscles strain, tired elastics, my bones ache, every part of me is sore from the movement, the exercise of art. The pain isn't unpleasant. It's nice to feel my body exist. To feel like it belongs to me.

"Take a bath," says Mim as I groan my way out of the day's clothes, which is the same black T-shirt dress Mim gave me on the day I was discharged from the hospital. I still haven't retrieved anything from Lily's place. Mim takes the plastic bag I use for my cast when I shower and tucks my arm into it, knotting it tight. "I'll go run it for you," she says, and skips off to the bathroom.

I step out of my underwear and toss it into a laundry basket. Then I open my closet to hang the dress. On the inside of the wardrobe, there is a mirror, a big full-length one that would let me see my whole body at once if I let it. I close the door quickly, not wanting to know if I have gained any weight, which I surely have, given that I have been eating—not much, but still, food—for the first time in years.

I read somewhere, maybe back in the facility, where the books were random donations, flotsam and jetsam from local strangers, that, in 2010, the Bolivian government granted all living things equal rights to humans. I also read that Bolivia was home to the world's largest mirror. I do not believe these two facts to be unrelated. Mirrors force you to see you.

When I started starving myself, I loved to look in mirrors. Not because I wanted to see my body, but because I wanted to see what wasn't there anymore. I wanted to see how much of me had been erased. I wanted to see how little of me remained.

Mim is sitting on the edge of the bathtub, reading the back of a shampoo bottle, when I get to the bathroom. She has one hand dangling in the water, testing the temperature, and, when I arrive, she turns the faucet off.

"Let me know if it's too hot," she says. I could have cried at it. When someone cares about you, really cares about you, they don't even want your big toe to be uncomfortable, not even for a glimpse.

I drop my towel, so accustomed to Mim seeing my body by now, even liking how carefully she watches me, and step into the tub, wincing at the warmth. It is too hot, but sometimes it's okay to be uncomfortable. Sometimes it reminds you how to be human.

I get used to the temperature and the water accommodates me, swarms around me, laps at my sore skin like a lover. I lower myself, sinking, until only my face is above the surface, and my submerged ears hear the sea.

Too hot? Mim mouths from up in the world. I shake my head at her and smile. She looks like something famous up there. Something divine.

She squirts a pool of body wash into her palm and rubs the soap into a lather. Then she lifts one of my legs and begins to wash me, feet first, her hands moving in quick, persistent circles, from my heels, ankles, calves, knees, she works her way up my leg and then back down the other. She washes between my legs, too, with such soft hands, while my blush spreads like something spilled. Mim doesn't stop until she has explored my whole body with her soapy fingers. Until I have been seen all over, she has seen me, and she is still here.

I reach for her T-shirt, wanting, and she pulls away.

"Oh, come on," I say. "That's not fair."

"Life isn't fair, babe," says Mim.

I watch her eyes as I tug the drawstring of her sweatpants, pull the knot undone, finger the string free. She smirks. I run my thumb around the elasticated waistband and dip a finger beneath the horizon of her underwear, where her pubis is rough with new hair sprouting. She swallows audibly. I smile, raise my eyebrows, asking for permission. She lifts the hem of her T-shirt over her head, holds it there, covering her face like an opaque veil. "Don't look at me," she says.

"Too late," I whisper, as she undresses herself, trying, and failing, to shield as much of her body as possible as she does so.

"Close your eyes," she says.

"No."

"Don't," she says, "please, just don't, just don't." And I don't think either of us knows what she means. She stands, one arm diagonally across her stomach, the other covering her thighs, crouched into a little fetal pose. Only a former thin girl would choose to cover such areas instead of what we are taught to be ashamed of: the vagina, the breasts. But Mim is beautiful. She still looks like a model. She is tall,

lean, but now she looks like a living person, someone who isn't hurting all the time, hurting herself all the time.

"I don't look the same anymore," she says.

"Of course you don't." I reach for her hand, but she steps away.
"You've changed. You've changed in so many ways, but they're all
good ways. You've become kind and caring and loving. And look at
you, you're healthy."

She wipes tears from her cheeks.

"You have changed," I say. "In such good ways. I'm trying to change,
too. To be more like you. The new you."

She looks at me. Vulnerable.

"You are so beautiful, Mim," I tell her. "Look at your arms. They're
strong. And your hips look like a movie star's. You are so fucking
beautiful standing there right now. I swear." There is an anger to my
honesty. I'd love every part of her she couldn't.

Mim snorts in the way she does, and then she slowly unfurls, like
some afraid stray animal being offered food by a stranger, her eyes
are on mine as she uncovers each part of herself, bares her flesh and
exposes her body to me, only me.

I reach for her, find her hips with my hands, and pull her toward
me. I kiss a belt across her pelvis, then down her hip, her thigh, her
calf, and lift her leg into the tub. She lifts the other in herself. When
she lowers her body next to mine, our limbs find each other, wind
around and around, tie themselves into knots that feel permanent.
I start to clean her, and I don't stop until my palms know all of her
parts.

39

The morning feels new, clean as fresh laundry, and we make coffee in the kitchen, side by side, and it is a scene that feels like forever. Like we could make coffee that way for the rest of our lives, stumbly with sleep, soft with echoes of the unconscious.

She steps around me for the sweetener and I duck beneath her arm for teaspoons and we brush each other's limbs, familiar as our own flesh, we each lift our mugs to our lips and breathe across the black surface, inhale the earthy scent, silent, a dance.

We step outside, so as not to wake Grace with our conversation, and once the screen door is closed, Mim takes a sip of coffee, sighs, the way she always does after the first taste.

I feel more human than I've felt in years. Being awake, really awake, tastes of toothpaste, the way it demands alertness. *I am alive and I am here!* Squinting into the morning sun, blinking, dazzled, so unabashedly here.

The Laysan albatross, after mating, often settles down to lay her eggs with a second female albatross. In Hawaii, about 31 percent of the species' population is in a same-sex relationship. The two mothers raise the offspring together. They stay together for life.

"Hello?" says Mim. "Hello?"

"Hello?"

"Welcome back," she says. "I'm Mim."

I smile.

"Where do you go when that happens?" she says. "Are you up

there?" She runs the pad of her thumb across my forehead, a blessing, a miracle.

"I'm usually just thinking. Just remembering."

"What was it this time?"

"I was just thinking about something I read once. It's stupid."

"What was it?"

"Oh." I shrug. My face warms. "Just this thing about albatrosses. About a third of them are lesbians."

"Really?" Jemima laughs, my favorite song in the world. "Lesbian birds? Lesbirds?"

I nod.

"That's fascinating."

"Is it?"

"I could listen to your facts all day, you know. You spend so much time up there in your head; you always have, even when we were kids. You and Lily always seemed to be able to talk without talking. You'd think things and she'd know I was jealous. I'm not a mind reader, Rose, I can't do what Lily did, but I do want to know everything. I love hearing your brain happen."

Hearing my brain happen.

"I want all of it, Rose. All of you."

Have you ever had someone want all of you? Animal and all?

We're quiet for a while, looking out over the ocean, watching the whole world happen. Then Mim clears her throat. "So I've been thinking."

"Are you sure that's a good idea?"

"Funny." She cradles her mug in her palms. "I think you should enroll in art school."

I go to take a sip, but Mim's hand is already there, covering the mouth of my mug. "No," she whispers. "Too hot."

I look at her. She smiles. "What! You're a baby about heat!" She laughs. "You would have complained about your burned tongue all day."

I set my mug on the porch railing and let it cool in the sea breeze.

"So, art school," she says, "is where you should be."

I nod. "I think I'd like that."

"Seriously?"

"Yeah. Why do you seem surprised?"

She shakes her head. Sips. Then points at my coffee cup. "You can drink it now." Then, "I thought you'd put up a fight. You don't usually like new things."

"Yes, I do!" I say.

"Oh, please," says Mim. "You hate change."

"No," I say. "I don't hate it, I think, I just think I'm afraid of change."

"So what's new, then? Why now? Why the change of heart?"

"I mean . . ." I take a sip. The temperature is perfect. "I need to do *something* with my life, don't I?"

Later, Mim helps me carry my newest painting, the one based on Lily's first story, to my sister's apartment, which is only a few blocks from the cottage. We lean it up against the front door, and Mim raises her fist to knock. I catch her hand before it makes contact. I'm not ready yet. I pull Mim away from the door.

"What?" says Mim. "I thought the whole point of this was to apologize. You can't apologize if you don't . . . you know . . . apologize."

"I'm not ready," I say. "I want to show her how much better I am. How I'm healthier now. For her. And I'm not ready yet."

Mim takes my head to her chest and strokes my hair. "You're doing really well," she says. "You are doing so, so well." She holds my face at an arm's length. "And I am so proud of you, Riz." She smiles.

Our embrace is broken by a stomping on the stairs. We turn to inspect our intruder, and I swallow when I recognize his face. He is sweating from climbing the three floors to Lily's apartment, his T-shirt patched with perspiration, hair slicked down on his forehead like an anime character.

"Rosie!" says Phil. "How nice to see you again!" His jaw glitches. His Adam's apple gulps, rises and falls.

"Phil." I clear my throat.

Mim reaches for my hand.

"What're you doing here?" I say.

"Oh," he says, laughing, "I live here now. I moved in as soon as you left."

"Lara kicked you out?" I say.

"Oh, Rose," he says, scratching his skin, static. "You're funny." He smiles. "And you're looking well!" he says. "Much healthier!" And he means fatter. And he knows exactly what he's doing. When I say nothing, he reaches a hand, sets it on my shoulder. "We miss you, Rose," he says. "I hope you girls can work it out one day soon."

I shake his hand off. His knuckles are bruised, and I don't want to know why.

"Would you like me to bring this inside for Lily?" he asks, pointing at my painting.

"No," I say, and start off down the stairs. "Don't touch it," I say, towing Mim behind me.

On our way home, we pass our old coffee shop, where we once sat, the four of us, stooped over a table, chugging peppermint tea and sharing dieting tips, fasting and exercising, laxatives and diet pills. Mim storms past in her usual battling-a-headwind style. I slow, peer into the window, and then stop in front of it.

"No," says Mim. "Oh no, no, no."

"Don't you wonder about Flee?" I say. "Whether she's still going?"

Mim shakes her head and then says, "Of course I do. Every single day."

"Why don't we try to help?" I say. "Call her."

"She can only help herself."

Mim pulls on my hand, but I'm stuck fast.

"Rose," says Mim, using my full name for the first time in a long time. I turn to her, and she repeats my own words back to me. "I'm not ready yet," she whispers.

The next morning, I wake to a clenched stomach and slick skin. I reach between my legs and find a wetness there. My fingertips are painted red. I smile as I start to cry.

Mim hears my weeping and comes running. "What's wrong?"

But before I can swallow the latest sob, she sees the stained sheets, speckled a deep and beautiful red, and sighs. "I'm so proud of you," she whispers. And I want to be happy with her, but a period means a healthy body, and health means an existence I don't feel ready for.

"This is so normal," says Mim. "You're learning to be human again." She leaves and returns with a tampon. I take it from her, and the gesture is doused with nostalgia.

40

Some days I still want to cry and stitch my lips closed. Some days I still can't get out of bed. One morning, maybe my fifth or sixth or seventh day at Grace's—time bleeds—the phone beside my bed rang. It rang and rang and rang, and no one picked it up. No one picked it up because it was right there, beside my bed, mine to pick up. I ran through the motions a hundred times in my head. Roll over, take phone from cradle, lift to ear, speak. But I couldn't. Answering the phone, a herculean task, and so I watched it bleat, helpless, until finally it quieted.

Most days, though, most days I can get out of bed. Most days, these days, I can answer the phone.

It's Christmas Day. I wake early. I plan to leave the house before Mim or Grace are up, but Mim hears me pass her room in the hall.

"Leaving?" she whispers, careful not to wake her grandmother. I nod. She holds up a finger, a *wait right here* finger, a finger that means *I'm coming with you.* Imagine someone wanting to come with you without knowing where. Without caring where.

A note: *Be back soon.*

We walk for forty minutes, hand in hand, then grow tired and take the bus the rest of the way. The house, my childhood home, looks older. The grass in the front yard has grown wild, the paint on the outside, browned. The path leading up to the front door is potholed.

"You okay?" says Mim, when I hesitate, my fist raised to knock. Lily answers before I make contact with the door. She looks bad. Her skin is pale and gray, her eyes sunken deep in her face, shy or afraid.

She's holding her arms across herself, holding herself together. Her body, unrecognizable.

"Hi, Lily," says Mim.

"Jemima," says Lily. Even her voice is the pith of itself.

"Lil," I say. But she turns away.

"Why are you here?" she asks, leading us down the hall, toward the living room.

"I didn't think Dad should spend Christmas alone."

"He spends every day alone," says Lily. "He *is* alone."

Dad is sitting in his usual corner of the couch. If he were to stand, there would be a fossil there. Archaeologists could determine his exact size and weight from that imprint in the cushion. He looks so old. He doesn't look up when we enter. There are beer cans at his feet, loyal little pets. There are cigarettes on the couch next to him, companions.

"Dad?"

"G'day, kiddo," he says. I don't think he knows which twin I am. It's probably harder to tell these days.

"Merry Christmas?" I say.

"Is it?" He smiles. I don't know whether he means Christmas or merry.

"Hi, Mr. Winters," says Mim. "I'm Jemima Gates. I'm not sure if you remember me. I knew your daughters growing up."

Dad says nothing.

"How are you doing, Dad?"

"Just watching the game," he says. There's no game playing. There are newscasters on the television, talking about some game past. The volume is too low to hear what they're saying. Still, he's fixated.

"Is there anything I can get you?" I say.

He lifts his beer into the air and shakes the can to indicate *empty*.

"I'll get it," says Mim. "You three should talk."

When she leaves, the air does, too. The room dehydrates, grape turned raisin. I grab my throat, hold my neck, breathe. We have nothing to say to each other, my family. I wish we had a dog or something, anything at all, in common.

"Merry Christmas," I say, for the second time.

"Merry Christmas," says Lily.

"Is it?" He smiles again. It's a joke. He doesn't laugh. No one laughs. He's missing a tooth, and the rest aren't in good shape. I wish he'd close his mouth.

"Rose was discharged from the facility, Dad," Lily says, but she won't look at me. "They let her out."

"S'great. You look good." He's looking at Lily.

"She's painting now," says Lily. "You should see her work. She's good."

"Lil," I say. But still, she looks only at him.

"I'm in a relationship," she says. "His name is Phil."

"Phil," Dad says.

"You'll meet him soon. He couldn't make it today."

"On Christmas?" Dad says.

"Right," Lily says. "On Christmas." Her voice is flattened as road-kill. There's nothing left to her. No life.

"Here's your beer, Mr. Winters," says Mim, handing over a condensation-coated can. He pulls the tab and smiles his terrible new smile.

"Cheers," he says, raising the can into our bad circle.

"We should get going," I say. "We've got plans."

"Plans," says Dad.

"Plans?" says Lily.

"Places to be," I say. "Don't we, Mim?"

"Yes," she says. "Places."

"I'll walk you out," says Lily.

Dad says nothing. Lily leaves and Mim follows her. I take one last look at my father, sitting alone in the dark, in the dust, a throne of trash and grime.

He clears his throat. "That your girlfriend?" he says.

I swallow.

He turns away from the television and looks at me. His eyes, yellowed.

"Yeah," I say. "It is. She is."

He nods and turns back to the set. "Good."

"Bye, Dad," I say. "I'll come back sometime. I'll visit." I stop at the door, and, without turning around, without facing him, I say, "Dad, why didn't you ever talk to me about it?"

"About what, girlie?"

"I had to figure it all out myself, Dad," I told the door. "I had to go through all of it alone, and you were right there, right in the next room, feeling the exact same way. All you had to do was talk to me."

He sighs. I hear the clatter of his empty can being crushed in his grip. "I still can't talk about it, Rosie," he says. I turn, but he's not looking at me, either. He's confessing to the silent television. He looks so small, sitting there. "You're stronger than me, girlie. Always have been."

"That's a cop-out."

"Yeah," he says. "It is."

"I'm happy, you know."

"Yeah," he says. "I can see it."

"You could be happy, Dad."

But he's not listening anymore.

41

In the following days, I relinquish the paintbrush and, instead, I use words. Writing is Lily's language, and if I want her to hear me, I have to speak on her terms. I don't write well, but I take the stacks of magazines Grace has stored in her garage. She kept every issue of every weekly that featured Absolute Abs, and there are hundreds and hundreds of glossy pages preaching calorie counting and juice cleansing and flash fasting. I cut those harmful words from their pages. Make puncture wounds, then great, gaping holes in every article. Words like *fat* and *flab* and *wobbly* and *lose weight fast!* I cut whole paragraphs that peddle the pros of substituting meals with a kale tea that clears the gut out quick as an earthquake drill. Then I cut images. I find magazines with Mim staring out, her old self, gloomy and looming on the page, so thin she looks serrated. I cut out her clavicle, angular as ramps, and paste the picture to a canvas. I cut "before" images of Grace, sad-faced and baggy-clothed, and the "after" ones, too, smiling a tooth-whitened grin beneath her pink-lipsticked mouth. I paste them side by side beneath the caption *LOSE WEIGHT FAST.* I cut and paste and cut and paste and I fill the whole canvas with supermodel legs and cavernous cheeks and bugging eyes and red-circled cellulite and the words *fat, thin, summer beach body!*

By the time I am done, the piece is a screen of dismembered bodies and body-related adjectives. I add the title, *YOURWEIGH: THE LARA BAX DIET,* and leave the art to dry.

Mim comes to Lily's apartment with me for a second time. I press my ear against the door and hear the television playing some sitcom with a laugh track. Lily isn't laughing along. I wonder whether she is even home. Sometimes she leaves the television on to deter thieves, because, she always says, thieves would think the voices in the sitcoms were people in the apartment. I never told her that I thought her logic would be sounder if the television were left on so thieves would assume that people were in there watching it.

I kneel to try to peer under the door, closing one eye and squinting, but I can see only the fibers of her carpet, tall as a whole forest from down here. I sigh and stand, leaning my forehead against her door.

Eventually, when the sitcom rolls into advertisements and then another sitcom, and because I can't do it, Mim slips my canvas under my sister's door. Then she pulls it back.

"What?" I say.

"She doesn't know how to contact you," says Mim. "When she's ready, I mean."

She takes a pen from her purse and bites the lid off, then writes her phone number, her grandmother's address, and her school email on the back of the collage. "There," she says, and she holds my hand as she bends to slip the art under the door for the second time.

I hold my breath as we leave, and Mim reminds me to inhale, exhale.

On our walk home, I find myself stopping outside the coffee shop again, staring into the glass. I check the time. It's six p.m., our meeting time, back when we were a *we* and an *our*, and I turn to Mim, who backs away from the café, eyes afraid.

"Come," I say, and reach for her hands, but she won't take mine.

"You've been helping me," I say. "Let me help now."

She rolls her eyes. "We're not keeping score," she says.

"What? I know that."

She looks through the café's window, at the crowd in there, and then she looks at me. "She might not even be in there," she says. "She might have stopped."

"She might have," I say.

"She might be all better. Cured."

"She might be."

"She might be dead."

"Don't," I say.

"Okay." She takes a slow breath, then walks toward the door, clenched fists, headfirst, and just as she is about to go in, she wrings her hands and spins back toward me, shaking her fingers as if to fling water from them. "I can't."

"I'm coming with you," I say. "I'll be right behind you."

"In front of me?"

"Sure, if that's what you need."

"No, I'll go first," she says.

I nod.

"No, actually, you go first," she says.

I nod.

"No, actually, can you just come with me?"

I nod.

"Like beside me?"

I nod. "Go," I say.

"Come," she says.

We stand at the door, hand in hand, our fingers interwoven in their own special padlock. The frame is too narrow for us to fit side by side very easily. We each hold our outside arm in front of us and have to sort of turn diagonally as we enter to fit together. It takes us longer than necessary to get inside the shop.

Flee is easy to spot. She's at our usual table, tucked into the corner, blue mug lifted to her lips, wet tea bag sitting on her saucer.

I stare at her, looking dead, wet hair limp against bony face, and I feel wholly and entirely good about recovery for the first time. Of course I miss hunger, the empty ache of a vacant gut, and the feeling of two-dimensionality after a long fast. I long for that sense of invisibility, that if I were to be hungry just a few more moments, I might fade away into nothing at all. I miss being hungry, but I don't miss this. This miserable existence, this life not worth living.

"Mim?" Flee croaks. "Is that you? And who is that, wait, is that fucking Riz, too?" Two of her teeth have gone, eroded, eaten by the bile she kept forcing up, through her mouth, out. "What are you doing here?" she says, trying to stand from her table but falling back into her seat. She looks like a sick baby bird, dirty and made of bones.

Mim breathes a long exhale and then says, "Hi, Flee." She turns to me, a flicker of doubt, quick as a faulty neon sign.

"You got fat, Mim," says Flee. There is a half-eaten SkinnyBar sitting on the table.

"Shut up," I say, defensive.

"Just saying," says Flee.

"It's okay, Rose," says Mim. "I'm okay."

Mim sits down across the table. She stretches her legs out before her and then tucks them under each other, like a kindergartner. She looks calm, as if she was prepared for this, as if she knows exactly what to do. I stand farther away, feeling like I might at a party of acquaintances. I had never belonged here, but I do belong with Mim, and so I stay, feeling like Michael Cera at almost any point in his life.

"You look fucking awful," says Mim. "Really fucking gross."

"Least I'm not fat," says Flee.

"Shut the fuck up." Mim laughs.

I smile at her strange vernacular. It's the Mim I had known. The Mim I knew from outside of her domestic self, so different from her cottage self and the Mim she is around Grace. The curse words are awkward from her lips at first, as if she were trying to pick up a language she had learned at high school and long neglected. But soon she is fluent again, the cusses spilling from her lips, natural as an exhale.

"This has to stop," says Mim. "I know what I said before. About needing to support each other's disorders. I know I said that, but I was stupid. I was wrong when I thought we could live this way. I'm saying now that nothing I said back then stands. You need help, Flee."

Flee looks hurt. She picks up the SkinnyBar, takes a bite, chews. "Zero calories," she says as her teeth squeak against the rubbery texture.

"I brought you here in the first place," says Mim. "I found you. I encouraged the dieting and the tea and the laxatives. All of it. And now I'm saying it's done." She is brave and fierce. I watch her wild eyes scan her small audience, attentive but despising. "We're done here."

Flee laughs, her autumnal mouth wide and possessed. "It's not that simple," she says, the laugh still echoing. "And you know that. Not all of us have famous grandmothers in cottages. Not all of us are rich white kids who can get checked into the fancy facilities like Riz, there. I have nothing. No house. No parents. No friends. I haven't got anyone left."

"You've got me," says Mim. "And you've got Rose. Riz. R . . ." She looks at me, questioning.

"Rose is fine," I say, wanting the sudden attention gone.

"And you've got Rose," says Mim. "And that's enough. We're enough."

Flee looks around the coffee shop. "So what?" she says.

"So we start meeting again," says Mim. "But this time they're recovery meetings."

"Recovery?"

"That's right." Mim stands, paces the perimeter of the table, taps her fingers against her thigh, plotting. "Recovery meetings. They'll be held in my grandmother's cottage. Same time, six p.m."

"You can't just come back and—"

"I just did," says Mim. She is so sure of herself. This was what makes a leader, this certainty in one's own existence. I watch Mim speak, entranced. "Are you joining us?"

"Why would I?" Flee sneers, holding her hip bones as if all that is holding them together is her own grip on herself. "You left."

"Because I want to help you recover."

"And what if I don't want to?"

"Then don't come," says Mim. "I'm not making you come. I'm not making anyone do anything. But if you're interested in getting better. Surviving. Recovering. Then my grandmother's house is open to you every day at six p.m. I'll provide the snacks," she adds. I am the only one who laughs.

Before Flee can answer, Mim takes my hand and starts heading for the door. "I hope to see you there, Flee," she calls over her shoulder. I turn back, and Flee's eyes are bright on Mim, as if she were walking in a spotlight.

That night, after I take myself to bed, a little earlier than usual given the big day, I feel a presence in my room. Not like a spiritual presence. Mim is standing beside my bed, leaning over me, her face hovering above mine.

"Can I join you?" she whispers, and I shuffle closer to the edge of the mattress to make space. The whoosh of air that accosts me when she pulls back the duvet makes me shiver and my body is alive all over. "Warm." She smiles into my back, pressing her body against mine.

"Bad dream?" I whisper, not wanting to wake Grace.

"Bad day," she says.

"Was it really so bad?" I turn and our noses touch. I feel conscious of the words I speak entering Mim's mouth as soon as they exit mine, like I'm feeding her, mother bird style.

"It was big," she says.

"It was," I say. "It was big."

She sets a hand on my hip, and I tuck my head into her neck and we lie still for many moments. "Thank you," I whisper. And I know that I could say it, I could say it over and over, but it would never be enough. I could never be grateful enough.

"Flee looked so . . ." she said, and she didn't have to finish the thought.

"You're not like that anymore," I said. "You're different now."

"Like how?"

"In so many ways."

She smiles against my skin. "Well," she says, "the body sheds all of its cells over a seven-year cycle, so technically, I'm not completely different."

"That's true," I say.

"You told me that," says Mim. "You don't remember telling me that?"

"No."

"Oh god," she says. "It blew my mind. At the time I thought, *I'll never forget that*. But you forgot telling me!"

"Sorry," I say. And I am. "I promise I'll remember this." I kiss her cheek, then the other one, her forehead, her nose. I will remember this.

"How mad is Grace gonna be when I tell her I invited my old pro-ana friend to her house?" Mim snorts into my hair.

"You're lucky to have Grace," I say.

I feel Mim's nod. "Yeah," she says. "I'm lucky to have you, too."

"What?" I say, pulling away from her. "Why?" I say to the dark, hoping that I am looking her in the eye, even though she has no way of knowing where my eyes are.

"I told you," says Mim. "You saved me when you checked yourself in. In saving yourself, you saved me. I didn't even know it could be done."

"No, you saved me," I say. "When you came to the hospital. I had nowhere to go. You saved me."

"No, you saved me," she says.

"No, you saved me," I say.

"No, you hang up first." She laughs.

"No, you hang up first." I join her.

Then she kisses me, and her lips are hungry. She nibbles my lower lip and then licks the bite better. She trails her fingers down my stomach, between my legs, takes my tampon out, and slides her fingers into me. I'm wet, a combination of blood and desire, slick and wanting.

"Can I taste you?" Mim says, and I moan in response.

"Wait," I say, as she licks her way from my mouth to my breasts, my torso, my cunt. "I'm bleeding."

She snorts her response. Her tongue is quick, and her lips are soft. She strokes her fingers so methodically inside me while her tongue circles my clit. I whisper her name when I come, and she holds me against her as I start to cry.

"Was I that bad?" Mim smiles into my neck.

"What?"

"Am I so bad at giving head that I made you cry?"

"Oh." I swallow my tears. "Yeah."

We fall asleep dressed in quiet smiles, her lips reddened with me.

42

We read about the death in the news. I get back from a sunrise walk one morning to find Mim on the porch, squinting at the beach, looking for me.

"What's wrong?" I say, panting my way up the stairs. I'm getting stronger, but my lungs are taking longer to adjust to my new routine than my limbs.

"Someone died," Mim says.

"What?"

"Someone on the YourWeigh diet died." She points at her phone where a news article is pulled up. She hands it to me and holds me from behind, arms lassoing my waist, her chin on my shoulder, as I read.

A woman. Rachel Parker. She had eliminated everything from her diet except for Lara Bax's SkinnyChips, which are made, the article explains, of almost the exact same combination of ingredients as fruit stickers.

She was twenty-eight years old. A single stay-at-home mother. Found dead. Fruit stickers are technically edible in small quantities, but they do not a diet make.

I use Mim's phone to dial Lily's number, and Mim leaves me to talk to Lily alone.

"Hello, it's Lily Winters here?" says her voice, so strange in its anonymous distance.

"It's me," I say.

"What is with that painting?" says Lily. "You did it?"

"I did it," I say. "That's not important. I read this article—"

"About the Parker girl? I already know."

"So you're quitting?"

"What? No."

"Lily!"

"Rose!"

I sigh, swallow to keep from crying. The waves are wild today, thrashing about on the shore like a tantrum, desperate to be soothed. "Lil," I say. "People are dying."

"Oh yeah?" says Lily. "One person died. And how many people died from your little diet?"

"My *diet*?"

"You heard me."

"You mean anorexia?"

Lily says nothing. I say nothing. This conversation is pointless. I know she is already too far gone to cede. I have been there. She knows I am going to keep pushing. We don't need to talk to keep the disagreement on the table.

I sit on Grace's porch bench, and I hear Lily, too, sigh into a seat. We stay on the phone until our breathing is synchronized, slow and steady. It's something Lily would do for me when we were in high school. When I was overwhelmed, starving and scared. We'd lie in our room, on our side-by-side beds, like two versions of the same person, existing in parallel universes. She wouldn't talk to me, because she was so angry about what I was doing to myself, to us. I wouldn't speak to her, either, because I wasn't going to change. But we would breathe together, and although we were becoming separate in almost every way, we still had that one primal, necessary thing in common: breath, and we remembered that twins was something we would be forever.

"I need you to stop trying to control me, Rose," says Lily. "You can't control me anymore."

I swallow. I know. I say, "I know."

She sighs.

"Jemima has been going to YourWeigh meetings," I say.

Lil says nothing.

"We came up with a plan to shut Lara Bax down."

"That's ridiculous," says Lily.

"We're trying to help."

"Controlling someone isn't the same as helping them," says Lily. "You know that, don't you, Rosie?"

"Yeah," I say. "I'm trying to know that."

Lily says nothing, but I hear her nod.

"I ran into Phil," I say.

"I know, he said."

"So you're still with him."

"Of course. I love him."

"He doesn't love you."

"He does. He loves me. He loves me so much he told me he'd kill himself if I ever left him."

What I say: nothing.

We breathe together. Mim leaves her phone with me, pressed to my ear, and goes off to live her day. Lily, since it's a Saturday, doesn't have to interrupt our silence to go to school.

Eventually, I hear a ding that means Mim's phone is running low on battery, and I inhale, count, exhale. I can hear Lily chewing her lip on the other end. The soft squelch of her flesh being mauled. She knows something is coming to an end, too.

"I'm eating," I tell her, battery dwindling. "Three meals a day."

"That's great, Rosie," says Lily. "I'm so proud of you."

"And," I say, "and I loved your stories. You're really, really good. You're a good writer, Lil."

A light laugh. "No one was ever meant to see that book. I only printed them for myself."

"They're amazing," I say, meaning it.

"Writing," says Lily, "really helped me. When you were going through all you were going through. It helped me get everything out." I can hear her tears, and I want to kiss her cheeks, wet with her very own seawater.

"I'm sorry you couldn't talk to me," I say. "I wish I'd been there for you."

"It's not your fault."

I inhale, count, exhale. "The stories," I say, "are all sort of related." I can hear her holding her breath. "They're not, you know, I mean, nonfiction, or, I guess, autobiographical, are they?"

"Which parts?" says Lily, and the tears surge up my throat like some chemical reaction.

"Oh god, Lil," I say.

"It's okay," says Lily. "It's okay. I really am okay."

"No," I say. "It's not."

"It's not," says Lily. "But I am."

I swallow sad soapsuds and say, "I can't believe you didn't tell me. You didn't tell me any of it. You know I would have listened. You know I would have been there for you."

I hear the rustle of Lily shaking her head. "You were dying, Rose," says Lily.

"But you were—"

"Raped. Yeah. I was. But you were *dying*."

"Raped," I say in an exhale, wanting to expel the word, wanting to blow it as far away from me as I could, out to sea, out to be beaten up by those ferocious waves. It sounds wrong coming from her, like she made the word up just now. The worst part is that I don't feel surprised. I knew Lily was going through something, back when she was in college, when she started seeing terrible men, and then terrible Tony who had squeezed her bicep like a fruit into juice. When she started eating with even more gusto than before, consuming anything, everything that she came across. I never asked. I never wanted to know. "I missed out on everything," I say.

"That seems like not the right thing to say here, baby sister."

"I'm sorry," I say. "I'm so sorry. I'm sorry. I think I knew, or, I mean, I didn't know, but subconsciously I think I knew *something*, you know?"

She says nothing.

"You were pregnant?"

"Yes."

"Lily, I just—"

"I know," she whispers.

"I felt it," I say, remembering. "That night I called, and you were crying? I called because of the pain. I'm so sorry."

"I know," she whispers. She swallows her tears in a gulp.

"But you were always telling me all of this other stuff and—"

"The light stuff. The trivial stuff. To get your mind off the hurt, Rosie. You were always going through something bigger. I just wanted to help you."

"Lil," I say.

"I just want you to be happy."

"Someone told me that you shouldn't rely on others for your own happiness. You should make yourself happy."

Lily snorts.

"Is that funny?" I say.

"No," says Lily. "Just difficult. It's hard to make yourself happy. It's hard to make yourself happy if you're, you know, not."

"You're not happy, are you?"

"No."

"Because of Phil?"

"I love Phil."

"Are you not happy because of me?"

"Not everything is about you." She laughs.

I laugh, too. But there is no joy in the sound. It's a diet laugh. A bad sugar-free substitute.

"I'm sorry," I say, when the laugh becomes a trailing ellipsis.

"I know," she says. "I know you are. But I'm okay. I meant it when I said the writing helped me. It's like a different language. It's like a way of communicating myself to myself. When something is too hard to understand, the writing sort of has a way of, I don't know, understanding it for me. That doesn't even make sense." She sniffs. "You're a really great artist, Rose," she says. "That painting. I hope art can help you, too."

"Thanks," I whisper. "And I know what you mean. It's like that with art. With painting, I mean. I understand."

Silence. The phone has a breath of its battery left, which means it's time, and I inhale until I'm so full of air it hurts. "I'm with Jemima Gates, Lil. Mim and me, I think we're, well . . . I think—"

"I know."

"Okay."

"You're happy," she says. "With her. I can taste it."

"Yeah," I say. "Yeah, I really am."

"How can you be with her after everything she did? How can you forgive all of that?"

"You forgive me, don't you?"

We go back to breathing together for the last seconds of Mim's phone's battery. When the call severs, the silence sounds like a peaceful death.

43

Grace and I cook dinner as we wait for Mim to get home from her YourWeigh meeting. I hate knowing she's there, with those hypnotized women, all dieting their way to self-acceptance. I imagine her buying into the scheme, getting caught up in the mania, the cult mentality. It's so easy to follow the people around you.

"Why is she so late?" I say as I chop carrots. "Do you think she's okay?"

"Be calm," says Grace. "She's fine."

"I am calm."

Grace points her fork to my face. "Your forehead says otherwise," she says. "You wear your emotions up there." She drops her fork to tap the skin between my eyebrows.

"She's taking a long time," I say, making sure to keep my expression even. "Just saying."

I go to the window and look out at the night, the moon, the slim crescent of a fingernail chewed from its root. It reminds me of Sarah. I miss her. I hope she's eating. She deserves so much more than the tiny existence of a starved mind. She could think thoughts so much more interesting than hunger. This, I realize, is how Lily has felt for so many years now. About me. My heart feels flat, an old soccer ball left in the yard to deflate. It's so much easier to wish well for someone else than to be well oneself. I go back to the kitchen and eat a halved carrot. Close my eyes and swallow. Every bite, a tiny war.

"You're doing well," says Grace, gesturing to my chewing mandible. I nod.

"It's going to be hard for a really long time," she says. "Eating is."

I nod.

"But it's going to get better. Easier. You're going to be okay, you know."

I nod. I know she's right. Just like every illness, recovery is a process, not a fix. But unlike every other illness, in which the body fights against the world, diseases, bugs, parasites, the enemy here is my own mind. To recover from anorexia is to beat one's own brain.

"It is worth it," says Grace. And I think she would give Lara Bax a run for her money at the whole mind-reading thing. "I promise." She sets her fingers over mine, and hers, swollen-knuckled and wrinkled, are warm against my eternal cold. I can't wait to feel warmth again. "You're going to have such a wonderful life," she says. "Such a full life. Once you let yourself start living it."

The front door opens and closes, and I turn to see Mim standing, hair wet from the rain, T-shirt darkened and damp, in the foyer. She wrings out her hair like a washcloth and then shimmies her whole body as if to shake herself dry.

"Brr!" she says with an exaggerated shiver. Then, "Ooh, what're you two talking about?" She points to my hands, still clasped with Grace's. "Secrets? I hope it's about me."

Grace starts piling the vegetarian stir-fry onto plates.

"Hi." She hangs her bag and walks into the kitchen, smiling, flushed, beautiful. "I missed you two today," she says, kissing me on the cheek, then Grace on the forehead, then taking a seat at the breakfast bar and pinching a piece of tofu from the pan, dropping it into her mouth, chewing. Even now, after weeks of living with her, I am in awe of how her relationship with food has changed since the last time I knew her. Sometimes, of course, she is still wary, still afraid, but most of the time she is casual around anything edible, treating meals like old friends.

Mim stabs a piece of carrot and airplanes it toward my mouth. She is giddy with the progress, and I, too, am dizzy, the good kind. I open my lips and let her feed me. Then she hops off her stool to set the table.

• • •

There are 821 million chronically undernourished people in the world, 98 percent of whom live in developing countries. These people do not choose to starve themselves. These people are starving. People are starving.

There is nothing redeeming about playing the victim.

We're halfway through dinner when Mim's phone rings. She looks at it. Frowns. Then holds it up for me to see. Lily's name is printed across the screen. I take the phone and press to answer the call.

"Lil?" I say.

"Hi," says a familiar voice. But it isn't Lily. "It's Lara. Lara Bax. Is this Rose?"

"Why are you calling from Lily's phone?"

"Rose, breathe," Lara Bax says. "Listen, I'm at Riverside Hospital. Your sister is hurt."

"What?"

"I think you should come down here and I'll explain."

"You'll explain now."

"I went over there, to her place, to drop off Phil's things. The door was open. I, well, she was just lying there. Lying on the floor. She's not dead."

"What?"

"I think Phil must've—"

I end the call before she finishes the sentence.

"We have to go," I tell the table, and Mim and Grace stand at once. Lily needs me.

44

In 2001, when the first World Trade Center tower was hit, everyone who was in the second one was instructed to stay inside. As if one would be targeted and not the other. As if one of the twin towers would fall without the other.

When Lily wakes, I'm at her bedside. We all are. Lara, Mim, Grace, and me. The doctors have come and gone. Lily is concussed. One side of her face is a dark purple, as if she's just partially in the shadows. We're all watching her breathe, the slow rise and fall of her rib cage. Life is just this. This slow rise, slow fall, and over again.

She looks just like me, lying there, thin as a string.

"Lily?" I say. My voice is the rough draft of one.

"Rose," says Lily, her voice frail, fatigued. "Jemima? Lara?" She frowns up at me, young and afraid. "What happened?"

"Phil," I tell her.

"Phil?"

"Lara brought you in."

"I need to call him. He'll be so angry."

"Don't you think he'd be here if he wanted to be?"

Lily blinks, and her tears are fat. I use my thumbs as windshield wipers, dry her face, and kiss her forehead.

"How are you feeling, Lil? Are you thirsty?" I lift a glass of water from the nightstand. But she shakes her head.

"Hungry."

"Do you want some soup?" I take a bowl of yellow liquid from the nightstand. One the nurse had delivered while Lily slept. "It's chicken, I think."

Lily nods and tries to sit up. Mim rushes over to lift her head, and Grace tucks a third pillow behind her back. I stir the soup gently, the soft clinking of metal on porcelain, then I ladle the liquid, blow on its surface, watch it ripple like a lake disrupted.

"Ready?" I ask.

She nods and I inch the soup toward her waiting mouth.

She parts her lips, takes a mouthful, and swallows. Watching her consume something feels so good, so good I can almost taste the meal for myself.

She finishes the whole bowl, and I set the empty dish on the nightstand. "I was so worried about you, Lil," I say.

"I was so worried about you," she echoes.

Something I have learned: to love is to worry about your beloved until you die.

Something else I have learned: to be loved is to have your beloved worry about you until they die.

A phone rings, and it's Lara's. We watch her examine the caller's name and then hesitate over whether to pick up.

"Answer it," says Lily, who, for now, is god, so Lara presses to accept the call.

We hear only the rumble of thunder, a masculine yelling, and Lara winces, grimaces, at the volume. She puts the call on speakerphone.

"Are you fucking serious, Lara? You deleted our Instagram? Because of that one fucking death? It was just one girl! That's our entire brand, you stupid goddamn bitch, you fucking crazy motherfucker, do you have any idea what you have done? Do you know how hard I've . . ."

He goes on and on.

Lara raises her eyebrows as Phil rambles.

"Is that Phil?" Lily whispers.

Lara nods. "Phil," she says, calm. Her voice even, amused. "I'm at Riverside Hospital right now. With Lily. I found her on the floor of your apartment this afternoon. She's got a concussion. What did you do?"

Shouting blears from the phone's speaker. As if he's right there, in the phone, caught and furious.

Mim takes the phone from Lara and hangs up. "There," she says.

"There," says Lara.

"There," says Grace.

"There?" Lily asks me.

"There." I nod.

Lily takes my fingers in hers, lacing us into one. I am in the midst of formulating an apology, when I hear her breath deepen, and she is already asleep.

Twinflowers are otherwise known as Linnaea borealis, and they were named by the same guy who coined the term *homo sapiens* for humans. His name was Carl Linnaeus, he was a botanist, and the twinflower was his favorite flower among any he'd ever seen. It's why they're named after him.

The twinflower grows from a single stem, a long stem, and then it forks into two slightly slimmer stems, with one pink flower growing from each. The two identical flowers hang beside each other, opening and closing together, functioning together. They share resources. Share sunlight. And if one dies, so too does the other.

I used to think that this was a good analogy for twinship, but humans are not flowers. For one, we cannot survive by consuming only sunlight. For two, we feel, we eat, we want, we love, we, human.

1994 (5 years old): When we realized that what we were tasting all the time were each other's emotions, we played restaurant.

"Feel sad," I'd demand, and she'd coax tears from her eyes. But it tasted of nothing, her performance of sadness.

"Feel happy," I'd say, but my mouth was empty.

"I think the feelings have to be real," said Lily. "I don't think we can fake it."

Then my sister pinched her arm, her fingernails carving smiles from skin. She pinched until she bled, until she cried out, until she wept; she hurt herself just to let me taste—

ACKNOWLEDGMENTS

Writing this book was a really difficult thing to do, but we can do difficult things, especially when we have people, like my people, to help us out along the way. My people include my incredible agent, Susan Golomb, and her assistant, Mariah Stovall, my cheerleaders from the beginning. Terry Karten, my unparalleled editor, who helped turn this book into the best version of itself. My thesis advisor and true idol, Roxane Gay, who read as I wrote, told it how it was, and supported me every chapter of the way.

Countless thanks to the team at Harper, including Lydia Weaver, for the impeccable eye, Caroline Johnson, for the beautiful cover, and everyone else who believed in this book enough to give it a life.

I want to thank my friends. Noah Baldino, Kelsey Wort, Charlie Peck, and the rest of my Purdue MFA-ers, who saw or heard excerpts of the first manuscript and who were nothing but encouraging. The faculty at Purdue, Brian Leung and Sharon Solwitz and Don Platt and Kaveh Akbar, have created a safe and supportive space and I'm so thankful for my time in Indiana, writing, reading, being.

My cohort at the University of Utah has been endlessly understanding and compassionate and gentle with me and my writing. Thank you, to my fellow PhD candidates, for being here, letting me be here, for growing alongside me. It's a beautiful thing, to grow.

I want to thank literary journals, in general. Thank you for loving writing and giving stories their homes. Thank you for the acceptances, the encouragement. Thank you for the rejections, the lessons. You're underappreciated, every single one of you.

My friends, the ones who have been here all along, who have stuck with me through the good and the not. I'm so lucky to have found my sisters, Sand, Soph, Stace, Moz. I'm so lucky they still want to hang out.

Bret, listen, I know you wanted a dedication, but an acknowledgment is going to have to do. Thank you for you.

My brothers, Nick and Andrew, are pretty good, as far as brothers go, and no one was more excited than they were to see this book in the world. My grandparents, Diane and Sidney, who are the best, and whom I promise to visit more often. My parents, to whom this book is dedicated, Mum and Dad, none of this, none of me, would be here without you. I love you for the world. Thank you.

Lastly, I want to thank *you*. This book is for anybody whose body is alien to them. Anyone who has ever felt out of place in their own skin. This book is for you, whose body is perfect just the way it is. Your body is a creature and it is yours to care for. It is your beast. Feed it. Love it. Be gentle with your body; be gentle with yourself. This book, first and foremost, is for you. Thank you for holding it in your hands.

ABOUT THE AUTHOR

DIANA CLARKE is from New Zealand. She is a graduate of the University of Auckland and Purdue University, where she received her MFA. She lives in Salt Lake City, where she is pursuing a PhD in English from the University of Utah. *Thin Girls* is her first novel.